MW00974503

The Inconceivable Life of Quinn

ABRAMS AMULET
NEW YORK

The Inconceivable Life of Quinn

MARIANNA BAER

Cataloging-in-Publication Data has been applied for
and may be obtained from the Library of Congress.
ISBN: 978-1-4197-2302-5

Text copyright © 2017 Marianna Baer
Book design by Alyssa Nassner

Printed and bound in U.S.A.
10 9 8 7 6 5 4 3 2 1

Amulet Books are available at special discounts when purchased
in quantity for premiums and promotions as well as fundraising
or educational use. Special editions can also be created to specification.
For details, contact specialsales@abramsbooks.com or the address below.

ABRAMS The Art of Books
115 West 18th Street, New York, NY 10011
abramsbooks.com

FOR BECKY AND BOOG, WITH LOVE

Where there is mystery, it is generally supposed that there must also be evil.
—Lord Byron

Memory is a mirror that scandalously lies.
—Julio Cortázar

THE DEEPS

a children's book by Charlotte Lowell

A still morning sea, the Deeps all asleep,
'til warmed by the sun they roll up the beach.
Some glide with a shush, *some crash with a* ROAR,
All eager to find what night left on shore.

Clamshells and starfish, smooth sea glass and stones.
Pieces of driftwood, washed pale as our bones.
Further and further, they draw up the sand,
Daring young Deeps, out exploring the land.

And look—someone's here. It's you, come to swim!
You kick off your shoes, run quick, and plunge in.
Hooray! cheer the Deeps, while lifting you high.
Let's play! you call out, now splashing the sky.

They tumble and toss you, upside and down.
You flip, flop and float, no feet on the ground.
The games go for hours, as happens with friends.
A magical day that you hope never ends.

But after some time, a voice calls your name.
The Deeps feel a pull from back where they came.
They slip out to sea, you wave a farewell,
From two different worlds, one story to tell.

QUINN

There was an ocean in her bedroom.

Brooklyn steamed with the thick heat of late August, and while Quinn had started her day off in the backyard hammock, book in one hand and phone in the other, it was soon too much of an effort to even turn the page or type a word. So she'd retreated inside, where she was now lying on a beach towel, eyes closed, misting herself with water as cold as the Atlantic. The distant traffic on Prospect Park West echoed the rhythmic shush and roar of waves. The salty sweat above her lip tasted like the sea. She was floating away . . . when the waves were interrupted by the ring of the doorbell and the familiar muted thumps of Jesse taking the stairs up to her room two at a time.

Quinn smiled but kept her eyes closed, too relaxed to open them quite yet.

Footsteps approached. The air above her stirred and shadowed, and Jesse's soft lips touched her own. She ran fingers through his hair and pulled his sweet coffee-flavored kiss even closer, a different type of heat sparking inside her. He had warned her that the visit was only a flyby, though. So, after a moment, sensing they were about to pause for a breath, she lifted her other hand and sprayed.

Jesse jumped back, face dripping with water, and said with a sputtering laugh, "What the heck, Q?"

"Just cooling us down," Quinn said, sitting up and grinning.

He shook his head to one side, sandy-brown hair flicking out in shaggy damp spikes. "Thanks. My ear canal was way overheated."

"I live to serve." She bowed slightly.

The water apparently dislodged, he sat on the floor next to her and stretched out his long legs—tan, bug-bitten, and with a few scratches and bruises from a summer of hiking and ultimate Frisbee. "Seriously, though," he said, "know what would really cool you down?"

"Iced coffee?" Quinn reached toward the plastic cup in his hand. He gave it to her.

"Camping. It's supposed to be thirty-eight degrees up there tonight. Thirty-eight! We're going to freeze our asses off."

"Don't rub it in." She took a sip, the coffee's sweetness dulled by the fact that she was about to spend the long weekend before school started without him. "You guys'll be making s'mores and I'll be making small talk with strangers."

"So come," he said, nudging her.

"You know I can't."

"I could kidnap you."

"My dad has friends in law enforcement. You'd get in trouble."

"Sadie could kidnap you. She's going to end up in jail someday, anyway."

"Ha." Quinn rested her head against his shoulder. "It's not just the campaign party. I have a check-up with my new doctor today, and I picked up shifts this weekend and Monday . . . Puttin' the labor in Labor Day." She gave an anemic fist pump.

"But I'll have to share a tent with Adrian and Oliver instead of you," he groaned. "It's tragic."

"Shakespearian," she agreed. "Hey, what's that?" A light blue shopping bag sat on the floor near his feet, partly hidden by scattered laundry.

"Oh. Your mom gave it to me downstairs. Something for you to wear tonight." He scooted the bag closer with his foot. The movement flexed his leg muscles and Quinn had to resist an urge to lean over and kiss the freckle between his right knee and the bottom of his shorts. "She said you should try it on. It's a size zero but the saleslady said it runs big."

Quinn handed back the coffee and pulled a crisp, tissue paper–wrapped packet out of the bag.

"Size zero," he mused as she unwrapped it. "Doesn't it give you an existential crisis? Like you're not really here?"

"If I'm not really here, you're the one we need to worry about, babe." She held up an oyster-white, gauzy cotton dress with a flared skirt and a pattern of delicate gold and silver seed beads around a halter-style neckline. Not something she'd have chosen—her favorite dresses were as close to T-shirts, hoodies, or flannel button-downs as possible. But it was pretty and she was grateful not to have to worry about what to wear.

"Be right back." She pushed herself up and slipped into the tiny adjoining room that was used both as her closet and for storage. (If she'd started disrobing in the room with Jesse, it would have guaranteed her little sister would burst in the door; Lydia had an uncanny sense for barging in at the wrong time.) She took off her shorts, tank, and bra, stepped into the dress, tied the halter strap behind her neck, and twisted her arm around to zip up. She could only move the zipper a couple of inches, though, so she went back out for help.

Jesse was standing, staring out the window. "Have you ever noticed that that pigeon is always outside my room?" he said.

Quinn peered across their backyards at his apartment building and watched the bird bob its way along the window ledge. "Let her in sometime. See what she wants."

"I doubt she wants the slobbery affection of a giant mutt."

"Maybe she does." Quinn loved videos of unlikely interspecies friendships. "Can you finish my zipper?" she asked, turning her back to him.

"I'd rather unfinish it."

"Tease. You're the one who can't stay long."

While she sucked in, he coaxed the zipper to the bottom of her

3

shoulder blades, the fabric squeezing her like a corset. The dress was sized much smaller than a usual zero, not bigger—that must have been what the saleslady meant.

She faced him, hands on her hips. "Too small, isn't it?"

"Whoa," he said, eyebrows raised. "It's . . . it's a dress, all right."

"Keen observation, detective. Is it a dress I should wear to my dad's campaign party?"

"And every day for the rest of your life."

She felt a hum of pleasure at his approval. "What, like Miss Havisham?"

Jesse shrugged. "She found something that worked and stuck with it. Nothing wrong with that."

Quinn laughed.

Her bedroom didn't have a full-length mirror, so she went down the hall to the bathroom, which was currently filled with jars of suspicious liquids for Lydia's "science" experiments. The air smelled dangerous, like it might spontaneously ignite. She flipped on the overhead light and shut the door so she could see the mirror.

Oh. A girl stood in front of her. But she wasn't Quinn . . . not really. The too-tight fabric had rearranged her flesh into someone else's shape. This girl had wham-bam hips and round, full breasts with a valley of shadowy cleavage, not her usual A-verging-on-B cups. Quinn knew she'd put on a bit of weight over the summer—courtesy of working at a way-too-good frozen yogurt store—but she hadn't worn anything that showed it off in quite this way. She turned from side to side, a little stunned by the effect. She looked older. Softer. Womanly.

A warm breeze snuck through the small bathroom window and rustled the skirt, as if the wind was admiring it, too.

As Quinn stared, listening to the waves of traffic shushing and roaring in the background, a fantasy flickered in her mind. Nighttime. Standing on top of a large, barnacle-speckled rock on the beach on

Southaven island; salty-wet wind fluttering the dress around her legs; moonlight painting her skin phosphorescent; waves crashing at her feet; her over-full heart speeding in her chest with anticipation; Jesse there, watching her, wanting her—

Suddenly, without warning, her thoughts skipped from fantasy to memory, from beach to dock, waves still crashing . . . and a boy's lips against her own.

A boy who wasn't Jesse.

Quinn caught herself with a start, a vicious stab of guilt twisting between her ribs. *God.* What was wrong with her?

Back in her room, cheeks burning, she quickly headed to the closet, avoiding eye contact. Jesse was thumbing through a pile of paper—Quinn's notations on the screenplay he was writing for an upcoming contest, a black comedy about a boy who thinks the girl who lives below him is literally the Devil. With the other hand he was rubbing her cat Haven's ears.

"You know," he said as she passed by, "you're allowed to comment on the things you think aren't working, too."

"I did," she said. "If you want me to be more critical, you need to write something worse."

Jesse pshawed. "Gonna wear the dress?"

"Too tight. Being able to breathe is kind of important." She untied the halter quickly, wanting the dress off her body and any lingering thoughts about Marco Cavanaugh out of her mind. For good.

"Hey, Q?" Jesse called. "I should probably go. Oliver's dad is picking me up soon."

"The sleeping bag is next to my desk," Quinn said. "And I baked some stuff for you guys to take along. In the Tupperware thing."

When she came out a minute later, he was already eating one of the peanut butter chocolate chip cookies. "Needed to make sure they weren't poisoned," he said, grinning. Jesse's face was angular and narrow, but his smile stretched from Park Slope to the Pacific; it brought out dimples that reminded her of what he'd looked like when he was new at school in fifth grade—rounder all over; hair straighter and shorter; shy, but still quick to smile. She'd thought he was the cutest boy she'd ever seen. She still did. Quinn placed the dress back in the bag and then went over and wrapped her arms around him from behind, breathed in his distinctive scent of sandalwood and grass tinged with sweat, and felt his ribcage expand and contract under her cheek. It was too hot to be pressed against another body, but she wanted the moment of simple closeness. She wished she could melt into him so they'd never be separated and hugged him even harder, as if that might make it happen. As if erasing any physical distance could banish the space between them where secrets lived.

"Oof," Jesse said. "How can someone your size be that strong?" He reached up and squeezed her biceps.

Someday he'll figure out that you don't deserve this kind of love. Enjoy it while it lasts.

"I'm sorry," she said, her voice muffled in the soft folds of his T-shirt.

"For what? Breaking my ribs?"

"For not going with you this weekend."

"Don't be ridiculous. And you'll be working; that's food for the whale, right?" They were planning an epic trip, to be taken whenever they could afford it: a full year off, backpacking around amazing islands all over the world—the Galápagos, Orkneys, Dalmatians, Tahiti. They religiously put money in a whale-shaped bank.

"So you forgive me?" she said.

"Q," he said, "there's nothing to forgive."

QUINN

Qui-iiiin! Doc-tor!" Lydia's voice bellowing up the stairs pulled Quinn awake. "Qui-iiiin! Qui-iiiiiin!"

"Coming! Jeez," she muttered, standing. Covered in sweat and vaguely nauseous, she reached out and steadied herself on her desk chair, then checked her phone. She'd been asleep for two hours. After Jesse left, she'd only meant to lie down for a moment, but the sun had draped itself all over her and *bam*, she was out. They had been happening a lot lately, these accidental naps, even when she got a good night's sleep.

She gave her face a spray of now-lukewarm water and headed downstairs.

"What took you so long?" Lydia demanded when Quinn reached the parlor floor of the row house. She was wearing a polka-dot bathing suit, plaid shorts, and high-tops Quinn had grown out of not that long ago. Ten years old, and she was almost as tall as her sixteen-year-old sister. Not that that was saying much. Lydia and Ben, their twenty-year-old brother, were built like their mother's family, which included a great-aunt who was six-two. Quinn took after her father's side, supposedly, though there were no living relatives aside from her dad as evidence.

"Why do you care?" Quinn said, retrieving her flip-flops from under the hall bench.

"I had to call you forever. And where's Jesse? I grew some mold I want to show him."

"He already left."

Lydia pouted. "I never see him anymore. Ever since he started being your boooyyyfriend you guys are all hidey-hidey in your room and stuff."

"That doesn't usually stop you."

The sound of quick footsteps came from the stairs that led up from the garden-level kitchen to the front hall. The narrow house had four modestly sized stories, with two main rooms on each, which made for a lot of up and down. "I lost track of time," their mother, Katherine, said, hurrying toward her daughters. "We're running late." She grabbed her bag from a hook next to the mirror, pressed a hand on Quinn's back, and steered her toward the door.

The minute Quinn stepped outside, the heat tried to push her back in. She paused for a moment at the top of the stoop, waiting for her mother to find her sunglasses in her large, overstuffed purse, which contained everything from pruning shears to three issues of the *New Yorker* and five tubes of the same shade of lipstick. (Quinn had counted in amazement during a recent search for gum.)

"You'll only be alone for an hour or so," Katherine said to Lydia, finally pulling out her glasses. "I'm going to see clients after I drop off Quinn. Ben will be here soon, though. You'll be okay?" She kissed her on both cheeks then wiped off the Rose Aglow smudges with her thumbs.

"Duh," Lydia said. "Except I'm starving. Is there food? And don't say 'kale muffins.' Those things are nasty."

"I shopped after my co-op shift last night," Katherine said, as she and Quinn walked down the steps. "There should be plenty in the fridge." She waved. "Be sure to lock the door when you go inside, sweetie."

The low, wrought-iron gate clanged shut behind Quinn and her mother. They started up the block, past the old brownstones, toward Prospect Park West.

"About the groceries," Quinn said. "You never unpacked them. They were sitting out all night."

Her mother glanced at her. "Seriously?"

"There were casualties."

"Crap." Katherine took out her phone and typed a quick note. "I can't wait for the election to be over so I can have my brain back. And our regular life."

Quinn's new doctor's office was near Grand Army Plaza; she and her mother only had to walk up PPW to get there. Normally, it would have been a nice walk—the trees and bushes of Brooklyn's equivalent to Central Park gathered on one side, elegant brick and limestone townhouses and apartment buildings lining the other. But the air was so boggy with humidity, Quinn had to shove it out of the way with every step, like she was forcing herself through a crowd of overheated, hostile bodies on the subway. That's what heat was like in the city: it made you feel like there wasn't enough room for you. (Although, it wasn't just the heat; in Quinn's opinion, the city landscape *never* allowed enough room for certain things—like thinking and breathing.)

While they crossed over to the shadier park side of the street, Quinn pictured the melted butter and ice cream she'd thrown out this morning, and wondered if her mom really thought they'd go back to regular life after the election. Quinn's father was running for Congress. He was a professor and had written books, two of which, *Urbanomics* and *ElastiCity*, were bestsellers that made him kind of famous—in an always-on-NPR kind of way. But even though he was already high profile in certain circles, life would be totally different if he won. (Which he had a good chance of doing; he'd already won the Democratic primary in June.) He'd live in DC for a lot of the year and would be even busier and more public than he was now. He'd be a friggin' United States congressman! What was regular about that?

Quinn wanted him to win, but she also knew that things wouldn't go back to normal. You couldn't go back. Like with Jesse. They'd been platonic best friends for years before becoming an official couple last spring. Now that they were "together," they could never go back to the way it had been before. Quinn didn't want to go back—not at all—but it made her sick down to her toenails to think that if the romance didn't work, she might lose the friendship, too.

She kicked a pebble. "I loaned Jesse my sleeping bag for the Adirondacks trip," she said. "His sucks."

"I feel bad you couldn't go. Are all the Dubs going?"

"Not Caroline—she's at an art thing on Long Island. Just Sadie and Isa." Caroline Williams, Sadie Weston-Hoyt, and Isa Weiss were Quinn's closest girlfriends.

"And the usual guys?"

"Adrian. And Oliver, obviously. Matt has soccer."

"You know how much Dad and I appreciate that you're coming tonight, right?"

"Yup."

"You've been great during this whole thing." Katherine ran her hand over Quinn's head as they waited for a troop of nannies pushing strollers to pass in front of them at the park entrance. "You make me proud, know that?"

"Don't be a dork, Mom."

"Were you sleeping again?"

Quinn followed her mother's hand with her own and felt a poufy rat's nest above her hair elastic. "Yeah, a little."

Katherine studied her face for a moment. "You're not depressed, are you, sweetie?"

"Depressed? No, Mom. God." It had been the best summer of her life.

They started walking again. "I didn't think so. But all this sleeping . . . I don't want to be the kind of mother who's oblivious."

"You're, like, the opposite of oblivious." Her mother loved to know what was going on with friends and guys and all of that—more than Quinn liked to talk about it. Quinn wasn't a big sharer with anyone except Jesse. The Dubs joked that she should join the CIA, if she wasn't in it already.

"I hope so," her mother said. "Anyway, I was serious about being proud of you. You're a good girl, Quinn."

"Ugh, Mom."

As Quinn said it, Katherine's phone rang, and she began talking to a client of her urban gardening business about replacing some diseased boxwood. Quinn spent the rest of the walk texting with Jesse and Sadie.

When they reached the large, sand-colored brick building where the doctor's office was, Katherine said, "I'm just going to come in to take care of the insurance stuff. Be sure to ask her to check your thyroid. Okay?"

"I'm fine," Quinn said, tucking her phone in her pocket. "It's the heat."

"And ask if you should try cutting out gluten."

"Mom. Stop worrying. I'm fine."

The door slid open, releasing a blast of icy air. Quinn shivered and stepped inside.

QUINN

After a chatty nurse named Emily evaluated her with all sorts of gadgets, Quinn waited for ages in a freezing exam room, wrapped in a paper robe that was big enough to cover her three times over but still somehow left her uncomfortably exposed. She was taking selfies, pretending to lick the intestines from a model of the digestive system, when the doctor finally knocked and then bustled in with apologies about the wait. Quinn sat on the edge of the exam table.

"I see the first thing I've done as your doctor is give you hypothermia," Dr. Kumar said. "Sorry about that." She fiddled with an electronic panel on the wall. "So, school starts on Tuesday? And you go to New Prospect?"

Quinn nodded. "I'll be a junior."

"I have a daughter there, but she's only going into second grade." The doctor sat next to a small desk and read over the forms Quinn had filled out in the waiting room, occasionally asking questions.

"Your environmental and chemical sensitivities—when did they start?"

"They were really bad when I was a baby," Quinn said. She always made sure to mention that so people would know she wasn't just neurotic, being allergic to ten million things. "We lived in Cincinnati, and I had a lot of trouble breathing in the city, so we moved to Maine and stayed there till I was seven."

"Maine? That's a pretty extreme solution."

Quinn shrugged. "My dad inherited a house there. By the time we moved to Brooklyn, I was much better. I try to avoid stuff that sets me off."

Dr. Kumar typed a note into the computer before checking the form again.

"And this unusual fatigue you wrote about, how long have you been noticing it?"

"I don't know. A few months? Over the summer, definitely. It's not a big deal. My mom wanted me to mention it."

"Your temperature is slightly elevated, so you might be fighting some sort of infection. But that wouldn't have lasted months. What were you doing this summer?"

"Working at a frozen yogurt store. I also volunteered at an environmental action committee and helped out with my dad's campaign. And I play ultimate and run and swim and stuff. I like being outside."

"Busy summer. When was your last period?"

"Um . . . I don't know. I only got it about a year ago, and it's never been regular. I guess the last time was . . . April? Or May?" Her mother's friend who was an OB/GYN said she shouldn't worry yet, since she was still settling into her cycle. And, recently, she'd had a feeling it was coming soon—her low gut had that constant sense of fullness.

Dr. Kumar typed a final note. "I'm going to ask you to lie down now, please."

Quinn scooched farther onto the exam table and then lay all the way back. Dr. Kumar started pressing on her belly; it made her need to pee. When the doctor was done with Quinn's gut, she asked if she examined her breasts regularly and told her she was going to do so. Quinn was holding her gaze on the crackled white iceberg of a ceiling and reminding herself that Dr. Kumar was a woman and did this all the time, when the doctor pressed the side of one breast too hard.

"Ow."

"Sorry. Sensitive there?"

"I guess."

"Noticed sensitivity in your breasts before?"

"No," she said. Although . . . She had recently started using a better sports bra; running in her previous, sort of flimsy one had gotten uncomfortable. "Well, maybe a bit."

Dr. Kumar finished up the poking and prodding and then told Quinn that she'd leave her alone for a moment so she could get dressed. Quinn put on her clothes and sat back on the table. She found a squishy salted caramel in the pocket of her cut-offs, its crinkly cellophane wrapper bringing a hazy memory of the stale lollipops she used to get at some doctor's office when she was little. A knock came at the door. She put the caramel back in her pocket.

Dr. Kumar pulled her stool across from Quinn and sat down.

"You said on your form that you're not sexually active. Is that correct, Quinn?"

"No. I mean, yes, it's correct. No, I'm not active."

"Many girls your age don't feel comfortable discussing it. Especially with a virtual stranger. And I completely understand that. But we need honesty between us. Okay?"

"Sure. I've never had sex, though." Quinn wished her feet were on the ground, not hanging in the air like a little kid's, flip-flops dangling.

"Okay. But in the past several months, have you been involved, sexually, with a male? Boyfriend or otherwise?"

"Well . . . what do you mean, *sexually*?" Did she really have to tell this random woman the explicit details of her romantic life?

Dr. Kumar folded her hands together in that "now we really have to talk" way.

"Quinn," she said, "I'd like to do a urine test for pregnancy. Your symptoms and my exam certainly indicate this as a possibility. Missed periods, fatigue, tender breasts. A slightly elevated temperature can also be indicative."

Pregnant? Hello?

Quinn tried not to act like Dr. Kumar was completely crazy and kept her voice neutral when she said, "In the past few months, I've only hooked up with my boyfriend, and we haven't done anything that could get me pregnant." She wasn't sure whether her face heated when she said this from just talking about it or from that "only with my boyfriend" part, which wasn't exactly true. "I'm not stupid," she added. "I know how pregnancy happens."

"Just humor me," Dr. Kumar said. "The urine test only takes a minute. All that will be wasted are the test materials."

By the time Quinn had peed in the cup and waited in the exam room again, she'd gone through a swing of emotions. First, an unexpected flash of worry. *Had* there been a moment with Jesse that might have been unsafe? Not actual sex, but something else? She thought back over the summer, as if she might have forgotten something, even though she knew perfectly well how far they'd gone: her shirt and bra off, some touching below the belt, but always with boxers and underwear still on.

The whole thing—becoming a couple after being best friends since fifth grade—had happened suddenly. Well, suddenly and not suddenly. For years, Quinn had harbored a painfully intense secret crush on him. The closer their friendship became, the more scared she was of risking it by confessing her feelings. (She had no idea if he *liked her* liked her. He'd never made a move, obviously, and fooled around with other girls now and then.) One afternoon this past April, they were in the park with his dog, Hugo, tossing a Frisbee. The air was soft and warm and heady with the perfume of flowering trees. Every time Jesse went up high for the disc, Quinn couldn't believe how long he hung in the air, like he was flying. At some point, he started wrestling Hugo, then he grabbed Quinn's leg and pulled her down, too, and in the play struggle that followed, she ended up on top of him, his wrists in her hands, pinned above his head. She was breathing heavily and Jesse's face was flushed, and all of a sudden she couldn't take another minute of it. Not another *second!* Agony outweighed fear a thousand times over.

"Jesse?" she said.

"Quinn?" he responded.

Her heart pounded, fear still there even though it was outclassed. "What would you do if I kissed you right now?"

He blinked, unreadable. "Depends where. Elbow? Big toe?"

Her ribs were going to break from the pounding. "Lips."

"Hmm . . ." He pretended to be considering it. "I don't think I'm self-aware enough to predict. I think you'd have to just do it and see." His tone was jokey, but as Quinn held his gaze, something shifted, and the look in his thick-lashed, hazel eyes told her what she needed to know: This moment was as big and as long-time-coming for him as it was for her. He wanted it as much as she did. This was happening. *Finally.*

She leaned down and kissed him. Every spring bud in Brooklyn bloomed.

Just like that, they were together.

Because they were already so close, it immediately felt like a "serious relationship." And if Quinn had listened to what her body wanted—if she'd given in to the ache for his touch—she'd have slept with him the day of that first kiss. Her brain, though, had told her to move slowly. To Jesse, she just said, "We have forever, right? Why rush?" But talking to Sadie in early May, loosened up by a couple of beers at a party, she found herself saying: "I'm scared of how much I love him, I think. I'm scared he's going to realize something's wrong with me and decide he doesn't want me, and if we've already had sex . . . I'll be even more devastated."

"What do you mean, he'll realize something's wrong with you?" Sadie asked.

Quinn hadn't thought before describing it that way; that's just how it came out. At Sadie's question, she regretted saying it, like she'd revealed something too personal, even though she didn't quite know what she had meant herself.

She tried to blow it off, but Sadie pushed. "You must have meant something," she said. "Stop being so mysterious all the time." (Sadie had been hurt that Quinn hadn't confided in her about her crush on Jesse. Apparently, Quinn had breached an unwritten friendship law: being "private" was okay; "secretive" was not.)

"Just general insecurity," Quinn hedged, honestly not knowing how to explain. "It's scary to be with the person you want to be with for the rest of your life; there's so much at stake. I want to be careful. That's all."

If you were so worried about what was at stake, why did you kiss Marco Cavanaugh? Quinn wondered now, still unable to shake the memory of that moment on Southaven. No, she was not a "good girl."

And no, she and Jesse hadn't done anything unsafe.

After Quinn dismissed that possibility, she started to get pissed at Dr. Kumar. Really pissed. Would she have acted like this with an older patient? Wasted the patient's time like this? No. It was because Quinn was a teenager that the doctor didn't trust her. Like how the woman who owned the neighborhood store that sold cool bags and doodads and jewelry always stink-eyed Quinn and her friends, as if they'd stolen something.

Quinn was fuming about this and trying to dislodge a chunk of that salted caramel, which had gotten wedged between two of her upper molars, when Dr. Kumar knocked and opened the exam room door. She quickly took her finger out of her mouth.

"Are we almost done?" she asked. "This is taking a really long time."

The doctor sat down, her expression concerned. "I'm afraid the test was positive, Quinn."

"Positive?" Quinn said, confused.

"For pregnancy."

"Right, but why would the test be positive if I can't be pregnant?" Quinn didn't try to hide her exasperation.

"These tests are very accurate. When women test at home, there are things that can cause inaccuracies. Here, that just doesn't happen."

"But, like I already said, I've never had sex, or had a guy . . . ejaculate near enough. Are you even listening to me?"

Dr. Kumar's sharp eyes remained fixed on Quinn's, so fatally serious that Quinn found herself having to suppress a sudden wave of laughter.

"I swear," she said, keeping it down. "It would have to be an immaculate conception."

"Well," Dr. Kumar said, "if it would make you feel better, we can do a blood test to confirm it. But I want to emphasize that given this first test, my exam, and the symptoms you've been experiencing, I'm very confident that you're pregnant."

"You can do a blood test, though?"

"Yes. I was going to have lab work done, anyway."

"You'll check my thyroid?" Quinn said, spoon-feeding her.

"We'll do a whole workup." Dr. Kumar stood and made some quick notes in the computer, then laid a hand on Quinn's shoulder and gave a small squeeze. "Just wait here. I'll have Emily come take blood. And I'll call you as soon as possible—by the end of the day—to discuss the lab results." A look of pity flitted across her eyes. "We'll discuss the next steps then, too. Okay? I'm here to help."

"Sure," Quinn said. "Whatever."

As she spoke, the chunk of caramel slipped free, giving her a choking feeling as it slid down her throat.

EMILY CLEMENTS

Watching the slight girl with the messy, chestnut-brown ponytail and heart-shaped face (who needed a little makeup and eyebrow shaping to live up to her potential, frankly), Emily Clements, the medical assistant who'd taken the girl's vitals and drawn her blood, nudged her coworker Marissa and whispered, "That's the girl. The pregnant one who said she's never had sex."

Marissa turned to see the girl hurrying through the waiting room toward the exit. "She really said that?"

Emily nodded. "I was drawing blood for the test and she was all, 'This is ridiculous. It's impossible.'"

"So how does she explain being pregnant? Mishap in the hot tub?"

"She says she's not pregnant. But give me a break. Pee don't lie."

Marissa laughed.

As they headed down the hall to get their stuff before leaving for lunch, Emily and Marissa discussed the strangest patients and ailments they'd ever dealt with. This was one of Emily's favorite things to talk about with other health care workers. She liked having a whole bag of stories about weird patients to reach into when conversation lagged at parties or wherever. There was even a "Freakers" chat thread on the private forum she was part of where nurses and techs bitched about their jobs.

"Pregnant virgin" would be a nice addition.

QUINN

The Cutlers were supposed to leave for Gabe's campaign party in fifteen minutes. Quinn's brother and her mother were arguing in the hallway outside her room. Quinn was trying not to listen, trying to do the clasp of her necklace, and trying to stop worrying for even one second. Failing on all counts.

Dr. Kumar had called: The blood test had come back positive, too.

"Why would you want me there?" Ben said. "You don't want me living in your house, why do you want me representing the family?"

"Don't be silly," Katherine said. "You know perfectly well we'd be proud to have you with us."

"What am I supposed to do when Mr. Richie Rich says how great it is that I followed my own path or some other bullshit? Lie?"

"Of course not. If you could just talk about everything without so much anger."

"Without making Dad look like a dick, you mean."

"Watch it, Ben. I'm not sure you realize how entitled—"

"Can I get by you now? I was on my way to the shower."

"No. Not until we've settled—"

Quinn couldn't take any more.

"Mom?" she called out. "Can you fix this for me?"

Katherine came in, her hair wet and pinned haphazardly on top of her head, wearing her black full slip but not the dress that went over it. She and Gabe had gotten home only about half an hour ago. Since then, they'd been running around getting ready and helping the kids get ready while taking phone calls and answering texts. And it had turned out that Ben thought he wasn't going, which was what led to the fight. Not that fights were unusual when Ben was around—

most often between him and Gabe. He'd moved out about a year ago after an especially big one (over Ben's decision to leave college to be on a reality show about urban surfers) and was only staying at home temporarily now; there'd been a burst pipe in his Bed-Stuy apartment and his floor was being replaced.

Quinn missed her brother. She didn't miss the fighting.

"Why does it smell like smoke in here?" Katherine glanced around Quinn's bedroom.

"Can you do my necklace?" Quinn said, ignoring her mother's question. She wasn't about to tell her that Ben had been smoking on the fire escape.

Katherine took the thick silver chain with a pendant of velvety aqua sea glass, murmuring, "This will be perfect." She attached the clasp and admired Quinn, who had ended up borrowing a sapphire-blue linen sheath dress from her. "I'll actually be surprised if your thyroid is off. You look so beautiful and healthy. When did Dr. Kumar say you'd get the results?"

"I don't know," Quinn said, rubbing the pendant. "Next week or something."

Her skin felt clammy at the lie.

Part of Quinn wished her mother had gotten home in time for her to talk to her about it. She needed someone she trusted to commiserate with her about Dr. Kumar's insanity.

But even though her mom would agree that the doctor was nuts, she'd probably be even more worried than Quinn was. And what could she do to help? Quinn had already done what could be done at this point. After researching online and confirming that there was no way she could have gotten pregnant through clothing, she Googled false positive pregnancy tests. While it did seem that false positives were rare, she discovered a site that said hormones created by a certain type of tumor could cause it to happen. *A tumor.* She'd tried not to panic and decided that the best thing would be for her to go back to her pediatrician for a real check-up. He knew her, and he'd be able to figure out what was really wrong. (*Please, don't let it be a tumor.*) She'd already left a message at his office, and there was nothing more her mother could do. No reason to tell her parents until after the party, when they weren't so stressed out.

As if on cue, her father yelled from the stairs, "Katherine! What's taking so long up there? I just got a frantic call from Suzanne!"

When Quinn was dressed and ready, she waited outside on the front steps to escape the tension. Dried brown leaves littered the ground prematurely. It hadn't rained in ages; the sky must have been punishing the trees for something. She dragged the heavy green hose from under the stoop, gave the plants in the window boxes and the pots on the steps a drink, and splashed some water on her arms and the back of her neck.

Everything was so still—air, leaves, even a squirrel perched on the wrought-iron gate—like they were all holding their breath, waiting for something to happen.

The party was in one of the newer apartment buildings in Park Slope—all glass and steel and cement. Something made Quinn's skin tingle uncomfortably. Probably whatever cleaner they used to keep the glass so spotless. After Gabe introduced the kids to the hosts, Mr. and Mrs. Simon, Lydia disappeared down a long, art-lined corridor with their similar-age daughter. Ben immediately began flirting with an attractive youngish woman, of course. A quick scan of the sprawling, semi-crowded room didn't reveal any high school–age guests for Quinn to talk to. She was probably too preoccupied to carry on a coherent conversation, anyway.

Normally, she would have surreptitiously messaged with Jesse or the Dubs, but none of them had cell service, so she tried to appear occupied by the art in the living room, moving from one piece to the next. She spent minutes focusing on the brushstrokes of one painting. They were the only things to focus on, really, since the painting was all black. The rhythm and gesture of the strokes made it look like the surface of the ocean at night, making her think of a secret midnight swim she took at the beginning of the summer, the feeling of freedom and electric joy that came with disappearing under the blackness. She stood, fiddling with her necklace and staring, wishing she could dive in and vanish under the waves. Words whispered in her head: *A still midnight sea, deeply asleep* . . . The start of a poem she once knew?

A touch on her shoulder made her flinch. She turned.

"They don't bite." Her father nodded his salt-and-pepper head toward the crowd. "Or if they do, at least they're not rabid."

"I know," Quinn said, making an effort to smile. "I was just look-ing around."

He studied the black painting. His eyes matched his shirt—the bright blue of a gas flame—and he had on the floral-print tie Quinn had given him for his birthday. He'd probably start wearing only solids and stripes if he won, like most politicians seemed to.

"I think we've seen work by this artist at the Whitney," he said. "I could ask Suzanne to come tell you about the collection."

"God, no."

He chuckled. "Right. Well, if it makes any difference, I'm really glad you're here." He rumpled her hair in that annoying parental way.

A few minutes after he rejoined the throng, servers started passing around flutes of champagne for a toast. Quinn's parents were both engaged in conversations; she couldn't catch either of their eyes to ask if she should take a glass. They were usually pretty relaxed about stuff like that, especially with toasts, so she took one.

The room quieted down when Mrs. Simon introduced Gabe. Quinn sipped her champagne and tried to stop worrying about what might be wrong with her as her father smoothly delivered a string of phrases she'd heard different versions of over and over since his campaign began. *Blah, blah, blah.* She only tuned back in when he said, "Also, some good news: The *Times* is going to run a feature on me next week."

Another article? What more was there to say? There'd already been ones on everything from his ideas on health care reform to his prowess at bowling to his childhood—something he never used to talk about because his mother had abandoned him when he was only four. Quinn had grown up being told that personal family business should never leave the house; now everything was fodder. (As long as it was spun the right way, of course—his mother's abandonment as the catalyst for his self-sufficiency and independence, etc.)

"The writer is not only a fellow Sloper," he went on, "he's joined us here tonight. Max?" He searched the crowd until his gaze landed on a youngish guy with chunky black glasses. The guy waved hesitantly, as if he hadn't wanted to be outed. "So if he tries to talk to you, be candid. But only about my strengths." Everyone laughed. Gabe finished up by thanking the guests for their support of his "champagne." "Freudian slip," he said, as people laughed again. "While I do appreciate our gracious hosts' support of my champagne, I appreciate your support of my campaign even more."

Quinn hadn't intended on drinking the whole glass, but she knew it would make small talk easier, and would maybe help her stop worrying, so she ended up turning her back to the crowd and finishing it. And she did begin to feel less uptight. She got a second glass from the cute bartender because the flutes were so skinny, and wandered down the empty hallway, pretending to look at the art while she drank. The bubbles were definitely lightening her thoughts. And, honestly, why was she so worried? She couldn't be pregnant, so that wasn't the issue. And the tumor thing had sounded really, really rare. Probably the whole thing was just a ridiculous mistake. She'd be telling all her friends soon and they'd be laughing. Dr. Kumar probably watched that reality show *Pregnant at Sixteen*, or whatever it was called. *"Teenage girl? Must be pregnant!"*

After downing her last sip, she went back to the main room, wishing she hadn't borrowed her mother's wobbly high heels. Could she take them off? No, bad idea. She set her empty glass on a side table and glanced around for someone to talk to. There was a buzzing in her head and she was weirdly aware of her eyelids blinking. Wasn't there anyone who looked friendly? Ben had already disappeared out the door toward the elevator, maybe just for a smoke, but probably for good. There, that older woman with pinkish-orange hair puffed on top like cotton candy, eating a deviled egg. She looked okay. Quinn went up and introduced herself. And yes, the woman—Mrs. Gilchrist, but Quinn thought of her as Mrs. Puff—was chatty and full of funny observations.

She told a story about how she and Mr. Puff had once accidentally grown marijuana in their garden in Arizona. They hadn't known what it was until they had some friends over and one of them was a cop. "Luckily he was a cop who appreciated the merits of a good doobie," she said, and she and Quinn both laughed.

And then there was silence. It was Quinn's turn to talk but she couldn't think of anything to say. The buzzing in her head was distracting. She was also a little dizzy.

"Pretty necklace," Mrs. Puff said.

Quinn glanced down. She'd been fiddling with the pendant again. "Oh. Thanks."

Silence.

"Meryl—my dad's mom—left it to me when she died," Quinn said. "A few weeks before I was born. She didn't even know me."

"Oh. That's nice, hon." A polite smile, then more silence. Quinn was going to say something else, about how surprised she was when her dad gave her the necklace on her last birthday, since he hated his mother so much, but Mrs. Puff waved at a man across the room and Quinn could tell she was bored with the conversation.

"Want to hear something funny that happened to me today?" Quinn said. The words spilled out, unplanned. All of a sudden she needed someone else to know. Needed to hear that, yes, it was crazy.

"You bet!" Mrs. Puff's eyes sparked. "I've been talking your pretty ears off."

Wait! Don't say it! "I found out I'm pregnant." *Shit.*

"I'm not!" Quinn clarified before Mrs. Puff could react. "Definitely not! But that's what the stupid doctor said even though I told her it's impossible. It's impossible because . . ." She lowered her voice. "I've never, *you know*. Not even close. But the doctor still insisted on testing me. Isn't that ridiculous? That's what makes it funny." She smiled to emphasize her point.

A furrow deepened between Mrs. Puff's penciled-in brows. "Well, darlin'—"

"I'm not pregnant," Quinn said again. "Look at me. Do I look pregnant?" She turned from side to side, smoothing down her dress. Almost bumped into a guy carrying a tray of glasses. Oops.

"Uh, no," Mrs. Puff said. "No, you don't."

"It's pretty funny. I mean, what if a doctor told you *you* were pregnant? It's just as impossible, right? So wouldn't you think it was funny?"

"Hon," Mrs. Puff said, "I don't think doctors make mistakes about things like that."

"Well, they must," Quinn said, getting frustrated.

"I really don't think they do."

"But I'm telling you, it's impossible. So obviously they do." This woman was as bad as Dr. Kumar!

"Okay, hon. Okay." Mrs. Puff touched Quinn's hand. "Have you told your parents about this, dear?"

"No," Quinn snapped, pulling her hand away. "Because it doesn't matter. Don't you get it? I don't care what the stupid doctor said! There's no way I'm pregnant!"

Mrs. Puff glanced around. Quinn followed her gaze. Everyone nearby was staring. Including her father.

His fingers pressed into her forearm as he led her down a hall, into the Simons' kitchen, and over by an open pantry, away from where caterers were refilling silver trays of hors d'oeuvres. His tight grip made her pulse pound. Katherine followed them. As Quinn explained everything, her father kept wiping the sweat that glistened on his forehead.

"I would have told you sooner," Quinn said. "But I didn't want to worry you before the party."

"So you thought you'd tell a complete stranger, instead?" Gabe gestured toward the living room. "You do realize everyone in there now thinks you're pregnant? Including Max Smith, the *Times* reporter?"

Champagne bubbles swelled in her stomach. "But I'm not. That's the point."

"Of course you're not!" he said, then added, "Are you?"

"No! I told you—Jesse and I haven't even had sex. I swear."

A crash came from across the room. Shards of glass and bright orange shrimp lay at the feet of a caterer. Ice cubes skittered everywhere.

Quinn had turned her head at the noise too suddenly. She rested her hand against the wall for balance.

"Have you been drinking?" Gabe said.

"I just . . . I had some for the toast. It was—"

"Can we back up a minute?" Katherine interrupted. She put a

hand on Gabe's shoulder and turned to Quinn. "Are you absolutely sure Dr. Kumar understood you're not sexually active?"

"Yes. I'm telling you, she's crazy."

"It's malpractice," Gabe said. "We should have her license revoked."

"Gabe," Katherine said, "I'm going to take Quinn home and try to get in touch with Dr. Kumar. Do you want to come with us?"

He pinched the bridge of his nose. "I need to stay. And we don't want to turn this into more of a *thing*. But call me the minute you speak with her."

Quinn followed her parents across the kitchen, avoiding missed ice cubes and a shrimp with its head still on that stared up at her accusingly from the black marble floor. The sound of people talking and laughing grew louder in the hallway. Quinn stopped. She had to say something before her father got swallowed up in there.

"Dad?"

"What?" he said, turning.

"I didn't mean to ruin your party. I thought it was funny. I wouldn't have said it if there was any chance it was true."

"Well," he said, his voice softening a bit, "look at it this way—it may not have been funny, but I'm fairly certain some people found it entertaining."

"They'll still vote for you?"

"Are you kidding? Would you vote for this face?" He pulled a mock-serious frown and held his chin between thumb and index finger. Quinn thought the anger might be gone from his eyes.

"Uh, yes?" She managed a smile.

"Well, then. Nothing to worry about."

Car chase. *Click.* Diamond earrings for $19.99. *Click.* People fighting on *The Preston Brown Show. Click, click, click . . .*

Quinn sat on the couch, next to her mother, who had her phone to her ear. Katherine hadn't been able to reach Dr. Kumar, since it wasn't a life or death matter, so she'd called her closest friend, Alex, an OB/GYN in Boston, and had Quinn tell her everything. Now Katherine and Alex were conferring. Quinn held the remote in one hand and was rubbing her pendant between her fingers with the other. The weather had broken. Raindrops pummeled the window panes. The situation didn't seem at all funny anymore.

She wanted to be in a tent with Jesse. Or somewhere deep under the waves in that black painting. Anywhere but here.

"I understand," Katherine said. "Of course, Al. I'll let you know. Thanks so much. Love you."

She put the phone down, took the remote from Quinn, and clicked the TV off. The only sound was the hammering of the rain. Neither of them spoke.

"Did she say it might mean something else is going on?" Quinn finally asked. "Like, a tumor—"

"No," Katherine said. "No. She didn't."

"Or maybe it's something to do with all my weird sensitivities. Maybe my hormones are screw—"

"Quinn." Katherine rested her hands on Quinn's knees and stared her in the eyes. "She said that you're pregnant."

Thunder rumbled. Every cell in Quinn's body was freaking out— hot, cold, numb, buzzing. She was ice, water, and steam, all at once. A physical impossibility.

PETER VEGA

Three hours later and ten rain-soaked blocks away from the Cutlers' house, Max Smith sat at his computer, determined to finish a draft of his *Times* article before going to bed. His roommate, Peter Vega, crouched nearby, placing an empty bucket under the air conditioner so water wouldn't pool on the floor the way it did when it stormed.

"He's obviously paranoid I'm going to mention his daughter," Max said. An email had come from Gabe Cutler a couple of minutes earlier, joking about the commotion and reiterating that it was a misunderstanding.

"Aren't you tempted?" Peter said. "Cutler wouldn't be so upset if she weren't actually knocked up." Peter wrote for the gossipy NYC blog *Gotham Gazer*, and he was tempted. Things like this didn't happen in Cutler's world of the New York liberal elite—especially not in holier-than-thou Park Slope. And to the daughter of a probable congressman? (A quick Google search had shown she was pretty, too, which always helped—big time.)

"I'll leave the public embarrassment of minors to you, thanks," Max said. "And the lawsuits."

Sadly, Peter knew Max was right. Not to mention that the girl would probably get an abortion tomorrow and make the whole juicy story disappear. It sucked, because Peter hadn't come up with anything good lately, and his editor had been on his case.

The wind picked up outside and water trickled into the bucket, confirming it was in the right spot. Peter stood. He'd done what he could do. For tonight.

QUINN

Quinn's bedroom was a mountainous landscape of all her clothes and possessions.

It was Wednesday morning. Today was her appointment with her mother's OB/GYN.

She'd been holed up for days. Called in sick to her job and the first day of school; sent a brief text to Jesse and friends saying she had a terrible flu; reread favorite books and binge-watched shows to distract herself.

This morning she woke in a panic before it was light, a sharp fear pulsing painfully in the middle of her chest. *A condom. There was a condom in her room. One handed out at school during health class. If her parents found it they would think she was lying about being a virgin.* Quinn's mind latched onto this thought and couldn't let it go, no matter how unlikely it was that her parents would ever be searching her room at all. She had to get rid of that condom.

She thought she'd hidden it in a small zippered pocket in a travel bag for toiletries. But, no, it hadn't been there when she checked. The back of her underwear drawer? No. The pain in her chest got worse.

Now, it was like Quinn had turned herself inside out—drawers and boxes and bags had all spewed their guts onto the floor. No hidden condom. Anywhere.

The only things that had been the least bit hidden—shoved way underneath her bed—were two shoeboxes, labeled "Quinns—dont tuch!" in her shaky second-grade handwriting. She opened them up. Childhood crap that she shouldn't even be saving—rocks and shells and drawings that reminded her of how weird and lonely and miserable she was the first year they lived in Brooklyn. She didn't have any friends until she transferred schools in third grade. By then, she'd learned how to talk and act like a city kid.

Looking at it all made Quinn even sicker. She shoved the boxes back under the bed.

Tears of frustration stung her eyes. Her breaths were quick and shallow. *Calm down*, she told herself. *You haven't done anything wrong. You are not a liar. You're not even pregnant. Just calm the fuck down.*

QUINN

A nurse entered the waiting room.

"Quinn?" she said, over the sound of an MSNBC report about an earthquake in India. "Follow me, please."

Quinn stood and found that her legs were shaky, like they would have been if she were in Mumbai right now.

"Good luck, Nicole," her mother said to the random woman sitting across from them who'd been talking excitedly about the experimental fertility treatment she'd come for from far away.

See how hard it was to get pregnant? It couldn't just . . . happen.

"Thank you so much," the Nicole woman said with a beaming smile. "God bless."

Quinn and her mother followed the nurse down the hall, under the buzz of fluorescent lights. The nurse's long, frizzy braid bounced against her puke-peach scrubs.

Katherine squeezed Quinn's hand and whispered, "Everything will be okay, sweetie. I promise."

If Quinn had ever believed that, she certainly didn't now.

"There it is. Hear that?"

A muffled, rhythmic sound. A distant drumming. Fast and strong.

A heartbeat.

A heartbeat that wasn't Quinn's own.

NICOLE ANDERSON

In her rented room in Manhattan, big enough only for a single bed and a small dresser, Nicole Anderson from Kalamazoo stood at the window and looked out at the city. She couldn't stop thinking about the teenage girl from the doctor's waiting room that morning, with the dark, thoughtful eyes under strong, slanted brows. Although Nicole knew it was foolish—her fertility treatments might not even work and she'd barely heard the girl say one word—she'd found herself hoping that someday she'd have a daughter just like her. She had no idea why. The girl was beautiful in an unfussy way, but it wasn't her appearance; Nicole didn't care what any of her God-willing future children looked like. So what was it about the girl that had struck her so deeply?

It wasn't until weeks later, when Nicole and the other believers stood outside the girl's house, that Nicole would realize her thoughts hadn't been foolish at all.

"God told me who she was that very first time I saw her," she'd explain to people from then on, as she described the waiting room encounter.

Despite how everything turned out, she thought about it often—a touchstone in the story of her life.

QUINN

Quinn watched herself from outside her body. A girl lying curled on the bed for hours—motionless, silent. Mother sitting next to her, father pacing, repeating the same things and asking the same questions over and over. *Why is she saying it isn't Jesse's? She hasn't been with anyone else, has she? She's so far along—over three months—how can she not have known? Why is she still insisting this isn't possible? Clearly it is! How can she still say she's a virgin? They aren't upset that she had sex—they just need her to admit it!*

Between unanswerable questions, they murmured to each other and on their phones. Quinn vaguely realized they were making arrangements to take care of this. Arrangements to make the nightmare go away. Because it had to be a nightmare. It couldn't be real. Virgins did not get pregnant. Except in stories.

QUINN

Morning. Impatient sunlight pried open her heavy eyelids. Her head throbbed; her body was drained. Why was she so—? *Oh. Oh, god.*

She nudged her cat, Haven, off of her legs and scrambled out of bed and raced to the toilet, making it just in time to vomit. When there was nothing more to come up, she sat on the cool tile floor with her back against the tub and her arms around her knees.

She needed to wake up from this nightmare. *Now.* She forced herself to stand, brush her teeth, splash water on her face.

At the bottom of the stairs, her parents' voices echoed out from the kitchen. Dread prickled through her. She had to talk to them about the next step, but didn't know how many more of their questions she could take. They made her own confusion even worse and filled her with guilt that was sharp but also fuzzy, since she wasn't quite sure what it was about.

"And after that?" her mother asked her father. NPR droned in the background.

"That thing at the Bridge. And then the community center in Crown Heights."

They weren't even talking about her. They were listening to *Morning Edition.* Regular life was going on.

"Hi," Quinn said.

Her father looked up from the *Times* spread on the table in front of him. Her mother turned from the stove. Dark circles formed bruises under her puffy eyes.

"Sweetie," Katherine said, putting down the bag of coffee and coming over to hug her. "Did you sleep?"

"A little."

Her father reached out. She went over and bent down for an awkward, one-armed embrace.

"I called school and told them you were still sick," her mother said in a falsely normal voice, as if her daughter just had a nasty cold.

Quinn sat at the table. "You said something . . . yesterday . . . about appointments?"

"At two today," Katherine said. "With a therapist here in the neighborhood."

That wasn't the appointment Quinn cared about. "What about . . . the other one?"

"Next week," her mother said. "Thursday. The clinic in Brooklyn Heights."

"That's a week away!"

"We were particular about which one to go to," her father said, folding the newspaper with precision. "They're busy."

"And because you're . . . far along," Katherine added, "it's three appointments. The first is just a consultation and tests."

That meant even longer to wait before the actual event. More time for the baby to grow. Quinn's gut clenched.

Her mother sat next to her. "Are you ready to talk?" she asked. "You seem like you might—"

"No," Quinn said, louder than she meant to.

"Quinn," her father said firmly. "We love you, you know that. But this not talking has gone on long enough. I'm not sure what the story is, but we need to talk about it. There is no other option. Understand?"

Quinn bit her lips. In the silence that followed came the click of the front-door lock turning, footsteps in the hallway, then on the stairs down from the parlor floor. Ben came into the kitchen. He was a mess. Hair all disheveled, shirt half in/half out, a stamp of some sort smudged on his cheek. He smelled of cigarettes and bodies and loud music and no sleep.

"Hey," he said. "Have you guys ever noticed how lame it is that you have to walk up the stoop to get into the house and then back down the stairs to get to the first floor? Total waste of precious energy."

No one spoke for a moment.

"I thought maybe you'd moved back to your place," Katherine said eventually.

"Nah. Just stayed at a friend's for a few nights. Didn't you get my text?" He grabbed a carton of orange juice from the fridge and glanced back and forth between Quinn and their parents.

"Man," he said. "I thought I looked like shit. Who died?"

The air in the kitchen froze.

"Fuck," Ben said. "Someone died?"

"Watch your language," Gabe snapped. "And as long as you're in this house, I don't want you living this way. All these different girls. When you're here, I want you to act like a responsible adult. Not out sleeping with different people each night."

"Jesus, Dad," Ben said. "I was at Zach's place. What's your problem?" He looked at Quinn and Katherine. "Seriously, what's going on?"

Quinn stood. "I'm sorry," she muttered, fumbled past the table and chairs, upstairs to the bathroom, then dry-heaved her guts out.

Physically spent, she lay on her bed and opened up the calendar app on her phone. Based on the ultrasound, the doctor had given her a two-week window in late spring when this had . . . happened: *her art teacher's gallery opening in Manhattan, Spanish tutoring sessions, Memorial Day weekend trip to Maine with her mother, Jesse, Ben, and Lydia*—those were the only entries. She stared at the mostly empty boxes, as if the answer was going to spontaneously appear under the laser beam of her gaze: *May 30—Impregnated! Abducted by aliens!*

Chosen by God, like the Virgin Mary! Ha! God would have picked pretty poorly if he picked her, seeing as she didn't even believe in him. Her family wasn't at all religious. (Except to voters. To them, they were "spiritual but unaffiliated.")

A knock came at her door.

"Yeah?" she called.

"Can I come in?"

Her father. She sat up, closed the app. "Okay."

"Everything all right, Little?" he said, shutting the door behind him. He used to call Ben "Big Ben," so when Quinn was born, she'd become "Little."

"Uh huh," she lied. But what a dumb question.

"I have something to—" He wiped his hand across his forehead. "It's like a jungle in here. I wanted to talk, but I'm going to melt."

"You can turn on the other fan or open the window wider." *Or just leave me alone.*

"Your window," he said, approaching it. "You don't have bars? Or even a screen?"

"Uh, no."

Palms on the sill, he leaned out a bit, glanced to either side, then shut the pane and locked it. "The fire escape is right there, Quinn."

Of course it was. So she could climb down if there was a fire.

"Someone could get in," he said. "Or out."

"If you're talking about Jesse," she said, "he uses the door. It's not like we've ever had to sneak around." This was mostly true. Quinn had snuck in and out before, but through the front or kitchen doors, not the window. And not to have sex. Just to hang out with Jesse and other friends in the neighborhood or to snuggle with him in the backyard hammock while whispering about the types of things you can only talk about outside, in middle-of-the-night darkness.

"We'll install an AC unit for you. So it can stay closed." He took out his phone and made a quick note on it, then wiped his forehead again. "Let's go down to the box. Fresh air."

Gabe's third-floor office was so small, the family called it "the box," and it was just as cold as the doctor's office had been. (AC wasn't Quinn's idea of fresh air.) There was one chair at the desk. Gabe sat in it before noticing Quinn was still standing. "Oh," he said. "You sit, Little." He stood.

She sat and looked up at him. His phone buzzed.

"This therapist you're seeing is supposed to be excellent," he said, ignoring the text. "She wrote a well-known book about adolescence. We had to pull some strings to get an appointment, so I hope you'll feel comfortable talking with her. Clearly, something's stopping you from being able to open up to me and your mom."

"It's not that—"

He raised his hand. "Just let me say a few things, okay? I'm not pressuring you to talk right now. I don't want you to keep getting defensive."

Quinn stared at her lap. "Okay."

"Okay," he said. "Let's start with what we know."

That was what he always said when he was talking about how to solve a problem that was too hard, or how he answered questions that he wasn't sure about during a debate or interview.

"We know that you were impregnated by a boy."

She bit her cheeks and nodded.

"Obviously, our hope—and assumption—is that you and Jesse weren't careful enough. Maybe you didn't even have sex, but just came close. I don't know. But if that's not the case . . . if you slept with someone else, other than Jesse, and feel guilty, you need to know that it's okay. You don't need to be scared to tell us. No matter who it was."

"But I haven't—"

He held up a hand again. "Let me finish. Okay? If it wasn't either Jesse or something else consensual . . . if someone did something to you against your will . . ." He rubbed his chin. "I know that victims often blame themselves. After a rape. And if that's what this is, you don't need to. Sexual violence is never, ever the victim's fault. No matter what the circumstance." He gazed down at her intensely. "Even if you were drinking or . . . or whatever. It would never be your fault. *Never.* You know that, right?"

"Uh huh," Quinn said. They'd had multiple assemblies at school about sexual consent, and her mother had talked to her about it, too. "But I don't remember anything like—"

"Quinn, please. All I want you to say is that you understand that we won't judge you, and that you'll try to talk to Dr. Jacoby. That you'll trust her to help you." He paused. "Okay? Can you do that?"

She restrained herself from saying she had nothing to tell the therapist, either. "Okay."

His phone buzzed again. "Sorry," he said, looking at the screen. "The photographer for the *Times*. She's coming today, of all days."

The article. "Is the reporter guy going to . . . mention the party?"

"No. I took care of it." He set the phone on the desk. "I'm sure I don't have to tell you the obvious importance of keeping this in the family, not including your doctors."

Of course. God knows she didn't want anyone to find out. She still hadn't answered anyone's messages beyond saying she was still sick. Jesse had come to the house to check on her, but her mom had sent him away and had promised Quinn she hadn't said anything suspicious.

"And by family," her father continued, "I mean us and Ben. Not Lydia."

"I know," Quinn said.

"No matter what the story is . . ." He squatted down in front of the chair so that he was eye level with her. "We'll always love you. There's nothing you could tell us that would change that. *Nothing.* Obviously, there's a rational explanation for this. Right? A rational explanation? And no matter what it is, we will still love you. Understand?" The blue of his irises was so clear and his gaze so piercing that Quinn felt like he could see something inside her that she couldn't even see herself.

She nodded.

"You need to tell us so we can help you," he said. "The only thing we want from you is the truth."

Eyes closed, Quinn lay in a bath to soothe her itchy skin. Out of nowhere, a vague childhood memory washed over her. Damp clothes. Bone-deep pain. A bumpy car ride. And her father's angry voice. *No more lies! No more lies, Quinn!* But . . . Although she couldn't pinpoint the exact circumstance, she remembered knowing that he hadn't wanted to hear the truth, either. Like now.

QUINN

D r. Ellen Jacoby's office was on the garden level of a brownstone in the North Slope, uncomfortably close to school. As Quinn and her mother waited out front to be buzzed in, Quinn kept her head down, long hair falling forward, and tapped a spiral notebook against her thigh.

The buzzer sounded. "Dr. Jacoby's supposed to be excellent," Katherine said, reaching for the door. "We were lucky to get an appointment."

"Dad told me."

A tall woman with close-cropped, grayish-blond hair and rectangular tortoiseshell glasses met them in the entryway. "Please, call me Ellen," she said. "Or Dr. Jacoby. Whichever you're more comfortable with." After a few words with Katherine about logistics, she led Quinn down a narrow hall to her office. She wore a slim gray skirt and silky orange blouse, all tailored and professional.

Floor-to-ceiling bookshelves filled two walls of the room; the back wall was mostly glass and had a door leading to a small, densely planted garden. The room itself was refined and precise. The only other type of therapy Quinn had ever been in was speech therapy when she was little, to help with a lisp, and now she remembered how chaotic that office had been—toys and dolls and bright colors everywhere. So different from this office, which was right out of one of her mother's design magazines. Ellen—*no, Dr. Jacoby*—sat in one of two modern armchairs and smiled. "Sit wherever you like," she said. Quinn picked the other chair instead of the sofa, because it let her look outside. She tried to calm herself by identifying the different plants in the garden: azalea, coleus, hosta . . .

Dr. Jacoby started out by telling Quinn that everything she said in the office was completely private.

"This is a safe space," she said. "If you decide you want to keep working together, I'm not even going to tell your parents what we talk about, unless I'm worried you might harm yourself. I'll be here for you, and no one else."

She had a steady, calm voice and seemed warmer than Quinn would have imagined from her appearance. Quinn almost wished she were more businesslike, more doctorly and authoritative. She didn't need a friend or confidant; she needed answers.

Dr. Jacoby asked what had brought Quinn to see her. "Your mother's told me a bit," she said, adjusting her glasses. "But I'd like to hear it in your words. Tell me what's going on and what you're hoping to get out of our time together, if you decide you'd like to continue."

"You know I'm pregnant?"

"I do. But assume I know nothing. Start at the beginning."

Quinn told the story of the doctors' appointments, and how she hadn't even believed she was pregnant at all. "Now, of course, I know that I *must* have had sex, even though I don't remember it, which is really impossibly weird. So I guess that I was probably raped and don't remember, because I was drugged and blacked out, or because I have post-traumatic stress disorder." After her bath, she'd spent a couple of hours researching online and making notes. She kept telling herself her father was right—there had to be a rational explanation. And those were the two rational options she'd come up with: raped while drugged or PTSD. With PTSD, your brain could apparently repress something that was too upsetting to know. "And I'm in therapy because I need you to help me remember. I'm not sure if we'll be able to find the man and press charges, but just so we all know, me and my parents. For peace of mind." She paused, and when Dr. Jacoby didn't immediately respond, she added, "Is that enough?" Saying all of this out loud—the very idea of having been raped—made her stomach crawl up her throat.

"If you're finished."

"I guess."

"So, what I'm hearing is that you've found yourself in this seemingly impossible situation and you want to find out how it happened. That you feel you need to know both for yourself, and for your parents."

"Right," Quinn said. "And I've already started doing some stuff." She opened up her notebook. She'd gone through everything she could think of—old emails and texts and posts online and notebooks from school—and had filled out a chart of her activity those two weeks, as well as possible. "It happened during this time frame," she explained. "So, if you hypnotize me and ask about those events, maybe I'll remember."

Quinn had circled a few things on the chart, like her art teacher's gallery opening and a music festival in Prospect Park that she'd been at with Jesse and their friends. She pointed at the entries. "Like, these two nights I don't remember how I got home. So if I was walking alone, at night . . ."

Dr. Jacoby spent a minute reading the pages. Quinn bounced her knee up and down, nervous, as if she was expecting her to immediately deduce what had happened.

Instead, Dr. Jacoby handed the notebook back, saying, "Let's put that aside for now. Okay?"

"Uh, okay. I know that there are a lot of empty time slots, but I did the best I could."

"You remembered a lot, Quinn. And although we'll definitely talk about what was going on in your life, and the work you've done will help, I'm not going to hypnotize you. I'm not sure if you know, but that's something only certain therapists do, and I'm not one of them."

"But . . . isn't that the way, you know, to get memories back? That's what I read online."

"Memory is a slippery fish, Quinn. Very complex. If you really are forgetting what happened, we can try to help you remember in healthier ways."

"What do you mean, 'if' I'm forgetting what happened?" Quinn asked, her chest twisting.

"Let's talk about that. You say you have no memory of what happened, yet you sound pretty certain you were raped. I'm wondering how you came to such a firm conclusion?"

Quinn thought of the ridiculous ideas she'd had. Alien abduction—please! "It's the only logical thing." She rubbed her pendant. "Right? What else would explain it?"

"Well, the most obvious possibility is that something happened with your boyfriend."

"We've never had sex, I swear. Or even come close." She was so sick of having to say that. "So since that really, really can't be it, what other option is there, aside from rape?"

"Does anything come to your mind?"

"I don't know. I . . ." This wasn't what Quinn was here for! She needed answers, not more questions. "When my mom told you what was going on, what did you think? How did you think it might have happened?"

Dr. Jacoby seemed to consider this for a second. "My first thought in a situation like this—about any girl in your position, not you specifically—would be that something accidental happened while she was being intimate with her boyfriend, as I already said. Or that she might not be ready to talk about something that happened with her boyfriend or with someone else."

"Lying?" Quinn said. "Why does everyone keep thinking I'm lying? I'm not. I swear."

"There are lots of reasons we all hold back the truth sometimes," Dr. Jacoby said. "Good, valid reasons. It wouldn't be any sort of reflection on you as a person, Quinn."

"But I'm not lying. I don't know how it happened! How am I supposed to figure it out if I'm telling the truth and none of you want to hear it?"

As Dr. Jacoby assured her that she wanted to hear whatever Quinn wanted to tell her, Quinn couldn't get enough air. She pressed a hand on her collarbone. "I really need this to not be more complicated," she said in a choked voice. "I just need us to figure out when I was raped, or whatever. Okay?"

Dr. Jacoby offered her a glass of water Quinn hadn't even seen her get. "Breathe a deep breath through your nose," she said.

Quinn did.

"And another."

She kept breathing and drinking. Her face was so hot she had to resist an urge to pour the cold water over her head.

"Quinn," Dr. Jacoby said, more softly, "I can't imagine how overwhelming this must be."

Quinn nodded, fighting back tears.

"By no means am I saying that you might not have been raped. I just want to keep our discussions as open as possible. And I don't want our sessions to only be about solving this mystery. You're going through some major emotional and physical stresses. I want to help you develop coping strategies for all of that."

"So, if you won't hypnotize me, what are we going to do?"

"Talk. Follow trains of thought. See what comes up for you, both emotionally and as far as memories go. Not just from those two weeks, but from anytime."

"Wait," Quinn said, agitated again. "Are you one of those therapists who's going to spend the whole time asking about my childhood? Because that has nothing to do with this. I need to talk about those two weeks, not about being a kid!"

"We'll talk about whatever you want," Dr. Jacoby said. "But our childhoods do affect how we react to later events, so we might find it useful to explore it."

"And you really think just talking will help? Because I need to know. Soon. Like, as soon as possible."

"I can't make you any specific promises. All I can promise is that I'm going to do my best to give you a place where you'll feel comfortable talking in ways you might not anywhere else. And I'm confident that will lead us somewhere." She paused. "I don't want you to get frustrated if it seems like things aren't moving quickly. With repressed memory situations, if that's what this is, there's really no way of predicting when it will come back. It will happen when you're good and ready."

"But I'm ready," Quinn said. "I'm ready now."

ELLEN JACOBY

The door closed behind her new patient.

Ellen tried not to make snap judgments, but at the same time, she liked to stay receptive to her initial gut impressions. This time, her impressions started before she'd even met Quinn in person.

Quinn's parents had both gotten in touch with her, separately.

When she called to make the appointment, Katherine Wells had made it clear that she thought it had to have been some sort of unlikely accident while Quinn and her boyfriend were together. "My daughter and I are very close," Katherine had explained, "so I'd definitely know if something traumatic had happened to her. No question. And she'd tell me if she'd had consensual sex. I've always been very sex positive with her. There's no reason she'd lie."

Gabe Cutler had left a message on Ellen's voicemail:

"A couple of points to cover here. First, I want to make sure you don't keep notes about patients online that could be compromised. Our medical records were part of that recent HealthOne leak, so we've already had trouble with that. For Quinn's sake, I want to make absolutely sure this will all be completely confidential. Also, this is probably unrelated, but I wanted to mention that my daughter had . . . an active imagination when she was younger. If she says anything now that seems upsetting or unusual, please let me know. I'm concerned about how . . . disconnected she seems. So . . . thank you, and please call me at this number if you need to discuss anything, not on the house or office lines."

Ellen's impression here was strong: Quinn wasn't the only one in the family who was, as Gabe had said, *disconnected*. It seemed that all three of them were—from one another, and perhaps from some aspects of reality.

QUINN

Quinn could tell her parents were disappointed—they'd been expecting one session with the amazing Dr. Jacoby to unbury the pristine truth from this shitpile of dysfunction.

"You'll keep seeing her, of course," her mother said. "But in the meantime, we're going to have you do a paternity test with Jesse. Okay, sweetie? I know you're convinced it's not his, but things happen."

Apparently, all they needed for the test was a single hair from Jesse—he didn't even need to know about it—and a blood sample from Quinn. Trace amounts of the baby's DNA would be in the blood. Her mom had already made an appointment for her to get the sample drawn later today. Fine. At least it would prove she wasn't lying about one thing.

Curled up on her bed, Quinn took out the chart of the two weeks she'd showed Dr. Jacoby and stared at it again. The answer was right there. How could she not see it?

She considered the two options—blacking out or repressing the memory. She'd read a book once where a random guy drugged a girl at an airport café, so she supposed someone could have done that to her at a coffee place or restaurant. But wouldn't she have realized the hours were missing when she woke up? How would she have gotten home?

Although the other option, repressing a traumatic memory, was hard to imagine, the idea of a random rape somewhere in the city wasn't impossible. This was New York: Being careful didn't guarantee safety.

There was the trip to Maine, too, but while she didn't rule it out, there were a few reasons it seemed unlikely to have happened there.

That weekend was the first time she'd been back to Southaven, her childhood home, since moving to Brooklyn nine years ago, so the trip had been special . . . memorable. Also, she'd been with Jesse or her family almost the entire weekend. The only two times she could think of when she wasn't with one of them were those brief moments with Marco Cavanaugh, and later that same night during the midnight swim at Holmes Cove—events that were seared on her brain in vivid detail. (Not that the coincidence of that traitorous, inexplicable kiss with Marco falling into this time period didn't give her a sick, sticky feeling. She didn't want to think about it, but forced herself to scan her memory: rickety dock, wind and waves, the look, the kiss, the hurried parting . . .)

Most of all, though, Maine seemed unlikely because Quinn's memories of that weekend were intensely happy. Even with the Marco incident, it had been one of the best weekends of her life. She had a hard time imagining how a repressed rape could be part of that.

So, for now, she concentrated on her days in the city. Thinking it was possible that whoever had done this had attacked other girls, too, she went online and skimmed through a year of weekly police blotters in the Brooklyn paper, looking for reports of rapes or attempted rapes in the area. There were a few—though nowhere very nearby—and she wrote down the details in her notebook, waiting for something, anything, to trigger even the slightest hint of recognition.

When nothing did, she found herself getting more and more frustrated. More and more angry at her cowardly brain.

Not remembering isn't going to make it not have happened, she told herself.

And whatever the truth was, it couldn't be as bad as not knowing.

In the middle of the night while trying to sleep, Quinn couldn't stop thinking about those police reports, couldn't stop imagining some random, faceless man following her down a dark street or a park path, hiding behind cars or bushes, waiting for an opportunity . . .

And when a breeze came through the slightly open bedroom window and touched her bare arm, she realized that maybe her father meant a stranger could have climbed in that way and hurt her. Here, in her own bedroom. *Could* someone have come in that way? Eventually, knowing she wasn't going to sleep, she slipped into the hallway, tiptoed past her sister's room and down the stairs in the dark (paranoid, thanks to her obsessing, that she could hear someone else's stealth footsteps on the stairs behind her own), into the kitchen and through the sliding doors into the garden. She looked up at the back of the house. The bottom section of the fire escape was slid up so that the closest rung was unreachable to anyone of normal height. If you were climbing down, you'd slide the section a few feet to reach the ground. But there was no way you could climb up on it from where Quinn stood. Unless . . . She supposed it could have been reached by standing on one of the patio chairs.

She turned and studied the backs of the buildings on the adjacent block and on Prospect Park West, scattered windows lit up here and there. The buildings were row houses and larger apartment buildings, fully attached to one another, and formed a sealed perimeter, meaning the area of backyards was a self-contained environment, not accessible from the street, only from the other buildings.

So even if someone had managed to climb the Cutlers' fire escape, no one would have been back there who would have done that to Quinn. (*You don't know all your neighbors*, a little voice said. *How can you be so sure?*) She took a deep breath. No. She refused to be scared in her own room.

She was about to go inside when her glance darted up to Jesse's dark window. The fact she'd barely been in touch with him for days was completely unprecedented. What was she going to tell him? She could keep lying and stick to the story that she had the flu. If she did, she'd have to go through everything—the abortion, therapy, trying to remember—without him knowing, which sounded impossibly lonely, not to mention logistically difficult. But if she told him, would he believe her story? What if he thought she'd cheated on him? What if she lost him?

Shhh . . . the ginkgo trees' rustling leaves said, trying to calm her. *Shhh . . .*

And then a tiny thought sparked in her mind.

Maybe the baby *was* Jesse's. Maybe, by some fantastic, beautiful miracle, it *was* his. Maybe he had superhero sperm or something, able to swim their way through any barrier. Even before she and Jesse were together-together, they'd talked about what they would name their kids if they had them some day—twins, a girl and a boy, Scout and Spock. Maybe they'd brought one of these pretend kids to life just by dreaming, because they loved each other so much.

Think of how relieved her parents would be if it were Jesse's. How much simpler everything would become.

She stood there, in the dark, listening to the reassuring whispers of the trees, and pressed a hand against her belly. *Please*, she thought. *Please, be Jesse's.*

Once back in bed, she left her window open, determined not to succumb to fear. It kept drawing her eyes, though, and she kept picturing someone out there. A minute later, she collected up some spiky seashells from where they decorated her mantelpiece and placed them in a row along the windowsill. Sentries.

LYDIA CUTLER

Lydia curled her hand and used it like a telescope as she stood in the garden staring up at her sister's bedroom. But she still couldn't see exactly what Quinn was doing. Putting stuff on the windowsill? In the middle of the night?

She'd followed Quinn downstairs, hoping to gather new information. Being the youngest meant Lydia was never told about anything that was going on. Her family either thought she was too young to understand or that there wasn't anything she could do to help. She had to figure out everything for herself.

Start with the things you know. That's what her dad always said

1. Quinn was sick with something that made her parents really worried and confused.

2. Quinn had been sick a lot when she was little, and she'd never gotten completely better. Maybe this was part of that. Except . . .

3. Her parents thought she caught it from Jesse, which meant it was probably something you got from kissing.

Lydia had expected Jesse to meet Quinn in the backyard tonight, like he sometimes did. All he had to do was go through the gate in the fence that separated their backyards, now that he lived so close. (He'd only lived there for a year or something, after his parents got divorced.) But he hadn't come tonight. Quinn had just stood there, alone. Looking around and around like a weirdo, rubbing her belly like she had a stomachache. After Quinn went back inside, Lydia had come out from her hiding spot in the kitchen to see if she could tell what her sister had been looking at. That's when the light had gone on in Quinn's room and she'd started doing whatever she was doing.

Up in her own room, Lydia had a hidden bag of things she'd taken from Quinn over the last couple years. Little things like folded up notes from friends and ticket stubs from movies. Sometimes, Lydia would empty the bag and sort through them, like pieces of a puzzle, trying to figure out her sister, who always seemed to be full of secrets. (What if her secret meant that she was dying? Lydia had always been scared that whatever weird illness her sister had meant she wouldn't live long.)

Standing there, staring up at Quinn's room, Lydia had a feeling that she was going to want to take one of those things her sister had just put along the windowsill.

Pieces of the puzzle. Because something was wrong, and if she could figure it out, maybe she could help.

Maybe she could save her.

QUINN

You'll be okay, sweetie?" Katherine asked Quinn as they pulled up in front of New Prospect's high school, an old brick building that looked like a mansion on one of Park Slope's historic district side streets.

Quinn and her parents had agreed she shouldn't miss another day. "This will all be over soon," her father had said. "No reason to fall far behind in your classes." Quinn couldn't imagine it ever being over, but she did want to at least pretend to get back to real life. Back to normal. She'd texted Jesse to pick her up so they could walk together, like usual. But she got sick after forcing herself to eat breakfast, and was still in the bathroom when he stopped by, so her mother ended up taking her on her way to a gardening job.

"I'll be fine," Quinn said, stepping out of the car. Her head ached; she'd barely slept at all.

Aside from the front-desk security guard, there was no one still lingering in the main lobby when she went inside—just the welcome-back fumes of fresh paint and cleaning products that made Quinn's skin itch. The polished dark wood floor gleamed and creaked under her feet as she headed up a flight of stairs. Other first-day-of-school memories crowded into her brain, like fifth grade, when she and the cute new boy (Jesse) were both wearing Coney Island T-shirts—hers from the Mermaid Parade, his from the Sideshow.

Room 203. Mr. Dellatoro's advisor group room. Quinn hesitated for a moment, stood up straighter, and opened the door.

Everyone sitting in the circle of chairs turned at the sound. In a moment of panic, she thought they were all looking at her because they knew. But no, of course not. They couldn't know.

"Quinn, hello!" Mr. D said. "So great to have you with us, finally." She was momentarily confused by his appearance, then realized he'd grown a beard over the summer.

"Hi," she said. "Sorry I'm late."

Jesse was sitting across the room, his posture uncharacteristically rigid. She gave him a small smile. His expression was worried, not happy or relieved.

Sadie jumped up and hurried over. "You're not contagious, are you?" she asked as they hugged.

"Only if someone touches me," Quinn said, face buried in her friend's enormous mass of dark blond curls. Sadie was obsessed with coding, and they all joked that she kept a couple extra laptops hidden in her hair.

"Let's save reunions for later, okay?" Mr. D said in a friendly voice as they broke apart. "Take a seat, Quinn."

Quinn scanned the circle again and slid into the one free chair, between Adrian Fama and Noë Becker. Adrian gave her a brief chin raise. "Hola, Cutler," he said, smiling his handsome, sleepy smile. "Hola, Fama," Quinn replied with a nod. Adrian had tutored her in Spanish last year. He was fluent in Spanish, French, and Italian. The romance languages, as he loved to point out.

Noë Becker—the school's unofficial PC police, currently wearing about eight rubber bracelets supporting different causes—offered her usual fist bump. Quinn returned it.

Mr. D was checking in with people about their plans for fall extracurriculars, since sign-ups were today. Quinn didn't hear much of what was said. She and Jesse talked with their eyes across the circle. Quinn told him how sorry she was. He asked if she was okay. She gave an almost imperceptible shrug.

"Quinn?" Mr. D said.

"Yeah?" she said, turning her attention.

"I asked if you were going to be heading up Adventurers again. I didn't see it on the list."

"Oh." She struggled to focus on real life. "Yeah, I . . . I forgot to send in the form." Last year, she'd started a club that went on weekend outdoor trips, hiking and canoeing and stuff. An excuse to escape the city as often as possible. Mr. D was the faculty advisor. "But yes. Definitely."

"Great. So you and I should meet about it. And Earth First?"

The environmental awareness committee. "Um . . . yeah. Everything I usually do." She rubbed her pendant. "Of course."

Minutes later, the bell rang for first class block.

"I'm so sorry I haven't been in touch." Quinn held on to Jesse's wrist as they walked out into the crush of the hall. "Please don't be mad."

"I'm not mad," he said. "I just want to know what's going on."

"Nothing," she said stupidly. "I mean—"

"Quinn, wait up!" Sadie grabbed her arm from behind. "You must have been so sick, poor baby!"

Before Quinn could respond, another voice called her name from across the hall. Isa was pushing through people to get to them, using her violin case as a battering ram, with the determination, big eyes, and small stature of a Chihuahua. "You look exhausted, Q," she said. "And we have so much to tell you! It feels like you've been gone for years." Quinn was still holding Jesse's wrist. She knew he wanted an explanation, but her next class was with Sadie and Isa, so she had no choice other than to let him go and say "See you later" as he got sucked down the hallway by the tide of bodies.

When she brought her books to her locker at lunchtime, a note in Jesse's handwriting was taped to the front: *Lounging. Come now. No food required.* There was a small cafeteria at New Prospect; the student lounge was where they ate if they brought their lunches or got take-out. This morning, packing a lunch had been the last thing on Quinn's mind, so she didn't have food anyway. Not that she was hungry.

The room was its usual lunchtime chaos—bags and books littered across the floor, chairs pulled up to tables unevenly as people crowded to sit with friends, laughter and voices filling the air. She found Jesse at a table by a window with the Dubs, Adrian, Oliver Chu, and Matt Rivera, a group originally brought together when they all started playing ultimate in seventh grade. (Except for Matt, who was Adrian's longtime friend, and Caroline, who Sadie and Quinn became friends with in an eighth-grade ceramics class.) By now, people had hooked up, broken up, crushed on one another, and everything in between. Quinn hadn't messed around with any of them except Jesse. The only other guys she'd kissed at all (aside from Marco) were an exchange student named Kai, who'd gone back to Holland, and some random friend of Caroline's at a party a year ago.

"Hey, everyone." She gave a brief wave. An enthusiastic chorus of "Hey, Quinn" echoed from the group.

"Thank god you're back, bunny," Caroline said, standing up to hug her. "We're all sick to death of each other already." Her blackish-brown hair was in two high side poufs, like Mickey Mouse ears, and she was wearing a vintage lace blouse and bright red lipstick. She was the only one in the group who aspired beyond jeans and T-shirts.

"I'll try to be entertaining," Quinn said, forcing a smile. A bunch of take-out containers were arranged between Jesse and the empty seat across from him, holding Quinn's favorite foods from a nearby Middle Eastern restaurant: stuffed grape leaves, hummus, spinach and cheese pie . . .

She sat down. "This is really nice, Jess. But I don't know how much I can eat."

"Because of the flu?" Jesse said. Their eyes met. He knew she didn't have the flu.

"You don't look sick," Matt said, waving a fry at Quinn, his white Real Madrid shirt in danger of being speckled with ketchup. "You look awesome, if you don't mind me saying."

"Of course he thinks so," Isa said to her, not so quietly. Isa and Matt had dated pretty seriously and now had a love/hate relationship. "Your boobs grew over the summer. A girl could be dying of consumption, and if her boobs were bigger, the guys would think she looked awesome."

Shit. Quinn's face heated in a flash. She forced herself not to glance down or adjust her shirt. "No, they haven't," she said. *Shit, shit, shit.*

"That's not what I meant," Matt said to Isa. "I'm not going to go around talking about her boobs in front of my man Jesse."

They don't know. No one knows. Everything is okay.

"If a girl was dying of consumption, I don't think her boobs would be very big, anyway," Oliver said, reaching over Jesse to snag a piece of falafel.

"What is consumption?" Matt asked. "Does your flesh consume itself or something?"

"It's TB, loser," Adrian said.

"Maybe it's what Oliver had over the weekend," Isa said, ignoring him.

"Gross! We're eating!" Sadie threw a cheese puff at her.

"And that was the opposite of consumption," Oliver said, which made all of them laugh.

The conversation redirected to private jokes about the camping trip, and Quinn's face returned to its normal temperature. *Everything is fine. You are still Quinn Cutler—a solid part of this group, Jesse's girlfriend, good student destined to go to a decent college . . .* She made a plate of food and tried to look like she was eating it. Jesse didn't seem to be eating much either. In the car this morning, her mother had reminded her about the paternity test. What was she supposed to do, casually pluck a hair off his head? Or off his shirt? Not even tell him?

And how incredibly disturbing that the baby's DNA was mingled with her own blood. Were they two people right now or one? Since all this began, she had tried not to think too much about the baby itself. But it was inside her. Right now as she sat here with her friends. It was either a boy or a girl, and it had fingers and toes and had been inside her for over three months. *Three months.* If she hadn't happened to go to the doctor, would she have been one of those girls who went all nine months without knowing? Because, clearly, there was something really wrong with her. She was really, really screwed up. And it was her fault somehow, she was sure of it. Otherwise, it wouldn't be happening to *her.* There wouldn't be a baby with fingers and toes growing inside of her—Right. Now.

"Quinn?" Jesse said. "Are you choking?"

Her hand was at her throat. She wasn't choking, but she couldn't breathe. She couldn't breathe at all, and she pushed back her chair and bolted up to go get some air. "Quinn? Are you okay?" Dizziness crashed into her skull. She put a hand out to steady . . . Everything tipped . . . The floor rose . . . fast.

Quinn was lying on the bed in the nurse's office. Her head was still spinning and she was full of nausea—dehydrated from the flu, she'd explained. The nurse forced juice and saltines on her.

"Can I see Jesse?" Quinn asked.

The nurse's lips tightened disapprovingly. "For a minute," she said.

When she ushered him in, he looked like he was the one who had fainted. His skin was the color of ash. Even his hair seemed to have paled.

"God, Quinn." He held her cold hand in his warm one. His

fingers were so long, it looked as if they could wrap around hers more than once. She loved his hands. He leaned over and kissed her on the forehead. "You scared me."

"Sorry," she said. "I didn't mean to."

"Q. Are you . . . are you dying? Like, from cancer?"

She smiled weakly. "No. Definitely not dying."

The nurse was talking on the phone in the outer room and the door was open just a crack. Jesse eased it shut, quietly, then sat on a metal folding chair next to the low bed. A sunstream from the window caught the light fuzz on his sharp jawline and brought out the flecks of warm gold in his eyes.

"So, seriously, can you tell me what's going on?" he said. "I'm going crazy here."

Her heart was jackhammering. She needed to tell him. This was too much to manage alone and there was no one she trusted completely other than Jesse. Also, they spent so much time together, she needed him to help fill in gaps in the calendar, help her figure out when and where something could have happened. He must have noticed her acting weird at some point. Her parents wouldn't have noticed because they'd been too busy with the election. But Jesse . . . how could he not have noticed *something*?

She'd say it when she reached three.

One . . . two . . . two and a half . . . Her lips were numb. She fiddled with her pendant.

"Quinn?"

Telling him the truth might make her more alone than ever if he thought she was lying about not having slept with anyone, or if he believed her and got too freaked out to deal with it. That could happen. People get freaked out when you tell them something they don't want to hear. People don't always believe your explanations. And if she had to live without Jesse . . . she wouldn't be able to breathe.

Still, the words were pressing up out of her chest, trying to get out, like her madly thumping heart. But she couldn't move her lips.

Two and three quarters . . .

"Quinn?"

She squeezed his hand again. "If I tell you, will you promise not to freak out?"

"Uh, I guess that depends."

"Will you promise not to leave me?"

"Jesus, Quinn. You're scaring me again. Can you just say it?"

Three.

JESSE KALBITZER

J esse's next class was pre-calc. He handed Mr. Evans his homework sheet. He sat down. Then, his brain exploded. It was a bit of a mess.

QUINN

Mostly to escape the deafening silence of her phone that evening, Quinn joined her family for dinner. They all acted as if they were happy to see her, but something was off, like when a movie soundtrack doesn't quite match the actors' lips. Except for Lydia, who was still oblivious.

Quinn moved her stir-fry from one side of the plate to the other. It had been hours since she told Jesse, and she still hadn't heard from him. She'd left school straight from the nurse's office, and during the afternoon the Dubs had all messaged to check on her. Even Mr. Dellatoro had emailed. But not Jesse. In the short time they'd had together before the nurse made him go to class, she'd only been able to give him the briefest outline of what was going on. He'd been too shocked to say much of anything except for, "That's not possible. How is that possible? What are you *saying*, Quinn?"

She'd sent him message after message:

Please believe me.

Know its crazy.

Theres a way to explain it.

Will find out what happened. Soon.

Don't be too weirded.

That was stupid. Of course youre weirded.

Please.

Believe me.

I love you.

She tried to shove down the anxiety, stabbed a piece of broccoli, and listened to Lydia talking about her new teacher, a Ms. McEvoy she wasn't sure she liked.

"I told her there was going to be a picture of me in the newspaper tomorrow, and she looked at me like this." Lydia tilted her head down, drew her brows, and scrunched up her mouth.

"What picture?" Quinn asked.

"In the article about Daddy. Duh."

"I didn't know you were in the photo," Quinn said. She'd forgotten the article came out the next day. Had forgotten about the article entirely, actually.

"Me and Daddy and Mommy," Lydia said. "It better be good. I'm going to bring it to school on Monday to show that disbeliever." She raised her glass of milk in the air. "She'll see I'm newspaper worthy!"

Ben snorted.

"What?" Lydia said.

"Not you. I just think it's funny . . ." He speared a forkful of stir-fry and looked at Quinn. "Oh, never mind."

Quinn knew perfectly well what he thought was funny: which of the Cutler children weren't newspaper worthy.

"You always laugh at me," Lydia said. "You'll see. Someday I'm going to be a famous scientist and live in Europe."

"No one is laughing at you," Gabe said as he pushed back his chair. "Sorry to desert you all. I've got to make an appearance at a function. Mom and I are going to a few block parties tomorrow, before a couple of more formal gatherings. Lydia, Quinn—you guys will join us. Ben, we'd be happy to have you for any of it."

"Gee, tempting," Ben said. "But I'm hitting Rockaway."

"You're going to the beach?" Quinn said, giving him a quick reprieve for being a jerk. "Can I come?" The last thing she wanted to do was spend the day at campaign events, with her parents worrying about her and having to make small talk. The beach was her favorite place in the world, especially when she needed to think: the rhythm and sound of the waves, the slow movement of the tide, the vast expanse of space. Watching the ocean even had a bit of a hypnotizing effect. She'd bring her notes about those weeks and keep trying to bring her mind back in time.

"I'm heading out early," Ben said. "Six."

"Early's fine."

"I want you with us, Quinn," her father said.

"I thought the Simons' party was my last obligation for a while."

"Ben's surfing. I don't want you there alone. You fainted today."

"Only because I hadn't eaten. And I'll invite Jesse to come, too. So I won't ever be alone. Please?"

She didn't let herself consider the possibility that Jesse wouldn't want to go.

"I don't think it's a good idea." Gabe rinsed his plate and put it in the dishwasher. "I've got too much going on to be worrying about it."

"Gabe," Katherine said. "I think it's fine if Quinn goes. As long as Jesse's with her. And she's careful if she swims."

"What's the big deal?" Lydia said to her father. "When we went to the beach this summer, Quinn was fine swimming, now that she's over being a chicken." She paused. "Do you really think she'd have *died* that time if Ben hadn't pulled her out, Daddy?"

Quinn had almost drowned in the ocean when she was seven, leading her to stop swimming in it completely until that midnight swim on Southaven over Memorial Day weekend. She'd still swum in lakes and ponds, just not the ocean. The drowning story fascinated Lydia, who never seemed to realize that it wasn't a good memory for anyone. Well, except maybe for Ben, who had been the hero.

Quinn sent her sister silent *Shut up!* vibes.

"I don't know," Gabe said gruffly. "And that has nothing to do with this."

"When you found her on the beach," Lydia continued, "after Ben went and got you, was she already dead and you brought her back to life? Or was she, like, just half—"

"Lydia," Gabe snapped. "Enough."

"I promise, Dad," Quinn said, "nothing will happen."

"You're right," he said. "Because you're not going."

GABE CUTLER

Nothing will happen. Gabe heard the words as he waited on Seventh Avenue for the B67 bus.

Nothing *would* happen if he let her go, most likely—he knew that. He also knew that he'd lied: His reaction *did* have to do with that day Quinn had almost drowned.

He wasn't sure why, but ever since finding out she was pregnant, he'd been having vivid memories of that day in Maine: a white-faced, eleven-year-old Ben telling them what had happened; his own frantic run down the wooded path to Holmes Cove; her tiny body lying in the surf. And when he thought of all that, he thought of everything that had come after that summer, Quinn's confused thoughts and imaginings and reckless behavior. And it was all tangled up with his memories of what his mother, Meryl, had said years earlier, before Quinn was even born.

Katherine had been pregnant with Quinn when Meryl had asked them to come visit her—the first time she'd tried to see Gabe since she'd walked out on him and his father almost thirty years earlier. Gabe's instinct was to say "No fucking way." But Meryl told him that she was dying, and Katherine said he'd regret not going, that he needed to process his anger. (Katherine was the only reason Meryl even knew how to contact him, having insisted on sending her occasional letters, when there was important news to share.) The morning of the visit had been strained, but fine, mostly occupied by Meryl showing them the house and land. As the day went on, she'd become incoherent and emotional, ranting to him about delusional fantasies, acting strangely and irresponsibly with Katherine . . . suicidal, although he didn't know it at the time. Shortly after they'd left the island, she had walked into the ocean with rocks in her pockets. That's what she'd meant when she'd said she was dying.

Standing there on Seventh Ave, Gabe was so lost in the unpleasant memories that he almost didn't notice when the bus rolled up and stopped with a mechanical sigh. He hung back as an elderly couple boarded, then stepped inside, inserted his MetroCard in the reader, and scanned the bus for a seat next to a constituent he could chat up.

He needed to stay focused. To live in the present.

He wouldn't picture Quinn's fragile, seven-year-old body in the surf. And he wouldn't let his mother's ominous words from that last visit keep poisoning his mind. They had nothing to do with this. Nothing to do with the day Quinn almost drowned. Nothing to do with anything.

Still, he heard them:

"Your baby . . . Your daughter . . . Listen to me. You must be the one to tell her, Gabriel. Help her understand. I won't be there to do it, and if you don't, things will go badly. Very badly. For all of you."

QUINN

Quinn crept downstairs in the morning when it was still half dark, careful not to wake her parents or sister.

She sat on the stoop with her beach bag, a black hole of worry in her stomach. Not about going to Rockaway (she wasn't sneaking—her dad had texted her from his event last night and told her that he'd overreacted) but about Jesse's continued silence. He'd sent one message: Will call. But he hadn't, not even in response to her invitation to the beach.

Of course he didn't believe her. Of course he thought she cheated on him. Why, why, *why* had she told him?

She closed her eyes for a moment and tried to fill the gaping emptiness with a deep breath so it wouldn't fill with panic.

Preoccupied, it took her a minute to register what was lying on the step below her feet. The *Times*. She shook it out of the blue plastic delivery bag and riffled through for the right section. There they were—her father, mother, and sister—under the headline, "Hoping to Put Bestselling Words into Action." She skimmed the article until her name jumped out. "Cutler's two younger children, Quinn, 16, and Lydia, 10, attend New Prospect School, a private school with campuses just blocks from the family's Park Slope home. Cutler says that he would have preferred all three of his children to go to public school, but that new zoning meant . . ." It went on to talk about school issues. That was it. Thank god.

The door opened behind her. "What are you doing?" Ben said as he stepped out. "Dad caved?"

Quinn stood up, tossed the *Times* into the foyer, and slung her beach bag over her shoulder. "Yup," she said.

Ben looked doubtful.

"What?" Quinn asked.

He shook his head. "Nothing," he said. "It's fine."

Quinn followed him to his ancient, beat-up, butter-yellow Mercedes station wagon, and waited in it while he made another trip to get his board and then fastened it on the roof rack. The neighborhood was still asleep under a blanket of haze, the pavement wet from rain during the night. Quinn always felt sorry for raindrops that landed on dirty city streets.

Ben checked the mirror and pulled out of the space. "I assume we're picking up Jesse at his mom's?"

Quinn swallowed. "Yeah, but I . . . I don't actually know if he's coming. He never answered."

"Seriously?" Ben said, glancing at her. "Fuck, Quinn. Dad's going to shit a brick if I take you without Jesse. And if something happens—"

"Nothing's going to happen. And Jesse will come. I know he will."

They were already turning onto the Kalbitzers' block. Ben pulled the car in front of a fire hydrant and idled. He hadn't been around much the last couple of days; this was the first time they'd been alone since finding out about the pregnancy. Quinn rolled down her window the whole way. Ran her finger over a rip in the seat. Birds twittered. *Anyone would have predicted this would be the other way around*, she thought. *Ben having gotten someone pregnant.* She wished they didn't have to talk about it at all, but she also wondered if maybe he could help. Finally, she just came out and said it.

"Have you ever blacked out?" she asked. "From drinking or drugs or whatever?"

He turned to her, his gaze sharp. "Why? Is there a night when you—"

"No," she said. "That's the point. There isn't. That's why I'm asking. I want to know what it's like. And whether it could have happened without me realizing. You know, if someone gave me a roofie."

"Oh," Ben said. "Well . . . I've never totally blacked out, but there are times when I've forgotten bits of the night. Like, how I got home or something."

"And the next day you realized you were forgetting stuff?"

"Yeah."

"Do you think I could have woken up after and *not* realized?"

He looked uncomfortable. "Well, yeah, sure. I guess so. But if it was a roofie, don't they make people black out for a big chunk of time? And feel sick the next day?"

"Yeah," Quinn said. She'd read a million websites about their effects. "But maybe there are milder ones? Or maybe I only took a couple of sips of the drink?"

Ben waited a moment before responding. "You know, Quinn, you can tell me anything, and I won't tell Mom and Dad. No one knows better than me what it's like with them. The pressure they can put on you to be a certain way. How judgmental Dad is. So if there's something you can't tell them—"

"There isn't," Quinn said, a bit short because he sounded just like them and everyone else, insinuating she was lying.

"Okay," he said, although she sensed skepticism in his voice. "Well . . . I just want you to know you can trust me. And that I'd do anything to help you. Anything at all."

"I know," she said. "And you are helping, by keeping me away from those stupid campaign events today."

Silence returned to the car.

Quinn focused out the window, willing Jesse to bound out of his building. The front door opened, but it was an older woman walking a dachshund. They waited ten minutes past when she told him they'd be there. A lump swelled in her throat. Ben started the car, pulled out—

"Hey! Wait!" A voice, calling from up the block. And then Jesse running down the street. Waving at Ben to stop.

During the whole car ride, Quinn reached into the back seat and held Jesse's hand so she'd know he was really there, not just a figment of her imagination. When he'd gotten in the car with them, she'd felt like she was about to float out the window. His smile was tight and his eyes guarded, but just the fact that he'd come . . . (He wouldn't have come just to dump her, would he?)

As they crossed over the bridge to the Rockaways, she tasted the ocean on the damp, briny wind. And the minute they reached the wide, flat expanse of beach, she kicked off her flip-flops and ran—heels sinking in the cold sand—down to the edge of the water, then stood, eyes closed. She didn't move, just stood there, arms out, and let the salt, seaweed, roar, rush, spray, seep into her veins. Freezing surf tickled her toes, then wrapped round her feet, trying to urge her in. Someone once told her that waves coming in were young ocean spirits, wanting to explore, and the undertow was cautious older ones pulling them back out. *Hello!* she splashed with her feet. *Hello! Hello! Hello!*

The morning air hadn't warmed up yet—there was a trace of fall in it, even—but she wanted to swim. First, though, she needed to talk to Jesse. As thrilled as she'd been to see him, the thought of what he might say made her a little sick. Wind plastered her hair across her face as she looked for where the boys had settled with their stuff. There—Ben putting on his wetsuit, Jesse fishing in his navy backpack.

When she reached them, Ben headed out with his board, grumbling about how the waves weren't as big as some guy said they'd be. Jesse was applying sunscreen. In the midst of all her worries, Quinn couldn't help thinking about how she'd like to be the one rubbing that lotion onto his abs. It felt like forever since she'd run her hands over his smooth skin.

Instead, she spread out a tapestry, anchoring down the edges with flip-flops and lotion bottles and cans of seltzer. After a moment, she realized she was fussing with stuff to put off the start of their conversation and forced herself to take a breath and sit. Jesse followed suit.

"Thanks so much for coming," she said.

"No problem." He poured a cup of coffee from a thermos he'd brought. He offered it to Quinn, but she shook her head.

"I'm sorry I didn't call," he said after a minute.

"That's okay. Were you . . . busy?"

He turned to meet her eyes. "Let's cut the shit, Q. I was freaked out. Obviously. You—Quinn—pregnant. It came as a bit of a surprise."

"I know," Quinn said. "I'm sorry." She bit her cheeks.

"You don't need to be sorry. That's not what I'm saying. I'm just saying that . . . that I have no idea what to say! I was in shock. It was like you threw a grenade in my head and I had to piece my brain back together before speaking to you." He pantomimed his head exploding, with sound effects.

"So, is your brain, uh, back together?"

"I think so," he said. "Took a while, given its enormous size."

Quinn allowed herself a slight smile. "And now," she said cautiously, "you believe me? You believe I have no idea how it happened?"

He dug into the sand with his feet. "Okay," he said. "Okay, so . . . no."

Of course he didn't. No one did.

He stared into her eyes again. "I get that you'd be scared to tell me you hooked up with someone else. But lying about it would be way, way, way worse. You get that, right? I'd rather a hundred times over that you just tell me the truth." His bottom lip was twitching slightly. "So . . . just tell me. Okay?"

Quinn reached up for her pendant but wasn't wearing it so fiddled with the drawstring of her hoodie instead. "I promise, Jess. I did not sleep with someone else. I absolutely swear." *You're not lying. You only kissed* Marco.

He kept his eyes locked on hers, and for once, she didn't like the feeling that he could read all her thoughts. "Swear on Haven's life?" he said.

"Swear on Haven's life."

A few beats passed. "Okay," he said. "Sorry for pushing, but it's kind of the obvious conclusion."

"I know."

"So you really, honest to god, have no memory of *anything?*"

"Honest to god," Quinn said. "I know it's impossible to believe. But I need you to trust me."

Jesse looked out at the waves. The wind ruffled his hair. "Well," he finally said. "It's pretty damn scary, and weird. Super weird. Like, David Lynch weird. But I trust you. So I guess that means I believe you."

Quinn's whole body softened at those words, except for a deep down tiny part that she swept into a corner. "Thank you, Jess," she said, hugging him and kissing the warm skin on his neck, tasting sunscreen. "You're the only one who does."

"So," he said. "What . . . you know, what happens now?"

Quinn explained about her upcoming appointments at the clinic—unexpectedly hit by a pang of sadness while talking about it— and then told him that her parents wanted them to do a paternity test.

"They wanted me to do it without asking. I'm not even supposed to tell you I'm pregnant—my dad would *kill* me if he knew I had. But I wanted you to know. All I'd need for the test is a strand of hair. I already got my blood drawn."

"No problem." He reached up and plucked a hair off his head, held it out to her, saying, "Take it now, if you want. But you realize my boys would have to be superheroes? Like, wearing tiny little capes and tights and doing impossible things."

"That's exactly what I thought," Quinn said. "Maybe they are." She rummaged through her beach bag and brought out her notebook, tore out a blank page and carefully folded it around Jesse's hair and put it safe in a pocket.

"And if they're just average citizens?" he said. "What then?"

She opened the notebook to the pages with the chart she'd shown Dr. Jacoby. "I need to remember every possible thing about these two weeks. I'm trying to fill this in." She held it out to him. "Could you look at your calendar or old messages or whatever and see if you can figure out any time when I might have been . . . I don't know, vulnerable? I guess any time I was walking somewhere alone at night would be most likely, right?"

He studied it, his eyes widening slightly. "Wow. I didn't realize it happened so long ago. You're really pregnant. Like, far along."

His gaze darted down to her belly for the briefest moment; she was glad she still had on the hoodie over her bathing suit. "Yeah," she said. "Anyway, I figure if we come up with some possibilities about where and when something might have happened, you can hypnotize me and ask me about them, try to make me remember. I've been reading about hypnosis, and it's not like you have to be trained to do it."

"Hypnotize you? Seriously?"

"I've read online about repressed memories, and some people say hypnosis works. There's a sheet in there," she gestured at the notebook, "something I printed out, with directions and stuff." A beat passed. With every step in the conversation, Quinn was bracing herself for him to run away from the whole thing. "Will you help? It might not work, but I have to *do* something."

"If you're sure," Jesse finally said. "I'll do anything you want."

"Thank you," she said, hugging him again.

When she pulled back, they both stared at the calendar.

She pointed at the night where she'd written: *Music fest in Park. Walk home?* "Do you remember us walking home that night?"

He paused. "Not off the top—Oh. Wait. I left early. Before the rest of you. Remember?"

Quinn shook her head. "Nope. But that definitely makes it more likely I'd have walked alone." She took a pen out of her bag, made a note on the page.

"What about that night in Maine?" Jesse said, pointing at the Sunday of Memorial Day weekend. Quinn froze for a split-second, but then he added, "You know, after we watched the movie, when we were on the deck and you disappeared? You were alone then."

"When I went swimming?" she said, breathing again. "I thought about that, but the thing is, I remember it so clearly. Swimming. And we had that whole conversation when I came back. You'd have noticed if I was, like, traumatized, don't you think? And you'd definitely have noticed if I was drugged, right?"

He thought. "Yeah, you definitely didn't seem groggy or drugged. You seemed . . . happy. Excited. Not upset. And totally clear-headed."

Although neither of them mentioned it now, Jesse was the one who'd been upset during that conversation.

He pointed to the calendar again. "We got a ride home from Isa's mom after Ms. Knowles's art opening, so it wasn't that night."

At the prompt, the memory of everyone piling into the car surfaced. "Yes!" Quinn said. "See? You're helping already!"

After making another quick note, she leaned over and kissed him overenthusiastically, jolting and spilling his coffee.

"Hey!" he said, setting it aside. "Watch it." He tossed a handful of sand at her.

"You watch it," she said, giving him a playful shove.

He shoved back, and soon they were throwing sand and wrestling and pretending to forget how unfathomably weird Quinn's life had become.

BEN CUTLER

en sat on his board, legs dangling in the water (shark bait position, one of his non-surfer friends called it), watching his sister and Jesse, completely fucking confused.

Being a sane human being, Ben knew that "true love" and "soul mates" were bullshit. But, sometimes, Quinn and Jesse made him wonder. You could almost see cables physically connecting them—like climbers, roped together.

Which made it impossible to understand why she'd been kissing Marco Cavanaugh that night in Maine.

Ben hadn't realized it was her until this whole fucked up pregnancy thing, when little parts of that evening gelled in his head: It was at a party at the Cavanaughs', the Cutlers' neighbors on Southaven—a good-bye party, since the Cavanaughs had sold their house. A barbeque followed by a bonfire. There were maybe twenty people at the bonfire, and enough of them were girls with long hair that when Ben saw Marco kissing someone on the dock, he hadn't thought twice. But later that night, Marco had been acting jacked up around him, and Foley Cavanaugh, Marco's older cousin, had said to Ben, "You got a live one there," while gesturing at Quinn. Ben had been too high or whatever to really wonder what the hell Foley meant. Now, though, it all made sense.

Well, not all of it. Not why she would have kissed Marco to begin with.

Those guys . . . Marco and Foley . . . Ben had been friends with them growing up on Southaven, but they'd never been especially nice to Quinn. Teased her, didn't let her hang out with them—normal older kid stuff. So it wasn't like there should have been some hot reunion.

The only thing that made sense was that Marco had coerced her to kiss him in some way. Which, of course, made Ben wonder what else he'd done to her that night.

Ben gripped his board. He should have had his eye on her during the party. But she'd been with Jesse, and Ben had been too fucked up to really pay attention. He'd been useless, just like his dad always said. Just like when they were kids. A terrible big brother. And he wasn't only useless, he was a liar. And he hated himself for it.

But he was going to make up for it now. He was.

He'd told a friend of his who was a survivor of sexual assault that something might have happened to his sister but she wouldn't talk about it, and his friend had said to let Quinn know he was there for her, but not to force her to talk about it if she wasn't ready.

Fine. He'd done that. But it wasn't enough. He wasn't going to just sit around and do nothing. Not this time.

QUINN

After talking to Jesse, Quinn practically skipped down to the water—strangely elated, even though nothing about their discussion changed how messed up her life was. The fact that he wasn't angry, that he was going to help, that she wasn't in this alone . . . It changed everything. And just the fact that someone believed her!

She stood shin-deep in the surf for a moment, easing in. The ocean's hands wrapped around her legs and pulled. *Let's play!*

She stopped teasing it—let it pull her farther out and dove in, through a wave, sputtering for a moment at the exquisite shock of the full-body cold. Quickly, she swam out to deeper water that came up to her chest. Waves barreled toward her. She flung herself up to the peak of the high crests, plummeted down on the other side. Again and again. Fly up, crash down. The waves seemed to get higher and higher, daring her to keep going, sometimes so big that she had to dive through instead of going over, fists pummeling her back and legs as the water thundered toward shore on top of her. She started thinking about the baby, wondering if it (he? she?) could feel all of this, too. If it was scared. Or maybe even having fun. She was sure a doctor would tell her that it didn't feel emotions, but she had seen pictures online of what a fetus looked like at this stage, and it totally looked like a tiny—if weirdly big-headed—baby. So it was kind of hard for her to imagine that it didn't feel anything. *Don't be scared*, she said silently.

She jumped and plunged and dove, forgetting about everything except the oncoming wave, knowing that fall was approaching and this may be her last swim for a while. And just when she was beginning to feel tired, the next waves weren't so exuberant—more rolling and gentle, as if the ocean were getting tired, too. She treaded water for a minute, catching her breath, then started to swim in slow, easy strokes, parallel to the shoreline.

She still couldn't believe she'd stayed out of the ocean all those years. When she took that midnight swim last May, it had been like a revelation. Her fear had been so wildly misplaced.

She could remember every sensation from that night in Maine. Lowering her naked body off the rock into the black depths, her pulse pounding with the thrill of doing something forbidden and dangerous; not only was she going in the ocean, she was at the very beach—Holmes Cove—where she'd almost drowned. But once she slipped into that ink-black water and her body disappeared, any sense of danger vanished, replaced by sheer exhilaration. Disappearing into that water had been like . . . like slipping out of her own skin into something that was both magical and massive, while still intimate and safe. Like she left her body and was just . . . Quinn. Yes. She'd felt more purely herself than she could ever remember. As if she'd found the part of her soul she'd left behind when they moved away. She'd thought she'd be too cold to stay in—swimming in the ocean in Maine in late spring was insanity—but she wasn't, maybe because it was so hard to tell where her body ended and the ocean began. The half moon had sparkled on the water, making it look like a whole school of those mysterious deep-sea illuminated creatures—lanternfish—had risen to the surface. Like she was swimming with stars.

She'd felt so alive. No fear, no guilt, just thrill.

The exhilaration lasted all the way through running back home on the dark forest path, the moss carpet springy under her feet, the secret of what she'd just done humming inside her. (Jesse was the only one she would tell. If her family—well, her father—found out she'd been swimming alone, at Holmes Cove, in the middle of the night? She'd have been better off drowning.)

Quinn stopped swimming now and turned over to float on her

back. The sky smiled blue above her. She placed her hands on her stomach and closed her eyes.

Float . . . float . . . float . . .

Water lapped against her ears, played with her hair, nudged her this way and that. She could almost hear it talking, telling her that everything would be okay.

This was the best—the most relaxed—she'd felt since this nightmare had started. Even aside from the relief about Jesse, everything felt so much easier when she was floating, weightless. Most people, it seemed, dreamed and fantasized about being able to fly like birds. Quinn hated the thought of flying—had panic attacks on airplanes. Quinn's fantasy, even during the years when she'd stayed out of the ocean, was to be able to swim like a fish, deep into the hidden world that was right here on the planet. Those lanternfish had always fascinated her—making their own light, thousands of feet under the surface. It must be so beautiful down there among them. She'd done a report on them in sixth grade and learned about bioluminescence; to Quinn, it was still magic.

She wished she could stay in this weightless world forever. She imagined swimming down to that mysterious place and releasing the baby into the water, watching it swim away, its path lit by those living lights. At the thought, an image appeared behind her eyelids. The baby, rocking inside her, like she was rocking in the swells. She pictured a round belly and tiny limbs, and wondered if being in a womb was like floating in the ocean, if the sounds were similar, and the weightlessness . . . the baby's own tiny ocean inside her, until it was ready for the real one. It probably felt just as safe as she did now.

How did you get here? Quinn asked. *Who are you? Why are you inside of me? Babies aren't supposed to be mysteries.*

She listened, trying to hear an answer, but none came, just the sound of the water.

Still, she had a profound feeling that the baby could understand her words, that it was listening to her just like she was trying to listen to it. *I need you to help me*, she said. *I need you to tell me where you came from.*

She listened again. Water . . .

She imagined it saying: *You know. You were there. I didn't exist yet.*

I don't know. Tell me.

Just the *lap, lap, lap* of the water against her, and the roar of the waves crashing on the shore.

I don't blame you. I just need to know.

Caaaw, caaaw . . . a seagull crying . . .

Lap, lap, lap . . .

It was beautiful. The words were inside Quinn, but weren't her own.

Are you Jesse's? she asked. Because that was the only beautiful explanation that Quinn could see.

Lap, lap, lap . . .

Beautiful. It was beautiful.

Water stroked her skin. Like it was comforting her. She lay so still and let it rock her, listening.

A still morning sea, deeply asleep . . . That poem again. It was "morning sea," not "midnight sea." A morning sea, like the one she was floating in right now.

The sound of the water was its own type of poetry. The *rush* and *roar* . . .

And inside her, a *shush-shush, shush-shush* . . .

A heartbeat. She wasn't sure whose.

QUINN

Hovering at the edge of sleep that evening, Quinn kept hearing the ocean and remembering the sensations from that midnight swim in Maine.

It had seemed like she'd plugged into the universe's electrical socket, like you could have powered every light on Southaven with the energy inside her, like anything was possible. She'd been one of those lanternfish herself. She could still feel the electricity now as she floated into sleep.

Later, deepest night, she woke up wet with saltwater. Sweat, not sea. Images from a nightmare fought to come to the surface. She'd been kissing Marco, underwater, and then . . . then Marco was gone and her father was yelling at her, telling her that it was all her fault and calling her a liar, and she was holding something. A wet—not just wet, drowned—kitten. No, not a kitten. Haven. Drowned. Dead. She felt frantically around the bed to make sure Haven was still there, alive. She was. Quinn lay still for a minute, hand pressed against Haven's warm, breath-full body, and tried to calm down, to remind herself the fear wasn't real. She tried to replace the nightmare images with actual memories of Rockaway. Of sand shifting under her feet, briny wind playing with her hair, of the ease of being in the water. And in thinking about it, she was overwhelmed by an urge, a need. Before she could consider the wisdom of it, she crept down the narrow staircase by the dim yellow glow of nightlights and found her mother's purse in the front hall. She hunted through the mess of business envelopes, tissues, campaign fliers, magazines, make-up, parking tickets. Just when she thought it wasn't in there anymore, she found the small, manila envelope she was looking for, the one she'd seen her mother put in there at the end of her doctor's appointment. She brought it back to her room, turned on her desk lamp, and took out the folded strip of paper—the series of ultrasound photos. Quinn hadn't watched when they were doing it, but after a moment, she could make out the shiny white-on-black image—big head, tiny rounded body, stubby limbs. Exactly like it was in her mind when she'd been swimming. Floating in an inky ocean.

She stared at the image with a hand on her belly. It was inside her. That baby in the picture. It had been created inside *her*.

"If we lived in the water," she whispered, tracing the shape of the tiny head with her finger, "I'd do this for you. But it would be too hard here."

Her entire body was thumping. It felt like fear, but she wasn't sure of what.

Maybe the baby was the one who was scared. It knew what was going to happen.

"How did you get here?" she asked again. "Can't you tell me? Can't you tell me who you are? I need to know."

The air around her seemed to throb like her body was throbbing. It was waiting for an answer, too.

"Please," she begged.

Nothing.

After a minute, she took away her hand, put the envelope in her desk drawer, and went back to bed. She turned over onto her side, tried to think about anything else—about how happy she'd be when she was back to normal, when her body was her own again. But she kept seeing the baby in her mind and wondering who it was and why it was inside her. And why she felt like it was a beautiful thing. Whose word had that been in her head: *beautiful?*

Mystery.

Oh, god.

She didn't know who this baby was, didn't know how it had gotten here. How could she get rid of it without knowing?

For the rest of the night, sleep only came in brief snippets. Shallow and uneasy.

The stretches between sleep were filled with uncontrollable thoughts, insistent as the tide. A plan: She could keep the baby but have it in secret, go away so no one but her family and Jesse would ever know she was pregnant, come back normal. Give it up for adoption. It would be hard, but she could do it. She had to do it.

She couldn't do it.

The morning light filtering through her blinds illuminated the obvious reality.

Of course she couldn't do it. She was a sixteen-year-old in Park Slope with a father who was running for Congress. What the hell was she thinking?

She got up and immediately went to her laptop, began searching again through those police blotters. Looking for anything she'd missed. Because if she could just figure this out, maybe it would go away, this feeling that was as strong as it had been sudden. But then—god knows how much later, in some sort of Internet search fugue state where she didn't even recall the chain of links she'd followed—she found herself on some random site, trying to figure out the New York State laws about putting up a baby for adoption when you didn't know who the father was. *No. No, no, no!*

She folded her arms on the desk and rested her heavy head on them.

A noise made her sit up with a start.

Lydia stood in her bedroom doorway, hands on her hips, wearing an old fedora from the costume box.

"Why don't you ever knock?" Quinn quickly closed the browser window.

"What're you doing?"

"Homework. What do you want, Lyddie?"

Lydia wandered farther into the room, picked up Quinn's sea glass necklace off the dresser, started fingering the chain. "I know something weird is going on," she said. "Something with you."

"No, it isn't," Quinn said. "I need to get back to my work, okay? I'm behind from missing so many days."

Lydia placed the necklace down and began fiddling with its cardboard jewelry box, obviously not ready to give up that easily. "I heard Daddy talking like you're still sick. He was talking about some problem you have. I thought you were better?"

"I am better," Quinn said. "I'm totally fine."

She still didn't leave. Kept playing with the box. Quinn opened a homework assignment on her laptop and began reading through it, realizing how far behind she really was. Maybe she should take the semester off entirely, pretend she was going away for some sudden internship opportunity. Or they could pretend her allergies were bad again and she had to leave the city.

"Who's Charlotte Lowell?" Lydia asked.

"Huh?"

Her sister held out a small, folded piece of yellowed paper that said *Charlotte Lowell* in scratchy black handwriting. "It was under the cotton. In the necklace box."

"I don't know," Quinn said, although the name rang a distant bell. "Meryl must have written that."

Lydia scratched her ear. "Maybe she was a lesbian."

"Dad's mother?" Quinn blurted.

"Maybe that's why she left Daddy and Grandpa. For . . ."—Lydia looked at the paper again—"Charlotte Lowell."

Quinn tried very hard to keep a straight face. "Dad would tell us if his mother had been a lesbian. No one cares that Uncle Ron is gay, right? And we know why she left—she had really bad depression." Bad enough to have killed herself, something Quinn hadn't even known until her father had to address it during an interview last year. Apparently she'd had a baby girl who died, before Quinn's father was born, and had never gotten over it.

"I'm sure it's just a random note," Quinn added. "Or maybe it's the name of the woman who made the necklace."

Lydia put the paper back in the box. "Just because I'm younger doesn't mean my ideas are stupid, you know," she said. "Why does everyone think that? Everyone. A reporter guy named Peter from Gotham something called on the house phone and I picked it up, and he didn't care at all what I had to say. He wanted Daddy or even you—"

"Lydia." Quinn cut her off, exhausted. "I don't think your ideas are stupid. I just really need to get back to work. Now. Okay?"

Her sister gave an exaggerated sigh and inched toward the door. She was halfway out when she turned to face Quinn again. "I'm excellent with problem solving, you know," she said. "Maybe *I* could help you."

The earnestness in her expression tugged on Quinn's heart.

"Thanks, Lyddie. If there's anything you can help me with, I promise to ask."

Quinn spent the rest of the day trying to remind herself of the life she'd be screwing up if she went through with the pregnancy. She played pick-up ultimate in the park and went for pizza at Smiling and ice cream at Uncle Louie G with the Dubs. Hung out at Sadie's and planned destinations for the Adventurers club, listened to Isa practice a violin piece for an upcoming audition . . .

She went to bed as soon as she got home, not wanting to be alone and awake with her thoughts.

But, again, her mind was swimming too fast to sleep. She tossed and turned for hours, the thoughts overwhelming her brain like waves crashing on shore during a hurricane. In desperation, she reached through the dark for her phone.

"Quinn?" Jesse said, voice groggy. It had taken four calls for him to answer. "What's wrong? What time is it?"

"Jess?" she said. Her mouth was dry. She was scared that saying it out loud would make it true. And she didn't even know what to say. "Jess?" she said again. "When you're writing a story, or your screenplay, and you want to describe something, but there aren't really words that describe it right . . . what do you do?"

"Quinn. It's . . . it's three a.m. What the hell are you talking about?"

She hesitated. Crickets chirped outside her window. A chorus: *be brave, be brave, be brave . . .*

"I think . . . I think I need to have this baby."

QUINN

There was silence on the other end for so long that Quinn wondered if the call had been dropped. She got out of bed and went to the window. Jesse was standing at his, the lamp on his desk casting enough light for her to see his silhouette.

"You . . . you mean . . . not get an abortion?" he said.

She nodded. "Yeah."

"Wow, that's . . . wow. That's huge. I mean, why? You weren't talking like this at the beach."

He was right. And she still didn't understand how her thoughts had changed so completely. "It's just . . . this intense feeling that I don't want to get rid of it," she said. "It's hard to explain." Again, she wondered what you were supposed to do when there was no word for what you wanted to describe. "And it's not like I'd keep it. My mother said we could discuss adoption. When she was talking to me about the abortion, she said choice is important, that abortion shouldn't be a knee-jerk reaction."

"You need to talk to her again," Jesse said. "And, I mean, I know that it can't be mine . . . but what if it is? Shouldn't we talk about it? It would mean a kid of mine was out there, too."

Quinn couldn't believe she hadn't even considered that aspect. How self-centered of her! "Of course," she said quickly. "Of course we'd talk about it. And we're getting the paternity test results this week, I think." She had given her mother Jesse's hair after the beach. "But what if it isn't yours? Would you think I was crazy?"

"Well, no. I've never been pregnant, so I don't know what it's like. But it'd be pretty hard, right? What would you tell people?"

"I'd leave town," she explained, "before I started to show. I'd live in the house on Southaven or something. I'd just disappear and come back normal. No one would ever know." She paused. "I don't know why it's here, Jess."

"Not to be mean," he said, "but is there a reason it would be here, ever? It's just a person. There are billions of us. Is there a reason that any of us are here?"

Quinn stared up at the city-starless night sky. "I don't know," she said. "Obviously, it's an impossible question. But what if there's even a tiny chance? It's not like I know the baby is a mistake I made. So what if . . . what if it's not a mistake at all? I mean, you believe in fate, right?"

He took a moment to answer. "I guess."

"Like, we were supposed to become friends," she said. "We're, like, connected. So, what if there's something . . . similar. A destiny. What if it's not a *bad* thing that the baby is here? And if it *is* yours, think of how crazy that would be. Impossible even! So what if it was supposed to happen?"

"I . . . I don't know," he said.

Quinn realized she was straying into territory that made her sound like she was high. It was frustrating, because what she wanted to describe felt so real inside her. She tried again.

"I mean, if we'd had sex without protection and I'd gotten pregnant, I'd probably be like, 'Okay, that was a mistake. We shouldn't have done that and this was not meant to happen.' I think I'd be okay with an abortion then, probably. But I don't know anything like that. How am I supposed to know that it's not here . . . for a reason?"

"Um . . . I don't know, Quinn," he said again. "I guess you don't."

On Wednesday, Quinn's biggest pair of jeans was fresh from the laundry, and for the first time, she couldn't do the button. Couldn't do it at all. She wiped her suddenly sweaty forehead, put the jeans aside, and found a pair of leggings that she could wear under a loose tunic. She'd have to buy maternity clothes soon. And how much longer could she stay in Brooklyn without anyone noticing? Whatever excuse she came up with would have to be really, really good for people to believe it.

She closed her eyes and took a deep breath. Maybe Dr. Jacoby could talk her out of this. (No. That wasn't going to happen. Quinn and Jesse had talked about it ad infinitum during the past couple of days and she hadn't changed her mind.) Well, maybe Dr. Jacoby could at least help her figure out how to tell her parents. Maybe Quinn could even tell them with Dr. Jacoby there as a buffer.

She went downstairs. Coffee was brewing, mugs were set out with milk to be warmed by the steamer, but neither of her parents was in the kitchen.

The house phone's irritating ring cut through the silence. Quinn answered.

"Hello," a man said in a friendly voice. "Is this the Cutler residence?"

"Mmhm," Quinn said, grabbing a Greek yogurt from the fridge. "This is Quinn." *Yogurt. That should be good for the baby. All that protein.* She had to start thinking about these things now. She was already worried about ways she might have unintentionally screwed up over the summer—drinking an occasional beer or two, not taking those special prenatal vitamins . . .

"Quinn," the man said. "Great. Hi. You're the one I wanted to talk to. Sorry to call so early, but I didn't know when to catch you. Kept getting your sister when I called."

Quinn sat down, more alert.

"Who is this?" she said.

"My name is Peter Vega. I write for *Gotham Gazer.* The online news site? I have a couple of questions for you."

"For me?" A chill scuttled down her spine. "Why?"

"Well, to start, how are you holding up?"

"Holding up?"

"With the pregnancy. Your dad said it came as quite a shock."

Quinn pressed down on her knees under the table to keep her legs from shaking. "All I remember is that his name is Peter and he writes for some website. I didn't tell him anything." She'd hung up immediately, not sure what else to do. "Lydia might know who he writes for. He said he talked to her."

Gabe was pacing. "Okay . . . Taylor will follow up with him. She'll know how to handle it. Tell him it's a lie, a rumor, whatever . . ." He began typing on his phone.

"What did he mean, you said it was a shock?" Quinn asked, still processing all of this. "You talked to him?"

"Of course not. He was trying to catch you off guard, pretend he knows more than he does. You think we can trust the people at the clinic tomorrow, Kath?"

"I didn't make the appointment under 'Cutler,'" Katherine said. She was at the table, next to Quinn. "I made it under 'Wells.'"

"Maybe we should consider getting it done somewhere out of the city, instead," Gabe said. "Just in case."

Quinn gripped her knees tighter. There was too much going on all at once. Too much to think about.

"So, um, the thing is . . ." she began. It had to happen now. "I don't think we have to worry about the people at the clinic."

Her parents turned their eyes on her. Her stomach dropped to her feet, through the floor and into the basement.

"I think I might want to keep it. I mean, not *keep* keep, but you know . . . go through with the pregnancy."

"*What?*" Gabe and Katherine said in unison.

"I'm in no mood for jokes," her father added. "Not now."

"I'm not joking. It's like . . ." Quinn struggled to find words that weren't as vague and watery as the ones she'd used with Jesse. "It's like, if there was someone at the door, and you weren't expecting anyone, you wouldn't just send them away without seeing who it was, right? It could be anyone."

"Someone at the door?" he said incredulously.

"Quinn," her mother said, eyebrows drawing together. "You're not . . . you're not saying you think the baby might be divine, are you?"

"Of course she's not," Gabe snapped.

"No," Quinn said. "I just . . . I don't know. I didn't make it on purpose. I don't know how it got here."

"We'll get the paternity test result in a couple of days," Katherine said. "Then we'll know."

"Only if it's Jesse's," Quinn said. "And even if it *is* his, it was created in such an impossible way. Even Jesse agreed—"

"Wait," her father said. "Jesse knows you're pregnant?"

Shit. Quinn nodded. "I'm sorry. I couldn't keep it from him. But he's not the one who told the reporter. I swear. He wouldn't tell anyone. And he's been helping me try to remember." Over the last couple of days he'd helped her fill in a few more things on the calendar, and they'd even practiced hypnosis in an empty study-group room during a free period. Not that it had worked—too many distractions, and it felt totally ridiculous. But it was a start.

Gabe took a deep breath. "Okay. We'll talk about that later. Right now we need to stay on track, because I'm not sure what's going on here. Have you been reading anti-abortion propaganda? Or what? Where is this idea coming from?"

"It isn't about abortion in general," Quinn said. "It's about the circumstances. The mystery."

"The *mystery?*" he echoed, biting the word. "Are you actually romanticizing this?" His phone vibrated on the table. He glanced at it, his jaw clenched, pulsing a bit on one side. "This is an emotional situation," he said. "But let's try to approach it with logic. Okay? Let's start with what we *do* know. Once again. Because this is not entirely a 'mystery.'"

"Okay," Quinn said.

"We agree that there's only one possibility here. You were impregnated by a man. That is how women get pregnant. Correct?"

"Uh huh."

"So in what scenario would this be a baby you want to keep? If it's Jesse's baby, you guys obviously aren't ready to have one. And if Jesse isn't the father, it's either someone you can't even admit to sleeping with, or you truly don't know how this happened, meaning someone probably hurt you. Is this someone whose baby you want to bring into the world?"

The same thought had gone through Quinn's head hundreds of times, and she didn't know how to argue against it. Partly, the problem was that she didn't *feel* any past violence, so had no emotion about it. After that swim at Rockaway, the pregnancy had stopped seeming *bad*.

"Not to mention what to do when it's born," Gabe continued. "You certainly can't raise it yourself, whether or not it's Jesse's."

"I know. I'd put it up for adoption." She turned to her mother. "You said we could discuss it."

"You said *what*?" Gabe barked at Katherine. Before she could answer, his phone vibrated again. This time he picked it up. "Not now, Taylor, okay? I'll get back to you in a few minutes." His voice was scarily calm, totally different from the one he'd just used. "Yup. Thanks." He set the phone on the table and directed his attention back to Katherine.

"I said we needed to discuss the abortion before she goes through with it," Katherine explained. "That it shouldn't be a knee-jerk reaction. That's what pro-choice is about. I never thought—"

"Jesus Christ. Which side are you on?"

"This isn't about sides, Gabe."

"If it's not Jesse's, I know I must have been raped," Quinn said, rubbing her pendant between her trembling fingers. "And I'm going to figure out by who, hopefully soon, and I know it'll be upsetting. Still, though . . . What if it's wrong to get rid of it? What if it's the wrong decision, and I regret it forever? There's no way to get it back."

"I guarantee," Gabe said, "that will not be your opinion. Once it's gone, you'll go back to being the girl you were. What about your grades? And college? The trauma has obviously impacted your judgment. You're not thinking through the consequences."

"I'll only be pregnant for five and a half more months," Quinn said. "Then it'll be over. I'm the one who'll have to deal with it."

"You really think your mother and I won't have to deal with it, too? Do you have any idea of the difficulties this will cause? At home and . . . out there?" Gabe waved his hand toward the buildings outside the kitchen doors. "I'm running for Congress, Quinn! You're sixteen years old!"

"No one has to find out!" Quinn explained, realizing she hadn't shared the most important part of the plan. "Before I start to look obviously pregnant I'll go away. Go live in Maine, or something. We didn't get new renters yet, right? Until then I can just wear baggy clothes. No one will suspect! And I'll leave before they do."

"You're not going to Maine!" Gabe was shouting now. "You're not going anywhere. Not since it's already leaked to *Gazer*. The lie would be obvious! And what about school? This is irrational, Quinn. Completely irrational. Don't you see that? Where are these thoughts coming from? What is *wrong* with you?"

"Gabe," Katherine said.

"I'm sorry," he said, not sounding sorry at all. "But she supposedly doesn't even know whose it is! And even if it's Jesse's, this is completely insane!" He reached out and grabbed Quinn's wrist, hard, pulling her hand away from her pendant. "Stop touching that damn necklace and tell me—what the hell is wrong with you?"

A chilly fear swept over Quinn's skin.

All she could say was, "I don't know."

What is wrong with you?

She'd heard those words before, in that same angry voice.

The memory flooded her as she sat in Dr. Jacoby's waiting room.

That summer she was seven. She'd been forbidden from swimming at Holmes Cove after the near-drowning scare in June, but she kept doing it because her friends did. Her mother caught her a few times. The last time it was her father.

Vivid details flashed in her mind: his khaki pants clinging wet to his legs as he charged out to grab her. Explosive pain in her arm socket as he yanked her from the water. That question: *What is wrong with you?* The blur of his hand coming toward her face. Her butt hitting the sand, hard. A puddle of accidental pee. That bumpy ride in the car: *No more lies! No more lies, Quinn!* Questions about her blackening eye at the doctor's office. The purple lollipop after her dislocated shoulder was reset. Its sweetness made bitter by shame.

GABE CUTLER

Gabe didn't know what he was looking for. Quinn was at the therapist; he was meeting her and Katherine there for a family session in an hour, to talk her out of this insanity. For now, he was alone in her bedroom, searching through the crap in her desk drawers. Looking for what?

Pictures or letters from a lover, someone whose baby she'd want to keep? Someone she couldn't tell them about. Someone older, maybe. A teacher? That one who chaperoned those weekend trips? Or a coach? That would explain it. Or maybe she had fallen for one of his campaign workers. She'd spent time at the office . . . Different men ran through his mind, fueling his manic energy as he sorted through her mess.

Looking for something. Anything. Anything to tell him that this wasn't what it seemed. That she was just plain lying, not that she was really having these irrational thoughts. Anything to get his mother's words out of his head.

But there was nothing.

Her laptop was password protected. He should have insisted on having access to his daughter's computer.

He got on the floor, reached under the bed. Pulled out stray socks and cat toys and dust bunnies the size of small children. Found a couple of shoeboxes way in the back. He pulled those out, surprised by their weight, and opened them: folded papers—drawings that looked like scribbles; some unremarkable shells and sand dollars and other junk from the beach; and rocks, probably those fucking rocks she'd dragged here from Maine. She'd used them to make a damned tide pool on the floor, filled it with water and dried seaweed, and had ruined the wood. She'd saved all of this?

The heat in his body built. Rage. Hatred. No. It was his mother, his mother he hated. Not Quinn. Never Quinn. He needed to get ahold of himself.

He stood up, brushed off. Put things back vaguely where he'd found them, but her room was such a sty she'd never know, anyway.

On his way out he noticed—how had he missed it?—on her dresser, the necklace. He picked it up and squeezed it in his hand. It wasn't what he was looking for, but taking it at least made him feel like he'd accomplished something. He never should have let Katherine talk him into giving it to her. It was part of Katherine's whole idea that he should be processing his feelings about Meryl, like when he'd made the mistake of going to see her. Katherine said he needed to stop demonizing her, to stop internalizing the anger.

But his mother had been a demon, in her own way. If he believed in curses, he'd believe she put one on his daughter.

QUINN

Things happened quickly. First, instead of school on Wednesday, a series of hastily scheduled appointments—with Dr. Jacoby and her OB—none of which changed Quinn's mind. But her parents refused to accept her decision as final until they got the paternity test back. "We want you to be very clear about the facts before you commit to anything," her father said. Since his explosion, he'd been using his professional "problem solver" voice with her, as if he didn't trust himself to talk as her parent. Just being in the same room with him made her insides tighten in a vicious knot.

The paternity test result was due on Thursday afternoon. All day at school, Quinn kept thinking about Scout and Spock, willing one of them to life.

"Maybe we should keep it," she said as she sat on Jesse's lap on a bench near the park a block up from campus when they should have been getting ready for ultimate practice. "If it's yours, maybe we should run away to somewhere tropical and live off rice and beans and never cut our hair or wear shoes. We can bring it along on our islands trip. Your film will be even better if we're teen parents," she joked. Jesse planned to make a documentary about the year they spent traveling.

Instead of ruining her fantasy, all he did was hug her closer and say, "I reserve the right to cut my hair, Q. Gotta look sharp for my lady."

Please be Jesse's, please be Jesse's, please be Jesse's . . .

Her phone rang at a little past three. She knew it was her mother without looking. Suddenly, she didn't want to answer it. She reached up for her pendant, forgetting she hadn't been able to find it today.

Jesse squeezed her hand. She climbed off his lap and took her phone out of her bag.

"Quinn, sweetie?" her mother said. "Get your stuff and meet me in front of school. I'll be there in five minutes."

"Is it his?" Quinn asked.

Katherine paused. "We'll talk in person." There was the slightest tremor in her voice. "Dr. Jacoby fit us in for a brief appointment. I don't want to be late."

"Oh, god." Quinn bent over. She didn't need her mother to say anything else. After hanging up, she drew a deep breath and pressed her fingers against her eyes. But the hot tears pushed their way through, and soon her face was wet and Jesse's arms were around her and her body was shaking with sobs, the first ones since this all began.

She made her final decision that night: It didn't matter that the baby wasn't Jesse's, she was still going to have it. Her parents accepted the announcement with white-lipped silence and, eventually, tightly worded promises that they'd support her.

In the morning, she went down to get breakfast early, hoping to avoid seeing either of them. But her father was already sitting in the kitchen. A laptop was open on the table, in the midst of a mess of newspapers and a couple of tablets and his phone. He looked like he hadn't slept.

She walked carefully over the eggshells that were between them now and headed to the fridge.

"He didn't wait," Gabe said. "My team and I are figuring out how to deal with it. I'm meeting people in a few minutes."

"Who didn't wait for what?" Quinn asked.

"That journalist. Blogger. Whatever. He didn't wait for our press release like he said he would."

He handed her one of the tablets.

The browser was open to a page on *Gazer* called "Gotham Glimpse," which featured short, gossipy morsels. The lead Glimpse said:

Which celeb Brooklyn Dem congressional nominee's sixteen-year-old daughter is carrying a future voter? Sources say she's going through with the pregnancy, so it won't be a secret for long. Will the baby daddy stay a secret, though? Apparently it isn't her longtime boyfriend. Oops!

Quinn's mouth went dry. "How do they know it's not Jesse's?" she said. "I thought we weren't going to say anything about who the father is?"

"Not sure. We weren't going to. And, like I said, he didn't even get the press release yet."

She swallowed. "Well, at least it's anonymous," she said, trying to keep her voice steady and unconcerned. "Right? I mean, who's even going to care enough to figure it out? Who even reads that dumb site?"

She put the tablet down and went about getting herself breakfast as if this weren't anything important. She hadn't really thought about how it would feel to see even this fleeting, anonymous mention of her most private life in a public forum. Her hands were tingling with panic and she had to purposefully slow her breaths. Of course, she'd known people were going to find out she was pregnant when her dad issued the press release. But somehow this . . . the gossipy tone of it, the speculation, the direct statement that it wasn't Jesse's . . . on a public forum! Had she made an enormous, life-ruining mistake, like her father said? Had she been a fool to think she was strong enough to deal with the consequences? Too late. Too late now.

As she buttered her toast—which she most definitely was not hungry for—her phone pinged with a message. From Sadie. And almost immediately after, one from Isa. Already? Was that possible? The blurb hadn't even said her name! *Shit. Shit, shit, shit.* She couldn't bring herself to read the texts. Just pressed the button to turn the phone off.

QUINN

A hush blanketed the hallway as she walked to her locker. Eyes darted toward her. Toward her stomach. Even though there wasn't much to see, she adjusted her shirt so it was hanging as loosely as possible. She should have worn something made of stiffer fabric, not this soft tee that clung. She hadn't thought about it when she got dressed, had just wanted something comfortable and familiar. Every person who looked at her, she wondered—*Does she know? Does he know?* But they all knew. Of course they did. Once one person knew something like this . . . Something like this. Ha! She'd heard of one senior getting an abortion, but that was it. No one ever, ever had attended New Prospect while openly pregnant.

She kept her head up and tried to walk like she didn't care.

As she stood at her locker, her hips felt strangely loose and her legs felt rubbery and weak. She stared at her combination lock, blanking on the numbers. Jesse appeared, nudged her out of the way, and opened it for her.

"Are you okay?" he said quietly.

"Depends what you mean by 'okay.'" She reached up for her phantom pendant.

"I'm so sorry," he said. "About my mom."

"Your mom?"

"Didn't you get my texts?"

She shook her head.

"Oh," he said, rubbing his nose. "The blogger guy called and talked to her and she freaked out and I had to tell her it wasn't mine and . . . she called him back and told him. She didn't want me mixed up in it. I'm really sorry."

"Don't apologize," Quinn said, realizing it didn't even matter at this point. "It's not like we were going to pretend it was yours. How did everyone here find out so quickly?"

"I'm not sure everyone—"

She cut him off with a *Don't bullshit me* glare.

"Michael P.'s dad reads that website. He told him. And . . ." He shrugged.

Quinn imagined the storm of texts that must have raged around the neighborhood and felt all the eyes in the hallway drilling into her. She needed space. "I'll be right back," she said. She needed to pee, too. She walked as quickly as possible to the nearest bathroom.

She shut herself in one of the stalls and sat on the toilet, her throat tight. *You will not cry again*, she told herself. *You're the one who decided to keep the baby. Now you have to deal with it. They don't know the weirdness of what's really going on. Being pregnant isn't* that *big a deal. Only Jesse knows the impossible truth.*

The bathroom door opened, and through the crack of the stall door she could see two girls come in. They started to talk; it was Sadie and Isa. They weren't using the other toilets, just the sinks. Probably they'd seen her come in and had followed her. And she should want to talk to them. They were her friends! She sat silently as Sadie tried to fix something about Isa's bra strap. First bell rang. Quinn still had to get her stuff from her locker. She flushed and went out.

"Quinn . . ." Sadie said.

"Hey, guys," Quinn said and began to wash her hands. She didn't want to turn the faucet off. Wanted to fill up the sink and climb inside, swim down the pipes and follow them to the sea . . .

When she was finished washing and drying, Sadie wrapped her in a quick, strong hug. "Are you okay?"

Quinn managed a smile. "Totally humiliated and screwed for life, but fine." She said it jokingly, hoping to lighten the moment.

"We thought you were still a virgin," Isa said. "I can't believe you didn't tell us. Even for you, that's crazy."

"I'm sorry," Quinn said. "I . . ." She shrugged.

"And it's not Jesse's?" Isa pressed. "Is that true? You cheated on him?"

Oh, god. Quinn struggled to remember her father's advice about answering questions like this. *Don't lie*, he had said. *That could come back and bite us.*

Don't lie. Don't tell the truth. If you couldn't lie and couldn't tell the truth, what did that leave?

"No, it's not Jesse's. It's . . . um, it's complicated."

"What do you mean, complicated?" Isa said. "Do we know him?"

"Uh, no."

"And you're not getting an abortion? Why? And why didn't you take Plan B? Didn't you know you might need to?"

"Don't you have to meet with Ms. Hilton?" Sadie said to Isa pointedly. "First bell already rang."

"Oh," Isa said, adjusting her books in her arms. "Yeah, I do."

"So . . ." Sadie raised her eyebrows.

"So . . ." Isa said, "see you guys later."

"I should go, too," Quinn said, but Sadie touched her wrist and said, "We still have a minute."

Watching Isa disappear into the hall, Quinn had a queasy sensation that reminded her of second grade, the year she'd had no friends. That sickly feeling of being different, wrong, weird.

Sadie gave her an uneven smile. "We all know that Isa isn't the most tactful," she said. "And I guess if you wanted to talk, we wouldn't have found out about it from some random website. But I just want you to know that . . . well, I want to be here for you in any way I can. I can't imagine what you're going through. I mean, it's so hard to wrap my mind around."

"I wanted to tell you myself," Quinn said. "Of course. But it all happened so quickly."

"I guess it explains why you haven't RSVP'd for my party. Pretty good excuse."

Sadie's birthday party. Her half-brother had had a bar mitzvah, so she'd wheedled an elaborate costume party at the Boathouse in Prospect Park for her sixteenth.

"I'm sorry, Sade," Quinn said. "I've been so distracted."

Sadie waved her off. "I was kidding. Obviously! Not to mention that it's still weeks away. But . . . do you not trust me or something?" she asked, more serious now. "Because, you know, I won't tell anyone else who the father is, if you don't want me to. I know how private you are—I get that—but I assume you need to talk to someone. Stuff must be beyond weird with you and Jesse. Are you even still together?"

"Uh huh," Quinn said. "And I'll talk to you at some point. I promise. I just need time. Okay?"

"Oh. Well . . . okay." Sadie turned toward the mirror and began running fingers through her long curls.

"It's not that I don't trust you. Really. And don't let this, like, freak you out," Quinn said. "I'm still me. I'm just going to be pregnant for a few months and then be normal. You don't have to worry about being wrangled to change diapers or watch me breastfeed at lunch."

"Can you imagine?" Sadie smiled into the mirror, but it looked forced.

Final bell rang.

"I'll talk to you about it as soon as I can," Quinn said, at a loss as to how to make the situation any less strange. "I promise."

JESSE KALBITZER

Second period had ended, and right as Jesse was about to round the corner into the dead-end hallway with the best vending machine, he heard Sadie's voice. Her tone made him back up a step, staying out of sight.

"She didn't tell me anything," Sadie said. "I swear."

Jesse should have known they'd be here. Their group of friends shared an addiction to these specific gummy candies that were only sold in this machine. It was a gathering place between classes to stock up and share news.

"Jesse neither," Adrian said, just above a whisper. "All I know is he's too fucking whipped. I mean, a guy's gotta have some dignity."

Jesse swallowed. He shouldn't be listening.

"We don't know the story," Sadie said. "Maybe . . ."

"Maybe what?" Isa said. "Obviously she hooked up with someone else. Someone she likes, since she's having his baby."

"I knew still waters ran deep," Caroline said. "But I can't even believe this."

"You know . . ." It was Oliver talking this time. "Jesse could have seen this coming. Not the pregnancy, per se, but the fact that Quinn had something else going on."

"What are you talking about?" Sadie said.

For a split second, Jesse had the same question. Then he realized and the back of his neck flared with heat.

Fuck this.

Before Oliver could answer, he stalked around the corner and straight to the vending machine, met by stunned silence. He didn't look anyone in the face. As he put money in the machine, Sadie started to speak, but he cut her off.

"You guys should be careful what you say here." He punched D12. "Anyone could be listening."

The gummies clunked into the receptacle. Jesse took the packet and walked away, steaming. He'd had a whole morning of his older sister telling him he was too loyal and not to be a doormat. He didn't need more of it.

And he didn't like the way other people's (uninformed) opinions brought out the questions he was trying to avoid, the things that didn't add up: Quinn's obvious happiness over the summer, the fact she didn't seem to have other PTSD symptoms . . . and, yeah, the condom Oliver had been about to mention. It wasn't that he wanted her to have been raped—god, no! But if he found out that she was lying . . .

When he started to think that way, it ignited his old insecurities. Years of thinking he was better off as the best friend, because Quinn could do much better than him. Not because she was so hot, which she was. But because while most of his friends were as interesting as, say, a Wes Anderson film, Quinn was an entire effing Fellini festival.

No, Jesse couldn't let himself dwell on questions and doubts. He was the one person she was counting on. Quinn kept some things to herself, sure. It was part of her appeal. But she wasn't a liar.

QUINN

When they arrived at lunch early, Jesse suggested they take a two-person table in the corner of the lounge, instead of saving a bigger table for the group.

"Won't that make us more conspicuous?" Quinn said. "Breaking our routine?"

"Eh." He shrugged. "I have a quiz next period I should study for."

As the room filled up, the air thickened with curiosity, making it difficult to eat. Still, sitting there with Jesse was better than the rest of the morning had been. Quinn's previous class block had been spent in a meeting with the Head of Upper School, the school counselor, and Mr. Dellatoro, supposedly discussing their desire to help her "negotiate the situation so it disrupts her New Prospect experience and her education as little as possible, and so she feels supported and secure." That's what came out of their mouths, at least. Their eyes asked all the same questions that Sadie and Isa had, their fascination just as undisguised. Her mind had gone back to second grade again, to sitting in the principal's office after she'd try to run away during recess.

As she opened a baggie of edamame, she saw Caroline scanning the room, then going over to join her art friends.

"Do you think if Caroline knew the truth, she'd think I was like Mary?" Quinn asked in a low voice.

"Huh?" Jesse said, flipping through his chemistry textbook.

"The Virgin Mary. She goes to church, you know."

"Uh, yeah. She's religious. Not stupid."

Would it be stupid if Caroline thought that? The way Quinn understood it, the whole point of religion was to see the world through the lens of your beliefs. If Quinn was religious, she was pretty sure that

113

she'd at least wonder in the back of her mind if it were possible. And, honestly, she was kind of sorry she wasn't. This all would have been a lot easier if she believed it was God's plan. Out of curiosity, she'd read what she could find about the Virgin Mary; it turned out that an angel (named Gabriel, ironically) had told her that it was God's baby at the beginning of the pregnancy. Mary was lucky she'd been clued in.

Quinn became aware of someone near the table and looked up. Noë Becker and her boyfriend, a senior named Sebastian, were standing next to them.

"Hey, Quinn," Noë said, hooking her thumbs in the pockets of her worn Levi's. "Sebastian and I just wanted to say that we're behind you one hundred percent."

"Uh, thanks?" Quinn said.

"All you did was have sex. If you were a guy who got a girl pregnant, it wouldn't be a big deal at all. It's a total double standard. You shouldn't be ashamed for one minute. I mean, we've had sex . . ." Noë gestured back and forth between herself and Sebastian. "And I'm not ashamed."

Quinn thought she heard Jesse choke on his milk. Sebastian appeared unfazed. Or maybe just stoned.

"And since you guys are obviously still together . . ." Noë looked at Jesse now. "I'm assuming you've got some sort of open relationship. Also cool. Seb and I have an open relationship, too."

Sebastian's face showed signs of life. "We do?" he said.

Noë rolled her eyes. "Duh." She extended her fist to Quinn. Quinn returned the bump, biting her lips.

After Noë led Sebastian back to their table, Quinn met Jesse's gaze. Without discussing it, they quickly packed up their trash and recycling and left the room, barely able to hold in their reactions until they made it outside into the small courtyard.

"Oh my god," Quinn said, when she could finally catch her breath after laughing so hard. "Am I Noë Becker's new cause?"

"I guess so," Jesse said.

"Unbelievable." Quinn tucked some hair that had escaped her braid behind her ears. "Of course, she'd be disappointed to hear that I haven't actually had sex." Seeing the look Jesse gave her, she clarified, "In the usual way." They sat for a minute, and the humor leaked out of Quinn like air from a balloon.

"I'm sorry people think, you know . . ." she said. "That I hooked up with someone else."

He leaned down to tie his sneaker, shaggy hair hiding his face. "Whatever. I know you didn't. That's what matters."

A cold breeze made Quinn shiver. "And what Noë said—people think I should be ashamed? Is that what everyone's saying behind my back?"

"She probably just meant those comments on *Gazer*." He pulled tight on the loops of the bow and then looked up at her. "Didn't you . . . ?"

"No. I didn't." Comments? Her father hadn't told her there was a comments section. She hadn't thought to even look. She reached into her bag for her phone.

"Quinn," he said, grabbing her arm. "Don't."

She shook him off. For a moment, she thought, *Don't do it. Listen to Jesse. It's out of your control.* But she couldn't help herself from pushing the button and watching the screen light up.

SuperSleuth: Didn't take long to figure out the pregnant daughter. Cutler. 9th district. That writer guy.

DD17: It's not even her boyfriends? Appalachia comes to Park Slope. Ha! Love it!

ToniB: Who cares? He's running not his daughter.

Sarasilbert22: I care if I might vote for the guy. Should have spent less time writing his elitest books and more time at home raising kids he could actually be proud of. Not like she can't afford birth control.

LMAO: Yeah, Brooklyn probably has an artisanal organic condom store she could have gone to.

Xocticbrand: Serves Cutler right for thinking his kids r too good for the NYC school system. The guys a douchebag.

Paula142: She's going through with the pregnancy? At 16? Please tell me Cutler isn't anti-abortion. I voted for him! He's a liberal Democrat! WTF?

Kizarrj: I don't know if he's anti-abortion, but he's clearly anti-parenting.

And more.

Across the kitchen table from Quinn, Taylor Bernstein—her father's campaign manager—*tap-tap-tapped* on her phone. The seriousness of her expression was emphasized by her tight bun and crisp blouse. Gabe was at a meeting and had asked Taylor to speak to Quinn about "several issues." She was the only person who worked for Gabe who knew the truth about the pregnancy.

Katherine was supposed to be there with them, too, but she was asleep and Quinn didn't want to bother her. She'd seemed completely blindsided by the paternity test result yesterday, like she hadn't even considered that the baby might not be Jesse's. Quinn was upset enough by her father's anger and disapproval; overhearing her mother sobbing in the bedroom was a million times worse.

"So," Taylor said, setting down her phone, "as you know, Quinn, we already issued the brief statement. And later today, your father is giving *The Lead* an exclusive interview. He's only going to talk about your family's personal issues a bit. He'll touch on how he and your mom expected you to want to terminate the pregnancy, but that you thought it through carefully, and that they support you in your choice."

She took a sip of coffee, her elegant, manicured hand out of place holding the childishly lumpy mug Lydia made in pottery class last year. *Poor Lydia . . .* She'd been so confused when they explained the situation to her. Of course!

Taylor continued. "He's going to steer the conversation to the fact that you're lucky to have had the luxury to make a decision at all. That you have good health insurance for prenatal care, live in a state where termination would have been accessible, and have a good support system." She went on about how he'd mention different issues relating to women's health, that the government needs to make services more available, etc. "He's still not going to address the issue of who the father is, except to say that it's a private matter."

Quinn nodded.

"So," Taylor said, "you can help by being a part of damage control."

"How?" Quinn asked. She'd do anything she could to stop people saying bad things about her parents. It hadn't even occurred to her that anyone would blame this on them until she read those comments.

"Well, we've already disabled all your social media accounts—Instagram, Tumblr, Facebook . . . Whatever you had."

"What?" Quinn said, taking out her phone to check. "You did that already? How?"

"Not my area," Taylor said. "Our tech guy, Hassan, did it. We didn't want other people posting on your accounts."

Sure enough, when Quinn tried to go to Instagram, she couldn't log in.

The same happened with Facebook as Taylor was saying, "Hassan did a thorough search and couldn't find any problematic photos posted anywhere. But have you sent anything to anyone privately we need to worry about?"

"Photos?" Quinn said, looking up. "You mean, like, naked?"

"Or whatever. Anything compromising or inappropriate."

"No. Nothing." She hadn't, had she? Something in Taylor's laser gaze made her heart beat a little harder, anyway.

"Good," Taylor said. "Also, it's good that you're staying close to your boyfriend. If people see that you're still together, it makes you more sympathetic. Avoid being seen alone with other boys."

"Are you serious?" Quinn said. "Who would even notice? Or care? Why does anyone care about any of this? They don't even know me. Lots of girls get pregnant!"

"Reasonable people won't care. But your dad is a public figure. And there will always be tabloids. So until this is off people's radar, better to be safe."

"Maybe we should just tell everyone the truth," Quinn blurted. "Tell everything, so people know I didn't do anything wrong and neither did my parents." For a moment, it seemed like a good idea.

"I assume you're kidding," Taylor said, alarm in her eyes. "Absolutely not."

"Are you sure?" Quinn said.

"Look, Quinn . . ." Taylor leaned forward. "If you take one thing from this meeting, let it be this: If the truth gets out . . ." She shook her head. "Trust me. This mess is *nothing* compared to the shitstorm we'll be facing."

EMILY CLEMENTS

Emily Clements sat on her couch in her Windsor Terrace apartment with a spoon in one hand and her phone in the other, wearing a purple lace bra and her scrub pants. Her u4me.com date had canceled at the last minute, leaving her alone on a weekend night. Asshole.

As she was taking a quiz—"What Type of Handbag Are You?"—and making her way through a pint of New York Super Fudge Chunk, a message came in from Marissa, the med tech she worked with.

U c this??? Its your virgin, rite?

Emily clicked the link, saw a blurb and picture of a handsome man with salt-and-pepper hair with a teen girl she vaguely recognized, read the blurb. Holy shit.

Yes!!!!!!!!!! she wrote back.

Oh, man. It was her! The daughter of a politician? And she was keeping the baby?

Emily put down her spoon so she could use both hands and went straight to the "Freakers" chat thread, where she'd already told the original story.

Guys!!!!!! she typed. *Guess what?* She pasted the link. *This is the freaking virgin!!!!*

QUINN

Sunday night, Quinn dreamed that she was underwater, surrounded by the lights of those deep-sea lanternfish. At first, she swam among them, happy. Safe. Until all of a sudden she realized the lights weren't fish, they were flashbulbs. She was swimming naked and people were taking pictures. And somehow she knew that they were going to show her father the pictures, and she panicked, trying to cover herself while swimming, and then she realized she'd been underwater too long and was going to drown and began flailing while the lights flashed and flashed.

She woke up, gasping for breath.

In the shame-coated dark came a memory.

The bumpy car ride with her father, but even clearer now. Her arm and shoulder throbbing, pain shooting with each jostle of the car, her cheek numb from the bag of ice she was holding against it. The smell of saltwater tinged with the scent of pee. Shame heating every inch of her from the inside out.

And her father's voice coming from the front seat.

Your grandmother died in the ocean, Quinn! Drowned. Do you want that to happen to you? It was the first time she'd heard that her grandmother drowned, Quinn remembered now. *Do you want to be like her? Do you want to end up like her and die in the ocean?*

Of course she hadn't wanted that. She knew almost nothing about her grandmother, but she knew she was bad. Knew her father hated her.

When we get to the doctor, don't say a word, Quinn. No more lies!

But then *he* had lied. Made up a story about how she got hurt, while she kept her mouth shut. Because he'd told her not to lie, but the truth wasn't okay, either. They couldn't know . . . what? That she'd been swimming in the ocean even though her parents had told her not to? That she was a bad, disobedient kid? That must be it.

She'd done something very bad, and she deserved the pain.

She deserved to feel guilty.

Her breaths were still tight, as if there wasn't enough air in the room. She got up and opened the window wider, leaned out into the night's soft arms. As Haven jumped up on the sill and head-butted her side, something caught Quinn's eye—ambient light reflecting off a spot on the fire escape. She leaned farther out, holding the window frame for balance, and grabbed what she now saw was a phone with a black rubber case. Ben's. He must have left it behind after smoking earlier in the night. She ducked back into her room and tossed it onto the floor. She'd give it to him tomorrow, not now; let him wonder where it was for a while. Punishment for making her and the baby and Haven breathe his stinky smoke.

QUINN

In the morning, Quinn was running late, rummaging through her clothes for something that would fit and not cling, but still look okay, so she'd have one less thing to worry about at school. After not sleeping well, she felt edgy and brittle. And it was only Monday.

"Quinn?" her father said. He was standing in the door to her room, already in a suit, but with a face that still had the crumpled look of having been recently pressed against a pillow. "Have a minute?"

"Uh, okay," Quinn said, stiffening.

Do you want to be like her? No more lies, Quinn!

He came in and sat on her bed, patted the spot next to him.

"Your mother told me you want to pick back up with your tutoring sessions for Spanish?"

"Just to stay on top of it." No way did she want to tell him how hopelessly behind she felt already, even though the school year was only two weeks old. Didn't want to give him more reasons to think she'd been wrong to go through with the pregnancy.

Gabe nodded. "Okay. But I want us to find another tutor. I got a recommendation through the alumni association for a girl who goes to Columbia."

"Why? Adrian helped me get that A-minus last year."

"I don't want you alone with Adrian, Quinn. Not with any boys from school, other than Jesse."

"I know," she said, restraining herself from rolling her eyes. "Taylor told me. But we can meet somewhere private, where no one will see us."

He looked confused. "I thought Mom and I had been clear about this. About safety."

Quinn was about to ask what he meant when it hit her like a fist to the gut. "Oh my god," she said. "Are you serious? It wasn't Adrian. Adrian didn't do anything to me." *This* was what her parents had meant when they gave her a talk about avoiding dangerous situations and not being alone with men?

"Unfortunately," her father said, "if you really don't know what happened, we can't be sure of that."

"Yes, we can! No one at school did anything to me. Especially not one of my friends! God, Dad. Why would you say that?" Heat surged into her ears and cheeks.

"It's the reality of the situation, Quinn. I'm just trying to protect you."

"I don't need to be protected from Adrian. That's disgusting!"

The squeak of a floorboard came from the hall. Lydia stood in the doorway, clenching the fabric of her dress in tight fists.

"How could you say that?" she asked their father, eyes wide.

"Lydia," Gabe said, standing again. "I don't know what you heard, but whatever it was was out of context."

"You said Quinn can't be friends with Adrian!"

"That's not what I said. Why don't you go to your room? I'll be there in a minute."

Her body was rigid with anger. "Don't lie. You said she can't be alone with him!"

"Please, Lydia," he said tiredly. "I realize this is confusing, but please just finish getting ready for school. I'll come talk to you in a minute."

"You're horrible!" she said. "I hate you!" She ran back into her room and slammed her door. The noise ricocheted down the narrow hallway.

"I didn't know she was listening," Gabe said, rubbing the back of his head. He shut Quinn's door quietly and then sat down next to her again.

Their thighs were almost touching; Quinn resisted the urge to shift farther away. "Wouldn't I know?" she said. "I mean, if it were someone I'd seen again, after it happened, wouldn't I know?" How could she have sat in a class with someone and not realized he'd done that? Or even just passed him in the hall?

"I have no idea. But isn't it better to be safe?" her father said. "The majority of sexual assaults are by someone known to the victim. Think about it. Date rape, kids at parties where there's drinking, coaches . . . Family members, but of course—"

"Ugh!" Quinn said, covering her ears. She knew that incestuous rape happened, obviously. That didn't mean he needed to say it out loud.

He gently pulled her hands back down. "I know, I know. I was saying that's *not* what happened here. But we can't rule out *other* people you know so easily. Including people at school."

She had seen some statistics. But . . . it hadn't even occurred to her to consider it.

"Look," her father went on, "just hang out in groups, with other girls along, too—okay? That way we won't worry."

They sat in silence for a moment. Between the roar of blood in her head and the heat on her face, Quinn felt like she'd been standing next to an explosion.

"Someone I know?" she repeated. "Someone I've *seen* since it happened?"

"You really hadn't considered it?" he said. "I would have assumed you'd have discussed it with Dr. Jacoby by now."

She shook her head. No. Of course she hadn't. If she was raped, it was someone in the park, someone on the street . . . One of those dangerous, nameless men out there. Not . . . not this.

She tried not to obsess over her father's words, but it was impossible. Adrian sat next to her at advisor check-in, and she couldn't stop looking at his hands (medium-size and strong, calluses from playing the guitar, one fingernail painted sparkly blue, probably by his little sister, a thin white scar at the bottom of his left thumb) and trying to picture them on her body. It was true that she'd had a couple of tutoring sessions with him during those weeks. And what about that night of the music festival? Maybe Adrian was the one who walked her home. (But she would know if he'd hurt her. She would. Wouldn't she?)

In every class, she couldn't stop herself from considering the boys in the room through this horrible new lens. Kevin Barnes? Scraggly red hairs curled down the back of his thick, pale neck in front of her. He was so shy. Too shy? Hiding-his-true-evil-nature shy? Or what about Raj Patel? He was hunched forward, drawing in his notebook. Supposedly he drank a lot and got out of control on the weekends. But he'd never given Quinn a second look. She went back and forth between telling herself it was sick to think like this and telling herself she was lucky that her father had snapped her out of her willful blindness. There was no way she was going to get any answers if her mind wasn't open to the ugly truth. That's what was wrong with her to begin with—her inability to face up to what had happened; her imagination telling her *It was beautiful.*

When she went to the library during a free period, supposedly to do research for a history project, she ended up using one of the computers to look up the statistics her father was talking about. The first site she found said: "Two out of three rapes are committed by someone known to the victim. Thirty-eight percent of rapists are a friend or acquaintance. More than half of all rape/sexual assault incidents were reported by victims to have occurred within one mile of their home or at their home . . ." Two out of three . . . that still left one third, of course, but he was right that the numbers were high.

She kept exploring the site, reading victims' accounts, looking for anything about a case like hers. There was one written by a girl who'd been roofied and passed out, but when the girl came to in the morning, naked, she recognized that she had blacked out those hours. Quinn couldn't find any stories where the girl couldn't even pinpoint the night when it had happened. She couldn't help feeling like reading a story more like hers would help her feel less like a freak. Less like this was happening because there was something wrong with her. But there was nothing.

As she padded across the library's carpeted main space, it was so quiet she could almost hear peoples' eyeballs moving in their sockets as they watched her. She sucked in her gut, hoping to minimize any bump that was showing. And then she started to wonder: Maybe the guy who did it was watching her right now. Maybe that's why she was feeling the stares so strongly. Maybe she was picking up on some sort of vibe he was sending.

Don't be ridiculous, Quinn. Still, she was about to venture a look at the nearby tables and carrels when, all of a sudden, a noise broke the silence. The screaming sound of a cellphone. From right near her. She turned around, looking for the idiot who'd leave their phone on in the library of all places. It screamed again. Now everyone's stares were openly directed at her, and she realized that it was coming from her bag. But it wasn't her ringtone. *Crap.* She reached in and felt around until her hand grasped Ben's phone. She'd put it in there that morning, meaning to leave it for him downstairs. *Crap, crap, crap.* When she brought it out of the bag, it was even louder. It rang in her ears as loudly as a fire alarm as she fumbled to turn it off, the librarian striding across the room like he was going to arrest her. The call was coming from Foley Cavanaugh, Marco's older cousin.

Before she could process this, the librarian was right next to her, his hand stretched out to take it. Quinn finally managed to decline the call and give it to him. The phone not ringing left a hole in the air, exaggerating the silence.

As the librarian huffed back to his desk, a guy coughed. Then another did. And before she could make her legs work, she realized it sounded a bit like they were saying "Slut." Or had she imagined it? A couple more guys made the same noise and she turned, trying to figure out who it was and whether she was actually hearing right: *Slut, slut, slut* . . .

Someone else, a girl, called out, "Shut up!"

The librarian said, "Shhh!"

But the coughs kept coming. *Slut, slut, slut* . . . And Quinn just stood there, her throat swelling. Eyes burning. Trying to breathe.

The first thing she did when she got home that afternoon was take a bath. Her skin itched horribly, as if that word, *slut*, was crawling all over it like tiny sand crabs. She spent the first while so reclined that her ears were underwater, wanting to block out the sounds of the day. Maybe if she listened hard enough, she could hear all the way through the network of pipes and into the sea with its comforting *lap, lap, lap*, and *shush* and *roar*. She rested her hand on her belly and reminded herself that Noë had been right—people were only giving her a hard time because she was a girl. If they saw her as a slut, and saw that as a bad thing, well . . . that was their problem, not hers.

(So why did it still hurt so much?)

She finished her bath, moisturized her itchy skin, and shuffled back to her room, thinking about asking her parents if she could increase her number of weekly sessions with Dr. Jacoby. If therapy was how she was going to figure this out, shouldn't she go as often as possible?

She didn't notice until she was a couple of steps into her room that Ben was standing at her desk and Lydia was bouncing on her bed, holding her rainbow stripe–covered iPad.

"What are you guys doing in here?" Quinn asked, annoyed. She tightened the towel that was wrapped around her. "I need to get dressed."

Ben held out his hand, palm up.

"Oh. Right." She found the phone in her bag, tossed it to him. "Your ring is really friggin' loud. I got in trouble."

"That'll teach you not to steal it again."

She rolled her eyes. "What about you?" Lydia was visibly excited, completely different from how she'd been on the way to school this morning after the scene with their father. Knowing how stubborn her sister was, Quinn had thought they'd be dealing with the aftermath for weeks.

"I figured it out!" Lydia said. "The great and wonderful Lydia figured it out!" She raised a fist in the air.

"The cure for cancer?" Ben said. "Peace in the Middle East?"

She handed Quinn her tablet. "Parth . . . parthenogenesis. It happened in a shark and in a python named Thelma, and it happened in you!"

Oh, god. Parthenogenesis. A cloning process, sort of. "Lyddie, it can't happen in humans," Quinn said, not even reading the article on the screen. She'd read about parthenogenesis already, during her searches about virgin pregnancy, and had definitely ruled it out.

"They didn't think it could happen in sharks, either," Lydia said, bouncing. "But it did! And in Thelma!"

"Yeah, but people are different. It really can't work with us. Doctors are positive."

"But I found all of these articles that say it can. It happened to ladies in England. That article was in a real medical journal. I can show you." Bounce, bounce, bounce. "It means no one hurt you. It means you don't have to worry and people can stop saying mean things."

"I appreciate you trying to figure it out. I do," Quinn said, getting frustrated that she wasn't listening. "But there's no way it's parthenogenesis."

"But there's an article from a real medical journal. You have to read it!"

"Lydia," Quinn snapped.

"What? Why won't you listen?" She stopped bouncing.

"Because. I told you. It's not parthenogenesis. End of discussion."

Lydia's jaw tightened like their father's. "If I was anyone else you would listen to me."

"No, I wouldn't."

She looked like she was going to explode, but she just stuck out her tongue and stomped out of the room.

"Way to encourage the budding scientist," Ben said, as they heard her door slam for the second time of the day.

"I was supposed to tell her she was right?"

He shrugged and headed toward the hall. "I have to pack. Going to Florida. Some show about bodybuilders." Ben had become friends with the producers of the urban surfers show (which never even aired) and worked for them as an assistant now. "But you can call me if you need to talk. About anything."

Quinn nodded. "I know. Thanks." He was almost out the door when she said, "Hey, Foley called you. Do you think . . . Do you think he and Marco know?"

Ben looked at her strangely. "Not sure. Why do you care?"

"I don't." But she did. She cared because she didn't want word to get back to Ben about what had happened with Marco.

"Well, I called Foley about something else. I'm sure he was just getting back to me."

"Oh," Quinn said. "'Something else.'" She made air quotes as she

said it. Ben had stayed in touch with Foley all these years and sometimes bought weed from him, she knew. Other drugs, too, probably.

"Right," Ben said. "Something else."

Quinn had just finished putting on sweats and was brushing out her
hair when Lydia barged back into the room.

She flung a drawstring plastic bag from Old Navy onto Quinn's
bed. "Here," Lydia said. "I don't want any of it."

"What—" Quinn began to ask. But her sister had already left.

She peered inside the bag, emptied the contents on her floor.

It looked like trash at first. On closer inspection, she realized that
they were all things of hers. She knew Lydia had the habit of filching
little things like barrettes and lip gloss, but hadn't known she'd taken
all of this totally random stuff, too. A silly toy car that Jesse had given
her because of a private joke. An early list of possible destinations for
the island-hopping trip. A smallish conch shell. A rock. A postcard of a
work by Andy Goldsworthy, her favorite artist, that Caroline had sent
her from London. A folded sheet of wide-ruled school paper, the kind
with dotted lines in between solid ones. She opened it, saw writing in
a kid's hand.

*The deps are my frends. we play games and won time so did my cat.
that was funy. Cats dont like water. The end.*

Quinn recognized it as something she had written, probably in
kindergarten or first grade. Lydia must have snooped in the boxes
under her bed. For a split second she thought "The deps" was talking
about the Dubs, but of course it wasn't, because she hadn't become
friends with them until years later. So she had no idea why she had
called her friends "the deps." (Maybe there had been kids on Southaven
whose last name was Depp?) The cat was definitely Haven, though.
Quinn remembered the day she'd come down to the beach and chased
the surf.

Reading it gave her a bitter taste in her mouth and a vague sense of guilt, like she'd gotten in trouble for writing the story. Like someone had told her it wasn't true. *No more lies, Quinn!* Maybe because it was so weird to think of a cat on the beach? Or maybe the feeling was just because so many of her childhood memories were clouded by a sense of having done something wrong. She folded it up and put it in the back of her desk drawer.

BEN CUTLER

Ben's phone rang at close to midnight.

"What the fuck, Cutler?" Foley said when Ben picked up.

"I don't know what. You're the one who called me," Ben said, lying down on his bed. (No, not *his* bed. The guest room bed. His parents had wasted no time converting the room when he moved out.)

"You know what I mean. Marco. I don't know what the hell you think you're doing. But I'm telling you, you better stop harassing him."

"Since when is sending a few messages harassing?"

"A few messages? You call that 'a few' messages?"

"I'll stop if he answers me."

Ben heard his mom out in the hall and hoped he hadn't spoken too loudly. God, he was so fucking sick of staying here. He'd had to sublet out his own place until he made some more money. Not that he'd told his family that. He wasn't going to give his dad the satisfaction of knowing that he was having trouble supporting himself, since that was exactly what Gabe had predicted when he dropped out of NYU.

"Look, Ben," Foley said. "He's here for baseball. You know that. If there's any word about him hooking up with some sixteen-year-old, that's gone." He paused. "Whatever happened that night was your sister's fault. So leave Marco out of it."

"What do you mean 'whatever happened'?" Ben sat up.

"Just what I said. Not saying anything *did* happen, just saying that we all know she was acting pretty jacked up."

"Why the fuck would you say that and then think I'd leave Marco alone?"

"Cutler, you're the one with the dad running for office. You don't leave him alone, I've got plenty of shit to tell the press. Okay? Like, the amount of shit you buy from me is more than what you'd use yourself."

"Fuck you, Foley. You're going to admit to the press that you sell?"

"Who cares about me? No one. You're the one with the family name."

"You are such an asshole. You always have been."

"Well, your sister's always been a freak, so I guess people don't change." With that, Foley hung up.

A vision of smashing him in the face jolted through Ben. He threw down his phone. Hands laced behind his head, he closed his eyes and took a breath through his nose to calm himself.

Whatever happened that night was your sister's fault. So something *had* happened.

He debated talking to Quinn again but didn't want to upset her and didn't trust she'd tell him the truth.

No, he needed to talk to Marco. He'd do it in person after Florida if he had to. If Marco was too big a coward to even answer the phone, Ben would go to Connecticut and see him in person. Fuck Foley's threat.

QUINN

oday will be better.

That's what Quinn said to herself every morning as she lay in bed, wishing she didn't have to get up.

Today I will feel normal again, like a regular girl at school.

Today my friends will be totally relaxed around me, without any of those uncomfortable moments where something calls attention to the pregnancy—like my frequent need to pee—or to the fact I'm still not telling them who the father is.

I won't hear whispers when I walk down the hall, or catch people looking at my boobs or my bump, which seem to get bigger every day. And if I do, I won't care.

I'll stop looking at the guys like they're all criminals in a lineup.

I won't be reminded about the ways this is making my dad's campaign more difficult. Won't overhear him talking about slipping in the polls or being snubbed by so-and-so or so-and-so. He's going to win. The Democrat always wins in this district.

Today I will figure out how I got pregnant.

None of it happened.

She felt like she was bobbing in the water, watching her identity as Normal Quinn float farther and farther away. As the baby was growing, she was shrinking into the distance.

Her grades were nowhere near as good as they usually were; she'd never recovered from falling behind at the beginning of the semester. She'd had to let Sadie take over running the Adventurers club, because she had therapy on Saturdays so wasn't free for the trips. She wasn't playing ultimate—too much chance of collision or falling on her stomach. She was still a member of Earth First but often missed the meetings, again because of her therapy schedule.

She and Jesse spent as much time together as they could, but even though they tried to act like everything was the same, there were differences: the cold shoulder his family gave her; the awkward tension with their other friends; the fact that while they still kissed, they didn't do anything else now—a change that had happened without any discussion. (Quinn's hesitation was that because of the baby it felt like there was always someone else in the room with them.)

And along with all of this *loss* was a constant simmering of anger under her skin, anger at herself for still not having figured it out. Sometimes it boiled over into fury. *What is wrong with you?*

But what more could she be doing?

Aside from her increased number of therapy appointments (three times a week), she'd done everything she could think of, including secretly going to one of the psychics on Seventh Ave, who had prattled on about helping Quinn figure out her romantic problems and then spent most of the time trying to sell her a more expensive reading. Clearly what she'd have said to any teen girl. Quinn had left feeling like an idiot for even trying.

Hypnosis attempts didn't go much better. No matter how hard she tried to take it seriously, and to believe that it could work, it never stopped feeling like a waste of time. Lying there, listening to Jesse recite the cheesy script: "Imagine you're in a sunlit field, safe and secure . . . Relax your feet . . . Relax your ankles . . . Relax your fingertips . . ." All it did was make her want to scream. (How the hell did you relax your fingertips, anyway?) They only kept trying because it was something concrete to do, which was better than nothing.

She felt like she might have more luck tapping into her memories alone, so she had started a new notebook full of writings about anything related to those two weeks. Whenever she had time before bed, she lay in a bath and wrote out every single thing she could remember, no matter how small, even if she didn't add anything new. She wrote in a stream-of-consciousness flow, like they'd done in the one creative writing class she'd taken.

Her idea was that if nothing came up during the actual writing process, maybe doing this before bed would spur her mind to think about it when she was asleep, and that maybe she'd dream something helpful, or wake up to a revelation. But the only dreams she ever remembered were guilty ones where people were calling her a liar, usually her father. Sometimes Jesse. One time, he said to her, "You didn't tell me what you were really like. I wouldn't have been friends with you. No one would have."

The emotions from the dreams lingered throughout the days, a layer of grime she couldn't seem to wash off.

QUINN

On a Saturday in October, the F train trundled out of the tunnel and into the bright sunlight toward the Fourth Ave and Ninth Street stop. Quinn sat with Isa and Sadie and Caroline on their way to Caroline's home in Cobble Hill. The girls had met up in the Slope at a church where Caroline had been volunteering at a book sale. One of Caroline's moms was starting a homemade organic beauty products line, and they were going to test out some of the facial masks and moisturizers. It was the first time Quinn had hung out with the Dubs in ages, and she'd been anxious all morning.

But as the train rumbled underneath her, Quinn was laughing. Laughing with her friends. She couldn't believe how good it felt.

Isa was wheezing. "I'm going to pee my pants," she said. "Seriously."

"Please don't," Sadie said, scootching farther away from her and closer to Quinn on the smooth, light blue bench seat.

Sadie had been telling a story about how she'd rigged her little brother's laptop to suddenly announce, "Take your shoes off. Now!" when he opened a certain program. It was so silly, but her description of her dumbfounded brother hurrying to take off his sneakers was hilarious. Sadie kept barking, "Take your off shoes, now!" and then mimicking her brother's face. The girls were laughing so hard that other people on the train kept giving them dirty looks, which made them laugh even harder.

"You know, Jesse is convinced you're going to end up in prison one day, Sade," Quinn said, while texting him a recap of the story.

Sadie smiled proudly. Her hacking had already gotten her suspended for replacing photos on the school's website with other images, like a picture of a lion tearing apart a carcass above a caption that said, "Students relax and socialize in the upper school lounge."

The joking continued through a detour to get pumpkin spice lattes and the longish walk to Caroline's family's duplex apartment, which was on the outskirts of Cobble Hill, close to the waterfront. Caroline's mother Juna wasn't quite ready for them when they arrived, so they got snacks and went to Caroline's bedroom. Caroline and Isa flopped on the bed; Sadie and Quinn sat on the floor.

"Oh my god," Isa said, head turned to one side, long black hair spread out around her. "Is that your peacock costume?" She pointed to the side of the room, where there was a pile of shiny fabric in different greens and blues folded up on a chair next to Caroline's sewing machine.

"Yeah," Caroline said. "But it's not nearly done."

"It's going to be so awesome," Sadie said. "We all know you'll have the best one." She turned to Quinn. "Speaking of which, you still haven't RSVP'd. You're coming, right?"

"Oh," Quinn said, a tug in her chest. "Uh, I'm not actually sure."

There was a charged silence. Sadie shifted into cross-legged position and said, "Why not?"

"I don't think my parents will let me. And . . ." She shrugged. "You have friends from other schools, Sade, and I don't know . . . I don't feel like being on display. It's hard enough being at school around people who see me all the time. And I don't have a costume."

More silence. "I understand," Sadie said. "But it wouldn't be the same without you."

"I'll help you with a costume," Caroline said. "No problem."

Isa stood up. "Let's just say it," she announced, looking back and forth between Caroline and Sadie. She turned to Quinn. "We didn't just get together to test Juna's products. I mean, we'll do that, too. But this is an intervention."

"An intervention?" Quinn said. For a shocked second, she wondered which one of them had a drug/alcohol problem or eating disorder and how she didn't know about it, before realizing they were all looking at her expectantly. "For what? I'm not getting an abortion, if that's what you mean." She pressed her hand against her belly.

"No! Of course not," Sadie said. "Maybe *intervention* is too harsh a word. We're just . . . We're worried about how isolated you're getting."

"We never know what to say to you," Isa said. "Because it's like this whole, huge topic is off-limits." She held her arms out wide for emphasis. "And we just think that it would be a lot healthier if you, you know, let us know what's going on."

"We're not blaming you," Caroline said. "We're worried. And we want you to know that you can trust us."

"You're our friend," Sadie said. "And we can tell you need friends. Other than Jesse, who really doesn't count in this situation. So we're forcing ourselves on you. That's the intervention."

Panicked by the intensity of their stares, Quinn briefly considered making something up. Some fantasy guy she had a one-night stand with. But then she remembered her father saying that if she lied now, it could hurt them if they eventually tried to press charges against someone. She'd be painted as a liar, an unreliable witness.

Part of her wished she could just tell them the truth, but a bigger part of her knew that it would be too bizarre for them to handle.

"I'm sorry," she said. "I love you guys. But I'm just . . . not ready to talk about it."

"It's been weeks," Isa said. "What's going to make you 'ready'?"

Quinn shrugged again, getting annoyed now. "I don't know."

For a few moments, the only sound was the muffled footsteps of the upstairs neighbor above their heads. Then Juna's voice came from down the hall. "Girls? I'm ready with masks for two of you. One for combination skin, one for oily."

The four of them exchanged glances. Sadie unfolded her legs and stood. "Isa, should we go first?"

"I don't have combination or oily," Isa said.

"You do now," Sadie said, taking her by the arm and pulling until she got off the bed.

After they disappeared out the door, Quinn pushed herself up and went over to look at Caroline's costume, so they wouldn't be sitting there not talking.

"This is beautiful," she said, fingering the top layer of silky fabric.

"Thanks," Caroline said. "You know, not to make you worry even more, but the weirdness at school is just going to get worse when you look really pregnant. Might as well try to make it as normal as possible now. Not going to Sadie's party just makes it more obvious."

Quinn turned to face her. "I'm really not sure I could go, even if I wanted to. My parents . . . they're pretty uptight these days."

"Well, if your parents will let you, you should go and you should wear something funny, that doesn't try to pretend you're not pregnant. Make use of it."

"What do you mean?" That sounded like a terrible idea.

"Something subversive. Like . . ." Caroline stared at the ceiling for a moment. "The classic pregnant Catholic schoolgirl, in a uniform? I don't know. Anything that lets you make a joke out of the pregnancy before other people do. That's one of the best ways of making people not tease you. Make fun of yourself first."

It did have a certain logic, Quinn supposed. "Maybe," she said.

She moved over to look at a bunch of small, brightly colored Mexican tin paintings on Caroline's wall, souvenirs from her family's annual trips to Tulum. Quinn's gaze lingered on a portrait of Mary and Jesus.

"Do you like going to church?" she asked, lightly touching the sharp corner of Mary's hem. "Your priest seemed nice." She'd met him today when they picked up Caroline at the book sale.

"Yeah, Father Bob is pretty cool. And it can be interesting, I guess. If there's a good sermon." Caroline paused. "You think you have it hard, imagine having been Mary. She was younger than us, and sex out of wedlock was a way bigger deal back then."

"Well, yeah," Quinn said. "But everyone knew it was an Immaculate Conception." It felt like dangerous territory to say the words *Immaculate Conception* out loud, even though Caroline couldn't possibly guess anything.

"You mean Virgin birth," Caroline said. "Not Immaculate Conception."

"What?" Quinn faced her again.

"Virgin Birth," she repeated. "It isn't the same thing as the Immaculate Conception. The Immaculate Conception is about Mary being made free from original sin so that she could have God's child. Not about Mary being a virgin."

"Wait, what?" Quinn said, still confused.

"Never mind, you heathen." Caroline waved her hand in the air. "Anyway, it's not like everyone back then would have believed Mary was a virgin. It's not clear when that whole story even started. And some people don't even believe it now. I don't believe it, in fact."

"You don't think Mary was a virgin?" Quinn said in surprise. "Isn't that one of the basic things in the Bible?"

"Well, yeah. But the Bible was written by people, and people don't always tell the truth, right? Do you believe everything you read online?" She stretched her legs out in front of her. "Some people think Mary was raped, and that Jesus's followers made it up so that he wouldn't be illegitimate. Or so he'd be all divine and cool, like some of the gods other religions worshipped. Lots of gods' mothers are supposedly virgins. And some people even think that the Bible was translated wrong, and no one ever even said she was a virgin at all."

"Mary might have been raped?" Quinn couldn't keep the shock from her voice.

Caroline shrugged. "No one knows. I guess that in the end, it doesn't matter if the stories are *true* true. It doesn't change what I think about Jesus's teachings. For me, you know, that's the most important part of my religion. I believe God chose Jesus, and he gave us those stories to teach us."

As Caroline spoke, questions crowded into Quinn's brain. Did Mary's parents tell her what to say, and make up the whole God thing, so people wouldn't know what really happened? Or did Mary hallucinate the angel, Gabriel, who told her the baby was God's? What did Joseph know? Did he think she cheated on him? Did she tell him the real story? Or did she not even know the real story herself?

"Basically," Caroline said, "I don't think it really matters if Mary was a virgin."

"It mattered to her," Quinn said.

Caroline laughed. "Good point."

All of a sudden, Quinn's hand flew to her stomach.

"You okay?" Caroline said.

She didn't answer right away. *There.* It came again. A distinct movement in her gut. A kick. Her heart kicked, too. "I felt the baby move," she said, just above a whisper.

Caroline sat up straighter. "Wow. Is that the first time?"

"Um . . . I've felt sort of flutter-type things, but couldn't tell if they were the baby or indigestion. But that . . . that was the baby." She'd had her twenty-week OB appointment a couple of days ago and had been told that this would happen soon, if it hadn't already. But nothing had prepared her for the moment.

"It's really in there," she added with a nervous laugh.

"Do you know if it's a boy or a girl?" Caroline asked gently.

Quinn shook her head. "Everyone thinks it's better if I don't find out, so I don't get too attached."

Caroline nodded, her mouth a solemn line, and then said, "The fact that there's a little life inside of you right now . . . that's all the proof I need that God exists. I mean, isn't it a miracle?"

Quinn rubbed her belly in a slow circle, imagining the baby swimming in its little ocean, underneath her hand. "It is," she said. "It really, really is."

For once, she wasn't lying.

QUINN

Quinn's parents said she couldn't go to Sadie's party. No surprise there. But she was ready with a plan, because there was no way she was letting her friends slip even further away. They would obviously see her absence as symbolic of how disconnected she really was. (And it's not like they were wrong. She was currently feeling more connected to some girl from over two thousand years ago who might possibly have had just as confusing a pregnancy.)

The Tuesday before the party, Quinn caught her father as he was on his way out to a meeting. She hated asking him instead of her mom, but he was the one she saw an angle with. "Dad," she said, as he put on his jacket. "Sadie's parents are really offended I'm not going. I think they're taking it personally since you're friends with them, and Sadie and I have been friends so long, and . . . *you know*." *You know* was referring to the fact that the Weston-Fines (only Sadie was a Weston-Hoyt) were big donors to her father's campaign. "I didn't know how to explain it to them," she added. "I'm pregnant, not on my deathbed. They don't know there's anything more to it."

The bluff worked.

Between schoolwork (which she was still behind with), therapy, and Earth First, she didn't have time to think about a costume during the week. On the day of the party, she brought an old clothes box from the basement and the dress-up box from Lydia's room into the bathroom, so she could try stuff on in front of the mirror. She rummaged through, hoping to find a random kilt for the Catholic schoolgirl idea, but she didn't, and nothing else she found was right. She wrapped an old blue sheet around her like a cape, looked in the mirror and considered Batgirl. But that had nothing to do with pregnancy, and while she had a black leotard and tights, she didn't have gold boots or a mask. She texted Jesse.

You done?

Mostly, he wrote back. *Need sunglasses.* He was dressing as Richie from *The Royal Tenenbaums.*

If have time come over and help? Emergency!

He was there within minutes and began brainstorming with her, totally in agreement that it would be best if the costume played off her pregnancy. He came up with a couple of good ideas—Mia Farrow in *Rosemary's Baby* or Ellen Page in *Juno*—but Quinn didn't have the right hair for Rosemary, and Juno wore the same type of clothes Quinn did, so she'd look like she hadn't bothered to dress up.

Quinn threw the blue sheet over her head in frustration. "I'll be a blueberry," she said into the fabric. "And since no one will see my face, I won't have to be mortified by the stupidity of it."

"Uh . . . Okay?" Jesse said, clearly not sure whether she was kidding.

"Arrgh!" She yanked off the sheet. Her hair was all messed up; she pulled it into a ponytail while glaring at her reflection, angry that she'd waited until the last minute to deal with this. And then, as she tightened the ponytail . . . the faint glimmer of an idea. She picked up the sheet again and brought it down over the top of her head so that it framed her face like a hooded cloak. She stared at her reflection and rested a hand on her firm, rounded belly. It was just a blue sheet framing her face and her center-parted dark hair. But she'd been to enough museums to recognize the visual effect.

Jesse's voice came from behind her. "What if we cut this—"

She turned around, holding the sheet together under her chin, and keeping the other hand on her belly for emphasis.

His mouth dropped open. All he could say was, "Holy shit."

✦ ✦ ✦

"I thought it was a costume party?" Katherine said when Quinn came downstairs that evening.

Quinn gestured at the shopping bag in her hand. "I have a sheet to be a ghost. It's all I could think of. I'll put it on when we're almost there, though. It's a pain to walk in."

"What else do you have in there?" her mother asked. "Aren't you just giving an envelope as a gift?" Sadie had requested donations to charities instead of presents.

"More clothes to wear under it, in case I get cold."

They walked down the stoop and closed the gate behind them. As they headed up toward the park, they passed a couple with a stroller. The toddler in the stroller was coughing loudly—frighteningly loudly for such a little body—and the mother had a hand on his chest.

"Excuse us," Katherine said to the couple, as she waited for the man to move over a bit so they could pass.

He moved out of the way, looking from Katherine to Quinn, a strange, surprised expression on his face. He held Quinn's gaze for a moment. Something about the look in his dark eyes froze her feet in place.

"Quinn," Katherine said from up ahead. "We have the light."

Quinn broke the man's gaze, and they hurried across Prospect Park West.

"Mom," she said, a bit breathless. "That man looked at me weird."

Katherine stopped. "What do you mean, weird? Did you recognize him?"

They both turned back. The man had one hand on the woman's arm and one on the stroller. Quinn studied him, but no further hint of recognition came. Just a middle-aged man out with his wife and kid. His kid who sounded really sick. They were probably walking to Methodist, the hospital down the street.

"No," Quinn said. "Sorry. I'm just . . . you know, always wondering."

"You're sure?" her mother said. "Should we go back?"

"No," Quinn said again, taking one last glance. The man and woman were now both squatting next to the stroller. "Let's just keep going."

"You're sure?"

"Yes," she said. "Positive."

They walked a bit.

"I really don't like you being in the park at night," Katherine said. "Even with other people."

"It'll be fine, Mom. I shouldn't have said anything about that man."

"Ben's going to be back from Florida today or tomorrow. He started the drive up already, but said he had to make a detour on the way. Anyway, I'm thinking of asking him to stay home long-term, so we have another person to be around for you and your sister." In the last few weeks, since the paternity test, Katherine had become totally focused on safety issues, never wanting the girls home alone, driving or walking them everywhere, talking about installing an alarm system . . . Quinn sensed it was the only thing that made her feel like she had control over any of this.

"What does Dad say about Ben staying?" Quinn asked.

"I haven't mentioned it yet."

With how tense the house already was, Quinn wasn't sure it was a good idea. The election was less than three weeks away, and while her father was still beating the Republican in the polls, there was a constant sense that he wasn't as far ahead as he should be for a Democrat in such a liberal district. His campaigning had taken on a frantic tone, at least behind the scenes.

After they took the loop road around the north end of the park, Katherine insisted on walking Quinn right up to the back entrance of the Boathouse. Through the glass door, Quinn could see down a short hallway into the softly lit main room, where people were standing around in small clusters.

"Put on your costume and we'll go in," her mother said. "I'm going to come say hello to Sadie's mom."

"No offense," Quinn said, "but please don't. I'm sure no one else's parents are here, and I'm weird enough already."

Katherine considered a moment then nodded. "Have a good time, sweetie," she said and gave her a kiss. "Be safe."

Quinn pulled the door open and was hit by the sound of echoing voices mixed with a pop song she didn't recognize. Before anyone could see her, she hurried into the bathroom just to the right. Luckily, it was single occupancy, not multiple stalls.

She locked the door, pulled out her phone and texted Jesse.

Here. Where you?

A second later he wrote back: *2 min.*

And, sure enough, in about two minutes a knock came at the door, along with Jesse's voice. "Q? It's me." Quinn opened it, partially dressed already. She had on a white bathrobe over leggings and a tank top, with a pillow stuffed into the waistband of the leggings. Although her bump was definitely noticeable, at almost five months it still didn't scream "pregnant," so she'd added some size. All she needed to do now was drape the blue sheet over her head and affix it with pins, like she'd practiced at home. It worked perfectly over the white bathrobe.

"Lookin' good," Jesse said.

He had on a pair of brown pants and an oversized brown button-down. After Quinn had settled on her costume, they'd come up with a new one for him, as well.

"You look like a UPS guy," she said, laughing.

"Hold on, I'm not done."

As Quinn arranged and attached the sheet, he tied a tan piece of fabric around his head, then took something out of his bag and worked it on, too—a brown beard held on by an elastic band.

"Joseph had one in all the paintings," he explained.

"Very convincing," Quinn said. A tidal wave of emotion swelled inside her; she leaned forward and kissed him. The matted synthetic beard smelled like chemicals and scratched her skin, but the touch of his lips spread warmth all through her. "I've never kissed a bearded man before."

Sound increased outside the bathroom. She felt a sudden surge of nerves.

"This is funny, right?" she said. "People will get it?"

"Definitely. We should probably go out before someone knocks, so we get to make a better entrance."

They gave each other a last once-over.

"Ready?" Jesse said.

"Ready."

Quinn reached for the door.

MARCO CAVANAUGH

Marco was deciding between a vintage button-down from a used-clothing store and his favorite worn-in Phillies tee when someone knocked on the door of his dorm room. "Yeah?" he called, slipping the T-shirt over his head. It felt right. He wasn't going to know a lot of people at his teammate's house party tonight and would be kind of nervous. This was a tee he felt good in.

Another knock. *What the hell?*

"Yeah?" he said again, this time pulling open the door.

Someone shoved him. He stumbled back as Ben Cutler barged in and kicked the door shut. Marco turned to grab something, anything, to defend himself. But Ben got him from behind, yanked his arms back, pushed him forward, against a wall, shoved him up against it hard, saying, "I don't want to hurt you. But let me be very clear. I will break your fucking hand into smithereens if you don't answer my questions, and you will never pitch again."

Marco nodded, cheek rubbing against the wall, pulse racing, trying to stay calm. "Okay."

"And if you go running to Foley after I leave, I will also break your fucking hand into smithereens. All you'll be doing is getting yourself in deeper shit. Get it?"

He nodded again. His shoulders hurt from the way Ben had his arms pinned.

"You have a sister, right?" Ben said.

"Uh huh."

"So you know what it's like to want to protect her. Meaning if you were going to bet on who's going to go further with this, me or Foley, you'd bet on me, right?"

"Uh huh." Yes. If Ben hurt Nell, Marco would kill him.

"So," Ben said, pressing even closer against him, breath hot against his face, "what happened with my sister that night on Southaven? And don't fucking lie to me. If you do, I swear to god, you'll never pitch again."

QUINN

The minute Quinn and Jesse stepped into the light of the main room, stage fright gripped her. Even though none of the zombies or superheroes or sexy cats were looking at them yet, all she could think was, *What have I done?*

"Quinn!" Sadie's voice rang out. It echoed off the patterned brick floor and vaulted ceiling and jumbled with the music and other voices. Quinn scanned the costumed people gathered along a row of round tables, and near the series of arched glass doors that led to a lakeside terrace, but couldn't recognize Sadie. "Quinn!" her voice came again.

Now people turned in their direction. For one excruciating moment, no one said anything. Just stared. Quinn wanted to run, but her feet were frozen as if she were the Virgin Mary statue in a church. She held Jesse's hand tighter.

"You made it!" Sadie said, finally appearing next to them, giving Quinn a side-arm hug. "Oh my god. You guys look great. I love it!"

"Really?" Quinn said. "You know who we are?"

"Of course!"

"You get that it's supposed to be funny?"

Sadie made a face. "Uh, last I checked there was a brain in my head."

"Told you," Jesse said to Quinn with a nudge.

Quinn smiled with relief. "You look amazing," she said, taking a moment to appreciate Sadie's costume. She was the Bride of Frankenstein, wearing a floor-length white gown, her hair dyed and piled on top of her head in an Everest-size bouffant.

Isa hurried up to them, dressed as a flapper. "I can't believe this," she said. "You guys are hilarious. Such balls!"

"I know it's kind of low-tech," Quinn said, aware of the obvious bobby pins along her hairline and the tips of her sneakers peeking out.

"Shut up." Isa smacked her on the shoulder. "It's awesome."

After Sadie and Isa filled them in on what they'd missed (Kevin got in a bike accident and wasn't coming; Adrian was flirting with Sadie's stepsister; Ryan had her pet snake with her), Quinn and Jesse made their way farther into the room, heading toward the table of drinks and food. Everyone came up to say hi and compliment their costumes, even people who hadn't talked to Quinn in weeks. Apparently, Caroline's advice had been completely right. Something about making fun of herself—flaunting the pregnancy, even—had changed the whole dynamic. She owed Caroline a huge thank-you.

"Do you have your phone?" Jesse asked, as Quinn looked around for the shiny fabric of Caroline's peacock costume. "Mine's out of charge and I want to get some pictures."

Quinn reached under the sheet into the bathrobe pocket and brought it out. When she turned it on, a text from Ben appeared on the screen.

Just saw Marco. Call me.

She paced next to the algae-smothered lake, its surface of solid green lit up by the large globe lights along the edge of the Boathouse veranda. The noise from the party was loud enough that no one could hear her, but she was far enough away from it that she could hear Ben. Most people were inside the glass doorways; only a few were outside.

"What do you mean, he saw me lying there?" Quinn said, trying to get all the facts straight, despite the pounding in her chest.

"That's what he said. He said he was walking along the beach and saw you lying on that big rock, naked, and that he thought you saw his flashlight. That's all. Do you have any memory of that? Of going to the beach in the middle of the night?"

"Well, yeah. I was down there."

"Doing what?"

She told Ben about her midnight swim. "So, I mean, I was down there, and I did go skinny dipping, but I didn't lie on the rock, and I didn't notice any flashlight. I got in, swam, got out, and ran home."

"Well, he said it was definitely you. Seriously, though, Quinn. This all sounds so weird. You were swimming alone in the middle of the night? At Holmes Cove? What the fuck were you thinking?"

For a moment he sounded like her father, and her throat tightened. *What is wrong with you? Do you want to end up like her and die in the ocean?*

"It was nice," she said weakly.

"None of this makes sense." She heard him take a deep breath. "And we haven't even talked about why you kissed him. Are you absolutely positive he didn't coerce you in some way? Why would you have done that?"

"I don't know. It just . . . happened." A surge of laughter came from the Boathouse. "Look, it's hard to talk about right now. But it was . . . I was happy. I was really happy that night. I know I was crazy and impulsive and I shouldn't have done either of those things, but I don't feel like something bad happened. I'm definitely going to think about it, and try to remember lying on the rock, but . . . I don't know."

"Well, obviously you don't remember it as well as you thought."

"How long did he say he watched me?"

"Not long. But it's not like he'd have admitted it if it *was* long."

She bit her lip and stared out at the lake. "I better get back to the party. When are you coming home?"

"Not sure. Might have to go back to Florida."

"Talk to you tomorrow, okay?"

"Okay," he said. "And Quinn? Just saying—from an outside point of view, that whole night sounds really suspicious."

QUINN

When she woke up on the screened-in porch of the Southaven house that last Sunday morning in May, sleeping bag kicked down to her knees in the unexpected, unseasonal heat, Quinn had the overwhelming feeling that something special was about to happen. Almost like that Christmas-morning feeling as a kid, except way more intense. The warm air had hummed with weird electricity . . . with possibility. She lay on the air mattress, listening to Lydia's breath from the other side of the room, and to the breath of the wind, and the whispers of the ocean, and to the cheeps and twitters of the birds. Energy filled her, starting at her toes, buzzing through her limbs, supercharging her heart. And in her still half sleep, she didn't question it, because it was excited anticipation, not nervous.

Something is going to happen.

As quietly as possible, she crept out of the porch and stood with her bare feet in the spiky, dewy grass, pausing to look out at the soft blanket of fog on the sleepy Atlantic. She'd just started toward the forest when the screen door slammed and Lydia ran up beside her. (That girl had supersonic hearing, even when asleep.)

"You promised to take me to Holmes Cove," Lydia said, bouncing on her toes. She had no memories of Southaven, having been a baby when they moved away. "Remember? Where you almost drowned?"

"I know what the cove is," Quinn said. It was where she'd been heading, anyway. She would have much preferred to go alone, but she knew there was no shaking Lydia now.

Even though it had been years since Quinn had walked on it, every root and stone on the quarter-mile path through the forest was familiar. After taking a sharp turn at the lichen-covered rock shaped like a sleeping dog, the path opened up to the water. Quinn's heart ran circles at the sight: large, barnacle-laced rocks surrounding an expanse of rough sand, small shells, golden-brown seaweed; the sweep of silvery blue-green ocean . . . All exactly as Quinn had remembered it.

And wait . . . There was someone standing in waist-deep water, facing the horizon. A boy—or man, she wasn't sure. Medium height, wiry. He must have been staying with their neighbors, the Cavanaughs, because no one else had easy access to Holmes Cove. He stood in the early sun, fog still lingering on the water, holding his long arms out to his sides, then dove in and swam straight out in a sure, strong crawl. "What's he doing?" Lydia said. "Doesn't he know about the current?" Quinn shrugged and sat at the top of the beach, a little worried for him. There weren't huge waves in the cove unless it was stormy; the ocean's movement and power were hidden under the surface. But after disappearing into the distance, the swimmer reappeared, and made it back to the beach without breaking his stroke. He stood and shook the water out of his hair, like a dog. Dark hair, close-set eyes, prominent ears.

With complete certainty, it came to her: Marco. Marco Cavanaugh, that's who it was. Their neighbors' nephew, who had spent summers there. One of the kids she used to play with, right here at this beach, during the best hours of her childhood. She had a sudden urge to run straight into the water and hug her old friend.

She stood and stepped forward. "Morning, Marco!" she called out with a wave.

Marco waved back, no spark of recognition in his expression.

"It's Quinn," she said. "Quinn Cutler. From . . . over there." She pointed in the direction of the house. "Ben's little sister." Marco was closer to Ben's age than Quinn's.

"Oh," he said. "Right. I heard you guys were coming. Been a long time."

"You shouldn't swim here," Lydia announced, stepping next to Quinn. "It's dangerous. My sister almost drowned."

Marco gave a goofy smile. "Looks like I survived."

Quinn smiled, too, through flashes of memory: laughter, splashing, seaweed wigs, diving for stones, swimming to the rock where the seals liked to lie . . .

"Well . . . see you later," Marco said, before loping toward the Cavanaughs'.

Quinn raised her hand to his back. "See you."

The fog had lifted. The water sparkled. The small, steady waves spilled up the beach to meet her . . . And Quinn felt a rush of joy and excitement so strong that she turned and grabbed Lyddie in a rough hug.

"I can't believe we're here," she said, even as her sister pushed her away. "It's beautiful, isn't it? The most beautiful place in the world."

Something is going to happen.

She had the feeling all day: as she and Jesse hiked in the nature preserve, biked to town for lunch and ice cream, as they visited the lighthouse and Quinn showed him all of the places she remembered from being a kid. That giddy anticipation fizzed inside her. She couldn't stop hugging and kissing him, bursting with affection.

The barbeque at the Cavanaughs' began on their deck and migrated to a fire pit down near the trees that bordered the water. Foley and Marco had brought a bunch of friends from college, and the party separated into two groups—the college-aged kids and everyone else. Quinn and Jesse sat a little on the outskirts of the college group, next to Ben. Quinn's chest still buzzed with that wild joy as she held Jesse's hand and listened to the hum of conversations, a girl playing guitar, and the sound of the waves. The night grew a little chillier, and when Katherine came over to tell them that she and Lydia were going home, Jesse volunteered to walk them back, so he could pick up a jacket at the house.

Alone for the moment, Quinn found herself wanting to get closer to the ocean. She followed the small path that led to the Cavanaughs' long, narrow, rickety metal dock. Cup of lemonade in one hand and the other on the dock's railing, she made her way down, staring out at the glittering surface of the moonlit sea. Only when she was about ten feet from the end of the dock did she realize someone else had had the same idea. Marco.

"What are you doing?" she asked as she approached, wind blowing her hair across her face.

Marco gazed out at the water. "I don't know," he said. "There's something in the air . . . like before a storm. I wanted to see if there were any signs of one. But it's so clear."

Something in the air. He felt it, too.

She was standing next to him now. She set her cup next to his on the railing.

"Electricity," she said.

And then she was looking up into his eyes and he was looking down into hers, the ocean wind dancing all around, the air full of salty perfume, and she felt it again—that overwhelming rush of happiness and excitement and *love*. Not love for him, exactly, but for the whole moment, the time and place—all of it. And she realized that she had *missed* him all these years. Her legs began to tremble—or maybe it was the dock trembling as the waves crashed against it. And, like a spontaneous expression of all the emotions inside her, Quinn stepped forward, sprang up on her toes, and kissed him—a long, full-of-love kiss.

"Whoa . . ." Marco said when they broke away. "I'm not . . . I have a girlfriend." He looked as stunned as Quinn felt.

"Sorry," she said, pressing a hand to her lips. "I . . . I don't know why I did that."

Without another word, Marco grabbed his cup and hurried down the dock to the shore. Quinn stood for a few minutes longer, listening to the waves, trying to calm her breaths and make sense of what had just happened. She knew it had been wrong—a horrible thing to do to Jesse. But . . . it had also been strangely beautiful, to be so full of those emotions . . . the spontaneity and tenderness of it . . . And she knew it would never happen again. Unlike her first kiss with Jesse, which had been a promise of *more*, she wanted nothing more from Marco. So as she walked back to the bonfire a minute later, she folded up the inexplicable, awful, lovely moment like a piece of paper and tucked it away. (Later, the guilt would hit her. But not then.)

Back at the bonfire, she searched the group for Jesse. He didn't seem to have returned yet, so she took her spot at the edge of the group and sipped her lemonade and kept her eyes down. Eventually, people started getting rowdier and drunker and Jesse was taking much longer than she expected, so she decided to go find him. As she was entering the forest path, she saw the beam of a flashlight approaching.

"Got lost on the way back," he said. "What's up? Ready to leave?"

She grabbed his hand tightly. "Yeah. Let's go."

It wasn't that late, so instead of going to their separate sleeping spaces, they found a DVD of *O Brother, Where Art Thou?* in the Cutlers' old collection and watched it outside on the deck, under the stars. But Quinn barely heard a word of it. As she lay there, her guilt still tucked away, the day's other emotions continued to swell. And so did the sound of the ocean. The rhythmic *shush* of the waves filled her like a heartbeat. When the movie ended and Jesse went inside the house, that mysterious thing she had been anticipating all day became clear: She wanted to be a part of that water. She wanted to forget her fear of the ocean and swim at Holmes Cove like she had as a kid. Suddenly, this felt like the most important thing in the world. It had to happen *now*.

Quinn ran down the forest path in the dark, roots and rocks letting her go without tripping her up. Once there, without even thinking twice, she shed her clothes and lowered herself into that liquid night; inch by inch, her body had disappeared, she slipped into that second skin, and she swam with stars. Everything else in life dropped away except for the sublime sensations of that very moment in time. When she was ready, she pulled herself out, tugged clothes over her wet skin, almost falling as she wriggled into her cut-offs, gave the water one last look, and ran home.

When she reached the house, there was Jesse, sitting on the deck, wrapped in a sleeping bag.

"Quinn," he said, standing up, his face pale with worry. "Where have you *been?*"

QUINN

Quinn headed back to Sadie's party feeling a sense of numb confusion, like her brain was waterlogged. She replayed everything that Ben had said. Replayed her memories of that night—so clear and so complete. Or so she had thought. No memory of lying on that rock. No memory of seeing Marco's flashlight.

"Everything okay?" Jesse said, breaking away from Oliver and Adrian, who were dressed as Star Trek characters Quinn was too preoccupied to identify.

She nodded.

"Want to go talk?" he asked.

"Talk?" she said, nerves jumping at his loaded tone of voice.

"You know what I mean." He raised his eyebrows.

Oh, right. They had planned to try hypnosis again, here in the park. While they had mostly given up on it, Quinn thought that maybe being in the location of the music festival would help her remember details of that specific night, that sensory input would jog her brain. It was one of the memory retrieval tips she'd read about.

"Oh. Uh . . . sure."

He took her hand and they went back outside, walked northwest of the Boathouse, and veered off the path up a small grass hill. Neither of them spoke.

Quinn was too sick about her conversation with Ben.

She couldn't believe he'd gone to see Marco.

Couldn't believe he'd known about the kiss this whole time.

Marco hadn't wanted to talk to him, Ben said. He'd had to "forcefully encourage" him to tell the truth. Quinn didn't know what that meant but imagined the worst.

If Marco told Ben the truth, she'd forgotten lying on those rocks. What else was she forgetting?

It just didn't make sense. She *remembered* that swim. She *remembered* running back to the house and talking to Jesse. She'd been filled with complete elation. Electrified. How could she have felt that way if something bad had happened to her?

"So," Jesse said. "Want to do it here? We probably shouldn't stay away for long."

They'd reached a relatively secluded spot, behind a tree and near where the grass was bordered by bushes.

"Okay," Quinn said, sitting and then lying down on a patch of dried leaves. Her pillow-stomach was disconcerting. She took it out from under her clothes and set it aside. Jesse took off his beard and headpiece.

After giving her a moment to settle into the space, he started reciting the now-familiar hypnosis script, trying to get her to relax and picture herself in a beautiful, peaceful landscape where nothing could hurt her and where all memories would be safe.

But all she could think about was that night on Southaven and the realization that she needed to talk to Jesse about it, to ask him again what she was like when she came back from her swim. And she knew that if they were really going to talk about that night, she needed to tell him the whole story. She needed to tell him what had happened with Marco. The thought made her want to vomit. If she put it off for even one minute, she wouldn't have the courage.

She sat up. "Um, instead of doing this, can we talk about . . . that night over Memorial Day? You know, when I went swimming?"

"Uh, sure," he said, sounding surprised. "What about it?"

She fiddled with the edge of the bed sheet. "So, you said I seemed happy when I came back?"

"Yeah."

"You're sure?"

"I thought you remembered all that?"

"I do. Or, I think I do. I just want to make sure I have it right. Did I look, I don't know, messed up at all? I mean physically?"

"You were wet. You know, your hair was all straggly. So, yeah, kind of." He tilted his head. "Why? I mean, why are you coming back to it now?"

Quinn chewed on her cheeks. "I need to tell you something. I want you to know that it . . . it has nothing to do with you. I know that sounds impossible. But it doesn't."

"What are you talking about?"

"That night at the bonfire . . ."

"Yeah?"

"You walked Mom and Lydia home with the good flashlight and then came back."

"Right, I remember that. I got lost."

"Yeah. And . . . while you were gone . . ." Quinn stared at her hands, which were twisted together so tightly the knuckles shone white in the dark. "While you were gone I talked to that guy, Marco."

"Who?"

"Um . . . the guy with the blackish hair? The Cavanaughs' nephew? You know, the people who were hosting the party."

"The baseball player?"

"Yeah. So . . . I walked down the dock, just to look at the water, and he was there. And . . . we ended up, um, kissing." Quinn thought her heart might have stopped beating as she waited for Jesse to speak.

"He kissed you?" he finally said.

"Um, yeah."

"While I was just, like, ten minutes away?"

"Yes."

"Wow." He raised his eyebrows. "What a fucking asshole. And, shit . . ." Now his brows were knit tight. "If he did that then, do you think he, you know . . . Quinn, of course! Why didn't you tell me before? I mean, if this guy came onto you, *kissed* you . . ."

Her tongue felt thick in her dry mouth. "Well . . . the thing is, it's not quite as obvious as that, because I kind of kissed him."

"What?"

"He wasn't hitting on me. He didn't *make* me do it." As hard as it was to say all of this, she didn't want to mislead him into thinking Marco had seemed like someone who would hurt her.

Jesse was absolutely still.

"I'm so, so, so sorry," she said. "It didn't mean anything, and it had nothing to do with you. It was just an impulse because . . . I don't know. I've tried and tried to figure it out but it never makes any sense."

"Nothing to do with me?" His voice was incredulous.

"No. It was . . . it was just a weird impulse. A moment. And you and I hadn't been together that long. Just a few weeks. I mean, not that that really matters." The minute she said that she regretted it.

"Holy shit," he said, like he'd had a revelation.

"What?"

"That night. When you went 'swimming.'" He made air quotes.

"No," Quinn said, shaking her head. "No, I wasn't with him. I wasn't."

"I'm supposed to believe you?" He stared off into the trees, eyes narrow. "I knew something was weird when you came back."

"What do you mean, weird? You just said I seemed fine."

"You were so happy, it was weird. Not like you'd just left me there like an idiot. You couldn't even hide it. Now it makes total sense."

"No, Jesse. I know I lied to you about this. I know I kissed him, but—"

"While I was there! Well, not right there because I was being a fucking gentleman and walking your mother and sister home."

"I know," Quinn said. "I know. I'm so sorry. It was a mistake. I have no idea why I did it. But why would I even have brought this up if I'd been with him?"

"I don't know. How am I supposed to believe you about anything?"

"It was just a kiss, Jesse."

"Right," he said. "So why *are* you telling me this now?"

She drew a deep breath, then explained what had happened with Ben and Marco, and how Marco said he'd seen her lying on the rock.

"And I have no memory of that. So . . . I was just wondering if I'm remembering other things wrong. I needed to make sure of what my mood seemed like when you saw me."

"So you told me because Ben figured it out," Jesse said. "And you needed to cover your ass."

"No," she said. "No, Jess. Please. I told you . . . I told you because I need to really know what I was like that night. Since it seems weird, what Marco said."

"So you need my help."

She looked down.

"I already told you what I remember. Your hair was wet and you were all weirdly happy and didn't seem to feel bad that you'd left me there like an idiot." He let out a choked laugh. "I can't believe I thought you actually went swimming. In that fucking freezing water."

"I did go swimming! No matter what else happened, that's why I went down there. I swear to god," she said. "I remember it. I think that Marco is the one who must be wrong. Or who must not have seen me for more than a second. And when I got back . . . I just didn't understand why you were so upset. I mean, I wasn't lying when I said I thought you'd gone to bed. You were in the house for a while."

"How could you not realize why I was upset? We were there on the deck, under the stars, and it's like the most romantic moment ever . . . And you brought that condom. What was I supposed to think? And then I said I'd be back, but when I come back out you're just gone."

"Wait, what?" Quinn said, startled. "What condom?"

"The one in your bag. I saw it earlier in the day, when you asked me to bring out your sunglasses. In that pocket."

Shit. That was where she'd stashed the condom from health class. That bag. "I didn't bring that on purpose," she said. "You thought . . ."

"Well, obviously I was wrong." He grabbed his hair with both hands and closed his eyes. "I'm such a fucking idiot. I even texted Oliver to ask if I should say something or . . . whatever. I was so nervous. Like a total asshole. Clearly you weren't bringing it to use with me."

"No," she said. "No, Jess. I promise. You can be mad at me about the kiss, but there's nothing else. I didn't bring that condom on purpose. And I'm sorry I didn't tell you where I was going that night. When you went inside, I really thought you'd gone to bed. I must not have heard you say you'd be right back." She'd been distracted, it was true. Distracted by the ocean calling her.

"Didn't you feel bad when we were watching the movie?" he said, lowering his hands and looking at her again. "You didn't seem upset."

She hadn't been upset; he was right. The guilt hadn't hit her until she was back in Brooklyn, as if she'd unpacked it with her clothes. "I knew it didn't mean anything," she said. "I knew I loved *you.*"

"I should have known," he muttered.

"What?"

"That this was too good to be true. That you don't really want me. I'm so fucking stupid."

"I do want you, Jesse! I do. I always have! You know that."

He stood up. "I need to go. Home. I need to go home. This just . . . sucks too much to be here."

Quinn stood quickly, too, her heart being shredded by every word. "Okay," she said, wiping under her eyes.

"Can you get one of your parents to pick you up?" he asked.

"Uh, no. Not soon. But I can stay until they're here."

"You want to stay at the party?"

She didn't answer.

"You can walk with me, if you want."

"You're sure?"

"Whatever," he snapped. "Do you want to stay?"

She shook her head.

"Then fine. Let's go."

It took hours—no, *days*—to reach her house.

As they walked through the park in suffocating silence, Quinn wondered if it was the worst she'd ever felt in her life. She wondered if feeling this bad did actual physical damage to her insides. Or, even worse, to the baby.

"I'm so, so sorry," she said, as they stood outside her gate. The bag she was carrying with her costume in it weighed a million pounds.

He didn't respond.

"Do you . . . Do you at least believe me that I wasn't *purposefully* with him when I went swimming?"

"I don't know. I don't know what I believe."

Quinn pressed her lips together and nodded.

"Are you going to go in?" he asked finally. "Because I don't really want to stand here with you."

"Oh," she said. "Yeah." Walking away from him, she felt like she was leaving behind a vital organ. She dragged her feet up the stoop, put her key in the lock, and then turned around. Normally, he'd have been waiting right outside the gate, making sure she got in safely, but he'd already started up the block. Something clutched at her chest, and she put down her bag and hurried back down the steps and through the gate, feeling like if she let him go she'd never see him again. He was at the top of the block, turning the corner, hunched over with hands in his pockets.

Before she had a second to decide whether to chase after him, a noise drew her attention to the sidewalk. A cup—one of those plastic sippy cups—lay by her feet, and a little ways away, a couple stood with a kid in a stroller. She picked up the cup and moved forward to hand it to the toddler, still looking up toward Jesse, willing him to turn around.

As she reached out, there was a brief flash of light, and then the woman standing with the child grabbed Quinn's wrist. Next to her, the man was holding up a phone to take pictures. It was the same couple that had been out there earlier in the night. The man who had looked at her strangely, with the toddler who had been coughing. Quinn was too shocked by the woman's odd, unexpected touch to try to pull away.

"It's you," the woman said, her voice breathless and amazed. "Isn't it?"

"Excuse me?" Quinn said.

"It's you," the woman repeated. "You're the Virgin."

ONE WEEK LATER

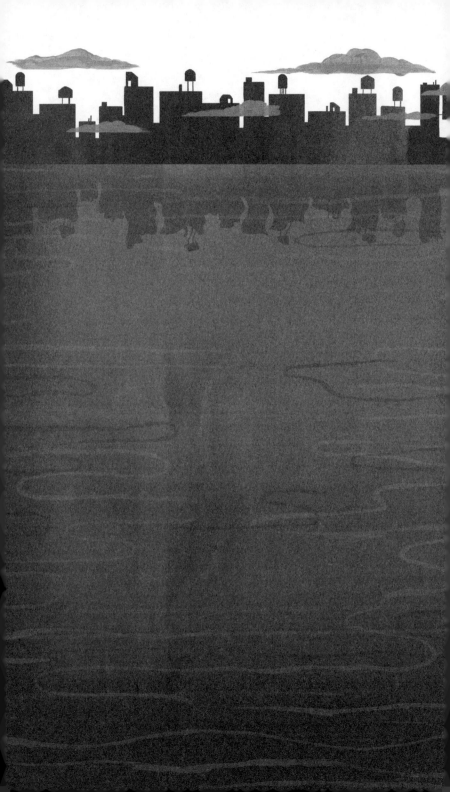

PETER VEGA

VIRGIN MOM MIRACLE!

By Peter Vega

If Democratic Congressional nominee Gabriel Cutler gets elected, he might have some pull in high—very high—places.

Not only is his teen daughter pregnant and, according to numerous sources, believes she's a virgin, now it seems that she's performing miracles, too. According to Ariana Lang of Woodside, Queens, sixteen-year-old Quinn Cutler's touch has cured her three-year-old child of an undiagnosed but serious illness that had been plaguing the child for weeks.

In an interview with the New York Herald, *Lang explained a chain of connections beginning with an online forum of medical workers that led her and her husband, Victor Lang, to hear about the virgin pregnancy. "No one else believed it," Mrs. Lang said. "But we went to the house whenever we could last week and waited. We both work, so it was hard. But we had faith, and then she came, and she touched him. On the head."*

Here Lang got too choked up to speak for a minute but finished by saying, "By the time we got home that night, his rash and fever were gone, his eyes and chest were clear. He was better. No medicine. Nothing has come back. It was a miracle, I swear to God."

The Herald *broke the story of Miss Cutler's supposed virgin pregnancy on Thursday. At that time, sources included numerous people, including a member of the family. But it was only after that story that the paper was contacted both by Mrs. Lang and by a medical worker, who wishes to remain anonymous, who disclosed that Miss Cutler insisted on her virginity right when her pregnancy was discovered. The medical worker refused to confirm or deny whether there was medical proof of the girl's virginity.*

The Herald *was unable to find anyone acquainted with Miss Cutler who had ever heard her give an explanation of the pregnancy. As seen in numerous pictures on Instagram dressed as the Virgin Mary, she certainly looks the part.*

It remains to be seen whether voters in Cutler's district will want to call in the big guns in the sky when voting next month.

Peter Vega held the print copy of the *Herald* in his hands—so fresh the ink was almost wet.

He couldn't get over it—a front-page story. And it was only his second story for the *Herald* ever. His first piece about Quinn, a couple of days ago, had been buried in the middle pages. Just a little item. Nothing like this lead article with a huge headline and photo and everything. (Seeing it had made him reconsider his opinion that print newspapers should be obsolete.)

Peter hadn't been surprised when *Gazer* had refused to post that first, short item breaking the Virgin story—they had ethical standards, after all, and the whole thing was based on a ten-year-old kid's say-so. (That poor kid, Lydia. She'd been so excited when she was the one to answer the phone that time he called. To get the chance to defend her sister. All he'd been hoping for was a little dirt. He'd had no idea Quinn supposedly didn't know how she got pregnant or about the Virgin rumor circulating online.) And he hadn't been surprised that the *Herald* would print it. Ethical standards? Not really the *Herald*'s thing. But readership? They had it in droves.

QUINN

Quinn stood behind the door, inside the shadowy entryway, hidden from the crowd of people gathered on the sidewalk in front of the Cutlers' house. She rubbed her belly, trying to calm herself with the rhythmic motion. The door was cracked open just enough so that she heard her father begin to speak from his spot on the stoop.

"I understand your feelings, your desire to believe in something," he said, his voice steady and even, the opposite of how he was a minute ago on the phone with some lawyer. The *chick, chick, chick* of cameras filled the spaces around his words. "But while my daughter is a wonderful girl, she's just a regular sixteen-year-old. A sixteen-year-old who is scared and overwhelmed by all of this attention. I'm sure you're all caring people, so I ask that you please show your respect by not making her uncomfortable in her own home. In addition, this is a quiet, residential street. My neighbors would also appreciate your consideration in not lingering on the block.

"For the media, I'll reiterate that I've made the only statement I'm going to about our private family issues. However, if anyone has a question about issues facing the city or my candidacy, I'll be happy to answer it."

A jumble of voices came all at once. "Over there," Gabe said, cutting them off. "Go ahead." A woman's voice said, "A lot of people are saying that the turmoil in your family is going to be too much of a distraction if you're elected. How would you respond to that?"

"First of all, this current drama will be short-lived, I'm sure. Secondly, we all fight many battles on many fronts every day. My wife and I have managed to raise three outstanding children while having extremely active and challenging careers. Next question. Here, in the front."

"Is it true your daughter told her doctors she was a virgin?"

"Okay, we're done here," Gabe said. "Thank you for listening, and for respecting my family's privacy."

Quinn scooted backward as the door opened. Raised voices were shouting out more questions as her father came inside, followed by her mother and Taylor, who practically lived with them now.

"That was perfect," Quinn said, trying not to let her voice shake.

"Unfortunately, if they were interested in reason, they wouldn't be here in the first place," Gabe said.

"How can they not listen?" Katherine locked the door. "This is our *home*."

Taylor answered a call and moved into the living room. Gabe headed down to the kitchen, came back up with an empty cardboard box, and went outside again, then returned with the box full of items people had left on the fence and sidewalk. Things people had left for *Quinn*. She watched as he sorted through them: flowers, candles, photographs, prayer cards (Quinn had never even seen a prayer card until yesterday), stuffed animals—these went straight into a black trash bag. He placed envelopes in a separate pile, not the trash; tied the garbage bag and left it in the hall; then took the envelopes upstairs. Minutes later, Quinn heard the whir of his shredder.

He'd used the shredder on hundreds of copies of the *New York Herald* a couple of days ago, when the tabloid published its first mention of Quinn: a short, mocking item in the "Weird News" section about the daughter of "bestselling author and wannabe congressman" Gabriel Cutler—a sixteen-year-old who believed she was a pregnant virgin. A photo of Quinn in costume, taken off of someone's Instagram account, was captioned: "Costume ain't no joke, folks." The article quoted guests from Gabe's campaign party and a member of the Cutler family who needed to stay anonymous, "for obvious reasons." (Yeah, because she was ten!)

Gabe had bought every copy in the neighborhood and sat in his office shredding and shredding. As if shredding a couple hundred copies would make any difference. And he couldn't shred the website.

"There are journalistic standards," he'd kept saying. "You're a minor. This isn't *news*." Every other phrase out of his mouth had been "legal action."

Taylor had explained to the whole family that the best thing to do was nothing. "Let it die a quick and natural death. It's not like anyone really believes she's a virgin." So Quinn's parents hadn't released any statement or response. To friends and family and people at school, the family brushed it off as ridiculous tabloid lies spurred by her costume.

But they'd never find out whether it would have died a natural death. Not after what happened yesterday.

Quinn had woken to a buzz in the house, a sense of more activity than usual. Downstairs, she found Taylor and a few other vaguely familiar people in the kitchen drinking coffee, talking on phones, and typing on laptops. The room smelled like cologne, coffee, and sweat, like they'd been there a long time.

Quinn had adjusted her robe so her belly was less obvious. "What's going on?"

"Quinn," her father said from behind her. "Let's talk in private."

She followed him up to the living room, which felt unusually stuffy and confined. Her mother sat on the couch in the light of a small lamp, reading a tabloid instead of the *Times*. Katherine handed the paper to Quinn, saying, "I wish you didn't have to see this."

The tone of her mother's voice iced Quinn's blood before she'd even looked.

"VIRGIN MOM MIRACLE!" the *Herald* headline shouted in big letters on the front page. Underneath, there was almost a full-page blowup of a better photo from the party. In this one, Quinn was gazing directly into the camera, a serene smile on her face. It seemed as if they'd even manipulated the photo to create a subtle, ethereal glow around her. It took Quinn a moment of shocked paralysis—*her own face staring back from the front page!*—to notice that inset into that photo was a smaller one, one Quinn didn't recognize: a grainy image of her reaching toward a stroller.

"Wait, is that . . ." Quinn said, pointing at it. Too stunned to speak.

Her father handed Quinn a tablet and tapped the screen. A video on the *Herald*'s website began to play—a couple being interviewed outside the Cutlers' house. The moment the woman started talking, the ice in Quinn's blood needled its way into her bones.

"I just picked up his cup," Quinn told her father. "I didn't touch him."

Her father rubbed his eyes. "It's that woman?"

Quinn nodded. She'd pulled away from the woman that night on the street, after Sadie's party, muttering a shocked, "I don't know what you're talking about," and had hurried inside. Her parents hadn't gotten home until the couple and baby were gone. There'd been no way to follow up or find out what the woman had meant or where she'd heard it.

"So, is this a big problem?" Quinn said, handing the tablet back to her father. She knew how dumb a question it was.

"Take a look." She followed him across the room to the windows, registering that the reason the room was uncharacteristically dark was because the drapes were closed. He pulled aside one curtain enough for Quinn to see. A small group of people stood gathered on the sidewalk, behind the low fence, which had bouquets of flowers resting on it, among other things. White news vans sat in the street, like sharks hovering near a colony of seals.

"What do they want?" Quinn had asked, staring at the people, her body frozen with horror.

Gabe shut the curtain. "They want *you.*"

Now, only one day later, people and offerings had multiplied with scary speed. While her father was upstairs shredding letters, Quinn peeked out the living room window again. His speech didn't seem to have made a difference; the people weren't leaving. They stared up at the house, all with the same expression on their faces: a sort of . . . hunger. Press photographers with huge-lens cameras and video cameras with raised microphones had turned their attention from Quinn's father to the group.

Because the story and the rumors had spread so fast yesterday, her parents had been forced to issue a written statement: "*No one in the Cutler family, including our daughter, believes that there is anything unusual about her pregnancy. We haven't released any specific information about it because there is absolutely no reason the public has a need for that knowledge. Comments attributed to our daughter and others are being presented out of context, as are photographs from a costume party. Quinn is healthy and has the full support of our family—that's all the public needs to know. Our children's private lives are just that—private—especially when involving something of such a personal nature. We insist that our daughter be given the privacy she deserves and that people resist spreading inaccurate information and salacious rumors.*"

Quinn kept staring out the window now, wondering if any of

these people—either the reporters or the religious ones—knew what the word *privacy* meant. She wondered why they were choosing to believe some random couple, who were obviously lying, over her father.

When she heard Gabe's steps coming down from his office, she let the curtain close. He took his jacket from the hook by the hall mirror and shrugged it on. Katherine came up from the kitchen, holding a travel coffee mug.

"They're all still there," Quinn said. "What should I do?"

"Absolutely nothing," Gabe said, straightening his tie, a striped one, over a plain white shirt. Quinn didn't know where he was going; he was busy all the time, at meetings both around the city and in the house. During the rare times Quinn saw him, he got an almost constant barrage of calls and texts and emails. Quinn had, too—tabloid reporters began calling after the first small article—but her parents had taken her phone away almost immediately. Supposedly, they were getting her a new one that could only make and receive calls to pre-programmed numbers, like you give to a little kid. As if that weren't humiliating enough, they'd also changed the Wi-Fi password in the house and disconnected the cable. "People are saying things that we don't want in your head," they'd explained. She'd had endless fights about it with them. None of which she had won. She was surprised they hadn't cocooned her in bubble wrap.

Her father looked in the mirror and brushed something off his lapel.

"Should I tell them I didn't touch that baby?" Quinn asked. "That I just gave him the cup?"

"No!" Gabe said. It was more of a bark than a word. "I've told you—I don't want you to have any contact with them. Not the press or those . . . people."

"So, what should I do?" She had to do *something*.

"Aside from going back in time and not wearing that costume?" he said. "Or not going through with the pregnancy at all?"

Katherine held out the travel mug. "You're running late."

He took the coffee in one hand and pinched the bridge of his nose with the other. Then he took a deep breath and looked at Quinn.

"Invisible," he said. "Be invisible. That's what you can do."

NICOLE ANDERSON

Outside the Cutlers' house, Nicole Anderson's heart was lit up like Times Square.

The girl—Quinn—was right there, inside those walls. Almost close enough to touch.

Yesterday, when Nicole saw the *Herald* at the newsstand on Fourteenth Street, she felt like she'd been hit by lightning. After the initial shock, it felt more like pure light. Like the lightning had turned into a warm, glowing presence inside of her.

She'd bought the paper with trembling hands and had to read it over several times to believe it. That girl. From the doctor's office. *That* girl. A pregnant virgin. Normally, she'd have ignored a trashy tabloid like the *Herald*, but the fact that it was *that* girl changed everything—it was too big a coincidence to be a coincidence at all. The fertility treatments—they'd been the call to New York City, but not the true call. They'd simply gotten her where she needed to be. It was no coincidence, of that, Nicole was sure.

Nicole had knelt down, right there on the dirty sidewalk in front of the newsstand, and begun to cry.

Since then, everyone back home in Michigan—her husband, her friends, other members of the Church of the Next Shepherds—wanted to know if God had told Nicole what to do, if she had a plan; they'd all been waiting for this moment, not just Nicole. But He hadn't, and she didn't.

Not yet, at least.

QUINN

Quinn paced the house, up and down the stairs. A rising and falling white noise of chatter could be heard from all the rooms at the front. It was like being near the scene of an accident: She was compelled to look, but when she did, queasiness shivered through her body.

They want you.

Finally, she couldn't take it anymore. She zipped up her hoodie and escaped into the crisp, cool air of the backyard, putting an entire building between her and the people. The garden hadn't been tended in a while—unheard of for her mother. Fallen ginkgo leaves smothered low plants. Quinn got a trash bag from the kitchen and began scooping handfuls of damp leaves and twigs into it.

A flash of blue peeked out from under a yellow pile. She reached down, pulled out a hard rubber ball. Jesse's dog Hugo's.

Quinn sat forward onto her knees.

The ache she felt when she thought about Jesse was almost unbearable. Like her heart and lungs had been torn out, and her ribs were collapsing into the empty space.

Since the party, he hadn't been acting angry or even giving her the silent treatment; the way he was treating her was almost worse than that. Complete indifference, like he didn't even care enough to be angry or silent. "Are you okay?" was said like, "Can you pass the butter?"

His eyes never met hers for more than a brief moment.

And no matter where she was, not more than five minutes could go by without something reminding her of him, or something happening that she wanted to tell him. Sure, the Dubs were her friends, but Jesse was her . . . person. Her other half. Everything was related to a discussion they'd had, to a private joke, an obscure movie he'd made her watch . . . A common library of references built up over the six years of their friendship. And it wasn't just about the past, it was about the future, all their plans . . . As she tried to not dwell on that aching emptiness, something was always bringing it back to her attention. The pigeon sitting on his window ledge had gutted her. An ad on the subway for Tahiti was worse.

She didn't blame him, not at all. It was her fault. But that only made the pain stronger. She deserved it.

And where had the information about Marco, and about her own behavior that night, gotten her?

She'd told Dr. Jacoby the whole story, told her that she'd been considering the possibility that someone had done something to her there on the beach. "I know it's possible that I might have been raped," Quinn said, "either by Marco or someone else, but I can't understand why my memories of that night are so . . . happy. And Jesse said I seemed excited when I got back to the cabin that night. So, I'm wondering if you can repress something that you . . . that you did voluntarily. Could I have done something willingly with Marco, either before or after swimming, and not remember for some reason? Maybe he's lying because he's worried, even though it wasn't rape?" It didn't make any sense, but it was the only thing she could come up with.

"Well," Dr. Jacoby had said, "if you felt extremely guilty about something you'd done, guilty about enjoying something you deeply believed was wrong, you might repress it. You'd have to have very strong feelings about it. Very deep guilt."

It was Dr. Jacoby's usual type of answer. Open-ended.

Then she'd added, "It's definitely worth discussing why you hadn't talked about that night to me in more detail before. Both what happened with Marco and an impulsive midnight swim in the ocean seem like important, unusual events."

"Because they were unusual I remembered them really clearly," Quinn said, hearing the defensiveness in her own voice. "I didn't think there was any point." Of course, saying it she realized how guilty it made her seem that she hadn't mentioned that night to Dr. Jacoby before. It was true that she'd thought the clarity of her memory meant nothing had happened to her, but she also knew that she hadn't wanted to admit to *anyone* what she'd done with Marco. She did feel enormous guilt about that kiss. Imagine if she'd slept with him! She wondered if the memory could be buried under such a huge pile of guilt that she couldn't find it even though she was digging in the right place.

"So what should I do?" Quinn had asked Dr. Jacoby.

"Let's keep exploring it, keep talking about that night, about Marco . . . Your history with him . . . What your mindset was about it over the summer . . ."

Quinn wanted to do more.

She thought about trying to talk to Marco, but she couldn't see any reason he'd give her a different story than he gave Ben. (Not to mention that Ben had told Marco he was asking about it because Quinn herself wouldn't talk. But how could Quinn explain her own questions? She absolutely couldn't tell Marco that she didn't know how she got pregnant. She couldn't take the chance that he'd go to the press.) She wished she could tap Marco's phone or bug his room, so she could hear his private conversations with Foley. They had to be talking about what was going on with her, what with all the publicity. Or she wished she could go back in time and see what he told Foley that weekend in Maine.

Go back in time. Fantastic plan, Quinn.

She tossed Hugo's ball into Jesse's yard and went back inside.

Later that night, after the people and news vans were mostly gone and the frantic energy in the house had turned into simmering tension, Quinn lay in the bathtub and prepared to start her ritual. She was still writing down everything she could remember about those two weeks, trying to coax out the truth—either in the actual writing or in later dreams. Since the party, she'd concentrated on that night in Maine, but the same old memories came up every time. Nothing about lying on the rock. No memory of seeing Marco's flashlight.

A couple of times, she'd tried making things up—stories about what *might* have happened. Her creative writing teacher had said that writers often don't even know they're writing about their own lives until the story is done and they step back and see it. But none of the stories Quinn wrote felt like anything other than grasping at straws when she went back and read them. Also, the whole exercise made her uneasy, like she might accidentally convince herself that something she made up was true. So she'd gone back to sticking with the facts. Or, at least, the facts as her brain remembered them.

None of the writing—fact or fiction—had led her to any sort of helpful dream yet. If anything, it had had the opposite effect. She'd begun to have a recurring dream, one that seemed to mock her efforts at finding the truth.

In the dream she was always outside—sometimes in the park, sometimes at the beach—and her body trilled with anticipation. A voice called her name, but she couldn't tell who it was. Suddenly, there was water surrounding her feet—a deep, velvety darkness, as if the universe had spilled a sea of liquid outer space all around her. She lowered herself into it, swimming down, down, down, her path lit by those illuminated deep-sea creatures, glowing like stars. And she always knew that somewhere among the dancing lights, Jesse was waiting for her. She knew he was there because he loved her. He was there because he needed her.

And every time, she woke up with a feeling of intense happiness thrumming in her chest.

But as she came to full consciousness, guilt and confusion and anger stormed in. She wasn't trying to remember something beautiful, and Jesse hadn't been in that water with her. And he wasn't the father of the baby. And he didn't love her or need her. And happy? Who was she to be happy?

Her brain was taunting her: *You think you can trick me into telling you what happened? That I'll let down my guard when you're asleep and reveal the truth? Ha! If you could handle it, you'd already know.*

The dreams made her feel like she was her own worst enemy.

QUINN

Monday morning brought damp, cold, and school. Outside the kitchen door, the gray sky hung low; the trees looked exhausted from holding it up. Quinn had worried that her parents wouldn't want her to go to school at all because of the *Herald* article and the crowds out front—that she'd be stuck here like a prisoner—but she'd overheard her father telling someone on the phone that keeping her at home made it seem like they'd done something wrong. "Why should we let these people dictate our lives?" he'd said. "Why should their insanity compromise our daughter's education?"

Thank god. She couldn't wait to not be trapped here with that constant crowd chatter coming from outside, the honking as cars tried to pass, the *whoot* each time a police car drove by, phones ringing nonstop.

Be invisible. As far as she could figure, the best way to be invisible would be to slip into her usual routine: going to classes, hanging out with the Dubs. Being as close to her pre-pregnancy self as possible. (Except . . . how could she ever be close to that self without Jesse?) Because her parents had taken her phone—and had only just given her the ridiculous preprogrammed one, which only had numbers for Katherine and Gabe, emergency, and doctors on it—she hadn't been in touch with anyone for days. Being without her real phone or Internet access was driving her as crazy as the crowd out front.

Her mother came up behind her. "Sure you'll be okay?"

Quinn nodded. "Better than staying here." She'd checked out the window on the way down to breakfast—the sidewalk was already a jumble of people huddled under umbrellas.

"Your father talked to the office at school again," Katherine said.

"They're confident no press or other people can get in the building. They had to deal with this type of security on a lower level for Elizabeth Chu." Oliver's sister, an actor, had starred in a couple of movies before graduating last year, and there'd been occasional paparazzi around her.

"I don't understand why I can't walk," Lydia said, putting on her raincoat while Quinn and Katherine waited. "No one's going to take my picture. Or try to touch me."

"Every other rainy day you beg me to drive you," Katherine said. "I'd think you'd be thrilled." She slid open the door. The wind blew a spray of cold drops through the opening.

"Oh, yeah," Lydia said. "I'm thrilled everyone thinks my family is a bunch of freaks."

Quinn bit back her reaction. Her parents had asked her to be patient with her sister; supposedly, her hostility was from guilt about having talked to the reporter, that Peter Vega guy. Quinn understood why a ten-year-old would have done something like that, but she still had to restrain herself sometimes.

To leave, they did the same maneuver Quinn and her mother had done on Saturday for an appointment with Dr. Jacoby: out the kitchen door, through their garden, into the backyard of Jesse's building, in the back door with the keys Quinn used when dog-sitting Hugo, through the building, and onto Jesse's street, where the car was parked. Like criminals.

They made it safely to the getaway car, let Lydia off first at the Lower School building, then drove a few more blocks to the Upper School. Katherine pulled into the small parking lot at the back, to avoid any reporters or people with cameras out front, then called the office. A minute later the fire-exit door opened. The front-desk assistant stuck out his head and waved.

"Call me if you have any trouble," Katherine said as Quinn got out of the car.

Quinn knew her mother really did want her to call if she had to. She also knew that she was probably praying she wouldn't.

Invisible girls didn't have trouble.

Inside the building, the first cluster of kids she walked past didn't seem to notice her. She searched the hall for a friendly face, and out of the corner of her eye, she saw some sophomore boy make the sign of the cross when she passed. The guys around him burst out laughing and copied the motion. Anger and humiliation swelled inside her, but she forced herself not to react, to keep walking, the same blank expression on her face. Invisible.

Instead of going to her locker, she went straight to advisor check-in, hung her raincoat on her chair, and kept her eyes on her notebook as the seats around her filled up. Sadie sat next to her and murmured, "Holy Mother of insanity."

"Yup," Quinn said, nodding slowly.

Jesse was the last person to arrive and had to take the chair on her other side. He didn't speak to her, maybe because Mr. D was starting to talk already. Quinn stared at the floor. He was wearing his Chucks. The green ones they'd bought after walking the High Line last spring, the weekend after they'd first kissed. Her foot ached to nudge his.

After check-in, which Mr. D ended by telling people not to let events out of school be a distraction during classes, Jesse seemed to hesitate before standing, but before Quinn could say anything, Sadie swooped in and ushered her into the hall where Isa was waiting. They flanked her like bodyguards.

"It's the craziest thing ever," Isa said. "You're famous! And I can't believe your parents took away your phone. How are you even functioning?"

"I barely am," Quinn said. "We had a huge fight about it."

"And did you know that our phones have to stay in our lockers all day now? No phones or even tablets outside of your locker *ever*. So people can't take pictures of you or anything. They're changing whole school policies because of you!"

"Sorry," Quinn said, not sure if that was the right response.

"Why did you touch that kid?" Isa asked. "The one they think you cured?"

"I didn't," Quinn said. "I just handed him back something he'd dropped."

"You didn't even touch him?" Sadie said.

"Why don't you tell the press that?" Isa said.

"My dad doesn't want me talking to them," Quinn said. She reminded herself to breathe; their curiosity was sucking the air out of the hallway. "The press twists everything you say."

"But there are all those people," Isa whispered. "In front of your house."

"I know," Quinn said, more loudly than she meant to.

"We're just worried about you," Sadie said. "It seems like . . . like you'd want to just tell everyone who the father is so it all stops. Wouldn't anything be better than this? I mean, the rumors are out of control. Some people think you really believe you're a virgin! Like . . . some people *here* . . ."—she glanced to either side of the hallway—"think you believe that. Like you really think your baby is the next Jesus."

"Isn't it kind of *asking* for attention, the way you're being?" Isa said. "Letting people think you believe it?"

Luckily, they'd reached the door of their math classroom. "I shouldn't even be talking about this," Quinn said. "I'm sorry, you guys." She went inside, anxious to sit and become just another student. And even though she didn't understand any of the numbers or symbols that Mr. Evans was writing on the board, focusing on something so far removed from her life, with no one looking at her, was a relief.

She was feeling slightly more relaxed when she went to English.

"I hope you all enjoyed the weekend," Ms. Bain said. "Unfortunately, for most of you, that warm and fuzzy feeling stops now." She flapped a sheaf of papers in the air. "Your quizzes from last week." She started walking around the large oval table, passing them back. "Do you want to go to the library and take it?" she asked quietly when she reached Quinn, who had been out of school on quiz day because of the second *Herald* article.

"I could use a bit more reading time, if that's okay," Quinn said.

"No problem. You can have until tomorrow."

After sitting back down at the head of the oval, Ms. Bain asked the class to go around and share their proposed paper topics and theses for *Tender Is the Night*. Quinn flipped through the unread pages, distracted by a series of especially enthusiastic kicks from the baby.

"Noë?" Ms. Bain said after Kevin finished a confusing explanation of his ideas. "What topic has Fitzgerald inspired you to investigate?"

"The virgin/whore dichotomy," Noë said.

Quinn froze, eyes locked on her book.

"Noë," Ms. Bain said sharply.

"What?" Noë said. "I want to discuss Rosemary as the virgin, his wife as the whore, and their influences on Dick's downfall. Obviously, the virgin/whore dichotomy is as prevalent today as ever, so I think it's a pertinent topic."

Quinn willed herself not to blush, but the heat was spreading impossibly quickly.

"Noë," Ms. Bain said again. "Keep other people's feelings in mind. I'll let you submit a new topic tomorrow. Oliver, let's move on to you."

"Quinn's feelings, you mean," Noë said. "Why do we have to act like she isn't here? I'm not trying to make her uncomfortable. I'm validating her experience."

Quinn was trying to sink into a crack between the floorboards. She stared at the sliver of dark space, praying for it to happen.

"No one's private life is a matter of discussion in this class," Ms. Bain said.

"It's all happening in public," Noë said. "The demonization of female sexuality. It scares them so much that she's a sexual being that they're willing to believe she defies the laws of nature."

"But Quinn's the one who said she's a virgin," a girl named Ryan chimed in. "She's demonizing her own sexuality!"

"No, she didn't," Noë said. "She never said that."

Please shut up. Please shut up. Quinn would have said it out loud if she hadn't already disappeared into the floor crack, going down, down, down, to a safe, dark space, like the depths of the ocean, like in her dreams.

"She did!" Ryan said.

"This discussion is over," Ms. Bain said loudly. "Let's move on to Oliver—"

"But it's not over," Noë said. "It's going on all around us." She pushed her chair away from the table and stood. "Isn't this what our curriculum philosophy is about? Analyzing current events and society in light of what we're reading and studying?" She hoisted her bag off the arm of her chair. "I'll take the unexcused absence. You've made a completely unfair attempt to stifle conversation."

There was a beat of silence.

"She's right," Ryan said, standing up. "So I guess I should leave, too."

"Sorry, Ms. B," someone else said. "But I'm with them."

A couple of other people followed. Quinn knew that not one of them cared that Ms. Bain had "stifled conversation"—well, aside from Noë, maybe. It was a joke to the rest of them. A story to tell later. A story about Quinn the freak. Or Quinn the slut. Take your pick.

✦ ✦ ✦

During her free, Quinn went to the library and headed to the computers, her fingertips burning with the need to search for all sorts of things online. She knew there'd be posts making fun of her and calling her a liar, calling her crazy, and it wasn't like she *wanted* to read them. But obviously everyone else had, so she wanted to get an idea of what was being said. Something was wrong with the computers, though. She tried two, and both said her student ID login was invalid. She went up to the librarian at the desk and asked about it.

The librarian paused uncomfortably before answering. "The thing is, we've been asked to facilitate your computer use for a while."

"You're doing that for everyone?" Quinn said, confused.

"No." He shifted in his seat. "Just you. At your parents' request, I think. Kind of a pain, I'm sure, but you should think of it as a silver lining. I'm a whiz at making research as speedy as possible. Want me to come over there now? What were you trying to look up?"

Quinn couldn't even meet his eyes. "That's okay," she said quickly. "It wasn't important."

The crowded, chaotic lounge spread in front of her like a minefield; the handle of her lunch bag was moist in her sweaty hand. Fortunately, she spotted a seat next to Caroline at a table with a few of her art friends. Jesse was nowhere to be seen. She mustered courage, navigated between tables and bags and chairs until she reached Caroline. "Okay if I sit here?" she asked.

"Of course," Caroline said, scooching her chair over a bit to make room. "You okay, bunny?"

Quinn nodded, willing back a sudden threat of tears.

"I'm sure you don't want to talk about it . . ." Caroline's voice was soft and low. "But I'm just going to say one thing: Those people outside your house are not representative of us normal, rational Christians."

"I know," Quinn said, although, honestly, she hadn't given it much thought. She hadn't even specifically thought of them as Christians— just as Them.

Quinn forced down a bite of her avocado sandwich. She didn't remember what it felt like to be hungry, despite the fact that all the pregnancy books said that at twenty-three or so weeks, her appetite should be huge. The emptiness inside her couldn't be filled by food.

In the corner of the room, a group of rowdy senior guys diverted her attention. One of them turned her way and stared at her with squinted eyes and a slight sneer. Another put a napkin over his head, like Mary's hood, and said something Quinn couldn't make out. The guys at the table leaned back in their chairs, hooting with laughter. Quinn's face heated up again. They were laughing so hard. Looking at her and laughing like whatever he'd said was the funniest thing they'd ever heard, like she was the funniest thing they'd ever seen. The heat burned all the way into Quinn's brain now. Her chest rose and fell more quickly.

"You okay?" Caroline asked.

Head burning and a roaring inside her ears, Quinn slid back her chair and walked to their table. She stood, arms crossed. She felt all the eyes from nearby tables on her, too. Screw invisibility.

"What?" one of the senior guys said. "No room at the inn?" The guys laughed again, and the heat in her head surged through her entire body. No response came to her, though, and she didn't even know why she'd come over here. She couldn't just stand here like an idiot!

"Hey," another said, "I've got wicked bad pain. Wanna cure it for me, Virgin?" He grabbed his crotch. Brett, his name was.

"Sure," Quinn heard herself saying. "Stand up." She was trembling, but her voice was steady.

"Huh?"

"You want me to cure you? Stand up."

The Brett guy looked nervously at his friends and then, with a laugh, stood up and came closer to her.

"Where'd you say it hurts?" Quinn asked.

He grabbed his crotch again. When he took his hand away and glanced back at the table with a smile, she took her opportunity.

Her knee landed right between his legs.

He doubled over with a groan, and all of a sudden, one of the other guys was up and in Quinn's face, pushing her away, and she was stumbling back and his hands gripped her shoulders. "Are you crazy?" he said. "Jesus, bitch. You are. You're fucking crazy."

She twisted out of his arms and ran from the room.

Driving home with her mother. Burning with shame.

And the shame brought her back to that memory, that car trip with her father to the doctor on Southhaven.

What is wrong with you?

Your grandmother died in the ocean, Quinn! Drowned. Do you want that to happen to you? Do you want to be like her? Do you want to end up like her?

When we get to the doctor, don't say a word, Quinn. No more lies!

What is wrong with you?

Do you want to be like her?

Quinn *was* like her grandmother. She was a bad person, making that scene, being the very opposite of invisible. Whether or not the guy deserved it, all she'd done was make her situation worse, giving people something else to talk about. Making them think she was crazier than they already did.

She couldn't control herself—kissing Marco, kneeing that guy, swimming when she wasn't supposed to . . . Her father had seen it way back then, when she was just a kid. Bad, just like her grandmother.

And what about her dreams, of going down, down, down in the ocean?

It was where her grandmother had gone.

She went into the room she used as a closet, pushed past her rack of clothes into the storage area, where her parents' cardboard boxes and plastic storage bins were piled high. She edged in as far as she could and scanned what was written on the sides, finally finding a series of large Rubbermaid containers labeled "Southaven" in her mother's handwriting.

The first bin she opened was filled with dishes and miscellaneous stuff: a radio, a flashlight, a bicycle pump; the next had towels and sheets with cans of cat food (*really, Mom?*) sandwiched between them; another had seemingly random books and folders containing tax returns and financial information from Katherine's gardening business on the island. In her mother's typical style, there was no order to what was with what. Quinn didn't know what she was looking for, anyway. Stuff of her grandmother's, yes. But what? Something to prove that Quinn wasn't like her? Or that she was? If this were a movie, she'd find an old journal of Meryl's filled with secrets. Filled with answers.

She knew so little about her. She knew that she'd grown up in the house on Southaven and that her father died of cancer when she was little. Knew she'd gotten married and moved to Cincinnati, where her baby daughter died from SIDS. Had Quinn's father and then moved back to Maine, leaving her family. Killed herself. That was all. (And most of it Quinn had only learned because of her father's interviews over the last year.)

By the time Quinn opened the final bin, she still hadn't found anything that might have belonged to her grandmother. The only things she'd set aside as being of any interest were a few framed photos. She brought them out of the closet room into her bedroom to see them better: her parents dancing at their wedding, young and happy and glamorous; Gabe graduating from Columbia Business School; Katherine holding Ben in front of their house in Cincinnati. The last one was of Katherine standing in the main living area in the Southaven house, toddler-age Quinn on her hip. Katherine's hair was long and in two loose braids, her face fuller than now. Behind her was a wall with a framed painting hanging on it. Quinn sharpened her focus, remembering it. A watercolor of the ocean.

A still morning sea . . .

The words came into her mind in her mother's voice. Clear as if Katherine were standing here now, as if she were reciting a poem or reading a book, like she'd done at Quinn's bedtime for years.

A still morning sea, deeply asleep, 'til warmed by the sun, it rolls up the beach. The words brought a memory of snuggling with her mother, wrapped in the satiny, ink-blue comforter that had been on Quinn's bed. And somehow the words were connected to that painting in the photo. Maybe they were from a poem or story Katherine had made up to go along with it? When they went to museums, she liked to linger in front of works and make up stories about the people in the paintings.

Quinn propped the photo on her bookshelf. *A still morning sea, deeply asleep, 'til warmed by the sun, it rolls up the beach . . .*

Late in the afternoon, Quinn was pretending to read *Tender Is the Night* at the kitchen table while her mother was typing on her laptop. Luckily, in this back part of the house, the only discernable sound from the scene out front was the occasional *whoot* of a police car.

"What was Meryl like?" Quinn asked casually.

Katherine looked up. "Where did that come from?"

Quinn shrugged.

"Well, I only met her once. She was . . . odd. And sad. No, not sad. Depressed."

"Because of her baby that died?" Quinn reflexively touched her stomach as she said it.

"I think she had clinical depression, and the death exacerbated it. She also had a lot of guilt about leaving your father, I think."

"So, what was odd about her?"

Katherine stared off to the side for a moment. "The one time we visited, she asked to spend some time alone with me, and she . . . told me things. She said we had to leave Cincinnati, before you were born. That we should move into her house after she died." She paused. "She seemed confused, mixing up her baby and our baby and saying Gabe would understand . . . She seemed to know that you'd have health problems in the city."

"She knew I'd have my allergies?" An uneasiness came over Quinn. A sense that Meryl had known because of some link, some similarity between them.

"She couldn't have, but it seemed like it, when I looked back after you were born." Katherine shrugged. "Anyway, that wasn't the only odd thing . . . While we were alone that day, before we talked at all, she asked if I wanted to swim with her."

"What's weird about that?"

"It was April. And I was really damn pregnant."

"Was she kidding?" *No one* swam in the ocean off of Maine in April.

"No. Definitely not. And . . . I actually went in."

"What?" Quinn said, shocked. "You only swim when it's ninety degrees out!"

"I'm not sure what came over me," Katherine said. "It was a sudden urge. I didn't stay in long, but it felt great." She seemed to lose herself in the memory for a moment before adding, "Don't ever mention that to your dad, though. I've never seen him so livid. And it was pretty stupid to go swimming in frigid water being that pregnant."

An image of her father dragging her mother from the water by her arm flashed in Quinn's mind. She shivered.

"The whole visit really upset your father," Katherine said. Her voice had become subdued. "I don't know what Meryl said to him, but somehow he came away from it with even more anger than before."

Hearing the change in her tone, and not even knowing what else to ask, Quinn turned back to *Tender Is the Night*. But she couldn't concentrate, and a minute later she found herself saying, "Do you remember a book or poem from when I was little, something that began like: *A still morning sea, deeply asleep . . . ?*"

A strange look passed across Katherine's face. "It was a children's book I read to you."

"Do we still have it?"

"No."

"Do you remember the title?"

"No. Why?" Katherine closed her laptop. "What's with all these questions? First your grandmother, now this? Dr. Jacoby isn't making you go into all this old stuff, is she? Because I don't see how that would do any good. Your father and I have been wondering what approach she's taking. And if she's spending too much time—"

The ring of the doorbell interrupted her.

"Dammit," Katherine said. "We've told them going past the gate is trespassing." She hurried out of the room and upstairs to the parlor floor. Quinn was surprised to hear her call her name moments later.

Sadie stood in the front hall, book bag on her shoulder.

Katherine headed back toward the kitchen, saying, "When you want to leave, Sadie, I'll take you out through the garden. I don't want you going out the front."

"Hey," Quinn said when her mother was gone. "I'm so happy you're here!"

"It's crazy out there," Sadie said, eyes wide. "I hadn't seen it in person yet. It's . . . creepy. People were, like, touching me. And this one guy begged me to bring out something you'd touched. I mean, ugh."

"I keep telling my parents it'd be a great day to have a stoop sale," Quinn said. She was expecting Sadie to smile at this. Instead, her expression seemed to sharpen from shock to something more pointed, as if she'd come out of a trance.

"What were you thinking," Sadie asked, "attacking Brett Lewis at lunch? Everyone's talking about it."

Oh. *That* was why she was here. "I . . . I wasn't thinking straight. I was just so pissed off. I wouldn't really say I attacked him, though."

"People are saying you totally lost it." Sadie folded her arms. "I think you better tell me what's going on, Quinn. I've been really patient with you and all your mysterious excuses. For weeks now. I need you to tell me the truth."

Quinn scratched an itchy spot on her neck. "I'm sorry. It's just . . . everything is screwing with my head. And Brett was being a total jerk."

"I don't mean the truth about why you attacked Brett. I mean the truth about this pregnancy." Sadie waited for a second, but Quinn didn't respond. "And you still haven't told me what's going on with you and Jesse lately. It makes stuff pretty awkward for us, you know, having no idea."

"I know. I just . . ."

"This is getting so old." Sadie shook her head. "Forget it." She turned to go.

"Wait." Quinn grabbed her arm, motivated by a surge of fear— she couldn't lose Sadie, too. And as her fingers wrapped around the cool nylon of Sadie's puffy jacket, a thought lit up in Quinn's mind.

It was a risk, but one that might pay off. She drew in a shaky breath and lowered her voice. "Will you come up to my room? Please?"

Once they were in her bedroom and the door was shut, Quinn

said, "I'm going to tell you the whole story. But you need to promise not to tell anyone. Not Caroline or Isa or any of the guys. Not anyone. It's really, really important. Like, life or death important." That didn't feel like an exaggeration, knowing how angry her father would be.

"I won't tell anyone," Sadie said. "I swear."

Quinn told her as brief a version of the story as possible, pacing around the room as she did, trying to play down the weirdness and to emphasize that repression of trauma wasn't uncommon. She didn't leave any room for Sadie to think she'd ever even vaguely considered she might really be a virgin.

Sadie sat on the bed, looking stunned. "I don't know what to say. That's so . . . horrible. And weird. And . . . horrible. I don't . . . I don't know what to say, Quinn."

"Now you can see why I haven't been able to talk about it."

"I'm so sorry we gave you a hard time. We all figured that because you kept the baby, it wasn't a traumatic story. I thought you were in love with the guy, whoever it was. An older man or someone. I thought it was something romantic."

"I wish," Quinn said.

"And, I mean . . ." Sadie's eyes were as round and glassy as marbles. "It's not like we'd ever have guessed *this*."

"I know," Quinn said, wanting to direct the conversation away from how weird it was. "So, listen—obviously I've been doing everything I can to bring back the memory, but it's really frustrating, because there aren't that many concrete things to do. And, well, maybe you can help."

When Quinn went to bed that night, she felt a spark of optimism— the satisfaction of having made a little progress. And of maybe having figured out a way to go back in time.

She'd had Sadie look at the calendar of those two weeks. Sadie had immediately remembered that the two of them had walked home from the music festival in the park with Adrian and Oliver. Another night crossed off. But more importantly . . .

Sadie had agreed to try to hack into Marco and Foley's email accounts to look at old messages and to check around on social media to see if they'd said anything after the party last May, or after Ben's visit to Marco. Or if they were saying anything about it now. It was a long shot, but if something did happen that night, any little clue could be the key Quinn needed.

SADIE WESTON-HOYT

Sadie's fingers sat motionless on the keyboard. She was supposed to be working on code for programming class. *Yeah, right.* No way was she focusing on anything tonight.

She kept reminding herself that Quinn had a therapist. That she, Sadie, wasn't responsible for . . . for what? Telling her how unhinged she sounded? Letting Quinn's parents know?

This wasn't what Sadie had bargained for when she pressured Quinn to confide in her. She realized now that a small part of her had even been jealous, before. Jealous of all the attention on Quinn, but also the fact that she was having this monumental experience that Sadie had assumed was the result of a doomed love affair with an older man or whatever. Something grand and romantic. Because, to Sadie, Quinn had always seemed like the heroine of one of those classic novels in which the woman is all upstanding on the outside but is roiling with passion on the inside, and ends up living a torrid, romantic life with some married nobleman.

Quinn wasn't the heroine of a romantic tragedy.

She was the heroine of . . . what? A horror story?

There was something scarily on the edge about her. The way she'd supposedly lost it in the lounge. And the way she was constantly scratching and rubbing her skin, as if she wanted to take it off. And the pacing, back and forth, back and forth.

But if she'd been raped, who could blame her for losing her shit? And if Sadie wanted to help, shouldn't she do what Quinn asked? To help prove it was one of those guys—Marco or Foley—if it was? She was Quinn's friend, not her therapist. And this whole time she'd been telling her she was willing to help.

Last year, this girl at school, Violet, had confided in Sadie that she was using serious drugs, and Sadie hadn't told anyone, out of some weird loyalty or girlfriend code. But she'd been wrong not to. So now she made a resolution. She'd do this one thing—she'd told Quinn she would, and she'd keep her promise. But if she saw anything weirder or more worrisome, she was going to make sure someone else knew. Quinn's parents, or her therapist . . . There were lots of rumors around that Quinn was completely losing it, and now . . . Sadie was worried they might be true.

QUINN

The dream was different this time.

Her mother was the one waiting for her underwater, and Quinn could see her, not like when it was Jesse and she just knew he was there. Her mother was holding a little girl, saying, "In the still morning sea, we're asleep in the deep." And then Quinn became aware that she—she, the one seeing this scene—was actually her grandmother, Meryl, and that she had told Katherine to go swimming, and that's why they were underwater together. And the little girl in Katherine's arms was Quinn.

"You're home," Katherine said, and released toddler Quinn into the water. But toddler Quinn couldn't swim. Her small limbs flailed and she began to sink. Quinn/Meryl tried to move to save herself/her granddaughter, but she was paralyzed.

She began to panic. Her granddaughter was drowning and she couldn't move to save her. *I can't get there!* she called out. *I told him I couldn't get there! You have to swim!*

And then lanternfish began to gather around them, more and more—they swirled around toddler Quinn in a frenzy of light. And toddler Quinn stopped struggling and the light held her up until she began to swim. And the lanterns glowed brighter and brighter and brighter until the whole ocean was made of light.

Quinn woke up, breathing heavily. But relieved. Everything was fine. She lay there for a moment, slowing her breaths, rubbing her belly. *Everything is fine. Better than fine—it's all made of light.*

Then the details from the dream seeped back into her brain like poison.

She had dreamed she was her grandmother.

✦ ✦ ✦

Taking a bath in the morning, she tried to wash off the dream's guilty residue. *It was as meaningless as the ones about Jesse*, she told herself. She tried to focus on other things, like the anticipation of seeing Sadie at school. She was anxious about both possibilities: that Sadie had been able to get into Marco and Foley's accounts and had found something, and that she hadn't.

But just as Quinn and Lydia and Katherine were heading out the kitchen door to drive to school, her mother's phone rang. "Hello?" she said. "Yes, hi Brian, it's Katherine." She left the room to talk, leaving Quinn and Lydia standing with their coats on and bags on their shoulders. After waiting a couple of minutes, they sat down. The table was a mess of breakfast dishes and a few days of the *Financial Times* and *Wall Street Journal*. Quinn began carrying dishes over to the sink.

"I'm going to be late," Lydia said angrily. "Everyone looks at you when you're late."

In the tense silence, it felt like forever before Katherine came back in. She'd taken her coat off and didn't have her purse with her.

"Change of plans," she said, sitting at the table.

She explained that school wanted Quinn to study at home until everything was less unsettled. The situation was too much of a distraction for the community, the head had said, and other parents were concerned. Apparently reporters had been hanging around outside the building, pressuring students to talk, following them down the street. School was going to arrange for Quinn to watch her classes on a live stream and conference with teachers on a message board—the system New Prospect used for students with extended illnesses.

"I'm not sure what we're going to do about you," Katherine said to Lydia. "I'm waiting for a call back from Ms. Dempsey." She was head of the Lower School. "But for today, you're not going in."

"But I have a presentation to give in science," Lydia said. "And what about my friends? I don't want to stay here with the Jesus freaks. Daddy says they're dangerous!"

"I'm sorry, sweetie," Katherine said. "I'm doing the best I can. And as long as we keep our distance, those people won't bother us. There's a police car around all the time. I promise we're safe."

Quinn unzipped her coat, not knowing how she felt about this. On one hand, after yesterday's scenes in English and at lunch, she was relieved not to be going back.

But how was she going to get in touch with Sadie? And was she just going to spend all day, every day, sequestered in the house mostly alone, with no way to contact people? Never talking to or seeing her friends? Even though seeing Jesse was painful, the idea of having no contact at all with him was worse. If she wasn't going to school, her parents would have to be more relaxed about the rules. They'd have to let her call and text her friends. And if she was going to stream her classes, she'd have to be connected to the Internet.

They couldn't expect her to be completely invisible.

Gabe was supposed to have been away from the house all day—the election was next week, the first Tuesday in November, and he was out campaigning and at meetings almost all the time. But he arrived home unexpectedly in the late morning, something about a mix-up with an event he was supposed to speak at. Quinn sat on the stairs outside the kitchen, listening to the clatter of dishes and his frustrated voice as he talked to her mother. She'd wanted to talk to them about getting her friends' numbers programmed into her phone, but this didn't seem like the right time.

"After all the crap I deal with out there, I have to come home to this mess?" her father said.

"You're welcome to do any sort of cleaning you want," Katherine said. "It's not like I've spent the morning sitting around doing nothing."

"All I'm asking is that it doesn't look like everything has gone to hell in here all the time. I've got people coming in and out."

"I can't believe you're complaining about this right now."

"It just seems that instead of anything getting taken care of, it's all exploding. We need to control what we can. Things like this matter."

"Are you talking about the mess, Gabe? Or what's going on out there? Because I have no idea what to do about that, and I'm just as upset as you are, so yelling at me isn't going to help."

"I don't think you could possibly be as upset as I am. Wait until you see Alicia's new ad." Alicia was his Republican opponent. Quinn wrapped her arms tight against her body.

There was a pause. Katherine's voice was quieter when she spoke. "We both knew politics meant being under a microscope."

"We're not under a microscope," he said. "We're being fictionalized. You do realize the corner that's been turned?"

Silence. What corner?

"There was no 'mix-up' today," Gabe continued. "And two of my afternoon meetings canceled."

Again, silence. Then Katherine, speaking softly, "Did you talk to Edward?"

At that point, they both lowered their voices to murmurs that Quinn couldn't hear.

Edward was their lawyer. Quinn didn't even want to know what her father needed to talk to him about. *The Democrat always wins in this district.* Her parents had told her a million times. *The Democrat always wins.*

She said it over to herself, like a prayer: *The Democrat always wins. The Democrat always wins.*

✦　✦　✦

She uncurled herself and walked quietly upstairs. In the foyer, she noticed something bright pink under the bench. A flower, sticking out of the box that was used to collect the people's offerings. Usually, her parents threw that stuff out right away. One of them must have gotten distracted after bringing it back inside.

She slid out the box and began sorting through objects: a plastic statue of the Virgin Mary, a popsicle-stick-and-yarn God's eye, flowers (mostly artificial), candles, prayer cards, small stuffed animals, photographs—bent and stuck together with tape—and envelopes. Lots of envelopes. Everything was damp from another drizzly day.

She took out a white, greeting card–size envelope, and ran her finger around the edge, staring at the smudged writing on the front: *Blessed Virgin*. The moist flap ripped open easily. Quinn pulled out a card that pictured an old painting of Jesus on the cross, the kind you'd find at the Met. Inside, in bubbly handwriting, it said:

Blessed Virgin,

People think you are lying but those of us with true faith are willing to open our hearts to the idea you are who you say you are. We send you love and we send your miracle baby love. In the end truth will be revealed as it always is. I thank you from the bottom of my heart for the sacrifices you are making for us all.

With love, Michelle DiGustera

Quinn set it aside and opened another, a drugstore-type card picturing a bouquet of roses. Inside, the handwriting was spidery and slanted, hard to make out.

My life is full of trials today. It gives me strength to know you are near. I wish you will pray for me & pray for my children, and the good outcome of my medical tests this week. And that my brother passes his exam. Knowing I can ask you this I feel full of more hope in tomorrow. Thank you so much. Love, D. Matthes.

The third card was handmade—a child's drawing of a big person and a small person and an unidentifiable type of animal. In kid's writing it said: *My cat is sik.* That was all. Quinn felt a twinge in her chest. She slipped the envelopes into her waistband and shoved the box back under the bench.

Later in the day, she heard raised voices coming from out front. Then a dog barking and a woman saying something that sounded like "Watch out!" Quinn eased back one of the curtains in the living room a couple of inches and cracked the window so she could hear better. The Cutlers' neighbors, a burly older man named Dave and his tiny wife, Georgia, were standing in front of the house with their Rottweiler. The people had backed up a few steps, forming a space around them. "You don't like it?" Dave said, waving an arm. "Get off the block! Go make a mess of your own blocks, assholes!" He stomped off with the dog. Georgia looked around and said, "This isn't the dark ages you know. They'll test that baby and find DNA from a father. How're you going to explain that? Huh?"

"God created DNA!" someone shouted back. "He can create whatever he wants!"

Georgia shook her head and followed her husband.

The people moved forward again. Around twenty of them. More women than men, mostly middle-aged; a couple of elderly; three children standing around a man in a wheelchair. A variety of races. No press at the moment—not that Quinn could see, at least. And while there wasn't anything outwardly pathetic about most of the people, there was still an obvious exhaustion . . . desperation . . .

She wondered if any of them had written the letters she had read.

You've got the wrong girl, she wanted to tell them. *I wish I could help you, but I can't.*

She shifted her gaze and unexpectedly met the eyes of one of the women. A youngish woman in a vibrant red coat and blue scarf. For a moment, Quinn was locked into eye contact. The look the woman gave back wasn't crazy or desperate. Her expression was calm and aware, like Quinn could have asked her any questions and she'd explain everything to her. There was something familiar about her, too. Quinn recognized her from somewhere else.

Footsteps echoed from the stairs up from the kitchen.

Quinn quickly closed the drape and moved away.

GABE CUTLER

eading upstairs after getting a cup of coffee, Gabe was reminded by the noises from out front that he should make a sweep of the "offerings" on the fence. He was annoyed to see that Katherine had left the box full of the last batch of crap in the foyer. How long had it been sitting there? He hated the idea of those things lingering, as if they had some sort of disease that would spread into the air of the house. He carried the full box up to his office.

After putting the objects into a trash bag, he sat at his desk, sorting through the cards and letters and notes, setting aside ones to pass along to his connection in the police department. The first bunch were harmless, as most of them had been since this all started. Pathetic, but harmless.

He unfolded a dirty piece of paper. One side was a printed flyer for a car wash. On the other side was handwritten: *Duderonomy 22:20–1 If however the charge is true and no prove of the girl's virginity can be found, she shall be brought to the door of her fathers house and there the men of her town shall stone her to death.*

Jaw clenched, he set it in the "Don't shred" pile, along with other threats and screeds about his disgusting, devil-worshipping daughter.

His shredder was jammed. He took the letters—the unthreatening ones that didn't need to be saved—into the living room and set them in the fireplace in a teepee arrangement. It was a damp day, though, and he had trouble lighting them. As he tried, he remembered another fire, lit years ago with a similar intent.

He'd lit the fire down on the beach at Holmes Cove, so there'd be no chance of it spreading. Had nestled the two thick envelopes—one meant for him, one meant for Quinn when she was older—in the middle of a group of stones. He'd gone through a whole box of matches. None would stay lit for more than a second, as if the fire was in cahoots with his mother. (*You must be the one to tell her, Gabriel! My father died before he could tell me. Listen to me, Gabriel!*) He'd gone up to the house and gotten the lighter for the fireplace, which had done the trick. Flames had eaten up the paper. Gone, as if the words inside had never existed.

As he watched the flames here in his living room fireplace, his phone buzzed.

"What's up, Taylor?" he said, tired of seeing her name on his screen. It was never good news. And the way things were going, probably never would be.

"That producer called again."

"Ben's?" Gabe began to pace, not wanting to think about the email he'd sent Ben that had likely ensured he wouldn't see him for a long time. Not that he wanted to see him anytime soon, but still . . . it didn't make him happy.

"No, no," Taylor said. "From *The Preston Brown Show*."

Gabe closed his eyes and rubbed them. "What if we get out now? Would that stop it?"

"I don't think so," Taylor said. "Gabe . . . it's going to be bad."

QUINN

The next day, her father's tech guy, Hassan, came over to configure Quinn's laptop. Thank god. Contact with civilization. She *needed* to get in touch with Sadie.

"So I'll be able to go online like normal?" she asked him as he worked.

"Huh?" he said, not looking away from the screen.

"You know, email and stuff?"

"Oh," he said. "No, not like that."

"No? Don't I have to be connected to Wi-Fi to stream my classes?"

He peered over his shoulder at her. "Sure, you'll be connected. But it's just going to be set up so you can access your classes and the message board. That's it."

"Seriously?" Quinn blurted. She'd have no way to contact Sadie. No way to connect with anyone outside the house. For *months*.

"Sorry," Hassan said with a shrug.

Her world was going to be as small as a drop of water.

She was taking an early evening bath trying in vain to soothe both her frustration and her skin, which felt like it didn't even fit on her body anymore even though her belly wasn't *that* big yet, when her mother knocked on the bathroom door. "Sweetie?" she called. "Jesse's here."

"He is?" she said, shocked. "Tell him to wait. I'll be right there." *Jesse is here?* She quickly got out of the bath and rushed through drying off and slipping into the same clothes she'd had on before—yoga pants and a hoodie, pretty much the only things she wore now. She towel-dried her hair but didn't bother brushing it, scared he'd leave if she took too long. *Jesse is here!*

She hurried downstairs, telling her feet not to outright run even though they wanted to, and took a moment to smooth down her damp hair and compose herself before going into the kitchen. He was standing with his arms crossed, a manila envelope in one hand, shifting from foot to foot. Her chest ached at the sight of his messy waves of brown hair and warm eyes. Like always, all she wanted was to kiss him and wrap him in a hug and smell his Jesse smell. She wanted to hug the breath out of him and never let go.

"Hey," she said. "What's up?" *You still love me? You miss me?*

"Hey." His expression was frustratingly neutral. "Mr. D asked if I'd be your 'liaison' for anything that can't be emailed. Books, that sort of thing."

"Oh." Quinn swallowed her disappointment that he wasn't here of his own accord. But at least this meant she would get to see him occasionally. That was huge. "Is that . . . Do you mind?"

"Whatever. It's fine," he said. "Makes the most sense, since I can come in the back way."

"Okay," she said. "Thanks. I really appreciate it."

"No problem. You wouldn't want anyone coming in the front door. Man."

"You walked by?"

He nodded. "I was glad there was a police car. Anyway, this is what Mr. D gave me for you." He reached forward to hand her the envelope.

"Thanks."

He hesitated, lips slightly parted, like he had something else to say.

"What?" she said.

"You . . . you smell like you."

The words squeezed her heart. "Shampoo," she said, pointing stupidly at her hair.

They stood, silent, awkward, until he said he better go.

After he left, she waited at the kitchen door and watched him make his way across the backyard. He usually bounced when he walked, like gravity had a hard time keeping him down. Today, gravity seemed to have won. Once he was out of sight, she opened the envelope with an irrational hope that there'd be something inside, a note from him, something he couldn't say out loud. There wasn't.

But there was an envelope from Sadie.

Sadie had gotten into Marco and Foley's accounts and found one thing: a photo that Foley had sent to someone of Marco, passed out and shirtless, with a paper crown on his head and graffiti scrawled on his torso, and the caption: "Behold, Prince Marco. A worthy farewell to his kingdom!"

It's from the day after the party, Sadie wrote in a note. *I guess all it proves is that he was wasted that night. Sorry I didn't come up with anything else. Love you. Hope you're okay. Call me when you can. XOXO*

Quinn stared at it, pacing around her bedroom. Marco had been messed up enough to pass out. Maybe he'd lost his reluctance to hook up with her? Decided it didn't matter he had a girlfriend? It still didn't explain why he'd have told Ben he saw her down there at all, of course, instead of denying everything completely. But it could mean something. It definitely could. Ben had said that Marco said Quinn saw his flashlight. Maybe he was trying to cover himself by admitting that he had been down there?

She needed to see Marco in person. She needed to judge her reaction to him, his reaction to her. And to ask him to do a DNA test, if it came to that. If he hadn't done anything, he'd have no reason to refuse.

Her mother was talking on the phone in her bedroom when Quinn found her. "Of course it's not true," Katherine was saying angrily. "How could you even—no, don't bother. Don't bother calling back if that's what you think." She hung up and looked startled to see Quinn. "Oh, hi. What do you need, sweetie?"

"I need Ben's number in my phone," Quinn said. "Now. And Jesse's and Sadie's, too." She'd asked a couple of times already.

"Okay, but I can't deal with it right now. I don't know how to program that thing anyway."

"Mom, it's important. I should be able to call my own brother."

"I know. I just . . . I'm sorry. When one of your dad's staff is here, we'll get them to do it."

Quinn felt the hum of panic beginning in her chest. "But I need to talk to Ben now. Today. You can't cut me off from everyone."

"Quinn!" Katherine snapped. "Did you not hear me? I said I'd get it done. Just give me a break here! There's more important stuff on my mind."

The unfamiliar sound of her mother yelling shocked Quinn into momentary silence.

"I'm sorry," Katherine said after a minute. "Here, use mine to call him." She held her phone out to Quinn, whose hand trembled a bit as she took it.

Quinn started out of the room.

"Call him from here," Katherine said.

"I can't have privacy?"

Her mother rubbed her temples. "Don't give me a hard time about this. We'll get his number in your phone soon, then you can talk wherever you want."

Quinn realized that her mother didn't trust her with a smartphone. Didn't trust her not to go online, probably. And it was obvious she wasn't going to give in. So Quinn called Ben as she stood there, hot with annoyance, not quite sure how she'd explain about Marco with her mother listening. She got his voicemail, anyway.

✦ ✦ ✦

That night in her dream, Quinn was holding her baby in her arms as she swam down, down, down into the watery depths.

Marco was waiting for them.

"You have to go away," Quinn said to him. "I'm not allowed to be friends with you."

"Can you call me?" he said.

Quinn held tighter to her baby. "No. You're dangerous."

And then, all of a sudden, Marco wasn't Marco. He was her father. "I'm not dangerous," Gabe said. "You're safe down here."

As he said it, the lanternfish began to swirl around them. "You're safe," her father said again. And Quinn let go of the baby, and it swam away, and she hugged her father.

Then, like the time before, Quinn realized that she wasn't herself. She was her grandmother. And somehow she knew that the baby that swam away was her baby that had died, before Gabe was born.

"You didn't tell her," she whispered to Gabe, her son, as she hugged him. "But don't worry. I forgive you."

QUINN

"You seem especially frustrated today," Dr. Jacoby said, narrowing her eyes a bit. "Is something going on?"

Quinn realized Dr. Jacoby was looking at where she'd scratched her arm raw. She pulled down her sleeve. None of the pregnancy books said anything about skin symptoms outside of places affected by pregnancy weight—belly, butt, hips—the places where Quinn was starting to see stretch marks. But Quinn's skin symptoms went way beyond that. It was so uncomfortable *everywhere* that she wanted to wriggle out of it entirely.

Not that that's what she was most frustrated about at the moment. She was frustrated with her brother.

He'd never called back on her mom's phone. She'd finally gotten his number (and Jesse's) programmed into her own and had spent the last couple of days texting him and leaving voicemails. She'd expected him to answer right away, but he hadn't. His voicemail was one of those pre-set ones, so she had Hassan double-check that he'd put in the right number. He showed her the number Gabe had given him, and yes, he'd entered it correctly. Which meant that Ben was purposefully ignoring her. Either that or he didn't get reception wherever he was traveling for work, but that seemed really unlikely.

He'd told her that she should call if she needed him. And now she had, and he was ignoring her.

She couldn't tell Dr. Jacoby about any of this, though, because she didn't want to admit that the reason she was so desperate to talk to Ben was so he could take her to see Marco in New Haven. Quinn wasn't sure if doctor-patient confidentiality would extend to something like that and couldn't risk Dr. Jacoby telling her parents. (She'd considered telling her parents about Marco, and her suspicions about that night, but had visions of her father taking action on his own, getting lawyers to subpoena Marco to do a DNA test, confronting him himself . . . Quinn needed to be a hundred times more sure than she was now that Marco was involved before setting all that in motion.)

Anyway, there were plenty of other things she was frustrated about to mention to Dr. Jacoby.

"I keep having those dreams," she said, standing up and beginning to pace. "You know, the underwater ones. And more often now, I'm my grandmother for at least part of the dream. And . . . the thing is that the dreams are so beautiful when I'm in them. And when I wake up, I'm so . . . happy. It's like my brain is purposefully avoiding reality."

"What do you think it means, dreaming that you're your grandmother?" Dr. Jacoby said. "Don't get me wrong, I don't believe there's only one correct interpretation. But I'm wondering what occurs to you."

Quinn sat back down in her chair. "That I feel guilty because I've messed up my dad's life as much as she did?"

"The guilt you feel might have something to do with it, sure," Dr. Jacoby said. "What about the fact that the dreams take place underwater? Your grandmother drowned, right? That's how she took her life?"

"Uh-huh."

"Were you thinking about her at all when you went for that midnight swim last May, after you kissed Marco?"

Quinn was confused by her train of thought. "What do you mean? No. Why would I have been thinking of her?"

"Well, it seems pretty risky to have gone swimming at night like that, alone, at a beach with tricky currents. So I'm just wondering if you remember thinking about the fact that she'd drowned."

"Wait," Quinn said, shifting in her seat. "Are you asking if I was trying to kill myself?"

"Not necessarily actively trying. But, yes, I'm wondering if you think you might have been tempting fate."

Quinn couldn't believe what she was hearing. "It wasn't like that. Not at all! I'm a really good swimmer. I didn't need to stay out of the ocean all those years. And I was *happy* that day."

Dr. Jacoby laced her fingers together. "But the last time you'd swum at that beach—the last time you were in the ocean at all—you almost drowned, didn't you?"

"Not the last time. I kept swimming there for the rest of that summer, until my dad found out and got mad." *His wet khaki pants as he charged through the water, the pain in her arm, his hand coming toward her . . .*

"He was mad because you were taking risks?"

Quinn nodded.

What is wrong with you?

"And, shortly after all of that is when you began therapy for the first time?"

"What?"

"When you were seven? That's when you started seeing a therapist, right?"

"What are you talking about?" Quinn said, a flush spreading up her neck. "I was in *speech* therapy. Not this kind of therapy. You must be confusing me with another patient."

"Oh." Dr. Jacoby looked flustered in a way Quinn had never seen before. "I'm sorry, Quinn. I thought . . . I'm sorry."

"And were you trying to say that I was trying to kill myself when I was *seven,* when I kept swimming there?" Quinn said. "Because that's crazy. Seven-year-olds don't kill themselves. And I wasn't trying last May, either. And I don't see what any of this has to do with anything!"

"Quinn," Dr. Jacoby said in an irritatingly soothing tone, "I can see that I've upset you. Do you want to look at why?"

Quinn stood up and started pacing again. "Because I'm not suicidal! I wasn't back then, and I wasn't last May. That's the exact opposite of how I felt when I went for that midnight swim. I felt happy. I felt *alive*! And it had nothing to do with my grandmother. I'm not like her."

Do you want to be like her? Do you want to end up like her and die in the ocean?

"If you had experienced suicidal tendencies, Quinn, there would be no shame in it. I was just trying to explore your thoughts about why you'd engaged in risky behaviors. Not saying that you were actually consciously trying to take your own life. And I'm sorry I was wrong about you being in therapy back then. I really do apologize."

Quinn felt hot tears behind her eyes but refused to let them out.

She wasn't suicidal like her grandmother. Wanting to die had *nothing* to do with her dreams about Meryl or why she'd taken that swim. If there was one emotion she'd felt that day it was love—she'd been bursting with it.

Start with what you know. This she knew.

ELLEN JACOBY

When her day of seeing patients was over, Ellen looked through her past session notes in Quinn's file, even though she knew Quinn was right—she'd never mentioned being in therapy before. Ellen had read it in some gossipy article and had said it before she realized. She'd been trying to keep abreast of what was happening around her client, and had read about her being in therapy as a kid, and had stupidly forgotten that's how she knew.

But now Quinn said she hadn't been in therapy at all. Another lie the press was telling. Unbelievable how out of control the situation was, how people were crucifying the Cutler family. Although, Ellen was the first to admit that she didn't completely trust what the Cutlers were saying, either. She'd seen their penchant for spin right from those first phone messages.

Reporters had been shameless in trying to talk to Ellen herself once they'd found out that she was Quinn's therapist.

"Dr. Jacoby, in general, what kind of patients do you see? Extremely troubled cases?"

"You wrote an article in 2007 about childhood sexual trauma. Is that a specialty of yours?"

"Do you treat adolescents with personality disorders? Schizophrenia?"

She was disgusted by their attempts to put together a picture of Quinn with the flimsiest information. She'd come to feel incredibly protective of her client. And along with her anger toward the press, she couldn't deny the anger she had toward Quinn's parents for not doing their job and protecting Quinn themselves. How deep that abdication of responsibility went, Ellen wasn't sure. She could only hope that the media's worst theories weren't true.

And weighing heavy on all of Ellen's thoughts was that no matter what the truth was, Quinn couldn't be isolated from what was being said forever.

QUINN

The next few days took years to pass.

Ben still hadn't called back, and Quinn had begun to worry that something was really wrong. Her mother said that she'd talked to him, so she knew he wasn't in the hospital or dead or something. All she could think was that he had decided he didn't want to help her for some reason. Didn't want to be in touch with her at all. But she couldn't think of why.

It also left her with no idea how to see Marco.

Stuck basically alone in the house, with no one to talk to except for Haven and the baby, Quinn found it almost impossible to keep from dwelling on the things Dr. Jacoby had said, on her bad dreams, on Ben. She watched classes on her laptop like a ghost but heard nothing the teachers said. She ran tedious miles on the treadmill they'd installed in the TV room, did prenatal yoga from videos, and took long baths. Being in the water was the only time her skin didn't feel like it belonged to someone else.

She paced up and down the stairs, trying and failing to fight the compulsion to peek outside. She made bets with herself: *If the man in the big plaid coat is still there, Ben will call. If there's more than one person in a wheelchair, I won't have any dreams tonight.*

Sometimes, when she was looking at the people outside, she'd think of those letters she'd read and then wonder what these different people wanted. Was it helping any of them to be here? Just because they thought they were closer to God? She hoped that maybe, in some small way, it did help. So something good could come out of all of this. That was possible, wasn't it?

When Jesse showed up on Friday, she had to fight an even stronger urge to hug him than ever. Not only was it Jesse, it was actual human contact. And this time, he asked if they could go upstairs to her room. On the way up, Quinn kept wondering what he wanted, whether he wanted to be friends again, or *more* than friends, whether he had forgiven her.

No, a voice deep inside her said. *He knows you now. He knows what you're really like. He'll never love you again.*

"I did something kind of stupid," he said when they got to her room. He took out a business-size envelope and a hundred dollar bill from his bag and put them on her desk.

"What the hell?" Quinn said. She fingered the bill.

"There was this woman in front of my building. She knew who I was, and she said she wanted to get this letter to you, and she was worried that you weren't reading the ones that people left outside. So she paid me to bring it to you."

"A hundred dollars?" Quinn held it up to the light, as if she'd even be able to tell if it were counterfeit.

"I know. Now I feel guilty for taking her money but also, like, worried the letter's a bomb or something."

Quinn put down the bill and picked up the envelope, a normal white envelope that had at most two sheets of paper in it. "That'd be one sneaky bomb."

"Anthrax? Ricin?"

Quinn knew he was basically kidding, but still asked, "Why are you even thinking stuff like that? Why would someone want to kill me? They think I'm carrying the messiah."

Jesse shrugged.

She set the envelope back on the desk and they stared at it some more. She wanted to keep talking about it so he wouldn't leave. It was the first actual conversation they'd had since . . . since the night of Sadie's party, probably.

"Are you going to read it?" he said. "Maybe I should just give it back, unopened."

"I'm sure it's just asking for a special prayer to heal her kid or something. Or maybe she's a reporter asking for an interview."

She picked it up again, ripped a messy tear across the flap, and pulled out a sheet of yellow lined paper. Unfolding it, she saw a full page of precise, attractive handwriting. She set it out so Jesse could read it, too.

Dear Miss Cutler,

My name is Nicole Anderson. We met briefly in the waiting room at the doctor's office weeks ago, and I've been praying outside your house every day since the Herald *article. I'm just writing to say that even when I saw you at the doctor's, I knew there was something special about you. God told me that you were chosen. So if you haven't been able to hear God tell you that because of all the other noise in our world (what a different world than in the Blessed Virgin Mary's time!) please know that I heard him for you. Do you know the story of Mary and the angel Gabriel? I'm not an angel, but I'd like to think I'm doing his work, if, as I said, you haven't been able to hear God yourself. Or perhaps you have heard Him, but other, outside voices are louder, telling you that you're wrong, or troubled, like happens to so many who are a special part of God's plan.*

The reason I know all this is because I was called by Him, too. I belong to a church in Michigan. The Church of the Next Shepherds. Our mission is to prepare the way for the new Messiah and protect him (or her) when he arrives. To be honest, I don't think many of us assumed this would happen in our lifetimes. We thought we were simply part of the chain of protectors, paving the way. Until now, we've just done whatever we can to make the world a better place—community service, teaching, etc.

But the minute I recognized your picture in the paper, I knew the time had come. I'm still not sure what that means—what role I'm supposed to play. But I know that I want to help you, protect you, and make things easier for you. And, right now, I see my role as helping you hear God's voice.

Listen deeply and you will hear the Truth.

With respect and love,

Nicole Anderson

"Whoa," Jesse said. "Do you know who she is?"

Quinn only took a second to make the connection. The woman in the red coat and blue scarf. That was where Quinn recognized her from: the doctor's office the day she'd had that first ultrasound. "Uh-huh," she said. "She's out there all the time."

She skimmed the letter again. " . . . *other, outside voices are louder, telling you that you're wrong, or troubled . . .*" Something jumped in her gut. The baby or nerves.

"I think I should give back the money," he said. "I don't feel right about it. And I don't want to get in the middle of all this. I kind of took it without thinking. Do you want me to give her the letter back, too? Tell her you didn't read it?"

"No," Quinn said automatically. For some reason, she didn't want him to take it. "That's okay. I'll just chuck it." She folded the paper, put it back in the envelope, and let it fall into the wastebasket.

"Okay," he said. "So . . . I guess I'll get going."

"You don't have to," she said, unable to hide the plea in her voice.

She sensed him hesitating. "I've got a lot to do," he said. "The deadline for the contest is tomorrow."

"Really?" Quinn said. "How's it going? Are you almost finished?" He'd gotten the idea to enter the screenplay contest last winter, had read piles of how-to books, and had spent hours with Quinn watching movie after movie, analyzing and taking notes, making her talk about what she liked and didn't like and hashing out his ideas with her. If he won, he'd get a scholarship to an intensive summer film program. The fact that she hadn't even known the deadline was tomorrow made Quinn's throat ache.

"I'll probably pull an all-nighter to finish," he said. "I still feel like I don't have a good grasp on a couple of the scenes. And Siobhan's character is still pretty weak."

"Did you have her keep the dog?"

"Yeah, but her motivation still isn't clear." He pursed his lips slightly in a way he always did when he was mulling over a problem. Quinn wanted to kiss them.

"I wish I could read it and help," she said. "But, you know, since I don't have email . . ."

He nodded. Silence billowed around them, swollen with everything that had happened and how they had gotten to this place.

Quinn followed him downstairs. When they reached the kitchen, Lydia was sitting at the table, alone, eating a pint of ice cream straight from the container. "Jesse!" she said, jumping up to hug him. "You're here!"

"Hey, Lyddie," he said. "I'm actually on my way home."

"Can't you stay for dinner? I haven't seen you in forever and there are a million things I need to show you. Did you know I got a turtle? My therapist said it'd be good for me, so they had to let me. I have a therapist now, too." She rolled her eyes.

"Sorry," he said, opening the sliding door, "I have to go."

"No." She caught him by the arm, keeping him inside.

"Lyddie," Quinn said. "He said he had to go. He'll stay for dinner another night."

"No!"

"Lydia." Quinn glared at her.

She let go of Jesse and crossed her arms. "Just because he doesn't want to see you doesn't mean he can't stay."

"I really can't tonight," he said. "Some other time."

Quinn followed him out into the chilly air. She said good-bye and wished him luck with the screenplay. "I'm sure it's amazing," she called out as he walked away.

Back in the kitchen, Lydia was gone, the pint of ice cream still on the table, unfinished. Quinn shoved the lid on and returned it to the freezer. Despite her father's complaints, it was still a mess in here: dirty dishes on the counter, an open can of coffee and box of cereal sitting out, banana peels overflowing out of the compost container . . . She took a few minutes to load the dishwasher and put away the food before heading upstairs. Lydia was standing in the front hall.

"I need to do research," she said, one hand resting on her hip. "I need to go online." Lydia wasn't streaming her classes; the lower school wasn't set up for that. She had a tutor with her full time during the day.

"Doesn't Annabelle do that stuff with you when she's here?"

"I need to do it *now*."

"Well, Mom's doing her shift at the co-op. Dad's here, but he's in a videoconference. And you know he won't let you, anyway."

"Your computer is online."

"Only the New Prospect site."

"You must have the new password."

"I don't. Hassan just put it into my keychain. I don't know what it is."

"So what am I supposed to do?"

"Can't you just wait until Dad is out of his meeting? Or maybe I have a book on it in my room. What's the topic?"

"The Gowanus Canal." Lydia raised her eyebrows. "You have a book on the Gowanus Canal?"

"Well, no . . ."

"I'm going to ask Daddy." She turned and began heading up the stairs.

"No," Quinn said. "Don't bother him. He said it's something important. Wait till he's done. Or just wait until tomorrow. Does it really matter?"

Lydia stopped and turned back to face her. "I hate this!" she said. "And I hate you. It's all your fault!"

"What is?" Quinn said stupidly.

"Everything! My life is ruined and Daddy's going to drop out of the election, and it's all your fault!"

"He's not going to drop out."

"They don't even want him to be the guy anymore!" Lydia said. "They're getting that woman who came in second to take over."

"No, they aren't," Quinn said, beginning to feel queasy.

"It's true. All because of you!"

"Lyddie—"

"And . . . and . . ." Lydia's face was pink, and she was so worked up she could hardly talk. "We don't ever see Ben or Jesse anymore. I'm not even allowed to have friends over. Because of you! And you can't even change the stupid cat litter even though she's your cat! And it's not fair!"

"This has nothing to do with not seeing Ben. He's traveling for work. And I'm sorry about the cat litter. You're not supposed to clean it when you're pregnant."

"Yes, it does have to do with not seeing Ben. It does! You don't know anything! You don't even know how you got pregnant. I hate you, and I wish you weren't my sister!"

She kicked the wall, leaving a black scuffmark on the pale yellow wallpaper, then ran up the stairs.

"Wait," Quinn said, hurrying after her. "Lydia!"

On the floor above them, their father's office door opened. He came out and shut it quickly behind him. "Girls," he said in a low, angry voice. "I'm trying to have a meeting."

"Isn't it true that they don't want you to run anymore?" Lydia said. "Tell her."

"You're not dropping out, are you?" Quinn asked.

He didn't respond, seemed at a loss for words. He was never at a loss for words.

"You are?" she said.

"Nothing is decided yet," he said finally.

"But they want you to!" Lydia shouted.

"Lydia," he snapped. "Don't raise your voice at me. I was going to say that not everyone thinks I should step aside. Some people do. We can talk about it later. Now, can I leave you two alone and go back to what I was doing?"

Quinn bit her lip. "Yes," she said. "Sorry we bothered you."

Lydia stuck her tongue out at Quinn and brushed past Gabe, stomping up the stairs to the top floor.

"We'll talk about this later," Gabe said to Quinn, a look in his eye that told her it wasn't going to be anything she wanted to hear.

Quinn was trembling a little after the confrontation. She shouldn't have been surprised about the election stuff, but she was. "Not everyone thinks" probably meant that most people did.

Didn't everyone know that the people outside had nothing to do with her father? And that they'd be long gone by the time he took office? It had no bearing on anything important. He'd clearly made a statement that the family didn't think the pregnancy was miraculous, so people couldn't think they were all nuts. Nothing had changed who he was or whether he'd be a good congressman.

He'd said nothing was decided yet. She knew her father; he was a fighter. There was no way he'd give up now.

But even as she told herself that, she couldn't get rid of the chill that had settled deep in her bones or the conviction that her father must hate her as much as Lydia did.

Upstairs in her room, she pulled out those shoeboxes of childhood stuff from under her bed and began sorting through it all. She held one of the rocks. A plain, gray, unexceptional rock from Holmes Cove. When they'd first moved, she'd made a tide pool with them right here in her room, along with a bunch of sand and seawater brought back from Southaven in a juice bottle. It wasn't enough water, though, so she'd added some from the tap, and then put the periwinkles and hermit crab and seaweed that she'd brought in jam jars. She went to school and left the bedroom door shut to keep Haven from eating the crab. When she came back, the water had leaked out between the rocks and all over the room. Her father had been so angry.

She unfolded one of the drawings from the box. Blue scribbles filled the whole page. A second and third drawing were the same, just done with different blue markers, like she'd been obsessed with drawing the sky. She remembered the feeling of frustration that went into making them. She could see it in the scribbles themselves. She'd wanted to draw something and couldn't. Like when she was trying to describe why she wanted to keep the baby but couldn't find the words. There had been something she wanted to draw but didn't know what it looked like. Which didn't make sense at all. If she didn't know what something looked like, why would she want to draw it?

All of this stuff . . . She'd been crazy back then, too, hadn't she? That's why she hadn't had any friends at her first school in Brooklyn. And why she'd hidden this stuff away, because her craziness made her father angry. He'd hated her then, too. And who could blame him—she reminded him of his mother.

CHARLES LOWELL

The photo of Quinn Cutler on the TV only looked a bit like Meryl Cutler in structural ways, but there was something in her expression that Charlotte "Charles" Lowell found uncannily similar.

"You must know the family," someone said to Charles, pointing up at the screen. "They as bad as they seem?"

Charles had headed over to The Shack for a beer and a bowl of chowder after a long day at the veterinary clinic. She knew everyone in there, all four customers. At this question, she realized that she was the only one who'd lived on Southaven when the Cutlers did.

"They always seemed nice enough," she said, stirring her chowder to cool it down. Her answer wasn't quite true: There'd been tension between Gabe Cutler and Charles's family.

"Don't sound very nice to me," the man said.

Even though Charles had tried to avoid taking part in the gossip, she was as fascinated by the situation with Gabe's daughter as everyone else. More so, probably. Just like she'd been fascinated by his mother.

Years ago, Charles had eavesdropped whenever Meryl Cutler came to the house to visit her grandmother, the original Charlotte. Listened to her tell stories of how she'd been sent away when she got pregnant at seventeen, how being separated from her home and then losing the baby had almost killed her. How she hadn't been able to return to Southaven when her mother was alive, so she'd married a man and had a son. Nothing had helped overcome her grief, though. She fell into a deeper and deeper depression, until she got to the point where she felt like her son would be better off without her.

When Meryl's mother died, she'd abandoned her family and returned to the island.

And then she'd reconnected with Charles's grandmother, a child-hood acquaintance, and read her book. To this day, Charles didn't know whether reading that book had been the start of some sort of recovery for Meryl or the catalyst for her disintegration. She'd killed herself, after all, so it wasn't like it had brought her peace.

Charles had always assumed that Meryl had been delusional about certain things. That she had grasped at straws to find answers in life. Like finding religion at your lowest point and clinging onto it. But now Charles couldn't stop thinking about those last days of Meryl's life, about the things she had wanted to pass on to the granddaughter Gabe's wife was carrying—Quinn. And Charles couldn't help wondering exactly what was going on behind the doors of that house in Brooklyn, and how it related to those strange beliefs of Meryl's that she'd always dismissed as fiction.

QUINN

Quinn was giving Haven an overdue brushing when her parents came to talk to her later that night. As they talked, she kept running the brush through Haven's long ginger fur, concentrating her eyes and hands on the task.

They explained that it was getting harder and harder to make people believe that Gabe wouldn't be distracted by this if elected, and that the Democrats were scared he was in danger of losing the election itself. A third-party independent candidate was complicating it. Gabe was falling in the polls and getting pressure from the party to resign.

"But it's not a done deal, right?" Quinn said, fingers worrying a stubborn mat in Haven's ruff. "Because you can't drop out."

"I'm officially withdrawing tomorrow," he said.

"No." She shook her head, back and forth, back and forth. "You can't. This doesn't make sense. The election is only a few days away. Wouldn't it be worse for some random person to be the candidate? It doesn't make sense."

"It's complicated," her mother said. "And the candidate isn't random. She has strong ties in the community."

"But this is a huge deal! Why are you guys acting so calm?" Quinn wasn't calm. Her pulse was thundering in her ears.

"Quinn," her father said firmly, "I did not make this decision lightly. I wouldn't be doing it if there were any other choice."

"But soon after you take office, the baby will be born and these people will be gone and, and . . . It's your whole career! How can you just drop out? Just because you have a pregnant daughter and . . . and some religious people have ideas? That has nothing to do with you being in Congress! Why would you drop out? Why are you acting like this isn't a big thing? Why are you doing this?" She wiped tears off her face.

"Jesus, Quinn—of course it's a big thing! It's the biggest disappointment of my life." His jaw pulsed. "There are things . . . reasons. It's the only option. I promise you that."

His phone buzzed. He glanced at it, said, "I have to take this," and left the room, phone to his ear.

Quinn and her mother sat in silence. How could Quinn ever make this better?

"He can't do it," she said, shaking her head again.

"You know that this isn't your fault, right?" Katherine said, resting a hand on Quinn's knee. "Dad is angry, but he isn't angry at you."

Quinn didn't respond to that. She sat thinking for a moment before saying, "You know Liz, the woman whose office I went to as a kid? During my year at 107? Was she a speech therapist? Or, like, a *therapist* therapist?"

"She was your therapist. You know that."

Ever since that strange slip of Dr. Jacoby's, Quinn had been having suspicions. "I remembered it as speech therapy."

"You did have a bit of a lisp," Katherine said, brows knitting, "but it went away on its own. You probably remember it as speech therapy because it was supposed to help you speak more. You weren't talking at school."

Quinn had never forgotten that, but had thought it was mostly because of her lisp. She thought she'd stopped talking because kids had made fun of the way she spoke, that it had marked her as an outsider. But no. That wasn't right.

"It was understandable," her mother added. "Moving here was a hard transition."

No more lies, Quinn! No more lies!

Now she remembered. She hadn't talked at school because all

she'd known to talk about was her life in Maine, and when she did, kids laughed, made fun of her, told her she was lying. That's why she'd stopped talking. Because if you couldn't lie and couldn't tell the truth, what did that leave?

She called Ben again. And again. And again. Even though, by this point, she knew that there was some reason he didn't want to talk to her. It was the only thing she could think to do. She had so many questions about so many things and needed answers. She needed to talk to someone. And she needed to go see Marco! She needed to do something other than talk to Dr. Jacoby and write out those stupid memories that weren't helping anything! *Pick up the fucking phone!* But he didn't.

She paced around her room, thinking about how unbelievably messed up everything was and wondering if the decision to go through with the pregnancy had been unforgivably selfish. All she'd done was listen to her gut, and look what had happened. This was her father's entire career on the line! No, there had to be something more to it all. Something that made it more than just a stupid selfish decision. Because she refused to believe that something she'd felt was beautiful and worth saving had really cursed the family like this. She refused for the baby to be born under that weight.

I know you're here for a reason, she said to the baby. *Even if no one else does. I know.*

As she paced, she spotted the envelope Jesse had brought over and fished it out of the wastepaper basket. With everything else going on, she'd forgotten about it. She took out the letter and read it again.

I knew there was something special about you. God told me that you were chosen. So if you haven't been able to hear God tell you that because of all the other noise in our world (what a different world than in the Blessed Virgin Mary's time!) please know that I heard him for you.

Was this Nicole woman insane? She didn't seem it, neither from the measured tone of her letter nor her expression when Quinn met her eyes.

. . . perhaps you have heard Him, but other, outside voices are louder, telling you that you're wrong, or troubled . . .

(*What is wrong with you? No more lies, Quinn!*)

Quinn was well aware that it was crazy to be considering anything this woman said, but . . . did she only think that because of what she'd been told while growing up? Had she been too closed-minded during this whole experience because of her parents' beliefs? No matter what he'd ever said publically, her father *hated* organized religion. He thought it was the root of the world's problems, all about power and money and controlling people's minds.

Was it possible that she'd had a connection to God back when she was a kid? Maybe she'd lost the connection because her father had told her it was wrong. If his daughter told him she had a relationship with God, wouldn't he have forced her to stop believing it? Told her she was lying? *No more lies, Quinn!*

And what about those drawings, those blue drawings? Maybe she'd been trying to draw . . . God. And all she could do was draw the sky. Her limbs began to tingle at how very possible that seemed. Because Quinn had never been taught about God, she wouldn't have had an idea of him as anything physical. Wouldn't have known how to represent him in a picture.

She found herself thinking about that midnight swim last May. She thought of that magical feeling in the ocean, the feeling of losing her body and becoming connected to something larger. Was it possible that God had been trying to tell her that night, but she hadn't been able to hear, because she had been told it was wrong to believe?

Listen deeply, Nicole's letter said.

✦   ✦   ✦

Sunday morning, Quinn woke late to the drumming of rain on the roof above her. Her nights were so full of dreams now that she never felt like she'd actually slept, but had just lived another, underwater life. As she lay in bed in the darkness of the storm, stroking Haven (who loved sleeping snuggled next to Quinn's firm, domed belly, as if communing with the baby), Quinn realized she couldn't stay inside this space one more day. Her father had officially withdrawn on Saturday, bringing a new wave of press to the house and filling the rooms with air so tight and tense it was hard to breathe. Lying there, it wasn't even a decision that she needed to get out for a while—it was an undeniable fact. Maybe her guilt was too big for the house; like trying to fit an ocean into a fish tank.

And there was somewhere she wanted to go.

After making an appearance downstairs to get a mug of tea, she told her mother she hadn't slept well and was going to take a long nap. Back upstairs, she dressed quickly in loose sweatpants, a sports bra that mashed her down to pre-pregnancy size, a tee and hoodie, an oversized windbreaker, sneakers, and a hat pulled low with her hair braided and tucked underneath. She considered sunglasses, but since it was raining, she thought that would just make her more conspicuous.

She put on music in her room, even stuffed clothes in her bed to make a dummy, and pulled the blinds to make it darker. On her way out, she turned around and left a small note next to her pillow: *Had to go for a run. Back soon. I have my phone.*

She slipped quietly down the stairs—knowing her father was shut in his office and her mother was on the phone in the living room—out the kitchen door, and through the garden and into Jesse's building, where she just missed running into one of the other tenants.

Once she was on the street, she had a moment of psychic

disorientation. It had been so long since she'd been outside alone! Her cells tingled with the freedom of it. *We could go anywhere*, she said to the baby. *Run the loop around the park, run to the beach at Coney Island, run all the way to Maine . . .* She yearned for the burn of fresh air in her lungs, the meditation that came with the rhythm of her feet. But there was something specific she needed to do, and she didn't want to risk being away from the house for longer than necessary. If she were caught this time, it would ruin her chances to sneak out again. They'd probably chain her to her bed. So instead of going toward the park or Coney, she headed down toward Sixth Ave. It was a fairly quick run, and soon she was approaching the stone church, walking now, suddenly aware of her rain-soaked clothes clinging to her skin. She put her hands in her windbreaker pockets to help hide her belly. There was a service going on. She stood to one side and waited under an overhang, bouncing lightly on the balls of her feet to stay warm and because she was nervous, both about being out of the house and about what she was doing.

People lingered, chatting, when the service ended. Quinn stayed over to the side with her hat pulled low until she saw Caroline and her moms leave. She kept waiting as other people shook hands and spoke with Father Bob, who seemed to be as friendly and cheery as the other time Quinn met him. When there were only a few people left, Quinn stepped forward. Father Bob saw her and smiled.

"I recognize you," he said. "Refresh my aging memory."

"Oh, I don't think so," Quinn said. She hadn't been expecting him to remember her, especially not with the hat on and her hair up. Or maybe he recognized her from the picture in the *Herald*? "This is my first time here. My name is . . . Lydia."

"Nice to meet you, Lydia," he said. "Did you enjoy the service?"

"Uh, I actually . . . I'm just here to see if I could ask you something. For a project I'm doing. But if you're too busy . . ."

"Not at all. Give me one minute to say hello to Mrs. Warner over here."

Quinn waited while he chatted with an elderly woman in a floral raincoat, taking deep breaths and trying to convince herself this really was for a project. A minute later, Father Bob was back.

"I'm sorry to bother you," she said. "But I'm supposed to get a priest's perspective about something, and I don't know any, and a friend told me you're nice."

He laughed. "I'm glad to know my reputation precedes me. What perspective can I offer?"

"I'm doing this thing . . . It's kind of hard to explain. But I need to know . . . Was Mary really a virgin? I looked at the Bible and there isn't that much about her. And then someone told me that today—you know, in our time—not everyone thinks she was a virgin. How could she have been one and still had a baby?" Her words tumbled out in a rush.

"Well, Lydia, the Virgin Birth is a mystery. It's something we can't understand."

"So, even though you're a priest, you don't know if she was?"

"There's a difference between knowing and believing. We *believe* in the Virgin Birth, but we don't know it in the same way that we know, say, the boiling point of water. So it remains a mystery." He laced his fingers together and rested the tips of his pointer fingertips on his chin. "Albert Einstein said that the most beautiful thing in the world is a mystery. The questions we haven't answered yet. Their mysterious nature doesn't preclude our belief in them."

He was even more evasive than Dr. Jacoby. Great. "Why would you believe in something if you don't know it's true?" Quinn asked.

"Mysteries do tell us a truth, in their own way. The truth told by saying, 'born of the Virgin Mary' is that God loves us." As he said this, Quinn noticed someone coming up the granite steps. Caroline's mother. Crap. She angled herself so Juna couldn't see her face as she hurried into the church. "God is everywhere. God is capable of doing things that people judge to be impossible. But they are possible, because God does them."

"Oh." Quinn's eyes kept darting to the door Juna had gone in. She bounced on her toes.

"Does this help at all?" Father Bob asked. "These are complex ideas. A lot to think about."

"Yes," she said, although she didn't mean it. She felt as if he'd talked around her question but hadn't really answered it. Couldn't *anyone* just tell her something straight? She was about to thank him and walk away when she decided she had nothing to lose and she might as well say it point-blank. "So, would a virgin birth, you know, like Mary, be possible today?"

Father Bob's expression became more serious. "Lydia, I'm wondering, is this something about all of the talk in the neighborhood about the young girl?"

"Sort of."

"Because I understand that the girl and her family are by no means claiming that this is a virgin pregnancy. It's quite a different issue. The people who are making a to-do out of it, well . . . their thinking might be a little confused."

"Oh. Right. But, okay, say the girl *was* saying it was a virgin pregnancy. Then would you believe it?"

"Well, of course it's possible," he said. "But to my knowledge, it hasn't happened for over two thousand years, so I'd have to ask myself, Why now? Why here in Brooklyn? When supernatural events take place, when the settled order of science and reason is disturbed, all believers must ask themselves to think hard. What is God doing here?"

He paused a moment and stroked one of his sideburns.

"It's also important to understand that God has given us all free will. The Blessed Virgin Mary said, 'Be it done to me according to your Word.' That was a yes to God. She made a decision, a choice. From the perspective of the Church, there has to be some communication, some consent, a *yes* in every relationship with God."

"Oh." Quinn felt her swollen belly underneath her hands, and thought about these ideas and questions. Consent. Had there been a moment when she said yes? Maybe her decision not to have the abortion? And why would it be happening here, now, to Quinn? Although . . . she supposed that was the question she'd been asking herself all along—why *her*?

"Does this make sense?"

"I think so," she said. "Thank you so much. I really appreciate you taking the time."

"My pleasure, Lydia." He stared at her face. "Are you sure we haven't met before? I feel certain I recognize you."

"No," she said. "I'm sure."

She walked toward the street; the rain had stopped. *A yes. A decision. A choice.* She started to run, her feet splashing in puddles, reminding her of her wet sneakers when she ran back to the cabin after swimming that night last May, filled with a sense of freedom, like she was now.

She couldn't piece together all of the different facts and opinions. Caroline, who thought Mary hadn't even been a virgin. This priest, who said it was possible but seemed super skeptical. The people gathered outside the house, who had no doubt. The strange coincidence of Nicole having been in the doctor's office that very day. Those blue drawings. Her troubles when she was a kid. Her feeling when swimming in that water. *And, of course, you,* she said, touching her stomach.

When she got near home, the idea of going back inside her prison turned her feet into bricks. Talking to the priest had opened up gates inside her that she didn't want to close . . . She finally felt the satisfaction of actually *doing* something. So, ignoring the voice inside her telling her how risky it was, she let herself run up the block that her house was on instead of heading to Jesse's building. She approached the group from the other side of the street, keeping her wool hat low and the collar of her windbreaker zipped up over her chin. Only one man looked at her as she stepped up the curb and joined them. Her breaths were as fast and shallow as if she'd run a marathon, not just a few blocks. She reminded herself that they'd only seen her from a distance, through a window, if they'd seen her at all. She stood a little to the side and looked up at the house, seeing it as they did, jogging in place the entire time.

"You a believer?" the man said after a minute. "Or a rubbernecker?"

"Oh . . . just running by," Quinn said, trying to think whether there was any way they'd recognize her voice. But no. People had heard her father talk, not her.

"I wasn't sure either," another man chimed in. "But I figure, can't hurt, right? Probably there's some other story, but what's it hurting, me trying to get a few prayers answered? Might as well try."

"You people are nuts," a woman walking by said, shaking her head. "Haven't you heard what's really going on?"

"Have you seen her?" an elderly woman standing with the group asked. "She glows. It's amazing. If you saw her, you'd believe."

"You got to stay in the back and wait your turn, though," the man in the plaid coat said to Quinn. "Some of us been out here all the time and we get the front spots. If there's anything happening we get first on line. You know what I'm saying?"

"Oh," Quinn said, surprised by his aggressive tone. "Sure."

"People can't just come in and expect to be first ahead of us. We've been waiting. There's a way it works out here." His face reminded Quinn of a hunk of raw beef.

"Okay," she said.

A few people over, someone turned toward her. Nicole Anderson. Their eyes met. And Quinn could tell immediately—without a doubt—Nicole recognized her. Quinn's blood froze.

Nicole's mouth got firm and she gave a little shake of her head—*no*.

"Where you from?" the man in the plaid coat said, now sounding accusatory.

"Um, around," Quinn said, still focused on Nicole. *No*, Nicole signaled again.

She was telling Quinn to leave, wasn't she? She was telling her this wasn't the time or place to talk, which, of course, it wasn't. And just like that, fear rocketed through Quinn. Mumbling something about needing to get home, she took off, running around the corner onto PPW and around the next corner and through Jesse's building. As she ran, she couldn't believe she'd let that happen, that she'd actually been out there, among them. And was recognized. Nicole could have done anything once she realized.

But all she had done was what was best for Quinn. Protected her, just like she'd said she would.

Quinn made it into the kitchen without being seen, ran up the stairs and into her dark room and flipped on the light and—

"Jesus!" she yelped in surprise, hand flying to her chest.

Lydia was sitting on her bed, holding the note Quinn had left next to her pillow. She stared at Quinn, eyes hard. "You went outside?"

Quinn swallowed. "I know. I just . . . I needed to get out, in fresh air. Please don't tell, Lyddie. Please. You won't, will you?"

"Why shouldn't I?"

This was bad. So, so bad. Quinn saw her bag slumped next to her desk and squatted down. "I don't know how much I have . . ." she said, searching through the pockets, finding a five, a ten, some crumpled ones . . . She smoothed them out into a stack and turned back to her sister. "Twenty dollars. It's all I have. Please, Lyddie? I know you hate me, but I really, really, really need you not to tell them."

Lydia looked at the bills, her jaw tight. Finally, she stood up and met Quinn's eyes again. "I don't want your stupid money. I just don't want you to go outside again. Promise you won't." Her gaze bored into Quinn, the same blue eyes as their father's.

"I promise," Quinn said. Was that it? She gave her sister a small smile. "Thanks, Lyddie."

Without responding, Lydia pushed by her, even though there was room to walk around. At the doorway, she turned. "Why are you so stupid? Daddy told us they're dangerous."

"I . . ." Quinn couldn't explain that from the letters she'd read and from her interaction with Nicole, she didn't feel in danger. "I wasn't thinking," she said. "That's all."

NICOLE ANDERSON

N icole's fingertips were pulsing, the way they did when her adrenaline kicked in.

Quinn. Quinn had been right there.

She scanned the group, nervous. Was it terrible that she was hoping no one else knew what had just happened? While she had compassion for all of them, and most of them seemed genuine and respectful, some of them scared her. A clique had formed, led by Samuel, that jerk in the plaid wool coat. The Entitled, she called them to herself. They acted like Quinn owed them something, and they were going to stay out here until they got it. Or until they took it.

This morning, she'd found one of them going through the Cutlers' trash under the stoop, looking for anything that Quinn might have touched. Nicole had told people over and over that stepping past the Cutlers' fence was trespassing. But not everyone cared. They didn't care about making this a sustainable situation—about being respectful and law-abiding so they didn't cause trouble, and so as many people as possible could benefit—they just wanted to get whatever they could out of it. She'd heard them talking about stationing someone on the other street, in front of Quinn's friend's building, the one that the Cutlers used to come and go. She felt like things were slipping a little out of control and was glad that there was usually a police car nearby.

Nicole didn't want to worry about any of this now, though. Because Quinn had made contact. She had read the letter—her friend had said so when he gave back the money—and now she had made contact. It was incredible. Nicole had worried so much about what she was doing and whether she was doing enough and whether the letter had been worded well and . . . everything! She felt so much responsibility. And to know that she might not be screwing up . . . That she might be worthy of this . . .

Tempting as it had been to hug Quinn right then and take advantage of her rare closeness, Nicole knew she'd done the right thing.

The energy out here was unpredictable.

QUINN

Why haven't we ever talked about the possibility that it could be an Immaculate Conception? Or Virgin Birth, whatever the term is," Quinn said while pacing around Dr. Jacoby's office.

She probably wouldn't have asked something like this before. But at this point, she had nothing left to lose. Her identity as Normal Quinn had floated so far away that it was now somewhere past the horizon, out of sight. Which meant she could say whatever she wanted.

"You mean parthenogenesis?" Dr. Jacoby said.

"No. Like, a God thing. Like the Virgin Mary."

Dr. Jacoby adjusted her glasses with a deliberate motion. "Is that something you've been considering?"

"Even if I haven't, isn't it kind of weird that we haven't talked about it, since so many people *do* believe it?"

"It's okay to tell me if you have been considering it," Dr. Jacoby said. "I'd completely understand."

"Well, it's just that I've been thinking about some things . . . like that night in Maine, the whole day, that swim . . . That whole memory is kind of . . . spiritual, you know? Like . . ." She went on to describe it in more honest detail than she had before—the emotional intensity, the almost supernatural beauty of the moon on the water . . . "What if that was all . . . God?" she said. "What if there really is a reason that the baby is here?" She tried to read Dr. Jacoby's reaction, but as always, her face stayed frustratingly neutral.

"Do you think that's why you're asking me this? Not because you actually think it's possible, but because you want to believe that this all has a higher purpose?"

"Of course. But does that mean it can't be true?"

"I think you know that I'm not going to tell you this is the answer, Quinn. But I also want you to know that it's totally understandable that you'd want it to be."

Quinn sat down and stared outside at the almost-winter garden. This refusal to even consider it was exactly the attitude that might be keeping Quinn from finding the truth. Just like Nicole had said in her letter.

"I don't want to drop this if you want to explore it further," Dr. Jacoby said. "But I do have an observation about the way you were just talking about that night in Maine." She wove her fingers together. "Lots of aspects of the experience—the intimacy you felt with Marco, the heightening of your sensory perception, the feeling of being connected to nature and the universe . . . the way you're describing it now, it all sounds like what could be a reaction to MDMA."

"What?" Quinn said.

"Ecstasy is the common form. Users often have those responses to it, and it can cause loss of inhibitions, as well, which would explain both kissing Marco and the swim."

Quinn sat forward a bit, shifting both her position and her mind-frame. "Can it make you black out, like, a part of the night?"

"It's certainly not impossible. Do you know if anyone at the party was taking it?"

Quinn shook her head. "I don't know."

"Well," Dr. Jacoby said, "I think this is worth following up on."

Ecstasy. Dr. Jacoby showed her the description of the effects in a book, and it did sound like her experience.

Not God. Drugs.

Except, how did it explain the fact that she'd felt that excitement and hyperawareness from the moment she'd woken up that day? And if something happened on the beach that night, with Marco or someone else, didn't it seem too convenient that she remembered everything around the event itself—running to the beach, swimming, running home, talking to Jesse—but not the event itself?

Are you actually questioning this? Quinn said to herself. *You want to believe it was God—something miraculous and supernatural—over this perfectly plausible explanation?*

She knew where the hesitation was coming from. She'd gotten attached to the idea that the pregnancy might have a special purpose, so some of her guilt would be alleviated. Like Dr. Jacoby had said when she suggested it. What she needed to do was face reality.

She couldn't wait any longer. She had to see Marco in person. Obviously, there was some reason Ben was avoiding her, so she couldn't rely on him. (Although, she did leave him another voicemail, asking if anyone at the party had been taking E.) But, assuming she didn't hear from him, she'd have to go see Marco alone. New Haven wasn't a hard trip—she'd done it before with the Earth First members for a climate-change event at Yale. She'd take the F train, transfer to the 6, and take that uptown to Grand Central, where she'd get one of the frequent Metro-North trains to New Haven.

Jesse came over the next day, and while she didn't mention the plan to him, she sent him with a note for Sadie asking her to please find out what dorm Marco was in and any other information (class schedule, maybe?) and a map and whatever else Sadie thought Quinn might need for a trip to New Haven.

Two days later, first thing in the morning, the doorbell rang. It was so early that Quinn had a surge of hope it was Jesse stopping by on his way to school with info from Sadie, momentarily forgetting that he came over through the kitchen now. She hurried downstairs, holding the railing, mindful of not risking falling and hurting the baby. Her mother had already opened the door. A man Quinn didn't recognize—tall, heavyset, ruddy-cheeked—was stepping inside while Katherine apologized to him about the crowd out front. "They're one of the reasons we need you, of course," she said. Quinn backed up onto the stair landing, out of view, and listened. The man was here to consult with her parents about an alarm system for the house. He enthusiastically described a high-tech system, with entry codes you had to use to get in or out—a different code for each person who was assigned one. All comings and goings were logged, and her parents would receive messages by phone whenever anyone came or went. As soon as Quinn heard that the alarm wasn't just to alert them to a break-in, but was going to alert them to a break-*out*, she knew: Lydia had told them. *Fuck.*

"That sounds like the one we want," her father said.

Quinn sank down onto the stair. The very moment she left the house, they would know. Going to New Haven would be impossible. Going *anywhere* would be impossible.

She sat for a moment and gathered her thoughts. This meant she couldn't wait any longer, not even for the information from Sadie. She had to go now. Today. Before the alarm was installed.

Without any further planning, she rushed through the same maneuvers as when she snuck out to talk to Father Bob: piled blankets to look like she was sleeping, darkened her room, put music on . . . A frantic energy filled her limbs as she did it all; she was already breathing heavily as she snuck back downstairs. But by the time she slid open the kitchen door, the energy had turned into the high-frequency buzz of panic. What was she doing? She didn't know anything about Marco's life at school, where he lived, nothing! What was she going to do, wander the campus, hoping to run into him? She didn't even have a smartphone.

She pressed a hand against her chest, her breaths too rapid, and looked out the door at the backyard, willing herself to be brave enough to run.

But even if she did find Marco . . . what if she had a flashback when she saw him in person? It could trigger some awful emotional reaction, and she'd be there alone, freaking out. Or—even worse—he could hurt her again, to keep her quiet. The possible ways this could go wrong crashed through her skull. There was smart brave and there was dumb brave; this was definitely dumb brave.

Reluctantly, she slid the kitchen door shut, feeling like she'd just closed the door to her own cell.

Quinn couldn't stop herself from storming up to her sister's room and asking why she had done it, why she had told their parents, making this place even more of a prison than it already was.

Lydia was sitting on the floor with her turtle, her hair in two messy braids she had obviously done herself. "I didn't tell them," she said, looking surprised. "I swear."

"So it's just a coincidence they're getting this maximum security system to trap me in here?" Quinn said, knowing her sister was lying.

"I don't know. I didn't tell them." She blinked her wide eyes.

The denial made Quinn even angrier. "I can't trust you at all, can I?"

She crossed her arms and stared down at her. And as Lydia stared back up, her chin began to quiver. "I promise I didn't," she said. "I know I told that Peter reporter guy about you, I know I did, and I know I ruined everything. But I was just trying to help." She spoke through sobs now. "I didn't want everyone to keep lying about you. I ruined everything, and I know you hate me, but I didn't tell about you going out. I promise. I didn't." Tears streamed down her face.

After a moment of shock, Quinn knelt next to her sister and wrapped her shaking body in a hug. "I don't hate you," she said. "I love you, Lyddie. None of this is your fault. None of it, okay?"

"It is," Lydia said. "I shouldn't have told him. None of this would have happened. It's all my fault. Everything. I was just trying to help."

Quinn moved in front of her sister and held her by the shoulders. Lydia didn't cry often, and when she did, it made her look so young. "Don't you ever think that," she said. "Please, Lyddie. I'm not sure why this has all happened, but don't ever blame yourself. It's not your fault. I promise it's not."

"I don't understand," Lydia sobbed. "I don't understand any of it."

Quinn hugged her again, wishing she could tell her that the baby was here for a reason, that something good was going to come out of all of this. But Quinn needed to stop relying on that fantasy. "Neither do I, Lyddie," she said. "Neither do I."

The alarm was installed.

Quinn was trapped. It heightened all of the emotions that had already been consuming her: loneliness, powerlessness, anger . . .

Although she craved human contact, she avoided her parents as much as possible; the tension and guilt she felt in their presence were overwhelming. Things were better with Lydia, at least, but that didn't make a difference during the long days when Lydia was with her tutor. She had no contact with friends, except Jesse, and seeing him still brought that aching emptiness in her chest.

He had given her something from Sadie the afternoon of her aborted escape, a note that said, "I'm sorry." Quinn wasn't sure what Sadie was sorry for, but she assumed it meant she hadn't been able to find any information about Marco. A moot point now, anyway.

She didn't let herself look out at the crowd anymore, didn't want to indulge that sort of thinking for even one more moment, even though it was still in the back of her mind, refusing to go away completely. Ecstasy, or some other form of that MDMA drug, made sense and was a realistic answer. So she spent hours and hours writing about that day on Southaven. Only that day. Waiting for the memory to surface.

And she took baths. Endless baths. Washing off the guilt and trying to soothe her skin and make it fit again. She didn't know who it belonged to, but it wasn't her own. She stared at her growing belly. Over five months now. When she was naked, it looked enormous to her. How was it possible that she still had a few months left? Was her body really going to be able to keep expanding? Sometimes, she found herself thinking evil thoughts. Blaming the baby. Wishing she could do something to get it out of there. The minute she caught herself, she always felt terrible. The baby was the innocent one in all of this.

She had to believe that. It was the only good thing she had left.

She was in the tub, barely awake, trying again to remember the words from that children's book: "A still morning sea, deeply asleep . . ." All of a sudden, the sound of a sharp explosion rang through the air and then the blaring siren of the alarm. *Wahh! Wahh! Wahh! Wahh!*

Quinn sat up, stood too quickly, slipping, grabbed at the wall to stop from falling. Stepped out and fumbled to put on her robe and hurried into the hallway. Lydia was coming out of her room.

"What was that?" Quinn said. The baby fluttered inside her.

"Stay up there!" Katherine called from below.

Wahh! Wahh! Wahh! Wahh!

"Was that a bomb?" Lydia yelled down.

Wahh! Wahh! Wahh! Wahh!

"Stay where you are!" Katherine said again.

Wahh! Wahh! Wahh! Wahh!

Quinn and Lydia stood together. "It wasn't a bomb," Quinn said, wrapping her arm around her sister. "A bomb would have been much louder." After a minute, they sat on the top stair. Finally, the incessant scream of the alarm was silenced. A police siren took its place for a moment, then that quieted, too.

"What's going on?" Lydia called downstairs.

Footsteps sounded on the steps and Katherine appeared, face drawn. "Everything's going to be fine," she said, sitting below them. "Someone threw a biggish rock through one of the living room windows. I'm not sure why. But he didn't run away. Your dad is out there with him and the police now. We need to just stay up here until it's all settled."

She rested one hand on Quinn's knee and the other on Lydia's. The air around them was especially still, in that way that follows a panic. Quinn closed her eyes, and with the warmth of her mother's hand on her knee, Lydia's body next to hers, and the baby moving inside her, for a moment, everything seemed okay.

Quinn sat with her parents in the kitchen. The crisis had been taken care of—the man arrested, the large window temporarily boarded up, a glass company called to come replace the broken pane. Gabe was explaining what had happened.

"He was agitated—I guess a bunch of them were—because they hadn't seen Quinn recently." His voice was even and measured. Tight.

Katherine got a confused look on her face. A sour taste rose in Quinn's mouth.

"Apparently they'd been seeing you?" Gabe said. "In the window? Word spread and that's what they'd come to expect. This man, I guess he'd traveled from somewhere and was angry because you didn't make any appearances."

"I don't understand. What are they talking about?" Katherine asked her.

Quinn swallowed, not sure how serious this was. "I haven't done it recently," she said. "But sometimes I'd just look out for a minute.

You know, out of curiosity. And boredom." She realized how stupid that sounded.

"Oh, Quinn . . ." Her mother rested her head in her hands.

"I didn't know something like this would happen," Quinn said. "I really didn't think it was that big a deal. I'm sorry. I'll pay for the window."

"I think you know this isn't about the window," her father said. "It's about your recklessness. Looking at those people? And making plans to sneak out, god knows where? We haven't even talked about that."

"My plans?" she said. So . . . Lydia *had* told them?

"Sadie told us," Gabe explained.

"She was worried," Katherine added.

Sadie had gone to her parents? The note: *I'm sorry.* Right. Now it made sense. Although, her parents hadn't mentioned Marco, so Sadie must not have told them everything.

"And maybe this . . . recklessness is our fault," her father said. "We've tried to protect you from most of what people are saying. But maybe that's been a mistake."

"What do you mean?" Quinn said.

"Hold on." Gabe left the room, went upstairs, and returned a minute later with a handful of envelopes. "These people aren't . . . they aren't in their right minds," he said, putting the letters down on the table.

He didn't realize that Quinn already knew the kinds of things the letters said. "Dad, just because they're religious doesn't mean—"

"Read it." He handed her one of the envelopes. It had already been unsealed. She took out a folded piece of dingy paper. No Hallmark card here.

To The daughter of G. Cutler:

You are a disgrace and a Danger to all. How can you be so proud? How can you disgust Him and his people so low? Do you not know the child you carry is the Devils child? And you portray yourself as like the Holy Mother performing miracle's. This is disgraceful and Disgusting. I for One pray that something happens to end this Blasphemous pregnancy before it brings the Devil's spawn to life. God will see to this, I am sure. If He does not We Will. Those who clame you perform miracles are also following the Devils path.

We are watching. HE is watching.

Dennis Loring

Bile rose in her throat. Gabe had already opened another one and laid it out.

All it said was: *LIAR! SLUT! SATAN'S WHORE!*

And another: *Punishment will come to this house. It's a true sin what unnatural force is at work in this house and there will be hell to answer for it. We do not back down in the face of evil.*

And another: *It is sickening the way you are abusing people of faith, people who know the truth, when you know nothing but lies and deceit. You are a whore, as far away from our Mother of God as you are from the sun. May you burn in Hell with Satan's baby.*

"No," Quinn said, shaking her head.

"No what?"

"This isn't . . . this isn't what they say, the people. I've read some. This . . . Where did you get these?"

"Where do you think? I go through all the letters people leave before I shred them. I share ones like this with the police in case anything raises real red flags. People who are going to believe something like this . . . they're not sane. The ones who think it's God's baby *and* the ones who think this is Satan's work. Both. And when you stand in the window and make it look like you're offering your blessings or whatever, it just encourages them. On both sides."

"But . . . I thought . . . I thought the religious people . . . I thought they think I'm good. That the baby and I are good."

"Still, Quinn. What were you doing looking out at them like that? I told you so many times. I told you to be invisible. It shouldn't have mattered what they think of you!"

Quinn's lips were cold. She reached up and pressed her fingers against them, like she had after the kiss with Marco.

May you burn in Hell with Satan's baby.

QUINN

The words crept under her skin and stayed there, crawling around like maggots. And what other things had people said? What else did they think about her and her baby? The curiosity worked up into a frenzy inside of her. She didn't care if the people were insane. She needed to know what they were saying.

She asked her father if she could see the rest of the letters.

"No," he said. "You've seen enough."

But it wasn't enough. When her father left the house to meet with a lawyer, she snuck into his office and shut the door quietly behind her. She didn't know how much time she had, so needed to get out as quickly as possible. First, she scanned the small room in case the rest of the letters were out in the open, in a box or bag or whatever. But she didn't find them. So she began methodically opening every cabinet and every file drawer—even though the room was tiny, her father was a packrat, and file cabinets were stacked on top of one another. Drawers were full to bursting with papers about taxes and mortgages and scrawled-on drafts of his books and articles and bank statements, and none of it mattered at all or held any answers.

Eventually she came to a drawer that held files about her and her brother and sister—medical records, financial aid applications for New Prospect, end-of-year teacher reports . . . No letters. She took out her report from second grade at P.S. 107: *Withdrawn . . . completely silent . . . extreme difficulty making friends . . .* What had her mother said? "It was understandable. You had trouble adjusting." But it was more than that.

She turned to Gabe's desk, opened those drawers, and found tape and staplers and checks and stationery and stamps and pens . . .

Nothing. Except . . . her sea glass necklace, shoved all the way in the back. Her father had taken it and not told her? He had let her think she lost it. Because it reminded him of his mother, she was sure. Crazy, both of them. That was why he had taken it. She took a moment to attach it around her neck. Not like he could be any angrier with her than he already was, and she had missed it, her fingers still reaching for it all the time.

She glanced around the room once more, in case she'd overlooked a stack of envelopes out in the open, but she hadn't. Maybe he'd given them to the police.

She was about to leave when she saw a pink Post-it note on the floor. She picked it up. *Preston Brown - 11/1*, it said in her father's writing. The date was underlined with three angry slashes.

The Preston Brown Show? That horrible, sleazy talk show where people revealed intimate details of their lives and yelled at one another in front of an audience? Quinn's lunch curdled in her stomach. Obviously, the episode couldn't have been about her since she hadn't been there and it was an interview thing. But why would her father even have been interested in it? For a split second, she envisioned her entire family on a talk show couch, being interviewed about her behind her back. But no . . . There was absolutely no way they'd ever have done that. If her father were going to be interviewed on TV, it would be by someone more serious, not Preston Brown. Still, the note meant something . . . Obviously.

She woke up her father's computer, which still had regular Internet access. It was password protected, of course. She began trying anything that occurred to her: combinations of the kids' names and pets' names and birth years and phone numbers. Her mind churned, and with every second that passed, she became more convinced she had to see the show. She was wasting too much time, though. She didn't have all day. *Think, Quinn, think.* What could it be? Book titles, ages, addresses . . . She typed and typed, her fingers hardly able to keep up with her brain, and then she realized that time was too short, and her father probably didn't even have a password she'd ever guess, and even if she got in, she wouldn't have time to watch. There had to be another way.

Only the windows on the ground and parlor floors were alarmed. Quinn's fourth-floor bedroom window wasn't, and her father had never made good on his threat to install an air conditioner. All that mattered was escaping unseen. She didn't care if she got caught on the way back. What could they do to punish her now?

She raised the pane all the way and stepped out onto the fire escape landing, keeping her breath as steady as she could and whispering to the baby that she'd be careful. She climbed slowly down the ladder, hands gripping the rough, cold rungs, feet slipping now and then, causing her heart to leap up her throat. At the bottom, she cringed at the loud, metallic scrape of the extension easing its way down. When she hit the ground, she ducked as low as possible and scurried across the backyard.

She knocked on the apartment door to make sure no one was home, telling herself that it wasn't that big a deal going into the Kalbitzers' when none of them were there. It wasn't like she was going to look through any of their stuff; she'd been alone in the apartment plenty of times. Hugo was barking on the other side of the door, and no one came to answer it, so she slid her dog-sitting key into the lock. Hugo was thrilled to see her—butt-waggy and kissy, shoving his snout into her hand. "Hello, my favorite boy," she said, hugging him fiercely, pressing her face into his shaggy, damp-smelling fur. "I've missed you. I've missed you so much." He followed her into Jesse's room, where she found his computer asleep but not password-protected. She tried not to be distracted by the familiar smell—a combination of sandalwood, dog, and laundry—or the sight of all his film posters, the map of the world with the thumbtacks stuck on the islands they wanted to visit, the whale bank with their savings . . . She didn't have time.

As she typed in the search terms, she had a moment of pause. Whatever she saw couldn't be unseen. But the Post-it note couldn't be unseen either, and she knew that her curiosity would just grow, that it would take over her brain. So she pressed Enter. The full episode was easy to find. November 1: Episode 308, *Immaculate Deception: Help! My Daughter Thinks She's a Pregnant Virgin!*

Preston Brown leaned forward, elbows balanced on the arms of his chair, fingers interlocked. The camera closed in on him. His penny-copper face, sculpted silver hair, deadly serious expression . . .

Quinn found herself leaning forward as well, elbows on Jesse's desk. Her palms were slick with sweat.

"It's a parent's worst nightmare," Preston Brown said to the camera, "finding out a teenage daughter is pregnant. We've had many families on this show struggling to deal with the emotional, financial, and spiritual consequences of teen pregnancy. But now let's add another element, one far more unusual and complex." The camera zoomed in even closer.

"As a parent, what do you do when your pregnant teenage daughter believes that she's still a virgin—and that the baby is the child of God?"

Quinn grabbed the arms of the chair to steady herself.

"Today," Preston said, "we're going to talk to several experts on adolescent psychology, a doctor, and a priest, as well, about this unbelievable situation. Of course, there is a case of this sort in the news these days. Unfortunately, the family didn't wish to participate in our show, so we won't have their direct input. However, we do have another mother and daughter—a daughter who insisted she was a virgin throughout her entire pregnancy. We'll talk to them a little bit later, and you'll hear that fascinating story. Let me introduce my first guests, who will shed some light on this topic from a medical and psychological point of view."

The camera panned over to show two women and a man sitting on a long beige couch. Preston introduced them and their credentials flashed on the screen. PhD, MD . . . *Trust them!* the labels shouted.

"Let's start with a little refresher course," he said, lightening his tone. "Dr. Osgood, can a virgin be pregnant?"

The doctor gave a half smile. "Well, I'm assuming our audience knows the basics. So all I'll say is that yes, there can be a situation where that is possible, but only if the female's genitals made contact with semen. That can definitely happen during intimate contact that doesn't include intercourse. It's not likely, but within the realm of possibility. And artificial insemination, of course, but I don't think that's what we're talking about today."

"So," Preston said, "if a girl said she'd never been intimate at all, in any capacity, but she was still pregnant, that wouldn't be possible? She couldn't have sat on a toilet seat or been in a hot tub or swimming pool? We've all heard stories like that."

"No. Some girls will insist that's happened to them, but I promise, it's not possible. Sperm can't survive in that kind of environment."

"Okay," Preston said. "So, we've got that covered. Now, Dr. Osgood, have you ever treated a girl who claimed to be a virgin, even though she was pregnant?"

"Yes," the doctor said. "I have." She went on to explain that in all of the cases, though, the girls were consciously lying.

"I just don't remember," Quinn said, as if they could hear her through time and the monitor.

But you've considered it, a voice inside her responded. *You even asked Dr. Jacoby about it!*

"So," Preston said, turning to one of the other guests, "is that the only explanation in a case like this, Dr. Sarandon? That the girl is lying?"

"No," he said. "It's possible that the girl truly believes she is a virgin. That she's not letting herself acknowledge the physical act that led to the pregnancy. In a situation like this, we have to assume that whatever happened was so traumatic that it caused a psychic rupture. Her brain has created a story to cover up what really happened because it was so painful."

"A psychotic delusion?" Preston said, the words melting in his mouth like rich chocolate.

"Let me emphasize, I've never spoken with a patient who actually has this belief, so I'm not talking about any one case specifically. Rather, I'm speaking in general about a case in which a girl might believe she conceived without intercourse or other very intimate contact with semen. We all know that's scientifically impossible. There must be sperm for a pregnancy to occur. So, yes, I would classify the belief that a pregnancy is immaculate as a psychotic delusion. It's serving the purpose of protecting the girl from a truth too awful to confront."

"That's not what Immaculate Conception means," Quinn muttered. Hugo rested his snout on Quinn's lap. She paused the show and took him out of the room, shutting him in the hall, then resumed play. She didn't want him to hear what they were saying.

"What sort of truth might that be?" Preston Brown asked.

"I would imagine it to be sexual abuse by someone the victim trusts, someone who would rock the victim's whole world if she acknowledged the person had hurt her in this way."

Quinn's guts began to rise up her throat.

"Most likely someone in the girl's family. Or a close, trusted family friend."

"I see," Preston said, his face a mask of concern. He turned to the third guest. "Would you agree?"

"Oh, yes," she said. "There's no understating the damage and trauma sexual abuse can cause when inflicted by someone trusted and loved by the victim. Our minds go to incredible lengths to protect us from the truth sometimes. Would you rather face the fact that you were raped by your father or brother, maybe brutally and repeatedly over a period of years, or believe that you were chosen by God?"

Raped by your father or brother. No. *No.*

"Over a period of years?" Preston said.

"Quite possibly. The victim would have a protective habit of dissociating during the abuse, separating herself from the physical reality of it. The delusion of a virgin pregnancy would be taking that to the next step, a cover story provided by her subconscious so she can keep out the truth. We live in a culture of 'specialness,' where young people are encouraged to think of themselves as being a special snowflake, as it were."

The words convulsed in Quinn's stomach. She wished she hadn't let the baby hear them.

None of it's true. None of it.

But even though she knew these people were lying, and she didn't want to hear another word, she kept watching, like she was bound to the chair.

"I challenge you," the psychiatrist said, "to find any mental health professional who doesn't hear a story like this and wonder if it is serious sexual abuse by someone the girl thinks she loves."

"That's quite a statement," Preston Brown said.

"We can also look at the girl's emotional and mental history for clues," she continued. "Has there been emotional disturbance in the past? Trouble in school? Depression? Withdrawal? Regression? Physical signs of abuse?"

"So, long-term psychological issues might suggest long-term abuse, which ended in pregnancy?"

"Yes. Most definitely."

By the end, Quinn was totally numb. This show, this show that millions of people watched and listened to and believed . . . On this show, people were talking about it like that was the only option, and anyone watching it would be thinking, "Oh, well, that explains the Quinn Cutler situation." How could those experts have pretended to know anything about her? And she was sure that the rest of her family had seen the show, or at least knew what had been said on it. Obviously, this was why her father had dropped out of the election. Who would vote for a monster?

And Ben. This was why he wanted nothing to do with her. Who could blame him?

Now that Quinn was here, now that she'd gone this far and had seen this much, she couldn't stop. She typed her name and "pregnant virgin" into a search engine.

When she saw the number of hits—1,781,570—the room tilted and spun as if she might pass out. She gripped the chair again and closed her eyes. Her heart seemed to wait for a full minute until deciding to beat again.

She started following the links. Link, after link, after link. She lost herself in the seemingly endless trail of blog posts and tabloid articles and even articles on more respected sites.

All of these people, all of these random people who knew nothing about her, they all thought they knew what the real story was. And while there were plenty who thought she was just a "lying slut" who didn't want to own up to her mistake, there were also plenty screaming that she was a victim, and that it probably was someone in the family. "What else would be so bad that she'd lie about it?" they all said.

"Who else would she care about protecting?" They thought her father had organized a massive cover-up.

And people knew she'd seen a shrink as a kid. How did they know that? Wasn't that kind of thing confidential? They were using it as proof. Long-term abuse. Troubled child. How did they know? And quotes . . . Quotes from parents of kids she'd gone to school with that year, in second grade. Talking about how withdrawn she was. How they knew there was something strange. They knew that she used to run away, that she'd run from school one day. Obviously, she'd been running away from an abusive home. Quotes from anonymous neighbors about how there was something off about her, something not right.

Troubled child.

Liar. Compulsive liar.

Taught to lie young by parents who lied.

No more lies, Quinn!

And—oh, god—a headline: *Report: Cutler Broke Daughter's Arm.* Holy shit. They knew about that? That was a one-time thing that had happened out of his fear. One time! He'd felt terrible. He wasn't a child abuser. And her arm hadn't even been broken—just dislocated. He'd been scared. She was wrong to be in the water and scare him. It had been her fault. She could have drowned.

And then there were the photos.

Pictures she didn't even recognize of herself in second grade. Always standing by herself, hands clasped in a worried way, looking off into the distance. Troubled child. Abused child. Where had they gotten these?

And photos from the last couple years. One of her stretching—bending forward over one leg propped on a fence—in her spring track uniform, those shorts that were like a bathing suit. A close-up of her ass, the bottom of one cheek peeking out . . . *Look how the slut dresses . . . Sexually promiscuous girls are often victims of childhood abuse . . .*

And the photos of her dressed as Mary, of course. Everywhere. *Delusional. Traumatized and delusional.* The trail of links was essentially infinite (1,781,570!), and Quinn found herself mesmerized, unable to stop looking. And she began to wonder . . . Which of these stories was true? Which of these versions of Quinn Cutler was the right one? Because she didn't know anymore. Maybe she was delusional. Maybe it was from trauma. Look at all this proof.

She knew it couldn't be what people were saying, though. No matter what the "experts" on that show thought. She may not have known who she was anymore, but she knew that her father and brother wouldn't hurt her. She'd known that right from the beginning.

Of course you think that—you're in denial! That's the whole point! Aren't you listening to what the people are saying? It makes sense, doesn't it? All your feelings of guilt as a child? And he did hurt you! Remember that pain?

There was an easy solution. An easy solution to this. Her hands trembled as she typed in different search terms related to incest and DNA tests. After finding out what she needed, she called her obstetrician's office and told the receptionist that it was an emergency, but not a life-or-death physical sort of emergency that an ambulance could help. The receptionist must have heard the desperation in her voice, because her doctor called back minutes later.

"You know the DNA test you did?" Quinn said, her voice shaky. "With my friend? The paternity test?"

"Well, yes," her doctor said. "I didn't run the test myself, though."

"But didn't you help? Like, I mean, didn't you send the blood and talk to the testers or something?" Quinn scratched her arm as she spoke, suddenly itchy all over.

"I did. What's up, Quinn?"

"When that came back, you'd have been able to tell if . . . if the baby's DNA wasn't right, right? You would have been able to tell, and you'd have told me, right?" Her words were coming out too quickly.

"What do you mean? If there were genetic abnormalities?"

How could she put this? "No. I mean, if there was too much, um . . . gene overlap, between me and the father."

"Oh," her doctor said gently. "Yes, Quinn. We would have been able to tell. There certainly was nothing to indicate that."

"Okay," Quinn said, letting out her breath. "Thanks."

"To be very clear, the father isn't someone closely related to you," the doctor said. "But Quinn? Is there a reason you asked? If you need to talk to me in person, about anything, I'm always—"

"No!" Quinn said. "No, I shouldn't have even asked."

She hung up and was hit by a wave of shame and dizziness and horror, even worse than before. She got cold and needed to vomit. She didn't make it to the bathroom. Puked on the hallway floor. The acid filled her mouth and burned her throat and tasted as ugly as everything she'd just heard. She tried to keep herself together, got paper towels from the kitchen, and cleaned up the mess. She brushed her teeth with a finger and swirled mouthwash and looked in the mirror—her hair was ratty, her eyes bloodshot, her face puffy. Had she really just called her doctor to ask that? Needed proof of something she knew in her bones? Oh, god. What was happening to her? Didn't she *know* anything?

QUINN

Quinn locked the Kalbitzers' apartment door behind her and made her way downstairs, clutching the bannister for support. She could barely feel her feet. She didn't want to go home. She wanted to go outside and run and run and never come back. She wanted to run to the ocean and swim out and feel the freedom of weightlessness, or maybe sink to the bottom or drown or whatever it would take so she could escape all of this noise. *The still morning sea, deeply asleep . . .* That's where she wanted to be, underwater in a still morning sea, asleep. Unconscious. Alive and safe in that underwater world, or just dead. Either one.

Like her grandmother.

As she reached the downstairs hall and wondered which way to head—out the front door to take off and escape somewhere (where?) or out the back door to go home—she realized that the one thing in this world that could make her feel better was Jesse. Despite everything, she wanted Jesse so, so badly. And unless he had other plans, he'd be home from school soon. There was no energy in Quinn's limbs to take her back upstairs. So she walked toward the rear door of the building and slid down against the wall, sitting with her knees up, in a spot where she could lean forward and see a portion of the front door, but where she wouldn't be noticed by people who were coming in.

The hallway was cold and dingy. Quinn squeezed her knees against her body and tried to think of anything other than all of the hideous words that everyone out there had been hearing and reading while she'd been in her protective cocoon, oblivious. "A still morning sea, deeply asleep. 'Til warmed by the sun it rolls up the beach." She whispered the words over and over. Finally, she heard the building door open. She leaned forward and peeked past the stairwell—just an old man. But as soon as she'd sat back, the door squealed again, and it was Jesse, thank god.

She was about to stand up when she noticed there was someone with him. Caroline. Quinn leaned back and closed her eyes. *If I can't see you, you can't see me.*

"Hello?" Jesse's voice echoed through the space. "Did you hear something?" he asked Caroline. Quinn must have made a noise without noticing it. She eased her way up to stand, then took a silent step toward the back door.

"Hello?" Caroline's voice this time.

Quinn opened the back door as quietly as possible, but it still emitted a wheezy groan. Once she was out, she ran.

"Quinn, wait!"

She kept going. Almost tripped over a cinder block at the back of his yard.

"Quinn!"

"Shhh!" She stopped and turned, and Jesse was on her already, his hand on her shoulder. "People will hear you."

"Well, just wait, then," he said, catching his breath. "Just wait a second. What were you doing in there? What's wrong?"

She stared into his worried eyes and couldn't even speak.

"What's wrong?" he repeated. "Why were you hiding in there?"

"I was . . . I was waiting for you. I just wanted to talk to you."

"So talk. You didn't have to leave. Or hide. Why are you so upset?"

She couldn't bring herself to say anything. Her jaw just hung a bit open. The voices of Preston Brown's "experts" and the words from all those articles and comments filled her brain. She imagined Jesse watching and reading and wondering . . .

A look of recognition passed across his face. "You went online," he said. "Didn't you?"

She nodded. "That show . . ."

"Oh, god, Quinn. I . . . I . . . God."

"You know . . . you know it's not . . ."

"Of course," he said. But he had hesitated before saying it, and Quinn knew that he had considered that it might be true. "Are you okay?" he asked.

She shrugged and pressed her lips together to keep them from trembling. They stood silently for a moment. She didn't know what she'd expected Jesse to say or do to make it better. There was nothing.

"I should go home," she said. "I'm not supposed to be out. Someone will notice."

"I'm coming with you." His hand was still on her shoulder.

"What about Caroline?"

"Don't worry about her. Matt was just locking his bike. He'll be there already."

They went in through the kitchen door using Jesse's alarm code; when her parents got the alert, they'd just think he was here bringing school stuff. In Quinn's room, Haven did her usual dance for him—pressing her side up against his legs. He reached down and patted her absentmindedly, his attention focused on Quinn, who had begun pacing.

"Do people believe it?" she asked.

"You mean people around here? At school and stuff?"

She nodded.

"No. No way. No one who knows your family would ever believe it."

"Are you sure?"

"Well . . . I mean . . ."

"Oh, god. I think I'm going to be sick again."

She held her stomach and hung her head, eyes shut tight. She was shaking. "We should have released the results of the DNA test. If my father knew this was happening, we should have told people. We can prove that it's impossible."

"It's okay, Quinn," Jesse said. "This isn't . . . No one believes it here. Not really. And . . . and it's all going to blow over." He moved closer and stroked the top of her head. "I mean, your DNA test results are no one's business. You shouldn't have to prove something with them. People just want a story, you know? The sicker the better. They don't know you. It's just a story."

"It's my fault," she said. "My fault for not being able to tell what happened."

"It's not your fault," he said. "None of this is. It's . . . it's people. They suck. The world is sick. Not you."

"Do you know what I've done? To my family?"

He was still stroking her hair, and she concentrated on the feeling, letting it soothe her. God, she'd missed him . . . "It's okay," he whispered. "It's all going to be okay." He repeated it, over and over.

After a few minutes, she opened her eyes and lifted her head, then turned so they were face-to-face. She reached her arms around his waist and hugged him tight, and he hugged her back, and she'd almost never felt anything as good as his body pressed against hers. She breathed in his smell, a little less sandalwood and a little more sweat, since it was the end of the day. And all she wanted was for him to stay with her. To never be left alone again. She pulled back from the hug, and, on impulse, rose up and touched her lips against his—hesitant, at first—both their lips a bit dry. But his were warm and soft and . . . Jesse.

Everything else disappeared. The world was just this—the touch, the connection, the love and safety and desire . . . All of the need and want from weeks without him surging inside her like a tsunami, swelling until it felt too big to fit inside her body. Her legs trembled underneath her. Blood *shush-shushed* in her ears.

Shush-shush. Shush-shush.

The rhythmic crashing of waves.

The shaking of her legs.

That other impulsive kiss, that night on Southaven . . .

The dock shook when the waves crashed against it. It made her legs shake, like they were shaking now. The dock shook as the waves crashed against it.

The waves had been crashing against it.

The waves had been crashing against it.

Quinn and Jesse pulled back from each other at the same time.

"Wait," he said. "This . . . this isn't . . ."

She held her hand against her chest to keep her heart from beating out of it. "Oh my god," she said.

"I know. That shouldn't . . . we shouldn't—"

"No," she said. "Jess . . . That night. That night in Maine. I couldn't have been swimming. I couldn't have been swimming at all."

Quinn stayed in her room while Jesse ran home. He'd left his phone there in his bag, and he needed it to check the Southaven tide charts for the previous May online to make sure that she was right. But she already knew. She was right. She paced back and forth, like the tide itself, back and forth. She couldn't be on both sides of the room at once. And if the waves had been crashing against the dock when she was with Marco, and the water was as high as she was picturing, then it was physically impossible she'd been swimming at Holmes Cove the way she remembered. It would have been getting near low tide, and at that beach the tide went far, far out and left a terrain of small, sharp rocks and shells interspersed with larger rocks covered with barnacles, and clumpy blankets of slimy, thin-ribbon seaweed, way too slippery to walk across. And even if you could get across all of that—next to impossible to imagine in the dark—the water was too shallow for too far out to swim in. High tide was the only possible time to swim off the rock the way she thought she remembered, lowering her body into the deeps . . .

The Deeps. *A still morning sea, the Deeps all asleep . . .*

That book. *The Deeps.* That was how it began. *A still morning sea, the Deeps all asleep, 'til warmed by the sun they roll up the beach . . .* But . . . Quinn shook her head to rid it of the digression. This wasn't important.

What was important was that she couldn't have been swimming. This detail—the impossibility of the tide—had been there the whole time in her description of that night, and she hadn't even noticed. Such a simple, simple thing.

She kept walking around her room, Haven warm and solid in her arms. If it wasn't true, she didn't understand where that memory came from: that clear, vibrant memory of swimming in the ocean that night, of swimming with stars. Of the electric cold that had somehow made her feel warm. Of such a sublime, even transcendent, moment. Of feeling more alive and whole and *Quinn* than she ever had before.

Had she made it up completely, to cover something ugly and horrible? Had she been drugged and hallucinating? Her brain hurt so much from the realization and all the questions it brought that her head felt as if it were going to burst. And as she was pacing and worrying, Jesse called and said that yes, she was right. If they were figuring the timing correctly—which they agreed they were—the tide hadn't been high when she was down there. She couldn't have been swimming. She'd been down there, in the middle of the night, naked, and she hadn't been swimming. Even though she remembered it as clearly as if it had happened yesterday.

"I can't come back over right now," Jesse whispered into his phone. "My mom . . . Give me an hour or so. Will you be okay till then?"

"Of course," Quinn said, although she wasn't sure she would be.

Her feet kept tracing a back-and-forth path as her mind went back and forth over the revelations and questions. Something definitely happened that night, down on the beach—there was no denying it now. Something had happened to her. Not that swim. Not that beautiful, ecstatic swim. The time was lost—it could be anything! And the fact that this memory was false proved one thing: It proved that nothing she thought or felt or believed could be trusted. If she couldn't believe herself, how did she know whom to believe? Someone had to be right. And it wasn't those people on TV or those people who said it was the devil.

Or maybe it was. Maybe Quinn knew she was bad because she was filled with some deep, primal evil. Maybe that was why she had worried that Jesse would realize something was wrong with her. Look what had happened to her family because of her. *What is wrong with you?*

But she felt the baby was beautiful, didn't she? Some deep instinct had told her not to get an abortion, despite all the challenges the pregnancy would bring. Where had that instinct come from? She had heard that voice: *Beautiful. It was beautiful.*

Too many questions.

All she wanted was for someone to give her the answers.

QUINN

The moment she stepped outside, a hush fell. The only sound was the soft thud of the front door shutting behind her. Even the air and trees paused and stood at shocked attention. From the top of the stoop, Quinn scanned all the faces, looking for the familiar red jacket and blue scarf. There. There she was, maneuvering herself forward through the momentarily frozen group of bodies down on the sidewalk.

"Quinn?" Nicole said, breaking the silence. "Are you okay?"

Before Quinn could say that she needed to talk to her, to ask her questions, to somehow figure out if she should believe her, the people came to life. There was a clank and squeal as the wrought-iron gate swung open, and the group surged through it and up the steps toward her as one solid mass of desperation. Quinn had no time to turn and go back inside; they were right up on her, and a hollow-faced woman was clutching her arm. Clutching it hard. Quinn stared down at the woman's bird-bone hand, confused by her strength, and by the sudden contact, and all of the voices and faces.

"I'm sick," the woman said. "My lungs. You healed someone else. Please. Please help me. I've been waiting."

The bodies were all around her now. Quinn tried to press backward, but the door was closed. *Breathe, Quinn. Breathe.* Where was Nicole? She'd lost sight of her. She moved her free arm in front of her stomach, protecting the baby from the groping mob.

"Just touching her is enough," someone called from inside the mess of people. "Get out of the way!"

"Blessed Virgin," a man said. He had worked his way one body apart from her, and he was dirty and smelled and Quinn tried not to gag. "Help me," he said. "Help me." He reached for her hoodie and got one of the pockets. His overripe stench curled in her nose. Panic gripped her chest as tightly as he gripped the fabric.

The steps were wide enough for a whole group to crush together on the top landing around Quinn. Calls of "Please! Please!" filled the air. "God wants you to help *me*," someone said. And now the man in the plaid coat, yelling, "Get outta my way! It's my turn!"

Quinn couldn't think what to do, how to open the door without turning her back on the people, without being crushed, trampled, torn apart. All of their desperate hands were reaching, touching, trying to get at any part of her. Even her feet. Nicole's face appeared in the midst of bodies—saying something Quinn couldn't hear. Then the door fell from behind Quinn, and she was pushed back as the crowd surged forward.

"Don't touch her!" Katherine yelled. "Get away from her!" She wedged herself in front so Quinn could try to get in the house, but the man still held on to her hoodie. Quinn tried to rip it out of his hand while her mother was yelling, and she was scared they were going to hurt Katherine because they were all shouting now, too. Shouting at her mother to get out of the way. Finally, finally Quinn got the fabric free and stumbled back into the entryway, and Katherine shoved at the mob, and Quinn didn't know how her mother would get inside without letting them in, too, but then there was the sound of a siren, and in that moment the crowd paused, and Katherine made it inside and slammed the door and locked it, leaned against it, breathing heavily.

Shouts from outside crashed through the door. People thumped on it with their fists, rattling the glass. The police siren wailed. Katherine grabbed Quinn's wrist and led her quickly through the hall and down the stairs to the kitchen. Even there, in the back of the house, they could hear yelling. They sat at the table, breathing, listening . . .

After a moment, Katherine said, "Quinn, what were you doing?"

Quinn was shaking all over.

"I'm sorry," she said. "I'm sorry." She kept repeating it, the only thing she could say.

"Why did you go out there?"

Instead of explaining, Quinn found herself saying, "Why didn't you tell me? About that show. And what people are saying? All the articles and posts and videos. Why didn't you tell me and why haven't you told them it's medically impossible? We can get my doctor to tell them. Why are you letting them say it? Why did you let it get so bad?" She stared at her mother through blurry eyes.

"You know about it?" her mother said.

She nodded and wiped her cheeks, tears falling heavily now. "I watched it at Jesse's."

"Oh, Quinn." Her mother reached over and hugged her.

"We should have released the baby's DNA information. Proven it's not true."

"We don't owe those people anything," her mother said. "We're following up on some things legally, but we don't owe them any sort of proof. It's just gossip. Disgusting gossip. We didn't tell you because we didn't want you to feel the added pressure. You're already in such a difficult place."

Her mother's words refocused Quinn's thoughts, reminding her what had really spurred her to go out front—her realization about the tide. "I need to go to Maine," she said, gathering herself. "Something happened there—I'm positive. I need to go and . . . I don't know, just be there so I can remember. Because now that I know, I can make myself do it. I know I can."

"Oh, sweetie," Katherine said. "I don't think so."

Her mother didn't understand. "I need to go to Maine," Quinn repeated. "That's the only way. I need to go to Maine."

✦   ✦   ✦

Hours later, Quinn lay in the bathtub, only her mouth and nose and knees out of the water. Snippets of conversation between her parents swam around her head. They hadn't tried hard to keep her from over-hearing, as if they thought she was so far gone, she wouldn't even understand the words.

"She's not going to Maine," her father had said. "Out of the ques-tion. That place . . . it's dangerous for her. Never again. Never."

"Not now," Katherine said. "That I agree with."

"Can we get Dr. Jacoby over here, since it's an emergency? She's not thinking straight. To go out there like that? After reading those letters even? Hassan already disabled her alarm code. Jesse's, too. But she needs something . . . a residential program, maybe. She can't stay here."

Quinn turned on the faucet again and lowered back down so her ears were underneath the waterline, trying to drown out the voices in her head, to replace them with the comforting sound of the gentle *slosh* and *whir* of the water. She shut her eyes and saw darkness and stars and somewhere deep and beautiful and protected. If that's where she was slipping away to, she was ready to go.

A still morning sea, the Deeps all asleep . . .

A still morning sea, the Deeps all asleep, 'til warmed by the sun, they roll up the beach.

Those words again.

Quinn hurried out of the bath and back to her room, fished around in her desk drawer until she found that story she wrote when she was little, the one that Lydia had returned to her. She pulled out the boxes from under her bed and took out the scribbled blue drawings.

"*The deps are my frends.*" That was what was written in the story, but she hadn't meant the "deps." It was just a spelling mistake. She'd meant the Deeps. And that's what this drawing was, wasn't it? The Deeps. Something in the ocean that Quinn used to believe in. Something written about in that children's book her mother used to read to her. *"A still morning sea, the Deeps all asleep."* The drawings weren't of the sky. They weren't of God. They were of the ocean.

No more lies, Quinn! The Deeps aren't real. There are no Deeps!

The only safe way Quinn could think of to get to Southaven without her parents' help was with Ben. Her father was shut up in his office. Her mother was in the shower. She crept into their room and scanned the night tables and dresser and then searched through her mom's discarded clothes until she found her phone. She didn't dare take the time to go upstairs to her own room, and instead just slipped into the hall and into the guest room.

"Mom?" Ben said when he picked up. "I saw something on the news. Everything okay there?"

"It's me," Quinn whispered. "I have to talk fast. I'm so sorry, Ben. I'm so sorry about everything and I wish I'd known and I completely understand why you don't want to talk to me."

"Hold on," he said. "What are you talking about?"

"I know you're mad about the disgusting things everyone is saying and that's why you haven't answered my calls or texts. I get it and I'm so, so sorry."

"Quinn, I don't know what you're talking about. I haven't heard from you in weeks. I tried to call you, but your phone just said, 'This number is restricted' or something. My texts were returned."

"You didn't get my messages?"

"No. None."

Quinn inhaled sharply. She didn't know what this meant, but they didn't have time to figure it out right now.

"Where are you?" she said. "You're not in Florida, are you?" *Please, no.*

"I'm at Zach's place. Why?"

"I need you," she said. "I need you to help me." She went on to explain her plan as quickly as she could. She couldn't go in and out of the front or kitchen doors because of the alarm situation, but the window was still an option. Her parents hadn't realized that was how she got to Jesse's to see the show.

"I don't know," he said when she was finished. "With everything that's going on, I don't think it's smart for me to take you away from home. I'm not exaggerating when I say I could imagine Dad issuing an Amber Alert. He . . . he doesn't want me around you."

"Ben. If you don't take me, I'll take a bus. I swear to god. You don't need to worry—I'll take care of Dad."

"Please don't take a bus, Quinn."

"I will. Tomorrow morning. There's no way I'm not going to be on Southaven by tomorrow night. With or without you."

She went to bed, not knowing whether she'd really have the guts to do it, not knowing whether having tried to talk to Nicole would bring a whole new wave of desperate believers to the house, and not knowing whether she'd ever be able to prove to people that what so many of them thought about the family wasn't true. How would she ever prove anything when her parents refused to release any information? And if people didn't know the real truth, didn't their own versions of it become more important? This story about her, written all over the Internet—it was there forever. Whatever people said was growing into the "truth." It was out of Quinn's control. It had everything to do with her, and nothing. Whichever group spouted their theory the loudest would win. She'd become who they wanted her to be.

✦ ✦ ✦

She finally fell asleep and had another one of her dreams, a bit different this time. She was running in a meadow—dressed in her track uniform—and a mob of people was chasing her. She knew they wanted something, but she didn't know if they thought she was good or evil, and she ran until she came to the edge of the meadow, where there was a sudden drop-off into the ocean, and she kept running off the cliff and landed in the water and sank down, down, down, into that starry blackness where the little girl was waiting. And this time Jesse was waiting down there for her, too.

He touched her shoulder. "Quinn," he said, shaking her. "Quinn." And then the touch and the voice became too real. There was a pressure on her shoulder, yes. And a voice. But she wasn't asleep.

Her body seized in terror and she started to scream.

A hand covered her mouth. She bit the flesh.

"Ow," Ben whispered, pulling away. "It's me. Jesus."

She sat up. "What the hell are you doing? You scared the crap out of me." She pressed a hand against her chest, heard herself thinking: *He's not going to hurt you. He's not going to hurt you.*

"I changed my mind," he said. "I trust you know what you're doing. I'll take you."

"What? Now?"

"While Mom and Dad are asleep."

The fright of being woken like that left Quinn alert and energized. She began shoving clothes from the floor into her backpack.

"How did you get in?" she asked. "The alarm . . ."

He gestured at the window. "Is there anything you really need?" he whispered. "Pregnancy medications or whatever?"

"Uh . . . just vitamins," she said, trying to think if there was anything else.

Courage. Clarity. Things she could only pray for.

QUINN

Soon after the sky started pinking, Quinn's phone rang. She pulled it out of her hastily packed bag.

"Thank god," her mother said. "Are you okay?"

"Fine," Quinn said. "I told you not to worry." She'd left a note explaining as best she could. And she did feel better than she had before. Her head and her intentions were clear now—much clearer than when she'd made the mistake of trying to talk to Nicole in front of all those people. She should have known something like that would happen. She'd just been so overwhelmed—the show, all the stuff on the web, the realization about that night on the beach . . . She'd latched onto the idea that Nicole might have some answers. But now, she saw her hope for what it was: another attempt to find an explanation that wasn't ugly, no matter how far-fetched it was. Nicole, and those people out there . . . they knew nothing about her or the baby. They were just looking for help wherever they could find it, making Quinn into something they could believe in, something that gave them hope.

"We want you to come back," her mother said. "Okay, Quinn? Right now. Let me talk to Ben."

"I'm putting you on speaker," Quinn said and placed the phone on the console between them. "You weren't going to take me, and I needed to go. So I asked Ben."

"Turn the car around, Ben," Gabe's voice said.

"Dad," Quinn said. "I need to be there. Give me one good reason I can't."

"The reasons are obvious. And they should be to Ben, as well."

"She's fine," Ben said. "I'll take care of her."

"I'm safer here than I am at home with all the people outside,"

Quinn said. "No one saw us leave. I don't really agree that the reasons are obvious. I can't even think of one."

"Quinn?" Gabe said. "I don't want you on that island. And I don't want you to go with *Ben*. Those are your reasons."

"It was my idea," she said. "Not his. He's helping me."

"Do you want to tell her, Ben?" Gabe said. "Or should I?"

"Dad," Ben said, "it wasn't what you thought."

"What?" Quinn said.

"Are you going to tell her?" Gabe repeated.

Ben glanced at her, a nervous, stricken look on his face.

"What?" Quinn said, apprehensive now. The baby kicked inside her.

"Dad misunderstood. I had nothing to do with it. The guys I work for, they wanted to do a . . . you know, a sort of TV thing—"

"A reality show," Gabe said.

"More like a documentary series," Ben said. "About you."

That was all? Quinn let out her breath. Of course they'd wanted to do that. Who could blame them? "So what?" she said.

"Your brother," Gabe continued, "was going to make money getting them access. Private information."

"I wasn't! They lied when they said I was on board with it." Ben's voice sounded to Quinn more like it did when he was younger, less like the older Ben who didn't care what his father thought of him. "I just don't get how you could believe them over me. How could you think I'd do that?"

"You haven't quit, have you?" her father said. "You're still working for them."

"Dad—" Quinn started. She didn't care about this or believe Ben would have betrayed her. But no one was listening to her.

"I can't quit," Ben said, maneuvering the car into the next lane. "It's not that easy. I need the money. Seriously—how could you believe I'd do that?"

"Because you've never protected her like an older brother should," Gabe said. "It probably did happen that weekend, while you were with her at the party. Who else was supposed to be watching her after your mother left?"

"But, Dad—" Quinn said. She was sixteen. She didn't need *watching*.

"She almost died," Gabe went on. "You were supposed to be watching her. You were old enough to keep an eye out for her. How the hell did she end up in the water? You were supposed to be watching her. We told you. Do you know what it's like to think your child is dead?"

What? Quinn was so confused, and her father's voice coming out of the phone was so loud and hard and what he was saying was so . . . so wrong and strange. She couldn't tell if he was talking about that night last May . . . or what.

After several unbearably long seconds, Ben said, "I was eleven. I was only eleven."

"She was only seven!"

"You're talking about that?" Quinn said. "Dad—"

"You think I haven't been trying to make up for it ever since then?" Ben said over her, and Quinn realized that they were having a conversation that had been waiting to happen, that she hadn't even known was festering underneath the resentment. And she had a hazy memory of Ben—eleven-year-old Ben—crying and her father yelling. But she didn't understand, because Ben had been the one who brought her in from the water. She remembered her panic when she realized she couldn't touch, and the water in her mouth, and then the feeling of his arms pulling her in, as if the undertow had shifted, pulling her to safety.

"How have you made up for it?" Gabe said. "By letting one of those guys do this to her?"

"That's why I'm trying to help her now," Ben said. "Okay? I'm trying, Dad. I'm trying to make up for all the lousy shit I did as a brother, including almost letting her die. Okay? How much more can I do?"

"How much—"

"You're the one who broke her fucking arm! What about that? You broke her fucking arm!"

"Stop it!" Quinn shouted, feeling like she was the sane one for a change, nervous about Ben driving while he was so worked up. "He didn't break it. And none of this has anything to do with anything! I'm with Ben, I trust him, and I'm going to Maine."

Now there was silence on her parents' end. Eventually, Gabe said, "Quinn? I know you're upset. Yesterday was . . . too much to handle, and you're confused. But everything's going to be okay. Just come home. Please? Maine is not a good place for you to be. You don't remember everything . . . but it didn't make you happy when you were little. You weren't yourself there. It was dangerous."

"I was happy there," she said.

"No. You were confused. You imagined you were happy. You've made up a story about it. I don't want you near that water, Quinn. Please come home. Please, Little."

"I can't," she said, closing herself off to the neediness in his voice. "I have to do this. I won't have to stay long. But I need to go now."

She ended the call and turned off her phone.

The two of them sat for a moment, the conversation still pulsing in the space of the car.

"You're the one who pulled me back that day," Quinn said. "You saved me. Why is he blaming you?"

"No, I didn't," Ben said.

"I mean, I know Dad's the one who did whatever—"

"I didn't do anything, Quinn," he said. "I saw you in the water, saw you not able to swim, and I just stood there until I ran and got

Dad. I didn't do anything. And he's right. I was supposed to be watching you before that. We all knew that you were obsessed with that beach. But I figured . . . I don't know. You knew how to swim. I was going to check on you."

"Wait . . ." Quinn said. "So who carried me in?"

"No one. I saw you out too deep, struggling, and I froze . . . I froze like a fucking idiot, just stood there watching . . . and then you were swept in with a wave, like you were bodysurfing or whatever. I watched the whole thing happen instead of trying to help."

"No. That's not right." Quinn didn't understand. She had memories of that day, including the feeling of Ben's arms carrying her. It wasn't clear—just a choppy, emotion-centered memory. But, still . . . And her family had talked about that day plenty of times. *Everyone* knew Ben had helped save her.

"I remember you," she said. "Your arms . . . And Mom and Dad said—"

"Mom and Dad told you that because you were freaking them out. I was supposed to go along with the story. Which, obviously, I did."

"What do you mean, I was 'freaking them out'?"

"Making things up," he said. "You know, your imaginary friends and whatever."

The Deeps. The Deeps all asleep . . .

Ben honked at a car that had cut them off.

"What do you mean?" Quinn said again.

"You know how you always pretended you had friends in the water you liked to swim with? Well, after I ran and got Dad, and he got you to spit up all the water you swallowed, you kept saying your *friend* pulled you back to shore because you'd gone out too far."

The deps are my frends.

"I still don't get why you all said it was *you*," Quinn said. "It was someone. I remember someone carrying me in. Some friend of mine must have been down there." She struggled to think of who that would have been.

Ben got a cigarette out of a pack in the glove compartment but didn't light it. "You didn't have any friends on Southaven, Quinn."

"But . . . I played with kids. At the beach. Like Marco."

"No, you didn't. Marco and Foley . . . you were just my baby sister to them. You pretended you had friends. Like . . . you wouldn't ever listen about not swimming alone, because you didn't think you *were* alone. And, well . . . your conviction about it was kind of freaky. And as for the drowning thing—I was there. No one saved you. You really believed someone had, though. So we pretended it was me."

"So . . ." Quinn ran her tongue over her dry lips. "You all lied to me? About you saving me?"

"I just said what they told me to," Ben said, sounding a bit defensive now. "It didn't seem like that big a deal. Your whole imaginary life thing was pretty weird, and . . . I don't know. It wasn't like I was going to go against them after you'd almost drowned because of me. I felt like shit."

"The Deeps. That's what I called them, right?"

"Yeah," he said. "Because of that book."

Quinn felt like a wave had swept into the twists and turns of her brain and was jumbling everything together, nothing in its right place. She couldn't believe that this seminal memory was fabricated. That she'd been told what to believe and had believed it all these years. It was one of those family stories, and a memory she returned to: her big brother's arms around her. And what about the fact that he was saying she had no real friends? She had no idea what was the truth anymore, about anything. What were real memories, and what were just products of stories?

Quinn was lying to herself. Other people were lying to her. About things from back then and now. And it was all getting mixed up together. The lies, the truths, the then, the now . . . one confusing mess.

Start with what you know.

She knew that there was lost time that night in Maine last May, time when she thought she'd been swimming. She knew that it was likely something had happened to her. She knew that someone must have been there with her. And she knew that to trigger the memory, she had to do anything she could.

"Ben?" she said. "We need to stop somewhere else."

Your brother's a hero. She could hear her father saying it. *Right? He's a hero, saving you like that. Right, Quinn?*

It was Ben. Ben carried you out. Don't lie and pretend it was someone else, Quinn. No more lies.

The Deeps aren't real, Quinn. Stop lying. There are no Deeps.

Do you want to end up like her and die in the ocean?

QUINN

It was still early morning when they arrived in New Haven. They parked in front of Marco's dorm with no idea what time he'd be up and out for classes.

"I can't believe you went for the stakeout cliché," Ben said, taking a bite of the doughnut Quinn had just handed him, along with a cup of coffee. He'd stayed in the car keeping an eye out for Marco while she'd gone to get sustenance.

"They're artisanal and gluten-free," she said. "Does that make them less cliché?"

"Nope. Just changes which cliché we're talking about."

Quinn was halfway through her tea and long done with her doughnut by the time a guy walked out of the dorm and Ben said, "That's him."

"It is?" she said, leaning forward. The guy had on a wool hat, down vest over plaid shirt, and jeans; his hands were in his pockets, backpack on his shoulder, and he was looking down as he walked. Right size, right dark curls and prominent ears coming out from the hat.

"Yeah. Definitely," Ben said. "You sure you want to do this? Alone?"

She sat up straighter. "Yeah."

"Okay, well, go now, so I'll be able to see you from here."

Marco was following a path that would lead him away from where they were parked if he kept on it. She needed to go now. She took a deep breath and reached for the door handle.

"Hi," she said, trotting up to him a moment later. "Um, Marco?"

He stopped walking, his expression showing no sign of recognition, like that morning on Southaven. Quinn would barely have known him, either, this time. Before, when she saw him standing in the water, she'd thought she was seeing an old friend. But now . . . he was just some guy.

"It's Quinn," she said, the same words she'd said back then.

His face registered a moment of shock. He glanced to both sides. "What the hell?" he said, quiet but hard. "What are you doing? You can't be here." His gaze went to her almost-six-months belly.

"Sorry," Quinn said. "I just . . . I needed to talk to you in person, and I knew if I asked, you'd say no."

"Uh, yeah. Yeah, I would have. You shouldn't be here. You really shouldn't be here. I already told Ben everything I know." He started to walk away, and she grabbed him by the sleeve. Students passing them on the path gave them quick looks.

"I just need to talk to you," Quinn said, her voice low. "Ben is sitting in that yellow car, watching us. You don't want me, or him, to make a scene, do you?"

Marco looked over at Ben, then back at Quinn. "Okay," he said. "But over there on the bench, not standing right here." They walked over and sat on a wooden bench at the edge of a path.

"Talk fast," he said. "I have class."

"I think I accidentally took some kind of drug, probably Ecstasy, that night in Maine," she began, "the night of the bonfire. That's the night I got pregnant." She figured the more confident and the less accusatory she sounded, the better. "So even though I know something happened, I don't know what. Can you tell me anything?" She forced herself to look in his eyes, to judge his reaction, which was definitely freaked. Her own reaction to him was still completely flat—no new memory, no fear, no revulsion.

"Wait," he said. "You don't know how you got pregnant?"

"I just told you. It was that night. But I was on something, so I don't remember."

He glanced to either side. "Like I said, I already told Ben everything."

"So when you saw me lying there later, it was low tide, right?"

"I don't know. It's not like I took a picture."

"How did you know I was okay?"

He shrugged. "You weren't crying. You were propped up on your arms, sort of. I don't know."

"Did you tell anyone I was there?"

He hesitated a bit. "No."

"You did," she said. "Didn't you?"

"No," he said. "I didn't."

Quinn waited for a guy and a girl holding hands to walk by before continuing. "Since I know something happened that night," she said, "I'd like to do a DNA test to make sure it wasn't you. You were really fucked up that night. Maybe you don't remember, either. Maybe there was something in that lemonade we drank. Do you know if anyone was doing E that night? I asked Ben, but he didn't know."

"No, I don't know. And how do you know I was fucked up?"

"Ben told me," she said, not about to admit she'd had someone hack into his accounts. "So, can I have a couple of hairs for a DNA test?"

"God, Quinn—"

"I'd like to ask Foley and the other guys you were with, too. Not just you. Anyone could have seen me down there."

"Foley? Good luck with that," he said with a dismissive laugh. "You realize I'm damned if I do and damned if I don't? If I don't, it looks like it's because I did something to you. And if I do, I risk getting caught up in all of this."

"Not if you do and it's negative."

"You think that's going to matter? How would I explain that you even wanted me to be tested?"

"No one would have to know. All I need to do is send the hair to this place. Your name won't be on it or anything."

He appeared to think about this for a minute. "I'm sorry," he said. "You're just going to have to believe that I'm telling the truth. I can, like, solemnly pledge, swear, whatever. But I won't do the DNA test. I can't get involved on paper like that. Stuff gets completely blown out of proportion. This isn't exactly a private thing anymore." He stood up. "And, if you remember, *you* kissed *me*, Quinn."

He pulled his wool cap over his ears and started walking away. Quinn watched him go. What more could she do, after all? She stood, too, and began walking in the opposite direction.

But only for a few paces. What was she thinking? She came all this way just to give up like that? To be no better off than she was before?

She turned back around and hurried after him.

"I don't want to be like this," she said when she caught up. "But if you don't give me a hair, I'm going to start screaming. I'm going to make a big scene. And . . . and like you say, it won't even matter if you didn't do anything. Because your name will be in all of this. And Ben saw us kissing, so it will totally be believable that something else happened. In other words, you're already mixed up in this—but if you give me a hair and it's negative, then no one will ever know unless you're the one who tells them. If you don't give me the hair . . ." She shrugged. "Not sure what will happen then."

MARCO CAVANAUGH

arco walked quickly across the green, head down, sweaty hands shoved in pockets, cursing himself for what he'd just done. But he hadn't had a choice, had he?

And it wasn't like the test was going to come out positive.

Although, what she'd said about the lemonade . . . Could that be true? Had he maybe been more fucked up than he'd even realized?

It would explain what he'd seen. Quinn, lying on that rock, moonlight glowing on her skin in this otherworldly way. The water lighting up with phosphorescence or something. It hadn't seemed real. More like something out of one of the fantasy graphic novels he read. A black-and-white illustration where the blackest blacks were so dense it seemed like you could fall into the picture, and the whites glowing like they'd somehow made the page whiter than paper.

It had seemed like a hallucination, but at the same time, he didn't think he was drunk enough that night to be so crazy. And he'd never hallucinated just from drinking. He didn't usually pass out, though, either, like he did later on in the evening.

And he'd been wasted enough that he'd told those guys what he'd seen. Had told them she was down there. Had told them she was naked, glowing. Even though she was obviously a messed-up girl from a messed-up family, he'd feel absolutely disgusting if it turned out one of them had gone down there and found her.

He shivered and shoved his hands deeper in his pockets.

Fuck.

QUINN

They made it onto the late afternoon ferry to Southaven. Usually, they'd have needed a reservation to get on with a car, and even with the reservation would have had to wait in a line for hours, but delivery trucks came in the mornings, and it wasn't prime tourist season anywhere in Maine, especially not the islands, so they had almost the whole boat to themselves.

Quinn stood at the railing; leaned forward over the silvery, rippled welcome mat that stretched as far as she could see; and breathed in the cold, wet, salty air. *Hello, hello, hello!* Gulls and wind and waves called out in greeting. The massive engine rumbled under her feet as the ferry left the dock. She felt everything inside her opening up as though she was emerging from a shell like one of the periwinkles in the tide pools at Holmes Cove when she'd hold it and hum softly, coaxing it out.

And somehow, this didn't make her feel more vulnerable, like the periwinkle. No, Quinn had the distinct sense that coming out of hiding would make her stronger.

After a little over an hour, the ferry docked near Southaven's village. The sun had set during the trip, making it feel later than it was. Quinn and Ben picked up supplies at Davis & Derry's, the one real grocery store, where she was relieved not to bump into anyone they knew. When they visited last May, it seemed like there weren't that many people they'd known who still lived here. Her mother had said that the island didn't have as many year-rounders as it used to. More wealthy summer people, instead.

Once back in the car for the final leg of the trip, Quinn felt like her body was a shaken bottle of seltzer. Even in the dark, she knew where the drive was taking them: first through the area with old Victorian houses, past the island's public school, library, and graveyard, and then into the stretches with mostly wooded areas and the occasional cottage or farmhouse in a clearing. Each twist in the road brought a different landmark that signaled they were getting closer to home: the sign for Big Bottom Quarry—the quarry where everyone swam nude, whose name made Quinn's family joke that you had to have a big bottom to swim there; the house with hundreds of old lobster traps in the yard; the hidden path to the island's lighthouse . . .

When they rounded the large curve in Upper Haven Road that passed the spot where Quinn had found Haven as a kitten, and then saw the three small signs at a narrow turnoff—the wooden CUTLER/ WELLS sign her mother had made underneath the painted metal one that said CAVANAUGH, and the official DEAD END sign—Quinn thought her chest might explode, her heart was beating so fast. Ben slowed the car and they shuddered over the bumpy dirt surface, down a hill and up again, first past the driveway for the Cavanaughs' and then, farther down, left at the turnoff into their own drive.

The two houses were on a peninsula, about a mile long and a half-mile wide, with only the one dirt road down it. Woods filled most of the land around and between the houses, which both sat on clearings that went down to the water. Narrow paths wound through the woods connecting destinations: the Cutlers' house and the Cavanaughs' were about a half mile apart. And about midway between was the path to Holmes Cove, more of a real beach than the waterfronts close to the houses, which had large rocks that were good for climbing, but not for swimming.

As Ben pulled up to the weathered-shingle cottage, illuminating it in the headlights, it looked asleep . . . unaware. No one had stayed in it all summer. Quinn unbuckled her seatbelt, opened the door, felt the gravel press through the soles of her shoes, and was home.

NICOLE ANDERSON

I n front of the Cutlers' Park Slope house, Nicole was squatting down, picking up offerings that had been blown off the fence and were now littering the sidewalk—snapshots mostly, a few wilted flowers, prayer cards—when Samuel, the plaid-coated leader of the Entitled, came huffing up the street. Nicole stood.

"She's at their other house," he said breathlessly to the group.

He had been staking out the block behind the Cutlers' and had followed Quinn's mother as she walked to her car, during which he overheard part of a phone conversation.

"I didn't hear where the house is," he said. "Or who she's with."

Angry murmurs spread. *They can't take her away. It isn't their right. God's grace isn't something you can choose not to share.*

"Maine," someone said after a few moments. "One of the articles says they have a house—"

"An island," another woman chimed in, holding up her phone. "It says here. Southaven island, Maine."

Nicole moved aside, not liking any of this—not liking the angry energy or the idea that Quinn had been so scared of them she had to leave. Because Nicole was sure that's what had happened after the disaster yesterday. Who wouldn't have been scared? And after the window was broken . . . Both things had happened too quickly for Nicole to stop them. She had failed.

And now she listened with increasing alarm as the group decided it was their right to go there, to follow her. They began researching options to figure out the best way to get to the island and how to find the Cutlers' house.

"What should I do?" Nicole asked her husband. She'd stepped a ways down the block to talk on the phone privately.

"Go with them, of course."

"But Quinn left to get away from all of this. I'm sure. You should have seen how everyone *attacked* her yesterday. It was horrible."

"She's not 'Quinn' to us," her husband said. "You can't see her that way. She's the Virgin carrying the child we're here to protect. What if her parents are planning to move her from there to somewhere else, somewhere we don't know about? To never give the baby back to the world? I've been reading about that family, and I don't trust them. They're not good people, Nicole. Definitely not God's people. They're the ones we need to protect the baby from. That's why God sent you to New York."

Nicole thought about what he was saying. Although she wasn't sure about Quinn's parents being the enemy, he was right about one thing: Somehow, she'd become attached to Quinn as a person. And her responsibility was larger than that, because at the end of the day, Quinn was not the important one. The baby was. That was what she had to remember.

QUINN

After settling in, building a fire, and having a quick, canned soup dinner, Quinn told Ben she was ready to go down to Holmes Cove.

"Want me to go with you?" he asked.

She shook her head. "I need to do it alone."

Outside, she lay down on the wooden deck where she and Jesse had watched the movie after the bonfire. The air was cold and damp enough tonight that it could have bitten her bare cheeks and ears, but instead, it just made her skin feel more alive. She almost couldn't hear her own thoughts because the chorus of the air, ocean, forest, and stars was filling her head.

But she couldn't pay attention to all of that now. She closed her eyes and thought back to last May, to the moment she'd decided she needed to swim. Although . . . why would she even have considered swimming if it wasn't high tide? It didn't make sense. In her (fantasy) memory, she'd felt a pull, an excited buzz in her body, a delicious sense of knowing the water was waiting and she was about to do something bold and crazy and forbidden . . . But if she'd known it was low tide, known she couldn't swim, what would the pull have been?

She took a deep breath of the salty, piney air and tried to tamp down her frustration. It wouldn't be good to arrive at the beach already discouraged. She stood and headed toward the trees.

In May, she'd run down the forest path in the dark, without a flashlight. Tonight, her feet weren't feeling steady enough to run, and how had she ever been able to run in the dark without tripping? So she turned on her flashlight and shone the beam on the mossy, root-woven path. The trees and forest animals were watching her, whispering encouragement. *We're here*, they said. *You're safe.*

It was a clear night with enough moon that when she emerged from the forest at Holmes Cove and turned off the flashlight, the seascape lit up in front of her.

She walked onto the beach, pebbles and broken shells crunching under her feet, and surveyed the scene, her heart beating fast. Here. It had happened here. How would this work? Was something going to come at her all of a sudden? A vision? Or a whole memory of the night, playing in her head like a movie? The memory lived in these rocks and shells and the water. She was sure of it. The question was whether it would appear all at once, like a crab startled out of hiding, or ease up slowly, like the tide.

She closed her eyes and filled her lungs with the sweet-brine air. It smelled like childhood—like digging for clams, clambering over rocks, watching for seals, poking through tide pools . . . And swimming and swimming and swimming . . . (She couldn't stop herself from remembering the swimming happening with friends, even knowing that she hadn't had any real ones. Her memories of being down here had no element of loneliness.)

Her ears filled with the gentle lapping of the ocean on a calm night. The sea breeze against her face was colder and stronger than at the house, but it still felt good. Her skin breathed here in a way it never did in Brooklyn. *Do you feel the difference in the air?* she asked the baby. *And do you know where we are? Do you remember?*

It was beautiful.

She saw herself in the black water, swimming with stars . . . Her body began to relax.

Then . . . wait . . . a noise. From behind her. She spun around, switched on the flashlight, and shone it toward the woods. But there was nothing. It must have been an animal. Fox, probably.

She turned back around and took another deep breath of the ocean air, trying to relax again, when she realized: these smells, sounds, feelings . . . they were the sensations of home and happiness in her mind. Which also meant that, at this moment, they were part of the problem. These fantasies—about having friends as a kid, about swimming that night in May—they were the stories covering up the truth.

Quinn pulled back inside herself and focused on why she was here. She had to be in a mind frame to remember. She had to strip away all the fantasies she'd constructed and try to remember the reality—the ugly reality—of what happened that night.

She walked carefully over the flattish part of the beach and climbed onto the rock where Marco had seen her. Swimming Rock, she had always called it, because it was the best rock for swimming off during high tide. She sat down, legs outstretched.

Since she couldn't remember what had drawn her to the beach, she tried to remember why she took her clothes off once she was down here. Had someone told her to do it? Forced her to do it? Or had she done it for someone (Marco?) willingly? Again, all she could come up with was the false memory she'd had this whole time. It was so stubbornly lodged in her mind—the feeling of freedom as she discarded her clothes by the trees and walked out to her rock, naked. Months of thinking about it had etched it into her brain, like grooves on vinyl.

She tried to imagine someone coming out of the woods—Marco, Foley, or just a faceless male figure, who had either seen her at the Cavanaughs' party and followed her or stumbled on her accidentally. She pictured the beach, no water to swim in, and tried to think where something might have happened. If she'd been here, on the rock, she'd have been bruised the next day, probably. And scratched up by the barnacles. Maybe up at the edge of the path, where the ground was softer? Maybe she went down to the rock after, in shock? And that's when Marco saw her? Or . . .

Nothing. Nothing was coming.

God, get over it, Quinn! Just deal with it! Forgetting wasn't going to change what had happened! Not knowing was worse than anything. Not knowing meant she was still ruining everything, that she was defective, that she was weak. Not only had she been victimized then, but she was too weak to remember now. She saw Preston Brown's face, heard all of the people on the show talking about how damaged someone like her must be, remembered all of the comments on the articles, people talking about what a strange girl she'd been, how sad it was that there was something so very, very wrong with her.

And as these destructive thoughts crashed into her brain, she found anger rising up inside her. Anger at everything. Anger at the stupid beach, at the pine trees and ocean, at the air, at herself. Anger at the scene that had stolen her memory and replaced it with fantasy. Why wasn't this working? This was supposed to be it! This beach! It was supposed to hold the answer. This smell and sound and touch was supposed to take away the fake memory and bring back the real one.

Because what was she supposed to do if it didn't? What was she supposed to do, as the world out there concocted their stories about her and as someone out there knew what the answer was and wasn't telling her? Because there was someone who knew. That was the one indisputable fact. Someone out there knew.

Maybe it was Marco. Maybe the paternity test would prove it. But maybe not. And even if it did, she wanted the memory. She wanted to remember what really happened, not have someone tell her. She wanted to know it, really *know* it, inside of herself. No matter how ugly it was.

She stood and closed her eyes and screamed as loudly as possible. All her anger and frustration roared out of her, waking sleeping crabs and seals and even mussels in their shells. And once she started, she couldn't stop. She screamed and screamed, hoping that it was being heard wherever memory was kept.

When her throat hurt and she'd emptied herself out, she opened her eyes and was momentarily disoriented. The tide seemed noticeably closer than when she'd looked before. Closer than it should be. Had she been standing here long enough for it to move that much? She really was losing her mind. She watched the small waves washing toward her and imagined walking out into it and never stopping. Because what was she supposed to do now? She was so tired. Deathly tired. She wanted to walk out and sink, sink, sink to the bottom.

Then it occurred to her: That's what her dreams were telling her to do, weren't they? The dreams were telling her to give up, to find peace at the bottom of the ocean, just like her grandmother had. Because peace wasn't going to come to her on land. Underwater was where she'd be safe, like her father said in the dreams. That's why it was so beautiful down there. Because it was away from all of this.

The water was closer; the tide was rushing in. A wave poured up the beach. The young Deeps, coming to explore.

All of a sudden, Quinn's body seized up. Her pulse rocketed and her whole body switched to flight mode. She tried to breathe through it, but anxiety gripped every cell and *no*, she couldn't be here. She couldn't be here. If she stayed here, she might do something. Something might happen. Her skin was twitching and she was hyperventilating and couldn't stay one moment longer. She turned and ran.

Her mother arrived on the late morning ferry the next day, after flying to Portland and renting a car so Gabe could drive up later. He had some meeting that he couldn't miss or reschedule and would also be the one to drop off Lydia at a friend's house in Westchester, where she would stay for the nights he and Katherine were away. Ben drove onto the same ferryboat that Katherine arrived on, to go the opposite direction across the water, heading back down to the city. Quinn felt guilt as deep as the Mariana Trench telling Ben and her mother that nothing had become any clearer during her visit to the beach. She'd made such a production of coming here, with all her assurances that it was going to give them the answers.

After she and her mother got home from the ferry landing, she sat in one of the old Adirondack chairs on the screened-in porch, bundled in coat and hat. She stared out at the slices of ocean interspersed between trees in front of the house. She didn't trust herself to go back to the beach, even though she wanted to. Its depths had beckoned last night in her dreams, and now when she was awake, too—she heard her name being called with every roar of a wave. She didn't know if she'd be able to resist walking straight out into the water and never coming back.

SAMUEL FERRIS

The bus seat vibrated under Samuel's thighs. Motion. Finally. There'd been some problem with the door, and it seemed like they might be stuck longer in Boston. But God had fixed it.

Samuel had been angry when the Virgin was taken away; now he knew the challenge would make it even better when they were with her again. Getting to prove their worth. That was God's plan, obviously. Show her they couldn't be shoved aside. Not after all the time they'd put in. All the crappy hours standing out there getting nothing. Not to mention the four-hour bus ride to Boston at six this morning, and now this four-and-a-half-hour ride to the ferry terminal in Maine. *Bet the Three Wise Men had it easier than this*, he thought.

Samuel didn't have a phone. Pissed him off not to be involved in the planning. The two guys sitting across the aisle from him were figuring the route they'd take once they got to the island. Samuel made them pass it over and show him the map. The Virgin's house was at the end of a long drive, the closest neighbors something like half a mile away. That was good. Space to camp near the house.

There'd be books written about this, Samuel was sure. A new Bible. And Samuel Ferris was damned if he wouldn't be in it.

QUINN

I can't figure out where anything is," Katherine muttered, opening and closing the painted teal cabinets in the kitchen area. "I know we left stuff, like a nice food processor and china . . ."

"There were renters here for nine years," Quinn said. "Maybe stuff broke." She was on the sofa, wrapped in her satiny blue comforter, with a copy of *One Hundred Years of Solitude* in her hand but not really reading.

"Ah!" her mother said. "That's it."

She went into her bedroom for a moment, and when she came back out, she had her set of keys to the house. Fumbling a bit, she unlocked the triangular storage space under the stairs. "We thought we'd be coming back in the summers," she explained to Quinn. "So we stored some of our stuff we didn't want them using under here." She ducked through the low door and emerged with a cardboard box.

Quinn stood up, letting the slippery duvet slide off her onto the couch, and padded over to her mother. She poked her head into the dark storage area. It smelled of musty pine and mildew. Behind some loose stuff, like a lamp and a tall, wood-framed mirror, there were several other stacked boxes.

"What else is in here?" Quinn said, wondering if there would be things from her childhood, not sure whether she'd want to go through them if there were. "More stuff you left?"

"Stuff of your grandmother's that we packed up when we first moved in. Books, mostly, I think. Probably stuff we should have just thrown away, but you know that's not my strong suit."

"Can I look through them?"

Katherine paused a moment. "I don't see why not."

Quinn pulled the dusty cardboard boxes into the center of the floor in the living area.

"I don't understand," she said as she tore brittle packing tape off the first one. "Why did we even move here if Dad hated Meryl so much? Didn't it remind him of her?"

"We weren't exactly rolling in money," Katherine said from the kitchen area. "And he inherited the house at the same time your health problems were getting worse. It just made sense. Clean air, no rent to pay . . ."

"Was it because of what she said to you that day, about leaving Cincinnati?"

"No," Katherine said immediately. "I never even told your dad about that."

"Why didn't you just sell this house and buy another one on the mainland? Especially once Dad got that job." He'd split his time between writing books and being a consultant for a Maine-based company.

A loud whirring sound filled the room. Quinn looked up to see her mother testing the food processor. After turning it off, she said, "Meryl's will stipulated that the house and land can't be sold. They can be passed down to direct heirs, or if there isn't an heir, donated to the Conservation Society. That's it."

"Oh." Quinn had never heard of anything like that before. "That's weird."

Katherine shrugged. "The property had been in her family for generations. She loved the island and hated the way it was being developed. People building big fancy houses. She wanted to protect what land she could."

Quinn turned her attention to the boxes again. Her mother was right: They were all filled with books. She went through volume by volume, finding everything from familiar favorites like *A Walk in the*

Woods by Bill Bryson and *My Family and Other Animals* by Gerald Durrell, to ones that looked really old and boring about American history and the history of Maine. There were a few about ancient mythology, Norse legend, Polynesian folklore. Books about the artists George Bellows and Winslow Homer. Novels by Stephen King, Jorge Luis Borges, Barbara Kingsolver . . . A bunch of Shakespeare. And there, nestled between *A Midsummer Night's Dream* and *Macbeth*, Quinn's hand discovered a very slim paperback—not part of the Shakespeare set. The minute she pulled it out her breath stopped.

The Deeps, written and illustrated by Charlotte Lowell. Charlotte Lowell. The name that had been in the box her necklace came in. It was a children's picture book. The cover illustration was a watercolor of a wave rolling up onto a rocky beach, similar in style to the one framed on their wall. Quinn's heart thudded as she carefully opened the slightly buckled cover. On the title page was a handwritten dedication: *To Meryl Holmes Cutler, Finest Kind. Charlotte Lowell.*

Quinn knew how the book would begin.

A still morning sea, the Deeps all asleep, 'til warmed by the sun they roll up the beach . . .

She couldn't have recited it, but as she read, she found she was rediscovering words that were already in her brain. Seeing pictures that she'd seen hundreds of times. Like meeting an old friend. This book had been a part of her. Still was a part of her.

It was a story of the ocean—of curious spirits in the ocean called the Deeps, coming up on a beach at high tide and playing with a little girl until the tide went back out and the girl's mother called her home. The illustrations were loose watercolors, the Deeps defined by subtle, expressive outlines. More gesture than actual form.

Quinn took it into her parents' bedroom, where Katherine was putting fresh sheets on the mattress. She held it out to her.

Her mother's face paled. "Where did you get that?"

"It's the one I was asking you about."

"We don't have a copy anymore. Where was that?"

"It was in with Meryl's books. The author, Charlotte Lowell, signed it. For her." Quinn paused. "Why are you so freaked out?"

Katherine wrapped her arms around herself, as if she were cold. "I was the one who always put you to bed," she said. "Your dad . . . he didn't realize Charlotte had given me a copy of the book. And that I'd been reading it to you. But then . . . you started pretending that you were friends with those . . . water people, or whatever. And your dad realized it was this book. And then you were refusing to stay away from the water . . . Going in any chance you could get. Talking like you had real underwater friends." She paused. "He blamed that book for putting the ideas in your head. Which, obviously, it did."

"Ben told me some of this. But . . . lots of kids have imaginary friends." Even as Quinn said it, she knew this had been different.

"No part of you seemed to recognize that they were imaginary," her mother said. "The way you insisted on going in that water, even after the accident. No matter how cold it was. We couldn't leave you alone for a minute. You'd have let yourself drown or freeze to death." She shook her head. "It was scary. You had no concept of the danger. You said they'd take care of you."

Quinn turned the book over in her hands. "Ben also told me that you all lied about him pulling me out of the water."

Katherine sighed. "We thought it was for the best, Quinn."

"So Charlotte Lowell lived here? On Southaven?"

"She was a friend of your grandmother's."

"And . . . what did this have to do with Meryl?" Quinn held out the book.

Her mother knit her brow. "Nothing, aside from the fact they were friends."

"But Dad . . . He told me not to lie about it. About the Deeps. And he asked if I wanted to be like her. Like his mother."

"If he said something like that, he was probably talking about her drowning."

Quinn turned back to the page with the handwritten dedication. *Meryl Holmes Cutler.* "Her middle name was Holmes?"

"Her maiden name."

"That's a weird coincidence. Holmes Cove."

"It's not a coincidence. It was named for her family, generations ago."

Quinn's mind was struggling to make sense of all this new information. There was something else. There was some other connection here between her grandmother and this story. Between her grandmother and herself. Quinn knew it.

Later, when she was helping make dinner and couldn't find a sharp knife, she opened a drawer in the kitchen and saw a copy of the regional phone book. On a whim, she took it out and flipped to the right page. There it was. Charlotte Lowell.

There was no cell reception here, so Quinn called from the landline while her mother was out getting firewood. She got a generic voicemail message that definitely wasn't a woman of her grandmother's generation. "Hi, um, this is Quinn Cutler," she said, flustered. "Calling for Charlotte Lowell. You don't know me. I'm Meryl Cutler's granddaughter, and I'm here on the island and . . . I found that book you wrote and illustrated and I had some questions, I guess. I'll try to call you again. Thanks." She heard call-waiting clicking on the other line. It was her father. She stiffened, imagining him having been able to hear her talking on the other line. But all he did was ask if she was okay and then ask to speak to her mother.

Katherine walked into the house with an armful of wood right then. She tumbled the logs next to the fireplace, wiped the dirt and splinters off her sweater, and took the receiver when Quinn handed it to her.

She left the room as she spoke, and came back in a couple minutes later.

"He missed the last ferry," she said. "He's not even past Portland yet. He's going to stay in Rockland and catch the one in the morning."

"Oh," Quinn said. "That's too bad."

Although, inside, she wasn't sure she really felt that way. She was sort of dreading seeing her father. She'd made such a big deal about coming here for answers, had practically promised him that she'd figure it out. And here she was, no closer to anything, and no idea where to go from here, except down.

"I'm not so disappointed," her mother said, echoing Quinn's thoughts. "We'll have a nice, cozy evening. Just the two of us."

SAMUEL FERRIS

They'd caught the last ferry. It docked on Southaven at 6:46 p.m., and Samuel was first on line to get off. The others—eight of them altogether—filed off right behind him.

"Supplies first," he said, his words getting blown away. The sharp, cold wind was gusting here. Marching with purpose, he led them up the slight incline to the main road. Pretended he knew exactly where he was going. God would show him the way.

"Grocery store closes at seven," one of the people said from behind him. "It's to the right."

God was working through a smartphone.

The sky was dead black. Too many clouds for stars or a moon. Samuel didn't like the rumble of thunder in the distance.

They piled into the small grocery store. It was empty, except for one cashier. Samuel grabbed a few packages of beef jerky, peanuts, and mini doughnuts. The cashier eyed the backpacks some of them were carrying and said, "You know camping isn't allowed anywhere on the island? And it's gonna be a cold, wet one tonight. Big storm coming."

"We'll be on a friend's property," Samuel said. "Or indoors, if it's stormy." As soon as the words were out of his mouth, he knew they were true. Somehow, it would work out for them to sleep in a dry place tonight. Maybe even the Virgin's house. God would make sure of that. It was only right.

QUINN

Katherine went to bed early. Quinn tried, but she couldn't sleep. She felt electrified, almost like that day in May. The baby was kicking and her brain was churning, going over everything she'd learned in the last couple of days. It was too much, all of this being heaped on top of her at once. So many things that had been hidden. Lies, false memories, secrets . . .

She knew she wasn't going to sleep. Wrapped in her comforter, she walked softly out to the kitchen and took the phone off its handset, praying Jesse would answer a call from an unknown number. He did. Her whole body warmed at his voice.

"It's me," she said, curling up on the couch.

"I knew it was," he said. "I've been so worried, Q."

She filled him in on as much as possible, overwhelmed by it all, nervous about mentioning Marco to him when she got to that part in the story, not wanting to reopen the wound. But he listened to the whole thing and didn't turn cold or sound hurt.

"Are you okay?" he asked. There was nothing "pass the butter" about the way he said it.

"I don't know," she said, truthfully. "And . . . about the other day. About, you know . . . kissing you. I'm sorry. I was just so upset after seeing all that stuff online. I wanted . . . I wanted you to stay. I wanted to be close to you." Quinn and her impulsive kisses . . .

"You don't have to apologize."

She rubbed her hand over her belly. "Jess?" she said, speaking around the knot in her throat. "What's going to happen with us? I can't . . . I can't keep going like it is. I know that we might not be together, but can we . . . can we go back? Can we really be friends? I

317

miss you. So much. I need you. I really need you. And maybe that's selfish, because I need you but you don't need me, but—"

"Of course I need you," he said.

"You do?"

She could hear him breathing. Was holding her own breath waiting for his answer. "Of course," he said. "I'm miserable without you."

Quinn smiled through tears. "You are?"

There was another moment of just breath. Then, "But I don't think we can go back," he said. "You know?"

Her stomach dropped. Of course they couldn't go back. She'd known that from the moment they became a couple. "Because . . . because you can't forgive me?"

"I've forgiven you for kissing the guy, Quinn," he said. "But it's screwed up that we were even in that situation. You should have said something if you didn't want to be with me like that."

"But I did want to be with you. I *do* want to. I mean . . . I don't know why I did that with Marco. It wasn't about *wanting* him. And it definitely wasn't about not wanting you."

"Are you . . . are you sure? You can still love me but not want me like that."

"Jesse," she said. "I've wanted you forever. Like that."

"So, um, why . . ." His voice was thick, like it was difficult for him to get the words out. "You seemed to pull back, sometimes, when we were together."

Quinn drew a long breath. "It was just that things happened so fast. And I was scared that you'd eventually realize, I don't know, something was wrong with me and you wouldn't want me. And if we'd gone too far, physically . . . I don't know." She stared up at the beamed ceiling. "I was scared of how much it would hurt."

"I've known you for years, Q. Why would I suddenly decide I didn't want you?"

Quinn pressed her fingers against her eyes. "I don't know," she said. "I think if you knew everything about me, you wouldn't love me anymore."

"Quinn," he said. "Why would you ever think that?"

Quinn couldn't answer. Didn't know the answer. It was just an elemental truth—if someone knew her completely, they wouldn't love her. They'd know something was wrong with her, like her father had known, right from the beginning. And as she struggled for words to explain this, something was released inside her and suddenly she couldn't stop crying, everything coming out all at once. She could still hear Jesse breathing on the other end of the phone. She tried not to make noise, wasn't sobbing loudly, but still couldn't manage to speak.

"I'm here," he said gently. "Don't worry. I'm here."

NICOLE ANDERSON

The wind flattened Nicole's trash bag poncho against her body as she pressed forward. Icy rain whipped her face. She wasn't sure how long they'd been walking now—it was slow going with the wind and the rain. Much slower than they'd anticipated. A storm like this hadn't been in the forecast.

"God's just testing us," that blowhard Samuel kept saying. "Making sure we're worthy."

Nicole wished she didn't have all this time to think. She was being torn in half. She heard her husband telling her that she needed to be near the baby to fulfill her responsibility. That letting the child slip away could mean losing it forever. He and the Entitled talked about Quinn as if she were just a vessel. And maybe that's the way Nicole was supposed to see her, too. But . . . she just couldn't. Even in the brief moments she'd connected with Quinn, she'd seen the girl herself. Not just some body carrying the baby. She'd seen her questions, her confusion, her fear . . . Nicole couldn't stop imagining how scared Quinn would be when she realized they had followed her here. Was being a part of that really how she, Nicole, could serve the baby, and her God?

"We're getting closer," someone called from up front. "I recognize this turnoff on the map!"

Nicole felt like a creature was holding on to her ribcage, trying to pull it apart. She kept listening for God's voice telling her what to do. But there was only the sound of the storm. And she didn't have time to call home or debate endlessly. She needed to choose a side.

QUINN

uinn woke with a start. It felt like deepest night, but according to the clock it was only 10:21, an hour after she finished talking to Jesse. She lay still, wondering what had woken her. Something was wrong. Was it the baby? Panic shot through her and she pressed a hand against her stomach. She couldn't sense anything different, though. Had no pain. But there was something wrong. Somewhere. She knew it.

She got out of bed and went to the window. Rain was battering the deck. And in the midst of the frantic drumming, someone was calling her name, a distant voice, like in all of her dreams. Maybe this *was* a dream. She got a flashlight from the kitchen, didn't bother putting on shoes or a jacket—there would be no keeping dry in this weather—and crept quietly out the door. Careful not to slip, she made her way across the slick grass and onto the wooded path, where the rain fell less heavily. That voice still called her name, and she picked up her pace, only realizing when she was at the rock that looked like a dog that she had never turned on the flashlight. She reached the opening at Holmes Cove, stared out at the rainwater becoming seawater, and listened. *There*, woven into the percussive symphony: *Quinn, Quinn, Quinn* . . . She set down the flashlight, walked out, and stood on Swimming Rock in her drenched nightgown. She knew it was cold out, but she was warm. And even though she'd had the sense that something bad—something wrong—was happening, she wasn't scared. Not this time. The baby was dancing inside her.

She could just make out the white foam at the edge of the water. It was hard to tell in the dark, but she thought it was almost lowest tide, a field of sand and mussels and seaweed between them. The *shush,*

shush, shush of the waves was an audible backdrop to the sounds of the storm. The waves were a bit bigger than usual in the cove, because of the wind, but still not huge. As Quinn stood there, she felt something tugging at her, as if a string had been tied around her sternum and was being pulled forward. Like the pull she had felt to come down here that night in May. And then, *wait* . . . the tide was higher than she thought. The forward point of the forward-and-back, forward-and-back motion of the edge was up to the rock the seals liked to sleep on. And then the pulling sensation in her chest got stronger. Wind wrapped her wet hair across her face. The baby kicked more forcefully.

When she pushed her hair out of her eyes, Quinn saw something impossible—so impossible that she knew that, yes, this was a dream. The ocean was sweeping farther and farther up the beach, much too rapidly. Like time-lapse footage of the tide coming in. It was spilling up toward her, as if she were reeling it in on a winch. As if that pulling sensation in her chest was something that attached the two of them together, and the same energy that had pulled her down here on this stormy night was now pulling the water closer to her.

She had never had this sensation in her dreams.

The wind whispered in her ear: *This is not a dream.*

She touched the wet fabric of her nightgown, the rainwater on her face, and felt the wind against her body. The sensations were real. This was not a dream. She was fully present in the moment. She knew both things—that it was happening and that it was impossible. *This is impossible*, she said to herself. But there it was, the ocean surging toward her. She wished the baby could see what she was seeing. To witness.

Within minutes, waves were lapping against the rock underneath her feet, the way they only did at high tide.

As she slipped into the ocean, the water again felt like a new skin. A new skin that fit so perfectly it was both covering her and inside of her—no separation between them. She couldn't see her body in the dark, couldn't tell where she ended and the water began, as if she wasn't made of flesh anymore, as if she'd become part of the ocean like the raindrops around her were. All she was was only emotion, thought . . . *Quinn.*

And then she remembered. It all came back, as if the ocean was telling her the story. That night last May . . . she *had* been swimming. She had felt that same call down to the beach, and when she had appeared, the ocean had surged up to meet her, just like tonight. She had slipped into the liquid night and there had been stars swimming all around her. Glowing like lanternfish. Welcoming her back. Welcoming her home. She remembered swimming among them, feeling both more like herself, more purely Quinn than she ever had, but also recognizing that she was a part of something larger, part of this mysterious world, a world that *needed* her. She had swum underwater, and those glowing lights had been dancing and streaking in the dark, no pattern to their movements, like sparklers being waved and swirled by kids through the night air. More and more of the lights gathered, building and building in intensity, until it wasn't like looking at stars from a distance but was like being right there in the middle of the Milky Way itself. Quinn had felt like she was glowing, too, from all of the reflected light. And then it was as if all those stars converged at once around her, and with a flash the whole sea lit up in one bright, blinding moment.

As she floated here now, remembering, she became aware of her body again and felt gentle, playful touches nudging her this way and that. Familiar touches. She was known in this place. She was safe. Tired, she let herself be rocked, wishing she could sleep. Until, suddenly, a pressure from inside her gut pulled her out of the moment. And then, through her legs, a brief flash of silvery light. She reached forward blindly in the water, felt something slippery between her fingers, pulled it out and saw that it was kelp. She dove under, eyes open . . . and there they were. All around her. The black water a universe of stars tracing glowing paths, weaving and swirling and looping. She held her breath for as long as she could, mesmerized. And when she knew she needed air, she felt a comforting touch nudging her toward the rock. She lifted her head out of the water, gulping at the rainy night, and let the waves gently push her toward land.

SAMUEL FERRIS

L ook!" Samuel shouted. His flashlight beam rested on a sign: CUTLER/WELLS.

"Praise God!" a woman called out.

Maybe now they'll shut up, Samuel thought. They were all wet, cold, and had blisters. All of them, including him, so they needed to just shut up about it already. Some of the crankier ones even moaned about wishing they'd gone with that Nicole woman, who'd been scared she was getting sick (*boohoo!*) and had gotten a ride back to town. Why walk a few hours just to give up? Samuel had never liked her, anyway.

Well, one less person meant more time with the Virgin for him. And according to the map, there was one last road—a mile long, at most—and then they'd reach the house. They'd reach the house, and he'd get everything he deserved.

QUINN

Quinn hauled herself on top of her rock and stood in the wind and rain—shaky, overwhelmed, and exhausted. She placed both hands against her belly, relieved to sense movement from within. She should have been cold. Beyond cold. She shouldn't have even been able to stay in the water for more than the briefest second. Somehow, though, she was only vaguely aware of a chill, just like last May. She took a deep breath, worried she might pass out. She needed to rest, to lie down. Like she had that night, she remembered now. She had rested on the rock, needing a moment to return to land life. But looking down now, she realized waves were skimming the top of Swimming Rock in a way they never did. Water lapped over her feet. The ocean had surged past the point of the high-tide mark. There was now a stretch of water between Swimming Rock and the forested land in a way she had never seen before. Quinn jumped back in and let the water sweep her up to the edge of the beach, then pulled herself out near the trees and watched as it kept going, making steady progress up, up, up toward the forest. Not with enormous waves, like during a hurricane. Just regular storm–size ones that kept pushing the edge up farther and farther.

Dread squeezed Quinn's chest. And she didn't understand. What was it doing? Where was it going?

You have to go back, she said silently, starting to panic now. No one could see this. No one could know. *Please,* she said. *Please, go back.*

She caught herself thinking this and was suddenly confused. What was going on in her mind? This had to be from the storm. Had to be a storm surge. What was she doing, talking to the ocean? The water kept coming, egged on by the wind and the rain, surging up over the lip of where it went from beach rocks to forest floor.

Soon the water was washing over her feet, where she stood by the edge of the trees. No, this wasn't a storm surge. Couldn't be. The ocean poured into the forest.

Please, she begged. *Please, no one can see you. They'll know. They'll know something's wrong.* This was a secret. It had to stay a secret. She wasn't quite sure what *it* was, but she knew that no one else should see it.

Again, she had the same thought she'd had when she woke: Something was very wrong. Something bad was happening.

Quinn's feet skidded on wet grass as she made her way along the edge of the trees. She hadn't been able to follow the ocean through the forest itself—she had watched as it surged from the shore through trees in a direction that would eventually lead to the road, but no path went that way. So she'd run back down the usual path and was now making her way in the cleared area around the cottage, moving the same direction the water was, hoping to head it off at some point, praying that it wouldn't come up this way toward the house. The entire time she was calling out to it silently, still begging it to stop, to return to where it belonged. She could hear it, though, moving forward, deep in the trees.

Forest and ocean weren't supposed to merge.

All of a sudden she lost her footing, caught herself on her hands, one landing on the flashlight it held, twisting her wrist. She stumbled back up and kept moving forward, ignoring the pain. Her flashlight beam illuminated the rain-thrashed tree boughs when she aimed it at the woods. She couldn't see the ocean, could only hear it.

She kept going until she reached the driveway, paused a moment to picture the trajectory of where the water would end up if it didn't stop. She ran along the gravel and then took a right when she reached the dirt road they shared with the Cavanaughs' house. She couldn't hear the ocean in the trees anymore, could only hear the howling wind and the rain hammering leaves, and prayed that meant it had stopped forward momentum. But she kept running down the road, to make sure, to see for herself that her secret wasn't spilling out of the forest.

SAMUEL FERRIS

The road in front of Samuel was flooded. A puddle, choppy like the ocean. Maybe twenty feet across. He couldn't tell how deep it was. As he got closer, it seemed to surge forward, toward him. Like a guard dog. It splashed over his shoes. Cold bit his ankles. He waded in. Even in such a shallow area, he could feel a pull like a current or tide. The wind howled. He backed up.

"What should we do?" a woman asked.

"What is it?" another said. "This doesn't make sense, water flowing from in the trees."

"It's a final test," Samuel said, realizing. He stripped off his trash bag poncho, which was catching the wind like a sail. "God's final test. Seeing if we're worthy. She's right there. Just gotta make it across."

He took off his shoes and rolled up his pants.

"Hey," he said. "Someone get a video of this."

QUINN

unning as fast as she could, Quinn reached the turn that was at the top of the hill where the road then dipped down to its lowest point. She rounded the corner and heard the rush of water, trained her flashlight beam down the hill and lost her breath. The flood stretched across the road, emerging from the ocean side of the forest and disappearing into the trees on the other side. From where she stood, Quinn had no idea how deep it was, but she could see the pattern of small waves rising and falling on the surface.

And . . . wait. There were lights on the other side of the water—beams darting in the erratic motion of people holding flashlights. The motion reminded her of those underwater shooting stars.

Quinn pressed a hand against her chest, which was rising and falling too quickly. She tried desperately to keep herself from going back to those crazy thoughts, those crazy thoughts about underwater stars and impossible floods. *It's a storm surge. A massive storm surge*, she told herself. But still . . . she couldn't stop herself from worrying that those people down there on the road, whoever they were, were seeing her secret.

Suddenly, her flashlight beam landed on a person in the group standing ahead of the rest, someone trying to move through the water. And then one of the group's beams landed on him, too. And held on him. And even from this distance, Quinn recognized something about the slump of his shoulders—and the shape and pattern of that big plaid coat.

SAMUEL FERRIS

I saw something," a woman cried. "At the top of the hill!"

"A light!"

"I don't see a light."

"It went off. It was there. I'm positive!"

Samuel squinted up the hill, the water pushing and pulling against his legs. He couldn't see anything. If there was a light, it could have been anyone. But he knew—it was the Virgin. Maybe she'd do something to help, seeing their devotion. Knowing she was right there, on the other side, made him even hungrier to get through this mess of water. He hadn't gotten to touch her, the other day, like some people had. Tonight, she'd let him.

He took another step forward.

QUINN

Quinn ran back in the pitch dark, letting herself give in to not knowing what was underfoot and trusting the land would let her get there as fast as possible, trusting no large rocks or roots would trip her up, splashing through puddles, which made her think of that man's legs in the puddle of ocean at the bottom of the road, pushing through, coming for her. *They want* you.

She reached the house and didn't try to be quiet as she opened the door and ran, dripping wet, across the creaky wood floor and into her mother's room. "You have to get up," she said, her breath ragged. She rested her hands on her belly, letting the baby know everything was going to be okay.

Her mother sat straight up, as if she had already been awake. "What's wrong? What . . . why are you so wet?"

"It's raining," Quinn said. "But that's not it. The . . . the people, they're here."

"What?"

"The people. From in front of the house. In Brooklyn."

Her mother's jaw dropped. "Here?"

"They're . . . they're on the road. Not at the Cavanaughs' yet. But soon. Once they're through the water."

"What? What water? Are you sure? How do you know?" As Katherine said these things, she was already up and throwing on warm clothes. She handed Quinn a towel that was draped over a chair. "Take off that wet nightgown."

Quinn did, while saying, "I just . . . I was looking at the storm and I had a feeling . . . it's hard to explain. But I took a walk, and I saw them."

"Put these on," Katherine said, tossing Quinn a sweatshirt and sweatpants. "What would they be doing walking at night in a storm like this? How would they even be here? Are you sure, Quinn?"

"I couldn't see them well, but yes, I'm sure. And . . . there's kind of a flood."

"What?"

"I can't explain right now." Her mother would see the flood, she would know that something wrong . . . something impossible was happening. But Quinn's thoughts about it were too fresh, too jumbled to try to talk now. The right words didn't even exist.

"Quinn." Her mother stared into her eyes. "Are you . . . all right?"

Had she lost her mind? That's what her mother wanted to know. And Quinn wasn't sure. "I'm okay enough to tell you that those people are really, honest to god here."

Katherine hesitated one more minute before saying, "Okay."

She moved with long, quick strides into the main living area and to the coat closet, getting out her yellow, fisherman-style raincoat. She picked up the phone. "Dead, of course," she said. Their phone service always went out in bad weather. This was like a horror movie. "You stay here, in the upstairs loft, okay? Keep the doors locked and all the lights off." After saying it, Katherine shook her head. "No, actually, I don't want to be separated. Come with me. They won't be able to see us if we're on the side of the road without a light. Right? If we don't get too close? I just want to see what we're dealing with."

"I don't think they'll see us," Quinn said, knowing she'd be scared to death waiting alone in the house, not knowing what was happening. She kept remembering being trapped on the stoop, with all of those people grabbing at her, wanting her . . .

Quinn put on boots and a sturdy, ankle-length raincoat that had been stored in the closet. Her mother pushed open the door, and they stepped out onto the deck that was still being battered by drops as big as bullets. Katherine held the flashlight in one hand and Quinn's hand in her other. They hurried across the deck and onto the driveway, the light bouncing in front of them. The wind was fierce, but it helped them on their way instead of fighting them.

When they had passed the turn off to the Cavanaugh's, Katherine switched off the flashlight, leaving them in rainy blackness. It was a noisy night, with the rain on the leaves and the wind and the sound of the ocean. They moved over to the edge of the road, still holding hands, and began feeling their way ahead. Eventually, their eyes adjusted a bit and they moved more quickly, finally reaching the turn and then the top of the hill. A couple of flashlight beams down below illuminated the expanse of water, that lone man still trying to cross it.

"Holy shit," her mother whispered.

They stood quiet for a moment. "What should we do?" Quinn said, the baby stirring inside her again.

"What *can* we do?" Katherine said. "No one has moved into the Cavanaughs'. We don't have phone service. We're not going to go down there and confront them. I think the only thing we can do is wait."

SAMUEL FERRIS

It wasn't that deep—just to his lower calves. But he still had only gone a couple feet in this whole long time he'd been trying to cross. The water wrapped around his legs, pulling him in more than one direction at once.

He wiped the rain from his face and tried again. The minute he lifted a foot to step, he was pushed off balance and stumbled backward. Okay, he thought, the harder the test, the greater the reward. That made sense. But the more he tried, the more exhausted he became. His legs were heavy as anchors. With some attempts, the only progress he made was in a backward direction.

Finally, somehow, he made it halfway across. A surge of energy spurred him. "Almost there!" he whooped, craning his neck to look at the others.

A strong force whipped through the water. A sharp *crack* sounded. Pain exploded in his shin. He crumpled, landing in the frigid water. "I need help!" he called. The water shoved him, tumbled him back to the edge, like wind blowing litter down the street.

People grabbed him and pulled him out. "Be careful! My leg! My fucking leg!"

Without looking, he could tell his left shinbone had snapped. "Need an ambulance," he said, panting.

"No reception here," someone said.

"Figure it out!" Samuel barked. Then, in the midst of pain worse than he'd ever felt, he imagined the story. The story they'd tell about the man with the broken leg who pressed on, who didn't let trials stop him.

"Wait," he said. "Forget calling. Someone . . . just wrap my leg. You'll carry me across."

As he said it, he realized it might not be the smartest plan. He wasn't sure he could keep from passing out.

At that moment, headlights appeared from behind them, from the main road, getting closer and closer, lighting up the flood. Look at that! God had sent someone to drive them across and up to the house! The vehicle stopped; someone got out and approached them. Backlit by the headlights, whoever it was looked like an angel.

QUINN

Who is it?" Quinn asked her mother. She could only tell that the man in the plaid coat had fallen, and the person in the vehicle had gotten out and approached the group. The light made it impossible to see much else.

"I don't know," her mother said.

"Do you think that it's one of them? That they got a car and are going to drive across? *Could* they drive across?"

"I don't know."

If the people got in that car and drove up to the house, if they went inside and waited there, Quinn and her mother would have to hide outside until her father arrived tomorrow morning, wouldn't they? Would they freeze to death in the wet and cold? Would she lose the baby? (No, she wouldn't even let herself think about that. She couldn't lose the baby.)

Quinn squeezed her mother's hand with all the strength she had left.

SAMUEL FERRIS

Looks like you need a ride," the driver called out. "Sorry, you can't all fit in the cab, but I've got dry tarps for the back."

"I need some help getting up," Samuel said.

The man and a couple others helped him into the truck's backseat, where he could sit with his leg stretched out. Two of the women got in the front seat with the man. Joe, he said his name was. The rest piled in the back of the pickup.

Samuel had entered an almost-trance state, with the pain, cold, and knowledge that God had sent this man to help him with the last bit of the journey. Samuel had shown his faith by telling them he wasn't giving up. God had seen the sacrifice he was willing to make.

Joe started up the engine. Samuel felt the movement of the truck. It began to reverse.

"No, no!" he cried out. He'd assumed the guy knew where they were going. "We're headed straight. Through the water. Up to the house."

The man didn't change direction.

"Did you hear me?" Samuel said, pushing closer to the front seat as best he could. "Straight."

"Sorry," the man said.

Wait. This wasn't right. "Stop. Stop the truck."

"Look," the man said, turning to face Samuel. "You can either shut up, or you can get out of my truck and walk on that broken leg. Your pick."

NICOLE ANDERSON

Nicole was still shivering, wrapped in the white tufted coverlet from the motel bed. She'd taken a hot shower, but the shivering was something deeper: fear of whether Quinn was okay, of whether they'd stopped the people in time, of whether she'd done the right thing.

Her husband . . . her husband had been so angry. He'd called her selfish, said he couldn't tell their friends and other parishioners what she'd done. "What if they take the Virgin away?" he'd asked. "And we don't know where the baby is?"

Nicole wished she could have told him that God spoke to her and had told her what to do, but she couldn't lie about it. There on that road, she hadn't heard God. She'd listened only to herself about what was the right decision. And if that was based on her compassion for Quinn instead of her devotion to the larger cause, well, that was a mistake she was willing to live with.

Who knew what would happen to the baby if they reached Quinn's house. Maybe Nicole's decision to turn back was all a part of God's plan. Maybe the reason He had put her in that doctor's office was so that she'd be on this island tonight. And while her husband and church would see it as a selfish betrayal, He would see it as what it was—a testament to her humanity.

QUINN

The truck's taillights had disappeared around the bend in the road several minutes ago; Quinn and her mother stood at the top of the hill, waiting to make sure the people were really gone. And it seemed like they were. Whoever had been driving that truck must not have been someone from the group.

Gradually, the wind and rain let up. The air stilled. The tree branches drooped tiredly. The only sound was the gentle sloshing of the puddle of ocean at the bottom of the hill.

"I'm glad we didn't need to go anywhere tonight," Katherine said, training the beam of her flashlight on the water. "I don't think we could have gotten out with that flooding."

The light skipped across the ripples on the pool.

It's not that we couldn't get out, Quinn thought. *It's that they couldn't get in.*

QUINN

Quinn opened her eyes and carefully shifted in bed so she was propped on her elbows. Her entire body ached. Sun peeked around the edges of the curtains—early morning sun, she could tell. She felt like she did when a fever broke, that sense of coming back to clarity. Last night's events ran through her head . . . Stranger than any dream.

Okay, though—what had *actually* happened?

She lay flat again and closed her eyes. Part of her didn't even want to think about any of this. It felt . . . enormous. Overwhelming. Inconceivable.

Was she really going to let herself believe what she'd been thinking last night? Believe that the ocean had come up to meet her like that? Believe that the presences she'd felt underwater were . . . something alive—the Deeps—not just the movement of the ocean? And that the ocean had surged through the forest to keep those people from reaching the house?

And the biggest question of all—if she was choosing to believe it, what did any of it have to do with her pregnancy? Because she couldn't help feeling like that memory from last spring, the swim she took that night . . . she couldn't help thinking that something she didn't understand, something magical, some moment of . . . creation, was what brought this baby to life inside her. That's what all of her dreams had been trying to tell her.

Her palms began to tingle with fear. She was crazy. She really was, wasn't she? Like, not just a little crazy. A lot crazy.

There were obvious explanations here that she was avoiding. She had heard about the Deeps in that book by Charlotte Lowell, and they had become part of her fantasy world. And the water last night surging through the forest . . . It was the storm. A huge storm surge. Maybe the coastline had eroded over the years, and the tide went farther up now than when they'd lived here. That was possible, wasn't it? And, with global warming, the sea level was rising—that was happening all over.

But what about the water coming up to meet her when it wasn't even high tide? What about the fact that she had gone swimming in the ocean off of Maine in November and hadn't been impossibly frozen? There was no physical explanation for it. And what about the lights underwater? Hallucinations?

There were some parts of the story that had rational explanations, yes. But other parts seemed completely impossible. Seemed to go against nature.

And, more than that, deep down, the crazy version was the one that felt true.

Quinn's limbs were stiff and sore as she made her way into the cottage's main room. She startled a bit at the sight of an old man sitting at the table, but then realized it was her father. Not old, just tired.

"Dad!" she said, surprised.

"Hi, Little," he said, smiling and holding out an arm. She went over to give him a hug, happy to see him despite having been dreading it. "Let's keep it down," he added quietly. "Your mom went back to bed."

"How are you here so early?" Quinn asked, sitting next to him.

"I came last night," he said. "Well, not here to the house, to the island. I stayed with Andy."

"What? I thought you missed the last ferry." Andy was a friend of the family, a lobsterman, and one of the island's volunteer firemen. He knew everyone on Southaven and was always helping out—the de facto guy to go to for any sort of problem.

"Andy called me when I was in Rockland to tell me what was going on. He brought the boat over and got me. But once we got to the island and drove out here, we couldn't get to the house, so I stayed with him and he brought me first thing."

"What do you mean, he told you what was going on?"

"With the people. Coming to find you."

"How did Andy know?" Quinn asked. "We didn't tell him. Our phone was out."

"A woman in the group had second thoughts. She made it to Good Tidings and asked where the police station was, and they gave her Andy's number." Good Tidings was the one motel on the island. There were no police on Southaven, just volunteer firemen and EMTs—the police force was stationed on the mainland.

Quinn was still confused. "So . . . Andy was the one who picked them up?"

"He had his brother Joe do it while he came and got me."

"Oh," Quinn said. "And then . . . you couldn't get here to the house . . ."

"Because of the flooding. We drove over, but once we saw the road, Andy didn't want to risk it."

Quinn's nerves tightened at the mention of the flood. So, her father had seen it, too, not just her mother. That was good. It meant . . . it meant he'd know what she was talking about when she said how impossible it had been. But how to begin? How could any of them talk about something that they had no words to describe? And while her parents would have had to see there was something extraordinary going on, they had no idea it had anything to do with her. Or the pregnancy.

"So . . . that was crazy," she said.

He stood and poured himself some more coffee. "Word is they left on the seven a.m. ferry, except one idiot who broke his leg and had to be air-lifted last night. I guess the others slept in the ferry terminal. Unfortunately, they didn't actually do anything illegal, so I don't think we can follow up. I felt so damned guilty that you and Mom were here alone. I never should have let that happen. I should have come up with her in the morning."

"We were okay," Quinn said. "And I meant . . . when I said 'crazy,' I meant the flood."

"Oh," he said, sitting again. "Right. Quite a storm surge. Major nor'easter." His face was unreadable as he stirred milk into his mug.

"Storm surge?" Quinn said.

"Hmm?"

"You said you saw it."

"Mmhm."

"Are you . . . Do you really think it was a storm surge? All the way down there?"

"I know. It's impossible to imagine. But clearly . . ." He shrugged. "It wasn't just a puddle from the rain, obviously. Not with that water level and force. Anyway . . . can I make you some breakfast, Little? Eggs or something?"

"That's okay," she said. "I'll make some toast."

Quinn got up and busied herself with filling the kettle for tea, slicing bread, and putting it in the toaster. But the whole time, she was thinking *He couldn't possibly believe that's what it was.* Was he really going to sit there and act like nothing strange had happened? It hadn't even been high tide.

The bread popped up. Quinn pressed it down again. It wasn't ready. Neither was she.

Maybe . . . maybe this was good. Yesterday, when the ocean had first surged away from the beach, toward the pine trees, she'd been horrified—so sure she needed to protect the secret. And if her father was going to believe it was a storm surge, well—here was her out. Here was the point where they all just agreed to believe in it, and Quinn wouldn't have to talk about it at all. He wasn't going to ask questions or investigate, so her secret could stay with her. All locked up.

The bread popped again. She took it out and got a mug for her tea and kept thinking . . . Keeping the secret would mean never telling them. Going along with the lies they told her whole life. And that hadn't worked! Look where it had all led. And . . . maybe once she began talking about it, it would all make sense to her parents, since they'd known her for her whole life, and had seen the water last night. Maybe her father just needed a push to see it all for what it was. Maybe she just needed to be the first one to state the obvious yet impossible truth.

"So," Gabe said. "I have some good news. Been a while since we've had any of that."

"What?" Quinn asked, sitting.

"I talked to my agent, and she's already fielded calls from my editor and other publishers about a memoir. Not about your experience, but about the political side of the story, and how the media exploited and twisted everything." He held up a hand. "I made it very, very clear that I wasn't going to get into anything personal about the pregnancy or our family. This would be a look at the media and Internet's ability to influence politics, destroy a career, all of that, using my personal experience for perspective." He took a sip of coffee. "She was talking very big numbers for the advance, given how high-profile the story was, and the sales numbers for *Urbanomics* and *ElastiCity*. But, more than the money, it's an opportunity to set things straight. Whoever I end up working with will definitely want to shoot for a pub date as soon as possible. I've already started writing."

"That's great," Quinn said, not sure if she meant it. She was relieved to see her father positive about something, but a book would just keep the story in the public eye.

She focused on her breakfast, her thoughts going back to last night. The toast was dry as sand in her mouth. She had to wash it down with tea.

"So," she said. "I . . . um, I have something to tell you."

"Hmm?" He was typing something on his phone.

She sat up straighter. "I think the Deeps are real."

"What?" he said, looking at her now, blinking.

"The water last night," she said, trying to make her voice more confident. "I don't think it could have been a storm surge."

"What do you mean?"

"It wasn't high tide. And the water had to go up and through the forest, for a quarter mile or something. I don't see how that's possible."

"I still . . . What are you saying?"

"I saw it happen. It . . . it was there on purpose, flooding the road. I think it was the Deeps. Keeping those people out."

His jaw went slack. "Oh no," he said. "No. We are not having this conversation. Quinn—"

"It happened before," she said. "Sort of. Not the flooding, but . . . Well, last May. I was down at the cove at night and the ocean . . . it was low tide and it came up to meet me. And I think that's the night I got pregnant. I think it—the Deeps—had something to do with it." A moment of deathly stillness followed.

Finally, her father stood up. "Okay," he said. "Okay." His voice had changed. It was now his problem-solver voice. He began pacing. "You've reached some sort of crisis point. Regression—isn't that a reaction to trauma? You're regressing to your childhood fantasies. Maybe this is good. It means that . . . that you can get through it and come out on the other side. You know? We'll . . . we'll call Dr. Jacoby. And we'll go back to Brooklyn. Today. I understand you believe what you're saying. I do. But here I am . . ." He walked over, knelt in front of her.

"Here I am. Real. Right? Your dad? And it's up to me, to me and your mom, to anchor you to reality."

The Deeps are not real, Quinn. There are no Deeps!

"So . . . how do you explain it?" she said, a bit more quietly. "It's come to meet me. I saw it. I felt it. I remember."

"You were either dreaming or . . . just imagining. Hallucinating. Going back to the childhood fantasy that book put in your head. The Deeps are a made-up story."

"But I was all wet. I'd obviously been swimming. Both times."

"The water was there for you to swim in, Little. High or low tide. You must have walked out to it. And the other things you remember . . . well, your brain made them up."

"But you saw that water last night. You know it was impossible. How can you say it was a storm surge? It was low tide!" She could hear the desperation in her own voice.

"Because between the choice of a supposedly impossible storm surge, and a . . . a *sentient* ocean, I'll take the storm surge!" He began to pace again. "And saying this has something to do with the pregnancy? You really think you're so special that this completely bizarre, supernatural thing happened to you? This thing that hasn't ever happened to anyone else?"

"Maybe it has," she said. "Maybe . . . Maybe Charlotte Lowell knew about it. And Meryl."

Her father stopped walking and fixed her with a cold stare. Quinn hadn't wanted to bring up her grandmother, but she was part of this. Quinn was sure.

"My mother was a very sad, very sick woman," he said. "And she has nothing—*nothing*—to do with you."

Quinn's mind groped for a way to make this better, a way to spin it into a story he could handle. "Wouldn't you be happy if someone didn't do this to me?" she said. "You keep worrying about me being someone's victim, about someone hurting me. Wouldn't you be happy if I wasn't?"

He looked at her incredulously. "You think what you're saying makes me *happy*?"

When he said it, she realized that no, of course he wouldn't be relieved. What he wanted was for her to be normal. If she was a victim, she could be saved. And a victim couldn't be blamed. Immaculate virgin, immaculate victim—either way, someone who hadn't sinned.

"I'm sorry if it's not what you want to hear," she said. "But it's what I believe. My pregnancy has something to do with the Deeps."

"Quinn. You can't get pregnant by the ocean. Am I really having to say those words?" He choked out a laugh. "You were impregnated by a man. Please—tell me you believe that. That's all I need to hear. That you believe me when I say you got pregnant by a man. Just tell me that, and we can talk about the rest. We can talk about the Deeps."

She shook her head. "I can't."

He closed his eyes and drew a deep breath through his nose.

"What about all the stories," Quinn said, "about mermaids and sirens and . . . stories about virgin births in different cultures, things like that. I'm not saying I'm some sort of mermaid or whatever—I'm not. I mean, I'm human, obviously. But what if there's stuff we don't know? Mysteries that don't go along with nature."

"Those are stories!" he said, eyes flashing open. "Myths! Written when people didn't understand how the world worked! People were looking for explanations, so they made up stories. That's . . . that's what myths are. But we don't need them now. We know how things work. We know how women get pregnant." He pressed his fingers against his temples. "We've known for centuries. It's not up for debate! And Charlotte Lowell made up that damned story about the Deeps."

"I know that. I understand. But . . ." She shrugged.

"Explain the physical aspect," he said. "How did this . . . make you pregnant?" He stared at her, challenging her. She was hanging off the edge of a cliff, and he was prying up her fingers.

"I don't know exactly . . . A moment . . . some moment of creation. There's . . . there's energy in the water. Light."

He raised his eyebrows. "Can you be more specific?"

She struggled to hang on. "If a boy and a girl grew up alone on a desert island without knowing anything about biology and then the girl got pregnant, they wouldn't be able to explain the process," she said. "I mean, isn't it always kind of a miracle that, like, two microscopic things come together and make life? And you wouldn't be able to imagine it yourself if you didn't know. It would seem impossible. You'd have a sense of when it happened but wouldn't be able to describe the actual process."

He shook his head in a way that showed he was too tired to explain the obvious again—that Quinn hadn't grown up knowing nothing, and that even though pregnancy has a miraculous element, we still know the biology.

Quinn felt herself drawing in, had a sharp memory of being a kid, of this same sense that all there was to do was collect your thoughts and ideas and beliefs like stones on a beach. Put them in a shoebox and hide them away under your bed. The only thing to do if you want to be loved.

"Obviously," her father said, sitting back down, "the trauma you experienced last May was . . . intense. And you're somehow susceptible to these thoughts. I've been thinking what could do that, what could have been bad enough that you can't even face it. Maybe . . . maybe it was that night, those guys at the party, and maybe it wasn't just one of them, maybe it was a whole group—"

"Stop it!" she yelled, hands over her ears. "Stop it! Why would you say that? Why would you want to make up something horrible just to put it in my head?"

He pulled her arms down with gentle insistence, keeping his fingers wrapped around her wrists as he spoke. "Because you need to confront the real-world possibilities," he said. "*Something* sent you over the edge."

No. She wouldn't listen to him. Not this time. She freed her wrists from his hold and said, "It's what happened. Whether or not you believe me. I've tried and tried to listen to you and to believe that it's something horrible, but it's just not true. I've tried to listen to everyone! But nothing has ever felt right. I've told myself stories and tried to have nightmares, and all I ever dream about is being deep in the ocean. I was there! I felt it! I've felt it my whole life. And you know it. You're the one who's always tried to deny it, by making up that story about Ben saving me. That was *your* lie, not mine. You're the one who lies!" Her last statement hung in the air for a moment.

"Okay," he finally said, placing his hands on his knees with emphasis. "Let's go down there. We'll go down to the beach at low tide and see it happen again. You'll . . . you'll do whatever you did. Call it in or whatever. And we'll see it happen together."

Quinn bit her cheeks. It wasn't like she had commanded it to happen before. And . . . well, there had been a reason.

"I don't think it works like that," she said.

"Oh?" He knew she was hanging on to the cliff by her last pinkie.

"It was an extreme situation. I can't just . . . call it."

"Okay," he said. "Let's . . . I don't think this discussion is getting us anywhere, Little. So . . . let's put it all aside. Okay? Let's put it aside, and when we get home to Brooklyn, we'll talk to your doctor and figure stuff out. Okay? No need to get all upset now. Clearly, no discussion is going to get us to see eye to eye on this. I am never, ever going to be able to tell you I believe you. I appreciate that you need this fantasy right now. That you're not strong enough for the real memory. But I can't pretend to believe you."

"You're wrong," she said, somehow finding it in herself to pull her body up and over the edge. "I *am* strong enough. That's why I remembered. And whether or not you believe me won't change what happened."

Later, she followed the forest path to Holmes Cove and sat on Swimming Rock. The tide was in between high and low, and . . . the water was exhausted. Quinn could sense its listlessness. Arms out for balance, she climbed off the rock and walked across slippery seaweed and mucky sand until she reached the lacy, foamy edge, then rolled up her sweatpants, took off her sneakers, and waded in. It was so drained of energy, she could barely feel any movement. There was the lightest of touch on her ankles, but that was it. The Deeps had spent everything last night. She waded farther out, until the water was up to the middle of her calves, and the touch became a bit stronger, a nudge acknowledging her presence. Nothing compared to before, but enough so she knew they were still there.

"Thank you," she said. "Thank you."

She realized now that they had tried to come to her that first night, when she arrived with Ben. The tide had started coming up to meet her, but she hadn't been ready. She'd been too committed to believing everyone else's version of the story, too focused on remembering a fictional trauma. The truth had started to come to her, and she had been too scared to see it.

"I'm sorry," she said.

She rested her hands on her stomach, where the baby was swimming around, not drained of energy at all. *You knew*, she said to the baby. *You tried to tell me.*

It was beautiful.

QUINN

The sound of a car's tires crunching the gravel driveway came from outside. Through the window, Quinn watched a red Jeep pull up. A stranger. Quinn stepped to the side of the window where she couldn't be seen. Her father was in town to use Wi-Fi, and her mother was asleep. A woman got out of the car. Maybe thirty or younger, jeans, navy down jacket, dirty-blond hair in a choppy pixie cut. Reporter? Probably. She seemed too . . . together, with the Jeep and all, to be one of the religious people. The woman glanced around and then walked up to the house. Quinn didn't move. *Shit, shit, shit.* A knock came at the door. And again.

Quinn didn't know whether she should wake her mother, or what, so she just stayed where she was, motionless.

Another knock.

When Quinn still didn't answer, a business card came sliding under the door.

Quinn picked it up as she heard the woman's steps go across the porch, back toward the Jeep.

Charlotte Lowell – Southaven Veterinary Services

Quinn opened the door, stepped outside. "Hello?" she called. The woman turned around and shaded her eyes.

"Hi," she said. "Quinn?"

Quinn nodded. The woman walked back in her direction. She moved with purpose.

"You're not Charlotte," Quinn said. There was no way this woman was old enough to have published a book in 1978, which was the date on *The Deeps.*

The woman smiled, emphasizing her wide, curved cheekbones. "I was, last I checked. But you probably mean that I'm not my grand-mother. And no, I'm not."

"Did I . . . Are you the one I called?"

Charlotte nodded. "My grandmother's been dead for a few years. Same name. People call me Charles, though. Childhood nickname."

"Oh," Quinn said, deflating. Charlotte Lowell, *her* Charlotte Lowell, was dead. "Sorry. I found the name in the phone book."

"That's okay. I tried to call back, but your phone line was down. I was out this way to check up on a patient, so thought I'd stop by." She put her hands in her jacket pockets. "As long as I'm here, is there something I can help you with?"

Quinn shook her head. "Thanks for coming, but no."

"I knew Meryl," Charles said. "Does that make a difference?"

Quinn made coffee and brought it over to where Charles was sitting on the couch looking at the book about the Deeps. She said she used to have a copy but hadn't seen it in years.

"I like your grandmother's illustrations," Quinn said, sitting in the chair nearest to her.

Charles nodded. "My house is full of her watercolors." After a moment she put the book down and took a sip of coffee. "Whoa. You make a strong cup."

"Too strong? I didn't taste it." Quinn had made herself mint tea.

"No, no. It's good." Charles took another sip, as if to prove she was telling the truth, then rested the mug on the table. "I know about your pregnancy," she said. "And some of what's been going on in the media. Just wanted to put that out there."

"Oh." Quinn rubbed her pendant. Of course this wasn't a surprise, but it made her sick to think of Charlotte—Charles—having read those things about her dad and Ben. She wanted to tell her they weren't true. But was she going to do that with everyone she talked to from now on?

"So," Charles said, interrupting her thoughts. "Where do you want me to start?"

"Charlotte didn't make the Deeps up," Charles began. "Well, I guess she made up that name—the Deeps. But the story is an old island myth, legend . . . whatever. Not just here. Other islands around the world have similar stories. My grandmother knew it from growing up here, and she turned elements of it into the book." She gestured at the copy on the table. "You know that feeling of the undertow pulling at you, or the current nudging you, or whatever?"

Quinn nodded.

"According to the myth, that's the ocean spirits. The waves coming in are curious young spirits coming up on land to explore. The undertow is the older ones pulling them back out. According to the myth, that's what causes the tides—the push and pull of young and old." Charles gestured a forward-and-back motion.

"And supposedly, a long time ago, there were people—families— that had a connection to these ocean spirits, passed down through the generations. They lived on islands and considered the Deeps their friends. I think the way my grandmother told it, their veins ran with saltwater instead of blood."

There was a flurry of movement in Quinn's gut, as if the baby was jumping up and down the way Quinn's heart was. Before she could ask any of her ten million questions, Charles spoke again.

"When women in the families were pregnant, their babies sometimes had two spirits—a human spirit and an ocean spirit. The mother would go swimming while pregnant and release the ocean spirit into the water. The ocean needed new young spirits for the tides to stay in balance, and humans needed the ocean to be healthy to maintain Earth's ecosystem." She reached for her mug. "That's the basic myth."

While Quinn's mind and gut and heart were all in a frenzy, she also felt a strange sense of calm, a feeling that everything was settling into place. As if she was hearing things she already knew in her bones, but hadn't been allowed to name. *The mother releases the ocean spirit into the water* . . . She remembered that silvery flash between her legs the other night, as she swam with the stars . . .

"So . . . do these families still exist?" she asked cautiously.

"The way you ask that is as if the myth were true," Charles said with a smile, setting her coffee back down.

"Oh, um . . ." How much could Quinn divulge to this stranger? "Did your grandmother think it was true?"

Charles hesitated. "No. But your grandmother did."

"She did?" Quinn said, not surprised in the least.

"Even though she grew up here, she'd never heard the myth until she saw a copy of Charlotte's book when she moved back here as an adult . . . you know, after leaving your dad and his father. But once she read it, she said she recognized what she'd felt her whole life. She told Charlotte. Charlotte filled her in on the rest of the myth. And Meryl started putting pieces together."

"What pieces?

Charles rubbed her chin. "I'm assuming from all your questions that you never got the letter."

"Letter?"

"From your grandmother."

Quinn shook her head.

Charles sighed. "I think we need more coffee. Tea, whatever."

Quinn took a moment to bring their mugs to the kitchen, pour more coffee, add more hot water and another tea bag. Her hands trembled the whole time. There was a letter somewhere. A letter for her! Even better than the idea of finding a diary or something in those boxes. There was a letter that would explain everything.

She sat back down and handed Charles her mug. "There's a letter?"

Charles nodded. "Meryl left it with Charlotte before she died." She paused. "Charlotte gave it to your dad, to give to you when you were old enough."

Quinn's hope sank like a rock. "Oh."

From the look on Charles's face, Quinn could tell that she understood what she was thinking: The letter probably didn't exist anymore.

"You didn't read it, did you?" Quinn asked.

"No," Charles said. "But Meryl wrote it at Charlotte's, and I was there. She was . . . agitated. She kept saying, 'It's supposed to be beautiful. But she should wait. She needs someone to tell her.' Honestly? I thought she was talking about losing your virginity." Charles smiled again. "Later, after Meryl died, Charlotte confided in me that Meryl thought her first pregnancy was . . . was with the Deeps, not related to sex at all. She thought that families like hers had lost the story of the Deeps somewhere along the line, that most had probably moved off of islands altogether, and that no one told girls like her what was going on. She thought that those babies with twin spirits were actually conceived in the ocean."

Quinn shifted forward in her chair. "But didn't she get pregnant with her husband?"

"The first time?" Charles looked surprised. "With the baby girl who died?"

"Yeah."

"No. She was only seventeen. She got pregnant while she lived here. She lived alone with her mother, and her mother was so upset about the pregnancy, Meryl had to move off the island in disgrace. She didn't meet her husband until later."

Jesus. "So . . . she was a virgin when she got pregnant? That's why she thought it was the Deeps?"

"No," Charles said. "She had a boyfriend. But . . . I guess, at the time, she'd been confused about how the pregnancy had happened. They'd used birth control or something."

"Oh." If Meryl wasn't a virgin, she could have just been crazy, thinking that it was the Deeps. "So, you don't believe any of this, do you?" Quinn asked.

"Like, actually believe it?" Charles said. "No."

"You think Meryl was delusional?"

Charles stared off toward the windows. "I don't know. I guess . . . I went to veterinary school, Quinn. I'm a science person. I'm not sure what was going on in Meryl's mind, but . . . I do know that she had a difficult life. Her father dying when she was young, and then the pregnancy, leaving home, and the baby's death . . . It took a toll."

"Why are you telling me all this then?"

"I debated about it. But . . . I don't know. I saw how unhappy your grandmother was, and I guess . . . I guess I thought . . ." She laughed. "I don't know, Quinn. Maybe there's some microscopic part of me that thinks, *what if.* You know?" She shook her head. "God, I can't believe I just said that. I mean, I don't believe it. I don't. But . . . still . . . I got your phone message, and . . ." She shrugged. "Maybe I shouldn't have."

"No!" Quinn said. "I'm so glad you did."

They both turned at the sound of a car pulling up the driveway.

"Shoot," Quinn said, standing. "That's my dad."

Charles stood, too, and pulled on her jacket hurriedly. "No offense," she said. "But I've never really liked him."

Gabe opened the door. His face went pale at the sight of Charles.

"Don't worry," she said to him. "I was just on my way out."

"What are you doing here?" he said, voice icy.

"I called her," Quinn said.

Charles rested a hand on her shoulder for a second. "Lovely to see you, Quinn. Take care." She walked out past Gabe without even looking at him.

"I don't want to know," he said to Quinn as he shut the door firmly. "I don't want to hear one word of the poison she's been filling you with."

"What happened to the letter Meryl left for me?"

"She was a sick woman, Quinn. And Charlotte . . . the older Charlotte . . . she wasn't much help, indulging her."

"Do you still have it?"

His silence was enough of an answer.

"Why didn't you ever tell me that she was a teenager when she got pregnant the first time?"

Gabe looked startled. "She was?"

"She was seventeen. Her mom sent her away."

"I didn't know that. I don't know much about her life. My father never talked about her."

"She wasn't married yet. And . . . later, when she found out about them, about the Deeps . . . she thought she got pregnant in the ocean. She wasn't a virgin, but still . . ."

Gabe appeared to be holding himself in check, eye twitching, jaw pulsing. Quinn didn't let his expression stop her. She told him everything Charles had told her about the myth of the Deeps and about Meryl.

"Quinn," he said. "Don't you think we'd know if girls all around the world were getting pregnant without having sex? If they were getting pregnant *in the ocean*, for God's sake?"

"No one's going to know about *me*, right?" she said. "We're not going to tell anyone. Also, Charles said lots of the families have moved off of islands. That they've lost the connection. Maybe it doesn't happen much anymore."

Quinn knew how this all sounded, of course. But the way she'd felt when she'd heard it, the way the words fit perfectly in the curves of her brain, in the chambers of her heart . . . Like water taking on the shape of its container, that's how well the story fit inside of her. There wasn't a way to explain how she knew it was true. She just knew.

"You'll never, ever know how sorry I am that whatever . . . whatever trauma you experienced has led you here," her father said, resting his hands on her shoulders. "All I want is for you to remember what you were like before all of this. In Brooklyn. When you were at school with your friends and happy and settled. That is who you are, Quinn. And who you still are. No one can take that from you. And we're going to get you the help that you need to find yourself again."

He squeezed her shoulders gently.

"Don't you understand what's going on here?" he continued. "You heard these stories when you were little. You wanted them to be true. You wanted friends. And now, in a time of crisis, you're going back to this . . . fantasy. It makes perfect sense, Quinn."

"So you won't even talk about Meryl? And the similarities? How strange it all is? You won't talk about it now, just like you never gave me that letter."

He briefly looked toward the ceiling. "Someday," he said, meeting her eyes again, "when you're better, you'll understand. You'll see that everything I've done has been to help you. Mom and I . . . we love you. And we need you here, Quinn, in this world. The real world."

QUINN

Her parents wouldn't let her stay on Southaven. She couldn't go back to the house in Park Slope, either, for obvious reasons. Gabe wanted her to go to an inpatient program, to try to find an antipsychotic drug regimen. Luckily, her mother and Dr. Jacoby were against that idea, both because she shouldn't take the drugs while pregnant and because they didn't see anything dangerous or harmful about her fantasies.

"She's not suicidal or self-destructive in any way," Dr. Jacoby said. "For the time being, she's found shelter in this story. I'm not saying that we should pretend what she's saying is real. But I don't think we need to go further than regular appointments—over Skype, if necessary—along with close monitoring and communication. If something changes, we can reassess."

"But what about whoever did this to her?" Gabe said. "One of those other guys."

Marco's DNA test had come back negative, just as Quinn thought it would. Her parents' lawyer said they didn't have enough evidence to demand DNA samples from Foley and the other guys who were at the party.

"If that's what happened, we let her come to it in her own time," Dr. Jacoby said.

In the end, Quinn and her mother ended up staying with Katherine's friend Alex in Boston. Gabe stayed with Lydia in Brooklyn, and the two of them went to visit Quinn and Katherine on several weekends, traveling in the middle of the night to avoid being followed. Gabe wasn't sure if anyone would be following them anymore. Now that Quinn wasn't at the house, people didn't gather in front any longer—just left the occasional snapshot or bouquet or letter. And without the people, there was no press, either. But, still . . . if the family had learned anything, it was that you could never be too careful.

Every so often, Quinn thought about lying. All she'd have to do would be to tell her parents that she'd come to her senses. That, of course, the story of the Deeps was just a myth. Tell them that she once again believed that her pregnancy was a normal one and that she probably had been drugged that night in Maine and had hallucinated the whole swimming experience.

She knew how much easier the lie would make everything. And sometimes she even told herself the lie so convincingly that she began to believe it. The logical explanations her dad had forced down her throat so many times began to seem as obvious as he said they were.

But she always came back to her memory of the water spilling up the beach to meet her, of it pouring through the forest and churning at the bottom of the road, keeping those people from coming to the house. (Breaking that man's leg!) That water had moved with purpose. With intention. Her father might believe that it was a storm surge, but she didn't see how she ever could.

And lying was what had started all of this to begin with. The lies she believed and the ones she told. Saying what people wanted to hear. Being who they wanted her to be. Wanting them to love her, even if the "Quinn" they loved was someone they had made up.

One day, when she was reading a book that she'd taken from her grandmother's boxes in Southaven, she came across a picture nestled between the pages, a picture she'd never seen before. It was in an envelope addressed to Meryl with a return address in Cincinnati. The picture was of Quinn's father at maybe four or five. While she didn't know for sure if the picture was taken before or after Meryl left him, she would have bet anything that it was after. He was standing in front of a slide at a playground, wearing pants that were too short and a striped top with an orange stain on it. His hands were together in front of his chest, one resting on top of the other, his elbows tight to his body. It was a strange pose that made him look insecure and nervous, but also defensive. Like he wanted to protect himself but wasn't quite sure how. His mouth was set in a small, straight line, and his eyes were both sad and guarded.

As she looked at it, Quinn remembered one of her dreams, one of the dreams in which she was her grandmother, at the bottom of the ocean. Her father had been there, too, and Meryl had said, "I forgive you." And Quinn wondered now if Meryl had been forgiving him for not telling Quinn about the Deeps, for destroying that letter. And Quinn wondered if maybe *she* should forgive him. Because, after all, his mother had hurt him in the worst, most primal way, and that last time he saw her, she had been talking about something that had no relation to Gabe's reality. Why would he have listened to her? Why would he have wanted to let her into his life again, let her into his daughter's life, after what she had done to him? His lies and anger had damaged Quinn, that was true, but maybe it was also true that those lies had seemed like the only way to protect her.

Maybe, in a way, his lies and anger had been proof of his love, not evidence against it.

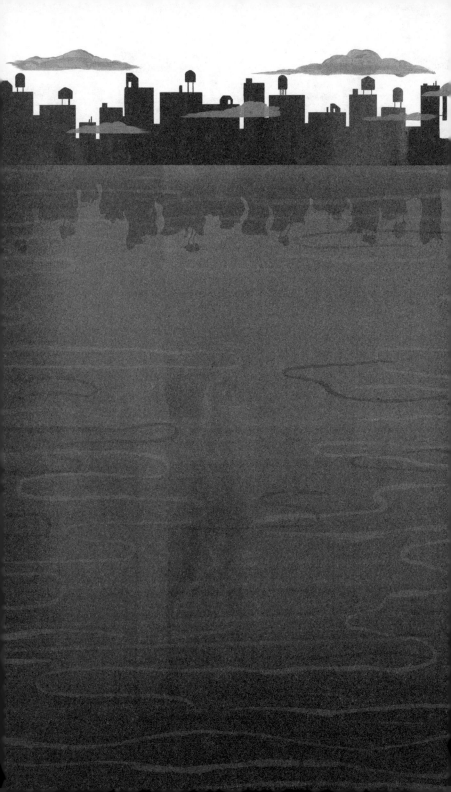

THREE MONTHS LATER

QUINN

The bone-splitting, muscle-shredding pain had stopped, but now Quinn's heart was bruising her ribs. Something wasn't right. Nurses and doctors were crowded around the baby, the baby that had just been born, calling out words and phrases Quinn didn't understand completely but understood well enough to know that they weren't good. She'd done a water birth in the special tub, and the baby had finally swum out between her legs, and everything had seemed fine, but now . . . now it wasn't.

"Is he okay?" she kept asking. "What's wrong? Is he okay?"

Her mother squeezed her hand.

The baby wasn't breathing. That was the problem. He wasn't breathing, and Quinn wasn't breathing either. It couldn't end like this. It couldn't. It made no difference that the baby was being adopted. She had fought to keep him and had carried him with her for nine months and needed him to live. *Please. Please.*

Then . . . "There, hear that?"

A sound—weak, at first, then stronger.

A tiny, life-filled cry.

PETER VEGA

M arch 1, Boston—Quinn Cutler, daughter of bestselling author and ex-congressional candidate Gabe Cutler, has given birth to a boy, according to an anonymous source at a hospital in Massachusetts. Secrecy was high around Miss Cutler's whereabouts over the last few months and the location of the birth, due to the amount of attention her pregnancy received when it was revealed that she thought herself to be a pregnant virgin. Tabloids and bloggers had speculated that she might be hiding the father's identity because it was someone in the family, but an accidental leak of a DNA test result proved that the father is not someone closely related to Miss Cutler. The baby is being adopted, and various people have expressed anger that "the next messiah" is being hidden away from the people who need him. Others have expressed faith that when the boy is older, he will "naturally fulfill his role as God's second son."

Gabe Cutler did not respond to a request for comment, but in recent weeks did say, once again, that the family does not plan on revealing the identity of the baby's father, as it is a private matter, but that his daughter is healthy, and that it was a normal pregnancy.

Cutler reportedly received a seven-figure advance for his upcoming memoir Political Virgin: The Disillusionment and (Near) Destruction of an American Candidate.

QUINN

They were lying on the cold sand at Coney Island, alone except for some seagulls, a couple of joggers, and a few old women walking up and down the beach speaking Russian. It was April, and while spring had already made a grand entrance in the park, here on the water, winter was hanging on for as long as she could. The sky was a blue as clear and sharp as glass. There was almost no wind, just a gentle touch now and then. The ocean was whispering instead of roaring. *A still morning sea . . .*

"So . . . what about Madagascar?" Jesse said. "Did we make a decision on that?"

"I think it's in the 'possible' column," Quinn said. She was on her back, staring into the blue above. It comforted her that wherever her baby was, he saw the same sky. And that if he could see or hear an ocean, any ocean, it was the same body of water as the one she was listening to right now. The same body of water where his twin spirit lived. These things felt important to her.

"Quinn?" Jesse said. "Did you hear me?"

She turned her head. He had gotten up and was standing on a rock, arms out for balance, like he was about to fly.

"No, sorry," she said. "What did you say?"

"I said they have those cool trees, on Madagascar. But it's not important." He jumped onto the sand. "So . . . I have an idea . . ."

"About the trip?"

"No. About him." Jesse didn't have to say who "he" was. They both knew that since Quinn gave birth six weeks ago, she'd barely stopped thinking about baby. The first weeks had been the worst, when her breasts ached and her milk came in, a constant physical reminder of the separation. She'd had to tell herself over and over that adoption had been the right choice, not just for her, but also for the baby, who wouldn't have been safe if people knew where he was. She cried more than she'd cried during all the trauma of the pregnancy itself. Now, she mostly worried. About who his family was and where he lived and whether he was healthy. And about whether he'd feel a connection to the ocean, and whether he'd sense the Deeps and not understand.

"I know you're not allowed to get in touch with him," Jesse continued. "So, I was thinking . . . It's a great story, you know, the story of the Deeps. The whole myth. And I was thinking—what if you made a movie or wrote a book or just posted something online about it? Tell your story."

Jesse never pretended to Quinn that he one-hundred-percent believed in the Deeps. But he loved the possibility that it *might* be true, loved how that made the world a bigger place. And he respected her belief.

"People have finally stopped gossiping about me," Quinn said, sitting up, "and now you want me to publicly announce that I'm nuts?"

"Of course not." He sat down next to her again. "First of all, you're not nuts. And anyway, you can use a pen name. And you can wait. Wait like five, ten years or whatever. Pretend it's fiction. Change all the details about your family, so no one knows it's you. The true part would be about your connection to the Deeps, and the myth."

Quinn wasn't following his logic. "Why?"

"You want him to know about it, right? But you're not allowed to have any contact with him. Well, if you write a book, or if we make a movie, maybe he'll see it. And your family isn't the only family like this, right? There are other families you think might have lost the story, but not the connection to the ocean. Other girls who should know what's going on. Some of them might read it and be like, "Holy shit! This is about *me*.""

Quinn remembered back to the first weeks she knew she was pregnant and her desperate search for a story that mirrored hers. She thought about her crushing disappointment at finding out her father had destroyed her grandmother's letter . . .

"I would like to find a way to share it with him," she said. "And others, if there are any. But I don't know if I want to tell everyone else." Even if it weren't written under her own name, and were written as fiction, she couldn't stand the thought of people tearing it apart, making fun of it, calling it stupid. It felt too sacred to her to open up to that. She felt protective of the Deeps. "Also, I don't know how I'd describe it. There's no scientific explanation. I don't have the right words."

"I could help you," Jesse said, leaning his body into hers. "Some people think I'm a decent writer, you know." He'd gotten an honorable mention in the screenplay contest, which guaranteed admission to the film program, and he was thrilled. So was Quinn.

"I've heard," she said, nudging him. "And maybe I will do it. Someday."

Maybe it was even her responsibility to bring the story back into the world.

She would never do it under her own name—never wanted that kind of notoriety again. But, at the same time, she'd reached a point where she cared shockingly little what people thought about her. She'd worried so much about the fact that other people were dictating how she was going to be seen, that other people were writing "the story of Quinn" in their tabloids and blogs and comments and talk shows. But it had turned out that what mattered was the story she told herself. Discovering the Deeps had changed her, making her feel like there wasn't anything "wrong" with her for the first time since she was a kid playing in the water at Holmes Cove. She wouldn't have thought change that elemental was possible.

"Is it my imagination," Jesse said, "or is that bird staring at me?"

The beach was almost exclusively populated by gulls, but sitting about two feet from Jesse was a pigeon, its small, round eyes looking right at him.

"It's probably the one from outside your window," Quinn said, only sort of kidding.

Jesse stared back at it. He stood up and began walking. The pigeon waddled after him. He walked faster. The pigeon flapped its wings and flew-walked to catch up.

"Seriously?" Jesse said, breaking into a jog. "You get to be friends with the ocean, and I get a pigeon?"

Quinn started laughing. And then laughed harder as Jesse began running faster, in big circles around her, and the pigeon followed, apparently determined not to lose him.

"It's an especially cute pigeon," Quinn called out. "If that helps."

He shook his head. "No, that doesn't help."

"How about a girl?" she said, standing up. "If a girl chased you, would that help?"

"Hmm . . ." Jesse stopped. "It might."

Quinn didn't even have to chase him, because he just stood there, waiting for her to reach him. Soon she was in front of him, on her tiptoes, hands on his shoulders, lips against his, body meeting and pressing into his warmth, everything melting together, like losing yourself in a midnight-black ocean, like swimming with stars . . .

When they broke away, he was smiling. "That helped," he said.

Before they headed home, Quinn walked down to the water to say good-bye. It was washing up in low waves edged in white lace and left a wide swath of sand glistening silver when it slid back. She squatted down and reached out her hands so that the next wave washed over them. The touch of the water on her skin whispered things to her the same way the touch of Jesse's lips on hers did. This ocean, and this boy . . . they *knew* her. And they loved her.

She stood back up and stared out at the rippled surface stretching out to the horizon, the glittering surface of another world. So much life hidden underneath it. So many mysteries.

It was the most beautiful thing she'd ever seen.

But after some time, a voice calls your name.
The Deeps feel a pull from back where they came.
They slip out to sea, you wave a farewell,
From two different worlds, one story to tell.

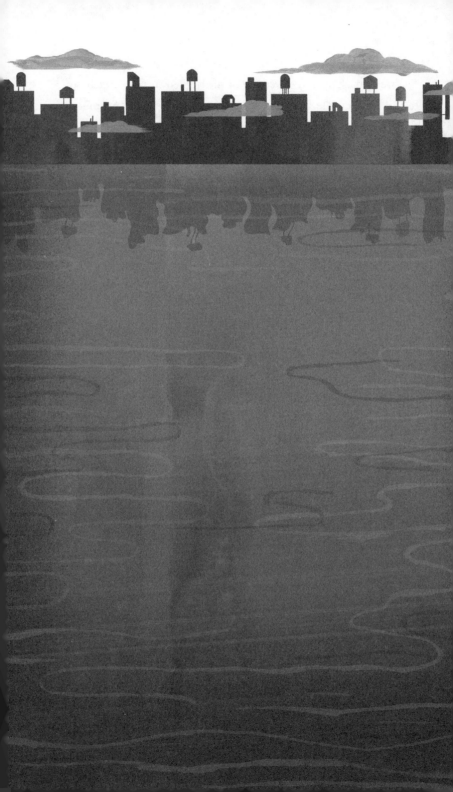

ACKNOWLEDGMENTS

Tsunami-size challenges arose while I was writing this novel. Many wonderful people kept me afloat, but two need special mention. Thank you to my amazing agent, Sara Crowe, for being my fierce supporter and champion, always. Her belief in me and in this book never faltered. And huge thanks to my dear friend Jandy Nelson: for her boundless enthusiasm and optimism—about Quinn's story and about life in general; for her sage advice and astute feedback; and, most importantly, for helping me have the courage to tell the story I wanted to tell. Sara, Jandy—I adore you!

I'm thrilled to have worked with my brilliant editor (and friend) Maggie Lehrman, who understood exactly what I was trying to do and how to help me do it. Thank you, Maggie! And thank you to everyone at Abrams Books, especially Anne Heltzel, Alyssa Nassner, Chad Beckerman, Samantha Hoback, and Susan Van Metre. For the most sublime jacket illustration ever, thanks to Christopher Silas Neal. Thank you to everyone who generously gave me critical feedback, especially on early drafts when the waters were truly murky: Tim Wynne-Jones, Marie Rutkoski, Jill Santopolo, Eliot Schrefer, Elizabeth Bird, Kekla Magoon, and Kristin Daly Rens. Much appreciation to friends who helped me with tricky story issues: Stephanie Knowles, Samera Nasereddin, and Signy Peck. And enormous thanks to my uncle the Reverend Robert J. Ginn Jr., whose perspective was invaluable.

The VCFA community cheered me on right from this project's beginning. Special thanks to Jill, Katie Bayerl, Kate Hosford, and my Beverly Shores peeps, whose counsel, kindness, and humor I rely on heavily. My friends in Brooklyn didn't forget about me when I disappeared into my writing cave for long stretches, so thanks to them for their loyalty and patience. Thank you to Alexandra Shor, my beloved best friend, for everything, always, and this time specifically for being my on-call OB/GYN. And thanks to her and Roz Zander for giving me a home on a magical island in Maine. To my father, Allan; my stepmother, Tamara; my sister, Rebecca; and my brothers Alexander and Henry: Thank you for making sure that I can't rely on personal experience when writing about difficult family members.

Finally, thank you to my mother, Lucy, for way too many things to fit on this page. Simply put, I wouldn't be a writer without your love and support.